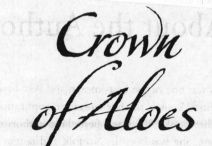

About the Author

Norah Lofts was one of the best-known and best-loved of all historical novelists, known for her authentic application of period detail to all her books. She was a bestselling author on both sides of the Atlantic. She was born in Norfolk and taught English and History at a girls' school before turning to writing full time in 1936. Her passion for old houses and their continuing history sparked off her much praised Suffolk trilogy, *The Town House*, *The House at Old Vine* and *The House at Sunset*. These were followed by the bestselling *The Concubine*, *The King's Pleasure*, a novel about the life of Katharine of Aragon, and *Eleanor the Queen*, a novel about the life of Eleanor of Aquitaine. Lofts wrote more than 50 books, including historical non-fiction and short stories.

Crown of Aloes

NORAH LOFTS

TORC

Cover illustration: *The Reception of Christopher Columbus by Ferdinand II and Isabella*, courtesy of The Bridgeman Art Library

This edition first published 2008

Torc, an imprint of Tempus Publishing
Cirencester Road, Chalford,
Stroud, Gloucestershire, GL6 8PE
www.tempus-publishing.com

Tempus Publishing is an imprint of NPI Media Group
By arrangement with Tree of Life Publishing
© Norah Lofts, 1973, 2008

The right of Norah Lofts to be identified as the Author
of this work has been asserted in accordance with the
Copyrights, Designs and Patents Act 1988.

British Library Cataloguing in Publication Data.
A catalogue record for this book is available from the British Library.

ISBN 978 0 7524 4469 7

Typesetting and origination by NPI Media Group
Printed and bound at Nutech Photolithographers

Contents

Author's Note

This book is very largely factual. The research was done by Frieda Lund of Bury St Edmunds who did a meticulous job and is not to be blamed for my mistakes, misinterpretations or inventions. In addition to the ordinary sources she used three books, not available in English. They are:

Crónica de los Reyes Católicos by Fernando del Pulgar
Libro de la Camero Real del Principe Don Juan by Gonçalo Fernadez de Oviedo y Valdés
Las Cosas Memorables de España by Lucio Marineo.

All three men were contemporaries of Isabella, and close to her; two were her secretaries, one an official in her son's household. It is from such hitherto unexploited sources that we learn not only the name of Prince Juan's dog, but also its breed and its behaviour when he died.

The Spanish Embassy in London was very co-operative in supplying information about such things as weather in various places, at different seasons.

Motives, thoughts, private conversations cannot, however, be recorded even by the most observant onlooker: to provide these, within the framework of known fact, was my job. For any misrepresentation I apologise to Isabella's shade, counting upon her well-known magnanimity.

The title chose itself, aloes being both sharp and bitter.

NORAH LOFTS

Prologue

The Royal Palace at Medina del Campo. 1504

'... mas suplice a su infinita piedad, quiera rescibir aquesta mi confesion dellos ...'

'... but I appeal to His infinite mercy, I would like Him to receive this as my confession.'

Last Will of the Catholic Queen Isabella

The last thing she saw was a friendly face, marked with grief. The delicate, gentle hands, always at her service, closed her eyes. Because she was dead.

The doctors had said it. 'Her Majesty is dead.'

A man sobbed with the harsh sound of ripped cloth.

For a second she toyed with the idea of saying, I can still hear! Surprise them all, as she had surprised sleeping sentries, drowsy pages, in her day. But the effort was beyond her, and not worth making. Why linger now? The priest had given her the last command, 'Go forth, Christian soul.' The holy oil was moist on her eyelids, her nose, her mouth, her ears and the palms of her hands, by its application absolving any sin committed through the senses. Her feet had not been anointed; she had said to Beatriz, 'My legs. Keep them covered.' A last gesture of pride?

Death was an old, familiar enemy no longer to be feared. What she did fear, lying there, officially dead, was the judgement of God. After death, the judgement. And in this timeless moment, in the time it took for the candles to be lighted, for Ferdinand to sob and Beatriz to weep—they were grieving though she had told them not to: 'Do not grieve for me; I am very tired and ready to go' —there was still time to think of herself as a failure. Inside the flower of success the worm of failure gnawed its inexorable way.

She had worked all her life for the unity of Spain, now, with her death, about to fall apart. She had advocated the gentle treatment of heretics, and the fires of the Inquisition burned more fiercely every day; she had freed thousands of slaves, but in the Indies another and worse form of slavery—worse because it was impersonal—was beginning to flourish. She had borne a son and carefully reared him to be King of Castile and Aragon and then, through a misjudgement, defeated her own plans. What a record of failure!

She tried to imagine the confrontation so soon to take place, but God had no face, no form. Christ had taken human shape and had been represented in every attitude, in paint, wood, marble, stone. Mary the Mother of God and all the Saints also had substance; but God Whom she had tried to serve, and Who had at times seemed so close, was outside the conception of the human mind, except in terms of light, a light to which the mid-day summer sun was but a candle. The disembodied soul was also difficult to envisage, and in fact when she imagined herself as she would be within a minute, it was something as small as an ant and as brown, in the Franciscan nun's habit, prostrate in the presence of ineffable light and glory and power.

There would be no need to say, God, I have failed. He would know that. She would say, Of Thy infinite mercy, forgive me; I tried and I failed.

Why? What went wrong?

What went wrong?

I

Arevalo. 1454

' ... fue criada doña Isabel con pocas riquezas, sin pompa, sin Halages,
y sin las otras cosas con que se suelen criar los hijos de grandes
principes y senores.'

' ... Doña Isabella was brought up with little riches, without pomp,
without flattery, and without the other things with which the
children of great princes and lords are reared.'

Las Cosas Memorables de España, Lucia Marino

I never wished to be Queen of Castile.

It is not true, as has been said, that I was born ambitious and
dreamed of the Crown, even in childhood. Such a dream would have
been ridiculous. When my father, Juan II of Castile died in 1454, he
left two sons: Henry, my half-brother, aged twenty-nine and married,
Alfonso my brother, a baby. I was three. As soon as I knew anything I
knew that two lives for certain and an unknown number of potential
ones were between me and the throne.

Also one does not dream of something one does not want. Free to
choose for myself I should have become a nun; not a mystic, given
to ecstasies and miracles; my nature has always been practical. With
my energy, common sense, ability to organise and—of course—my
rank, I should have been made abbess, and I should have ruled a
good house, my nuns living neither in luxury nor squalor, taking no
lovers, bearing no bastards. As head of a convent similar to that of
Santa Ana in Avila I should have been happy.

Final repudiation of the idea that I had always had my eye on the
Crown must surely lie in the fact that I once refused it. In 1468, when
I was seventeen, I stood in the nuns' parlour at Avila and a deputation,
representing the majority of the nobles of Castile, knelt and offered
me the Crown; begged me to take it, and I refused, saying—the
words are on record—that I would never accept the Crown while
one person more entitled to it was alive.

It may be that I was mistaken. Had I been more ambitious and less scrupulous some bloodshed might have been avoided.

It is an irony that I shall be remembered, if I am remembered at all, as a queen almost constantly at war. Yet I hate bloodshed, even in the bull-ring. But in my life irony seems to have a wholly disproportionate part.

Back to the beginning.

The beginning for me was in 1454 when we were banished from Court and went to live at Arevalo. I was three years old, and that is where my memory, my self-awareness, seems to start. I cannot remember my father's death, the obsequies or any of the ceremonies connected with my half-brother's ascension, but I can remember with the utmost clarity our arrival at the castle; the almost empty great hall, bare-walled, bare-floored, with uncovered stone stairs clinging to the wall. Very bleak and very chill. I remember saying, 'I do not like it here.' Mother said, 'It will look better when it is furnished.' Alfonso, in his nurse's arms, began to cry and I said, 'Fonso doesn't like it either.' Doña Maria, Mother's one remaining lady-in-waiting, said, 'That will be enough about liking or disliking, Your Royal Highness. We none of us like it, but grumbling does not help.' In all my memory of her I do not think that Doña Maria ever failed to give me my title; nor did she ever fail to administer a rebuke.

'We must make the best of it,' Mother said. I remember her in those days as a gay, high-spirited woman, a Princess of Portugal, briefly Queen of Castile, now reduced, banished and poor; poor as she once said, 'in the worst way. A position to keep up and little to do it with.'

It was worse for Mother and for Doña Maria who had known comfort and luxury in many palaces than for me, too young to have any standard of comparison and only knowing that even when some extra furniture was installed the castle at Arevalo still had a ringing emptiness that made every voice, every footfall sound loud and yet hollow, and even in the height of summer no warmth seemed to penetrate the thick walls or enter by the narrow windows; it was an unfriendly place ...

'I will pay her,' I remember Doña Maria saying, 'and send her packing first thing in the morning. We can't have such tales being spread. Don Pedro can find us a girl from the town. Or, if it comes to the pinch, Your Majesty, I can take charge of His Royal Highness. Had I been born a peasant I should now be tending my grandchildren ...'

They were talking, I gathered, about Alfonso's nurse. Don Pedro I knew, he was the keeper of the castle and lived, with his daughter Beatriz, about my own age, in some apartments above the gatehouse.

Alfonso's nurse vanished and was not replaced. Mother, Doña Maria, and I, as I grew, shared the care of Alfonso who—it was gradually borne in upon me—was a very important personage indeed. He might be as dirty, and presently naughty as any other little boy, but unless something extraordinary happened out in the world, beyond the sheep country of Arevalo, Alfonso would one day be King of Castile. From the beginning I was reared to believe in the near-holiness of direct royal descent. The something extraordinary which might push Alfonso aside would be that our half-brother, Henry, should beget a child of his own.

Another scrap of conversation overheard. 'Impotent with one, impotent with all,' Doña Maria said in her didactic way. 'This new marriage will be no more fruitful than the old one.' She danced Alfonso on her knee. 'We shall see our little boy recognised as heir to the throne and ourselves back at Court.'

It lasted for years, this hope, the constant iteration, mainly from Doña Maria—'When we return to Court we must not appear rustic! Your Royal Highness strides about like a stable boy.' Apparently at Court ladies took such little mincing steps that they might have not feet but well-oiled wheels under their skirts. At Court ladies never raised their voices, lost their tempers, needed to answer any call of nature in precipitate fashion ...

I half-accepted, half-repudiated what Doña Maria stood for. But Mother was there, living proof of the fact that everything Doña Maria said was right. Mother, even when she joined in our games, as she did in the early days, never took large strides or shouted; and her temper was always under control. Rage might make her white-faced and tremulous but no more. I tried very hard to model my behaviour on hers because it was royal behaviour, and because I loved her, but I often fell short of the ideal because I forgot, or was too much absorbed in what I was doing.

I was fortunate in having Beatriz de Bobadilla with whom to share games and lessons. Doña Maria found her just acceptable as a companion for me, there being no other, but she disliked it when Beatriz used my given name—as Mother had suggested she should. I was also fortunate in having a friend who was not easily dominated. We were of an age but I was bigger, more active, more boisterous, more anxious to excel; when I had done so Beatriz would smile, shrug her narrow shoulders and say, 'It is only a game.' Her attitude towards lessons was equally casual. 'So long as one can read for pleasure and write a letter. We are not going to be clerks.' She embroidered beautifully—and made me do so, too, for I could not bear not to equal her in Mother's eyes.

In many ways Beatriz was more knowledgeable than I. Don Pedro always behaved to her as though she were made of something very frail and delicate, but he talked to her as though she were grown up. She heard the gossip of the gatehouse kitchen, too. I was not allowed in our kitchen quarters, and in any case our servants never stayed long, with the exception of an old couple, man and wife, both lame and both surly. Don Pedro was very grateful to Mother for teaching Beatriz, and when we were six he reciprocated by producing two well-mannered ponies and teaching us both to ride. That was the beginning of my love of horses and delight in riding. Beatriz could stay on her pony's back but she never mastered the art of mounting or dismounting.

We were all fortunate that there were many books in the castle. That was because it had been my father's custom to spend some time there each summer, living like a private person. When about a year before he died he decided never to visit Arevalo again and gave orders for most of the castle's contents to be removed, the books had been overlooked. Much of what I know about history and about distant places I learned in those long evenings at Arevalo: winter evenings with the snow whispering down; summer evenings smelling of thyme and of sheep.

It was a healthy, happy life. Occasionally—but more rarely as time went on—visitors came; and then everything was very stiff and formal and Mother would occupy a chair with a canopy which Doña Maria had ordered. She said that the canopy was to exclude draughts, of which there were plenty, even in the relatively small rooms which we occupied. I know now that the canopy, like so many other things in Doña Maria's life, was an echo of the past when Mother had been Queen of Castile, a gesture towards the future, when Mother would be Queen Mother of Castile ...

Plans for the future concerned my education, too. Mother regretted the fact that she could not teach me Latin, the common language of Christendom, or French which was an accomplishment like playing the lute; but when I was eleven I should go to the nuns in the Convent of Santa Ana in Avila, a house of Bernadine nuns, famous for its orderly way of life, and for learning.

When this plan was first proposed I was neither more nor less religious than any girl reared in the Christian faith; orthodox in my beliefs having never examined them; regular at confession, at Mass; faith in God the Father, God the Son and in the Blessed Virgin Mary, Mother of God, had come to me, by precept and example, as effortlessly as breathing. But the idea of living in a convent where everything, the hours of the day and of the night, the clothes, the meals, everything was religious, appalled me.

I said to Beatriz, 'When I go to Avila next year, will you come, too?' She said, 'Isabella, I think I could not. My father would not consent. He ... he has other plans for me.'

'What plans?'

She said lightly—I remember how lightly, 'For marriage. As Father says, a girl must be married and nobody is going to bang on the castle gate and ask if a marriageable girl lives here. But Father's family is extensive. I have many relatives ... an aunt by marriage in Segovia, Doña Léonare de Cabrera; she has arranged many marriages, and will arrange mine.'

A jump from happy, carefree childhood into the adult world. In a sidelong kind of way we both knew what marriage meant. It was simple, wholesome knowledge, shared by every country-bred child. God in His infinite wisdom had made male and female, animals, human beings. The two shapes fitted together—as everything that God who made Heaven and earth, the sun, the moon and the stars, and the waters under the earth, fitted—and by fitting, bred. Too simple to merit much attention, except for the difference; a ram mounted a ewe and trotted away, his duty done. People had to live together ...

I said, 'Beatriz I do hope, with all my heart, that your aunt by marriage finds you an amiable man.'

'And that is my wish for you—when the time comes ...'

I remember that conversation, partly for its content, partly for its timing; late autumn of the year 1461; the last ride on our matched ponies; the last time that Beatriz's life and mine seemed to run together; change in the air.

'The wind blows sharp from the north,' Don Pedro said, 'it will snow tomorrow. And that will be a pity, for I have this minute received a new horse, a real horse for Your Royal Highness.' Even as he spoke to me, fulfilling my long-felt wish, a real horse that could run, he lifted Beatriz down and said, 'Indoors with you!'

Beatriz went away, indolent, graceful. I said, 'Don Pedro, where is he, my new horse?'

'It is a mare, Your Royal Highness; full Arab breed and responsive to her name—Sasha meaning distinguished in the Arabic.'

Distinguished Sasha certainly was. I said to Don Pedro, 'I want to see her,' and he led me to the place where she was stalled. Sasha was beautiful, creamy gold in colour, with silky mane and tail just a shade darker in colour and the slightly hollowed out head and the lithe, light lines of her breed. But what mattered to me, more than her looks, her indisputable pedigree, was that she recognised me, instantly. Don Pedro said, 'There she is, Your Royal Highness. Be a little careful. She has made a long journey, and has not yet settled.' I spoke her name softly and she turned, nuzzling me, her soft nose quivering between my ear and my shoulder. Mutual love at first sight ...

The snow came down in a blizzard that lasted two days and a night. Doña Maria took a heavy cold and was obliged to retire, unwillingly, to her bed. 'A cup of hot wine, a hot brick to my feet and I shall be well in the morning,' she said, bravely. Mother said, also being brave, 'You are not to think about our servantless state, my dear. We can manage.'

I saw Alfonso to his bed; he was eight years old, quite capable of looking after himself, but he liked to be waited on. We made a game of it—he was King, I a gentleman of the Bedchamber. Then I went down to join Mother at the embroidering of an altar cloth, her gift to the church for Christmas. Secretly I was rather pleased to have her all to myself and determined to stitch so diligently that Doña Maria's contribution would not be missed. Poor Mother, she had such a generous heart, such a desire to give, and so seldom anything to give except time and the labour of her hands. In fact this altar cloth had cost her a gown. The money spent on the crimson cloth, the threads of silk and gold, should have been spent on a dress for me, I was growing so fast, so Mother cut down a gown of her own—seven years old, but still splendid—to fit me.

We sat close together to take advantage of the small heat given off by the charcoal brazier. There were few trees around Arevalo, and they all fruit-bearing. So logs for fires, hauled from a distance, were expensive. Charcoal weighed less and was a little cheaper.

On this extremely cold evening the supply of charcoal in the basket was low and Mother, stitching away, said, 'Old Jaime cannot carry much these days.'

'Why do our servants never stay? Over at the gatehouse there have been no changes for as long as I remember.'

Mother looked up and gave me a measuring glance as though estimating how much cloth would be needed to make me a cloak.

'You may as well know. Stupid people believe this place to be haunted.'

The word in itself is a frightening one; pleasantly frightening in a book or a tale, less so when used about one's home, insufficiently occupied, on a November evening. But mother had spoken lightly. I endeavoured to do the same.

'What by?'

'The ghost of a man, Alvaro de Luna, for whose death I am responsible.'

I was astounded. Mother! Then I remembered those rare, white-faced, rigidly controlled fits of rage.

'By ... accident?'

'No, darling. With the utmost deliberation. He was a very evil man. He exercised enormous influence over your father and used it for the worst possible purposes. Fortunately he was also extremely

16

dishonest. I managed to expose him and your father was so deeply shocked by the disloyalty ... he had him beheaded.'

'Here?'

'No. In Valladolid.'

'Then why ... I mean, I thought ghosts walked where ...'

'Isabella, don't speak as though you believed in such things! It is a stupid tale, concocted partly by those who think I deserve to be haunted. Also, your father and de Luna used to spend summers here, pretending to be private gentlemen ...' A look of disgust, scorn, mockery changed her pretty face for a moment and she took a few jabbing stitches. 'It did not need a ghost to punish me. Failure did that ... I thought that with de Luna dead your father would listen to me; but he pined for his ... favourite, and outlived him only by about a year. And he left me Arevalo in his will. It was the kind of joke, a sour joke, they both enjoyed. To be displaced; to be told by Henry, 'Go live on your property. Take your children with you.' Misery enough without de Luna wailing and clanking his armour.'

'Is that what he ... I mean, is *said* to do?'

She noted the correction and gave me a warm, approving smile.

'Why the armour,' she said, reverting to her light manner, 'is a puzzle. I believe he did once fight in a battle. I never saw him except in silk and satin. His mail doubtless stands rusting somewhere, and his soul must be in Hell.'

As though to mock her there came a long wailing howl, muted by distance.

'Alfonso,' she said. 'That tooth again!'

My first teeth had dropped out painlessly and toothache was unknown to me; but one of Alfonso's had stayed rooted, a blackened hollow which had lately given trouble.

Mother snatched up one candle. 'I don't want Doña Maria disturbed. Darling, run and ask Theresa for a clove.' That was the cure; a clove, well chewed and pushed into the hollow.

'There's none left, Your Royal Highness,' Theresa said when I gasped out my request. 'No cinnamon neither, nor nutmeg. I couldn't find any such things, no, not if Our Blessed Lady herself wanted it.'

In order to tell me this, Theresa paused in the bandaging of her swollen leg.

'They'd have some over at the gatehouse. Come what may, Don Pedro is paid—and no bad hand at looking after himself.'

The shortest way between castle and gatehouse was along the curtain wall. Eight steps and there was the platform on which, in time of war, archers stood to shoot their arrows through the narrow slits in the wall. The platform at some far distant time had been roofed over and there were still, despite some collapses, long stretches which in bad weather made good playgrounds. Why shrink from the thought of using it now?

'Where is Jaime?' I could not suggest that Theresa, bandaging her leg at the end of a day in which she had done three women's work, should go.

'In bed. He took this cold and unless I'm careful with him it'll be on his chest till Easter.'

I said, to myself rather than to the old woman, 'I'll go.'

'It's a clear night and full moon.'

Think of Mother, trying to pacify Alfonso; think of Alfonso with toothache, awaiting the cure.

No time to find and light a little oil lamp, or a splinter of pinewood for a torch. Candle quite useless, it would blow out as you ran. And what is the matter with you, Isabella Trastamara? Afraid of the dark?

Yes! The garderobe at Arevalo, as in all old castles, was placed in a distant corner at the end of a passage dimly lighted by an oil lamp on a wall bracket, half-way along. The garderobe itself, to which one must make at least one necessary errand after dark, was quite brightly lighted, being small and having its own lamp. Sometimes to move out of this narrow, well lighted though evil-smelling space, and brave the comparatively dark passage and the positively dark stairs, had required a definite effort of will. Once indeed it had taken me so long to make the effort that Doña Maria noted how long I had been away and asked was I in need of a dose! Senna, another thing which came, like cloves from the East, and which, administered by Doña Maria, gave one the sensation of being disembowelled.

Tonight I did not even have to face darkness, except on the steps, up which I ran, holding the front of my skirt high. The stretch of platform lay before me, sharply striped with light and dark, narrow strips of white near the arrow slits, wider strips where the roof had collapsed.

The moonlight was useful, I could see where I was going, but I realised that there is no comfort in the moon. I began to run. I told myself that I was running not because I was afraid but so that Alfonso's suffering should not be prolonged.

I was half-way along, and in a light, roofless part when just ahead of me and to my left, the wall side, there was a rattling clank and a terrible howl. I stopped. Everything inside me stopped, my breath, my heart. The paralysis of terror gripped me so that I could not even lift my hand to make the sign of the cross. Only the surface of my body moved, hair bristling, skin crawling. I stood there, rigid, staring into the next dark patch, waiting ... If de Luna, mailed and wailing, if Satan himself had emerged from the darkness, I could not have moved out of his way.

Then the sound came again and I knew what it was. A wolf in a trap near Don Pedro's sheep-pen at the base of the wall. There are fewer wolves now in Castile, a modest reward for a freshly severed head has reduced them, but in those days they were a great nuisance, especially in sheep country like Arevalo.

Once I knew, I could move—but not run. I moved rather feebly, shaken with a peculiar hiccupping kind of laugh. I kept saying to myself—this must stop or I shall not be able to ask for the clove.

I reached the door at the end of the platform, the stout nailed door which opened directly into the gatehouse apartments. I beat on it with my fist and rattled the heavy ring of the handle. To be kept waiting now! I banged and rattled harder.

'Who is there?' Beatriz's voice, very cautious and timid. 'Isabella. Let me in. Let me *in*!'

The rooms of the gatehouse were smaller and lower than ours and were therefore always warmer and seemed better lighted. The warmth and light engulfed me now as I said, 'Can you let me have a clove? Fonso has toothache again.'

'You can have a dozen.' She looked at me and said, 'Is it raining?' Only then did I realise that fright had made me sweat in what Doña Maria would most certainly have called a most unladylike way. My hair was plastered to my skull and there were drip marks on the front of my bodice.

'I've just had a fine fright,' I said. 'Get me the cloves, Beatriz.'

She went in her leisurely way to a small chest which stood upon a big one, opened it and threw up the lid, revealing a number of small lidded compartments. Into one she dipped her very slender, tapering fingers. 'What frightened you?'

'I thought it was a ghost, but it was a wolf. I'll tell you all about it in the morning. Oh, Beatriz, be quick. Fonso is screaming.'

The sweet scent of cloves and other spices wafted out of the chest and hung on the warm air. She came towards me, her narrow palm cupped around a dozen cloves. I wiped my own hand on my skirt before taking them. I said, 'Thank you very much Beatriz.' I did notice that she looked different, her dark hair all loose and her clothes peculiar. But I had no time.

She said as we went towards the door, 'All the servants are at a wedding. And Father is making his last round ...' I thought impatiently—and what is that to me? Then we were in the doorway. I saw her face change from creamy pallor to the bluish white of skim-milk; and it tightened. She looked out along the light- and dark-striped passageway and said, 'I will come with you, Isabella.' She said it with an effort, but she said it ... And I knew that I had much underrated Beatriz de Bobadilla.

I said, 'Thank you for offering. But you'd catch your death of cold. And I am not at all frightened.'

Suddenly and blissfully it was true. That stark terror—and I still think that there is no fear quite like fear of the supernatural—had taught me in one short sharp lesson that the thing to be afraid of is fear. And it is not unlike the smallpox, if you survive a genuine attack you are free from it for the rest of your life. I do not mean that I did not know fear again, I have feared many things, but no fear ever paralysed me since; I have always been capable of thinking that the wailing ghost in clanking armour could only be a wolf in a trap. And for that reason I have always tried to see that young recruits, however trained and promising, do not go into battle without a good leavening of veterans, men who have faced fear and overcome it.

Mother said, 'What a time you took! I almost came down myself.'

So all this had happened in the time she regarded as a slow journey to the kitchen! Another lesson; time is not constant, though clocks and calendars and church bells do their best to measure it out as though it were wine, or flour.

In the morning, when Beatriz and I were alone, working on the altar cloth, and I had told her about being scared of nothing, she said,

'Did you notice what I was wearing?'

'You looked very pretty.' Possibly the first downright compliment I had ever paid her, but her offer to come out into the cold, the dark, the unknown, had touched my heart.

'The clothes belonged to my grandmother. She was a Moor.'

I knew, from my reading of history that long, long ago, in the eighth century the Moors, infidels, worshippers of Allah, had come from the East and overrun the whole peninsula. One of the chronicles said that of the Visigoths—my direct ancestors who had taken Spain when the Roman Empire collapsed—only about thirty families had escaped slaughter and taken refuge in distant, mountainous places like Asturia. (One pleasing little legend said that the Moors could not live anywhere where the olive tree cannot live and certainly in that country, swept by the rain-laden winds from the Atlantic, no olive tree could live.) The Moors rushed across the Pyrenees and would have taken France, but Charles Martell defeated them at Tours. They were also defeated in Portugal. A lot of English Crusaders, on their way to the Holy Land put in at Lisbon for water and supplies, and the King of Portugal sent them a message—No need to go to Palestine to fight the Infidel; fight him here and now.

Then, from Asturias, the descendants of those thirty families, hard, mountain-bred men with nothing much to lose and everything to gain, began to attack and to beat the Moors. Bit by bit, here a castle, here a town, the country had been recovered until now the Moors held only the Kingdom of Granada in the far south-east.

There was nothing shameful about having a Moorish grandmother—from time immemorial men of the conquering race have taken wives from the conquered. Always the way, from the taking by the Romans of the Sabine women, of which the old, extremely badly written but luridly illustrated, stories told; kill off the men, marry or enslave the women ...

'I found the clothes one day, in an old chest, and put them on—for fun. But Father said they suited me, and that I could wear them when he and I were alone.' She sounded rather defensive and I said, emphatically, 'They do suit you.' My memory produced details of what I had not been conscious of noticing the satin skirt made in two parts, like ankle-length breeches, very full and gathered in at the ankle; the little, heavily embroidered jacket. I said idly. 'Made in some stouter material, such clothes would be just right for riding, wouldn't they?'

'How people would stare!' Beatriz said.

The end of the truly happy time ...

2

Madrid, Ocana, Segovia, Toledo. 1462–5

'Besides it is notorious and generally believed that Doña Juana is the daughter of Don Beltran de la Cueva. When she was born certain taps were administered to her on the nose, in order to give it the form of the nose of King Henry IV, and so make her resemble him ...'

Memoir of the Privy Council of Castile

The man who came was of no importance. Alfonso and I were not called upon to show off our manners, but the news he brought was important, and to Mother and Doña Maria, very bad indeed. Queen Juana of Castile, my half-brother Henry's second wife, after years of childlessness was now pregnant.

Between themselves, Mother and Doña Maria might say that they could not believe it, that it could not be true, that there was trickery somewhere; but they did believe it. Mother's resolute gaiety vanished and Doña Maria ceased to use the words, 'When we return to Court ...' The hope upon which they had lived for more than seven years had vanished overnight.

In almost every other country in Europe there might have been some hope left—the hope that the Queen would bear a girl. But in Castile the right of the female to succeed to the throne was acknowledged.

Once Doña Maria said almost savagely, 'We must not despair. There are miscarriages, and still births.'

'Oh, don't. Don't wish ill to the unborn,' Mother said, and broke into the weeping that came so easily to her in those days. As well as being lachrymose she seemed to lose interest in everything; she would sit down to work on the altar cloth, make a few stitches and stop, needle poised, eyes fixed in a stare of such despair that it hurt to look at her. Any attempt to comfort her was worse than useless. I tried. I would put my arms round her and kiss her and say things like, 'So long as we are together ... So long as we are in good health ...' She would then clutch me to her so hard that I could scarcely breathe, and say, 'It is the future I dread. What is going to happen to you both?' She spoke vaguely about some betrothal that concerned me, made long ago, and now never to be honoured. She made vague, dismal-sounding plans—at least they sounded dismal to Alfonso and me at that time. I could go to a convent; Alfonso must work harder at his lessons and qualify for holy orders. He might attain a bishopric. A conventual life had no charm for me then; I liked the open air, riding, dancing, archery even; I was greedy about food, such wine as we had; I preferred secular books to religious ones, and merry music to solemn. I was also, though this surprises me to remember, fond of fine clothing. The hyacinth-blue velvet gown that Mother had made to fit me had given me extraordinary pleasure. As for Alfonso, he disliked such simple lessons as had hitherto been forced upon him and the idea of serious study appalled him. 'I shall just run away, Isa, and be a soldier.'

It was a very long, very gloomy winter. Only Beatriz had anything cheerful to say. 'If you can avoid taking the real vows, Isabella, I am sure that my aunt, having found me a husband, will do the same for you. Or I will do it myself, once I am married ...'

So April of the year 1462 came; the best time of year in central Castile; green grass springing up after the winter rains, fruit trees in flower, the air full of birdsong and the cries of newly dropped lambs. On a blue and gold, blue and green, blue and white morning we all—Alfonso, Don Pedro, Beatriz and I, came back from a ride to find the castle court yard all astir; a lot of men in livery, and a lot of horses, all good ones but not one like Sasha.

Doña Maria was on the look-out for us, 'If only we'd had an hour's warning,' she said, hitting Alfonso and me with wet cloths and brushes, though we now had—and that was irony, too—servants again. They all came from Galicia and spoke a dialect which made them almost foreign, so they could not gossip, and did not associate with the people of Arevalo who might tell them about the ghost.

When we had been roughly made presentable the stubby young man who acted as page flung open the door of the room in which we had huddled, peasant fashion, through the winter and spoke—as though it had been something he had learned by ear—our names.

Mother sat in the canopied chair. Her eyes were bright and her face, so pale of late, had a delicate pink flush which made her look young again.

She said, 'This is His Grace, the Archbishop of Toledo. Your Grace, my children.'

Alfonso bowed; I made my curtsey. The Archbishop looked us over keenly and made favourable remarks about us being well grown and handsome. He was handsome himself, more like a soldier than a cleric. He had a florid face, bright greenish-brown eyes and a mouth which was petulant, except when he smiled. He smiled as he said,

'I have come to take Your Royal Highnesses to Court.'

'To Madrid,' Mother said joyfully. 'We can leave immediately after dinner. We have so little to pack!'

In later years people wondered why I bore so much from Alfonso Carillo, Primate of Castile, the childish tantrums, the arrogance, the downright treachery. Such people were not there when he said, gently,

'Your Majesty, I fear I must have misled you. You are not ordered to Madrid at this moment.' Mother blanched and wilted. 'It may be that His Majesty had been led to believe that you were not in good health—a notion which I shall correct immediately, I assure you.'

She began to cry. 'They are too young. I cannot let them go alone.'

'Not alone, Madam. They will be in my care. I promise, I will look after them as though they were my own. And at the first possible opportunity ...'

'I should have known. To take from me all that I have!'

Most people when they weep are faintly repulsive, sobbing and gulping and snuffling. Mother was different; tears simply flooded her eyes and spilled. I flung myself at her and forgetting all I had been taught, shouted, 'We won't go! Don't cry, Mother! If we can't *all* go together, we will *none* of us go.' Alfonso, near tears himself, came and embraced us both, one arm around Mother, one around me, and said, croakingly, 'We won't go!'

Mother disentangled herself from our clinging arms and said, 'Darlings, you must. It is an order from the King, whose subjects we all are ...'

The Archbishop had tactfully turned away and stood, looking out of the narrow window; now he turned back and said,

'That is so ... And it may be only a short separation. Once the ceremonies are over ...'

Mother said, 'Not back here, to rot in obscurity! Puppets taken out to make a show and then put back in the box. Not that! That least of all. They are the children of a king. Let that not be forgotten. And I must speak to my daughter. Privately. She has not yet had her eleventh birthday but she must not go into the world in ignorance.'

Those were perhaps the last coherent words she ever spoke. When we were together, in private, what she said to me was all muddled and sidelong, as though I had been going about with my eyes shut. Had I actually been as ignorant as she assumed me to be, I should, when she had done, have been little the wiser, except for one remark, something she would never have said in her right mind—'Darling, there is no joy in it. It is like being poked with a stick.'

So, this was the Court of which Mother and Doña Maria had, until last November, spoken of as though it were Heaven on earth. Like a beehive disturbed; dozens of people all busy, or pretending to be.

Henry, the King, our half-brother, to whom Alfonso and I

knelt when presented, was kindly. The extended hand, the words, 'Welcome to our Court.' But even kindliness could not mask his ugliness; an over-large head on an over-thin neck and between the true Trastamara eyes, a nose running flat from left to right, then a hump, and right to left.

Whoever broke that poor little baby's nose in order to establish her likeness to the king who was supposed to have fathered her, was not only a brute, but a fool. Even I knew better. Henry had broken his nose when, as a boy, he had fallen from a wall. It had been badly set. But whoever knew an old soldier, with one arm, one leg, one eye, one ear, come home from the wars and beget a child similarly maimed? There were several old soldiers in Arevalo and all their children were sound. There was a leper, too, not in the town itself, hovering on the outskirts; he had no nose at all, and few fingers, but his children were healthy and whole and never failed to put out food for him, on a boundary stone.

However, perhaps whoever broke the baby's nose had never lived in the country, near to reality. For my half-brother Henry's Court was about as far removed from reality as a place could be. And much nastier than any place should be.

I was puzzled at first. I was given over to the care of Doña Elvira de Guzman, extremely strict, but it was she who said, laughing, 'If only God had given the Marquis of Villena a womb, we should not have waited so long for a christening!'

Another lady said, 'Villena is green with envy. It is with Beltran de la Cueva that His Majesty must share everything—even his Queen!'

Sometimes an awareness of my presence would cut short such talk; often it did not; and when I partly understood, and overheard some sly horrid remarks about the Marquis of Villena having a fondness for very young boys, and a desire to inspire jealousy in the King to avenge his favouritism for Beltran de la Cueva, I became very worried about Alfonso whom I had seen only twice since our first evening at Court, and then only to smile and wave to across a crowded hall. And on both occasions, I now remembered, the Marquis of Villena was near by. Of the Archbishop I had seen nothing. I felt that I must do something; so I planned the first campaign of my life.

Every day after dinner the ladies not in actual attendance on the

Queen—whom I had not seen yet—took a siesta and then had long sessions with dressmakers and shoemakers in preparation for the forthcoming christening. I had already been fitted out with one new gown for ordinary wear, tawny satin, with square-toed shoes to match, and my crimson velvet for the great day was in the making. (The clothes with which I had come to Court, even Mother's lovely cut-down dress, had evoked glances and sniffs of scorn.) Planning my secret errand I had the little extra confidence that the knowledge of being well dressed can give to the young.

The Archbishop had his own palace in Madrid; he owned, I was to learn, more palaces and castles than the King himself. I was surprised to find, when I approached the place, no men in the Archbishop's livery in the forecourt or at the wide doorway, one half of which stood open. I paused and drew a deep breath and rehearsed once more the difficult thing I had come to say—difficult because it seemed to hint that the promise to Mother had not been fulfilled. I was ignorant of all diplomacy and intended to say frankly what I had overheard and what worried me.

Just inside the door an old woman, wearing a coarse apron, was washing the marble floor. I knew as soon as I entered why the place was apparently deserted; there was that unmistakable stench of garderobes and drains being cleansed. Even at Arevalo, inhabited by so few people, the process had been necessary and nobody wished to be within doors while it was going on. The Archbishop would not be here this afternoon. I was about to ask the old woman if she knew when he would return, but she spoke first, resting her red, swollen hands on the bucket's rim.

'You're a day early,' she said, in a disrespectful way. Early for what?

'I wished to speak to His Grace. Can you tell me when he will be here?'

'You weren't bespoken then? I don't know,' she said, shaking her shaggy head. 'Every time your sort get younger and bolder. Trying to get in first; eh?'

'I do not understand you. I am the Princess Isabella and I wished ...'
She gave a hoarse cackle of laughter. 'And I'm the Queen of Sheba! Not a bad trick though, it might have got you past the door. Except

27

that everybody knows where the Princess is. Over there,' she jerked her head in the direction of the palace. 'Being made use of. Made to stand godmother to La Beltraneja.'

I said, 'I *am* the Princess Isabella. And you should stand up when you speak to me.'

She looked at me, narrowing her eyes. 'You been taking something? You know what I mean—unless you've had too much. It can addle your wits besides making you good and ready.' Something like pity touched her harsh face. 'Be warned by me. It's no sort of a life, dearie. Fine clothes and fine gentlemen to begin with; then shopkeepers, then soldiers, and if you aren't dead at forty, you end scrubbing floors. Get out while you can. That's my advice to you.' She put her hands back into the scummy water and groped for the cloth.

I did not understand her at all. What I did understand was that she did not believe me. Perhaps *her* wits were addled.

Out of it all—when I had swallowed the humiliation, which could have been avoided by the presence of a single page or waiting-man, and which I had brought upon myself—something emerged. The old woman had used the term, La Beltraneja, and the ladies of the Court used it too, sniggering. She had also said the Princess was being *used*.

I had taken the arrangement that I should be godmother as perfectly right and in order. Who but a king's daughter should stand sponsor to another? This feeling of correctness had blinded me to what lay behind the sniggering gossip. Now I knew.

I went blundering on, rather like somebody learning a strange language. Looking back I can see now that I was not only ignorant but arrogant in a clumsy way. In part it was the result of our upbringing—I say 'our' because Alfonso shared the attitude. At Arevalo, despite the poor food, the cut-down clothes, the clumped shoes, we had never been allowed to lose sight of the fact that we were royal. If our half-brother, Henry, had gone about more cleverly in his design to reduce us, make us subservient, he would have kept us at Court where we should have been ground down in the mill of etiquette and protocol.

As it was I saw no reason why I should not approach Henry, and ask him a direct question. He was King, I was his subject, but not his slave.

The palace was becoming crowded; more and more people arriving to take part in the baptismal ceremony. The King was receiving nobles from distant places, prelates, delegates, ambassadors; I could not even see him, leave alone get near enough to talk, until late evening when he went—I imagined—to his private apartments where a rather haughty-looking young page was overlooking the replacement of candles. In answer to my question he said that His Majesty was in his laboratory.

'And where is that?'

Shocked boy broke through the official manner.

'Your Royal Highness could not intrude there. Nobody is admitted.'

I said, 'Direct me.'

He led the way to a part of the palace unknown to me; rooms that communicated, passages, and finally into a small octagonal anteroom, one side of which was taken up by a door, covered with leather and heavily nailed. It had no guard; it had no handle.

The boy said, 'Really, I wouldn't, Your Royal Highness. His Majesty would be angered. And old Don Philipino might put a spell on you—turn you into a frog!' He spoke with earnestness.

'If he does,' I said, 'pick me up gently and put me in the nearest pool.' Such flippancy offended him. He said,

'It is not a matter for jest, Your Royal Highness. Don Philipino is an alchemist and a magician. Fear guards that door.'

I went towards it and pushed. It opened slightly, heavy against the hand, and something was released, a warmth, a strange sweet scent and a definite feeling of secrecy, of the forbidden thing. It was powerful enough to halt me for a second. It was a different fear from the one that had assailed me on the night of the clove and the wolf, that had taken me unawares, no time even to call upon God, or upon St Michael, the protector from evil. I had time now …

The boy said, 'If you will go … I will come with you.' His face wore the white, tight look that Beatriz's had worn on that night.

I said, 'Thank you for offering; but two frogs could not help one another!'

I pushed the door farther and saw that immediately beyond it a staircase spiralled down. The walls were hung with tapestries and velvet and strips of parchment bearing strange signs. At intervals little lamps burned on wall brackets, and gave off a sweet odour as they burned. I went down and down; not consciously being brave for I did not believe that Don Philipino—or anyone else—could turn me into a frog. That was fairy-tale stuff. My need to have talk with my half-brother, and curiosity, dominated my mind.

The stairs ended with another door, one of fine ironwork of the kind called Moorish or Arabesque because it was formed into formal patterns, no recognisable shapes. All very old buildings, dating back to the days before the re-conquest, had balconies or window screens of such work. I pushed and it did not yield. Here again there was no handle. I leaned close to the door and looked into the space beyond. The stairway, thickly carpeted underfoot, and so well hung, so well lighted and so sweet-scented, gave way at the iron gateway to a kind of dungeon, not unlike those at Arevalo, unused for many years and explored by Alfonso and me once, and no more; there was the same smell of stone, wet stone, and of the inedible fungi and moulds that grow in such places, needing no light. Yet this place was lighted.

A narrow table ran the length of the room; on it there were flasks, scales, things I did not recognise, a clutter but orderly. About half-way along the table, with an oil lamp and a candlestand, the one casting a steady, the other a wavering light, my half-brother, Henry King of Castile, sat confronting a greybeard, Don Philipino. Between them lay what looked like maps to me and there was also another of the unrecognisable objects, a sphere on a stand, not solid but made up of intersecting circles.

Henry was crying. I had never before seen a man weep like a woman. He leaned forward, holding his heavy head in his hands, and sobbed.

The old man said, coldly, 'I am sorry. I have cast it three times, hoping I was mistaken. There is no escape. The glass tells the same tale. The pity is that you did not believe me, ten years ago, when I told you you would die without issue.'

'I was trying to secure an undisputed succession,' Henry said.

'Choosing the worst way. All you have made certain is disaster, bloodshed—and finally, for her, death by poison.'

Henry made a sound, half-sob, half-groan, 'Poor child! Poor child!'

He raised his head a little and said, 'I am an evil man. Vice always came naturally to me but ...'

'It was in your stars,' Don Philipino interrupted. '... but I am not so vile as to contemplate without sorrow such a fate for an innocent child.'

'It could be mitigated,' the old man said. 'It is the *combination* of her stars with yours that spells calamity.'

'How can I disown her now? With every Grandee of Castile come to see her baptised?'

'She could be dead in her cradle tomorrow morning.'

'I will not have murder,' Henry said, sounding, for the first time something like a king.

'A substitution, then. I could arrange it. A dead baby is easily come by—picked up on any midden.'

Henry dropped his head again and was silent. Finally he said,

'It would disappoint the people, already discontent enough.'

'Will the baptism of a bastard content them? Once the meat is eaten and the wine drunk? As for the Grandees, they will take their oaths, but with reservation. How can they do otherwise when the child is already called La Beltraneja, in every tavern?'

That angered the King. 'They can say what they like, they cannot *know*. Nobody *knows* except you, and the Church takes a stern view of witches and warlocks. I am King of Castile; if I behave towards her as though she were my own, she will be accepted.'

'With the results that I have foreseen.'

'What must be, must be,' Henry said. He stood up and I prepared to hurry back up the stairs. But he turned in the other direction and opened a door in the dimness. The draught stirred the cold, cellar smell, and a skeleton that hung on the wall rattled a little.

Well, I was answered. I went more upon Henry's words, *as though she were my own*, than on the old man's use of the word bastard. And if the Grandees of Castile could swear Oaths, with reservations, so could I. I understood the term—it meant that when something was forced upon you by some outside pressure, you did it, or said it, with a silent appeal to God for forgiveness and understanding: I had read of it being done by prisoners of war held for ransom, and asked to swear not to attempt to escape.

As I went up the stairs I realised that I had also learned something else of importance—the fallibility of witches and warlocks. If Don Philipino had possessed half the occult power that he claimed he would surely have known that somebody was there, on the other side of the grille, watching and listening.

The boy was in the little octagonal space, his face bonewhite.

'You waited,' I said. 'That was very kind.'

He grinned, making mock of his fear now that fear was over. 'I had in mind a pleasant pool—with water-lilies.'

'Well, as you see ...' I smiled. Then a thought occurred to me.

'You are a royal page. Do you have contact with my brother?'

'I see him—sometimes,' he said cautiously. 'He is not lodged with us. I could take a message if Your Royal Highness wished.'

I thought quickly. 'Early tomorrow. At Prime. By this pool into which you proposed to put me. Will you ask him to meet me there? Say it is a matter of importance.'

'I will do it.'

I said, 'I am much indebted to you. What is your name?'

'Inez de Mendoza,' he said, with rightful pride. The Mendoza family was one of the foremost of Castile. 'Younger son of younger son for three generations,' he added wryly, and I understood; he meant that despite his great name he had his own way to make in the world.

It pleased me to think that I was able, in the end, to repay him for that evening's kindness.

It was such an innocent morning, giving promise of a fine April day. Alfonso, still sleepy-eyed, looked as young and innocent as the morning and I suddenly realised the enormity of what I was about to say.

'Mother?' he asked anxiously. We had left Mother in a dreadful state, held up by Doña Maria and weeping hopelessly. But so much had happened since that—God forgive me for being so unfilial—I had forgotten her, sometimes for hours at a time.

'No. We should have heard, from Doña Maria, or from Beatriz. What I wanted to say—of course I wanted to see you properly, Fonso, and I am glad to see you—but, well ... it concerns the Marquis of

Villena ...' It was difficult to say, difficult to find the right words. What words?

'Oh,' Alfonso said, astounding me. 'Pacheco the Pederast. That is what they call him. I was warned about him the first day. Twice. A big angry boy was extremely rude to me; he said I was not to think that because I was a prince, and handsome, I could displace him in the Marquis's favour. If I did, he said, he'd black my eyes, split my lip, spoil my looks. Then another boy explained it all to me. I could hardly believe my ears. It sounded so ... so silly. How did *you* know, Isa? I should have thought ladies ...'

'They talk, too. Never mind. just so long as you remember not to be alone with Villena—or any other man who seems to take too much interest in you.'

'Trust me,' he said. 'You see, Isa, if you do *that*, you can't have any children ... At least that was what the second boy said. He said the King did it and that was why he had no children. The baby is not supposed to be his. Did you know *that*?'

'I have heard it said ...' Like a smack in the face came the knowledge that I could never tell what I *knew* without disclosing that I had eavesdropped in a peculiarly dishonourable way, almost as though I had lurked and hidden when a confession was being made. Thrusting that distasteful thought away I explained to Alfonso what 'with reservations' meant when taking oaths.

He said, 'This is a strange world. So much to learn, Isa. Sometimes I wish ... I wish we were back at Arevalo.'

'So do I.'

All my tears were shed long ago and with good reason, but now and then, when I look back, a feeling near to tears comes lumpily into my throat when I remember that morning. Nothing personal; the two children who stood by that pool where later the water-lilies would flower, have gone their different ways and vanished. Even Alfonso, having undergone the final change, can hardly have vanished more truly than Isabella, to whom change came more slowly and in the end more completely. But they were real once, two children ripped from their mother, and the world they knew, plunged into a corrupt society, and wishing themselves back in Arevalo.

When it came to my turn to hold the baby I did so tenderly. She was so swaddled and draped that she felt like a wooden doll rather than a living baby and her swollen nose, which later grew as straight as mine, somewhat marred her looks. But I looked on her with pity, not because Don Philipino had foretold a bad fate for her, but because in streets and taverns she had been given a scornful nickname before ever she was recognised as a child of God and given her Christian name—Joanna.

The nobles swore the oath of allegiance to her and the Cortes of Castile, similar to but much more democratic and representative than the Parliament of England, met and recognised her rights as heir to the throne. This was a passing over of Alfonso's rights, but only the King, Don Philipino and I could be *sure* of that; perhaps the Queen herself was uncertain who fathered her child. Alfonso's informant had been mistaken in linking perversity with sterility—Villena had a son—so perhaps the Queen did believe the child was Henry's. I knew even then, that if Henry died without *indisputably* begetting an heir I should be greatly troubled in my mind, but Henry was still King and there was nothing I could do except conform. Indeed for quite a long time absolute conformity of behaviour was a necessity for me, for fear someone should say—She is as mad as her mother! For that is what had happened to my gentle, gay, high-spirited mother: she was deranged. At first Doña Maria tried to hide the fact from me and Alfonso: 'I am writing because your mother, the Queen, is not feeling well today.' My letters, which I tried to make cheerful and interesting, and Alfonso's, briefer, but fond, evoked no reply from Mother; there were mentions of headaches, stiffness of the fingers, a heavy cold. Then Doña Maria ran out of excuses and wrote to the King, telling him the truth and asking him to break the news to us gently. He shirked the task and left it to Doña Elvira, as ungentle a tool as he could have chosen. I am not aware of ever having given her any reason to dislike me, but she did and seemed to derive some pleasure in informing me that my mother had fallen into melancholy madness, took no interest in anything, scarcely spoke and when she did talked incomprehensible nonsense. And ever after that Doña Elvira would remind me from time to time: 'Your Royal Highness reads too much. It is not good for the mind.' When I asked whether lessons could be arranged for me, she said that that was a *mad* notion, giving the word emphasis.

Alfonso and I once asked for leave to go and visit Mother. It was refused for contradictory reasons; she would not even know us; the sight of us would upset her.

Beatriz had never written anything about Mother's condition, until she knew that I knew and then she wrote very sweetly, saying that Mother had lost her mind, but seemed happier in her mindlessness than in the last months before our departure or the week or so after it. 'She no longer cries and her expression is placid. Melancholy may have brought her to this state, but she is not melancholy now.'

It was almost like hearing that Mother was dead, but less simple, for when the mind is gone where is the soul? Could one pray for the soul of a woman still alive? Would a woman who did not know her own children be able to perform even the simplest of religious duties? Pray? Confess? Observe holy days?

'Your Royal Highness looks very glum,' Doña Elvira would say, when in fact I was thoughtful or—as frequently happened—disapproving at the scurrilous talk which seemed to me all the worse because it was a matter for mirth; 'I hope you are not turning melancholy.'

I led a very lonely life in the midst of the crowd. My great comfort at this time was my confessor, Father Tomas de Torquemada. I must admit that the idea of Torquemada being a *comfort* to anyone seems strange—strange now even to me. He was a member of the Dominican Order, well known for its austerity, but his asceticism surpassed even the Order's rules. He never ate meat, or used a bed, or wore anything but a hair shirt next to his skin. He imposed the heaviest penalties for quite trivial sins and for that reason was avoided as a confessor. Yet his very sternness was a comfort. When at last I ventured to ask him about Mother, about the connection of mind and soul, he behaved to me as though I had blasphemed. Even to ask such questions, he said, revealed a regrettable lack of faith in God, and an equally regrettable degree of spiritual pride. God had, in His infinite wisdom, seen fit to darken Mother's mind, and that had no more to do with her immortal soul than if her physical sight had been darkened. 'The activities of the mind, no less than those of the body, can endanger the soul. From such sins of mental error, your mother is now immune. You can leave her soul to God—and look to your own.' He said a lot more, much of it beyond my understanding. What did emerge dearly was that trust in God, complete submission to His will, was essential; and complete submission meant not questioning, even in one's mind ...

So three years passed.

I had noticed, as the Court moved from Ocana to Segovia, from Segovia to Madrid, and from Madrid to Toledo—Castile having no fixed capital city like Paris or London—that it grew less crowded. Notable absentees, the Archbishop of Toledo, the Marquis of Villena and Don Faderique Enriques, Admiral of Spain, all had valid excuses for lengthening absences, the one his plurality of livings, the other his huge estates, the third his naval duties. It came therefore as a shock to everybody, most of all to the King, to learn that these three, with many other of the Grandees, were plotting open rebellion unless Henry accepted their ultimatum, issued from Burgos, a town in the extreme north.

I was present when my half-brother burst into the Queen's apartment, papers in his shaking hand, frenzy in his shaking voice, 'Look at this!'

3

Ocana, Olmedo, Segovia, Arevalo, Cardenosa, Avila. 1465–8

' .. y todos los Grandes y Cabelleros y las Ciudade y Villas estuvieron divisas en dos partes, la una permanecio siempre con este Rey Enrique, la otra estuvo con aquel Rey Alfonso, el cual duro titule de Rey por espacio de tres anos, y murio en la edad de catorce anos.'

'and all the Grandees and cavaliers, the cities and towns were divided into two parties, the one always staying with this King Henry, the other with that King Alfonso, who held the title of King for three years and died at the age of fourteen.'

Los Claros Varones de España, Pulgar

I was there on that morning partly on account of my age—fourteen—partly on account of my status, and partly because both the Queen and the Princess Joanna had taken an unaccountable fancy for me. The child's liking for somebody still just young enough to play was understandable in simple human terms, the Queen's was more complicated; favouring me she administered snubs to other of her ladies. She was no fool, she knew what was said of her, and who said most of it; also it pleased her to see me, indisputably a Princess of Castile, crawling about on my knees to retrieve a ball or some other toy, thrown by her daughter, another Princess of Castile whose claim was not quite indisputable. On my side I was not sorry to get away from the ladies' apartments and into something that often resembled private life and I was fond of Joanna, my godchild; she was so pretty, so lively and yet amenable and affectionate.

Irony again! The will of God? That La Beltraneja and I, born to be enemies, should have loved one another once. I had never *admired* Queen Juana, she was vain, soft, voluptuous, idle and immoral; but on that morning my mild liking for her, slightly, I admit, contemptuous, did take another turn.

She took the papers, read them and said,

'How *dare* they? How dare they send this to you, their King? How dare they? They call me whore, our child a bastard. As God is in Heaven, my brother of Portugal will avenge this insult! He has twenty thousand men ready for the field. Send back to them, these rebels, say that we do not care that,' she snapped her fingers, 'for them and their demands.'

My half-brother said, 'It would mean war.'

'Then let it. It was meant to be. An ultimatum is a challenge. A challenge must be accepted.'

'It would mean bloodshed. That, at any cost, I would avoid.'

Juana said, 'There speaks the half-man I married, God help me! The meanest peasant, cowherd, swineherd would take spade or fork to avenge such an insult.'

'And provoke a family feud; no more. This, unless I agree, would bring civil war. Compromise. We must compromise.'

His idea of compromise was to agree to everything and then retract. In a way his behaviour made the Queen's understandable—after that year she became shamelessly promiscuous.

Henry agreed to accept Alfonso as his legitimate heir; he agreed to banish Beltran de la Cueva from Court and strip him of all honours; he agreed to allow the Marquis of Villena and the Archbishop of Toledo to take charge of Alfonso so that his education might continue away from the distraction of life at Court. He made a number of other concessions on minor matters, such as getting rid of his ostentatious and incredibly vicious Moorish guards and 'amending his way of life'.

Alfonso, before he went to Cabezon, the place named by the rebels for his acknowledgement, came to say farewell to me. At twelve years old he had lost his dangerous pretty-boy looks; he was tall, thin, awkward, his nose too large for his face, his feet and hands too big for the rest of him, and although he did not yet need to be shaved his chin and cheeks were fluffy enough never to look quite clean; he was spotty, too. Physically he was neither man nor boy and his manner, his whole attitude reflected the half-way state; portentous dignity, childishness alternating. But under it all was a cynicism, something down-to-earth, a trifle caustic which made me think that if the rebels thought that he would be easily manipulated they might presently have reason to think that they had the wrong cat by the tail. I did not fear *for* him so much as what he might *do* in one of those royal-dignified spells. I told him that he must never forget that Henry was King; that anything which detracted from the mystique of royalty diminished us all. I said, 'Alfonso, you must never do anything to undermine the throne which you are now heir to.' He said, 'Oh, never. And how could I? I am really nothing more than a prisoner, held as hostage. I know that.'

Before the summer of 1465 he was much more.

The scene—shocking to me and to all genuine Royalists took place outside Avila. On a platform built high enough to be visible to a great crowd, the rebels set up an effigy of Henry in royal robes and with all the regalia of monarchy, replicas complete to the last detail. The Archbishop said Mass; then he mounted the platform and removed the crown; other rebel nobles took away the sceptre, the sword and the clothes and tumbled the naked dummy down to be mauled by the crowd. Alfonso was led to the throne, crowned and pronounced King, to the sound of trumpets and shouts of 'Castile! Castile for the King, Don Alfonso.'

When the King heard, he wept. The Queen raged, 'So much for your compromise!' I was grieved that Alfonso had been forced into such a masquerade; I was also alarmed. If a rabble, headed by a few malcontents, can make a king, they can equally well unmake him. I wrote to Alfonso, not reproachfully, for who knew what pressures had been brought to bear, but frankly and warningly. The letter may never have reached him: he did not reply to it.

Several large towns, including Seville in the south, declared for Alfonso, and so began the civil war which Henry had tried to avoid. My position became even more unhappy; I was sister to the usurper, and therefore suspect. I became aware of being constantly watched; the Queen withdrew her favour. I should have been thoroughly unhappy but for the fact that Beatriz was with me.

In every letter she had ever written to me she had expressed a wish that her father would make up his mind to send her to her aunt in Segovia so that at least when the Court was in that city, we might meet; finally Don Pedro braced himself for parting with her and she came to Segovia and we had two brief meetings. Then Beatriz changed her wish—she wished she could live at Court in order to be with me and her aunt, that arranger of marriages, was able to arrange that, also. There was a member of the de Cabrera family, Don Andreas, at Court already, occupying the responsible post of major domo; he was also Governor of Segovia. A word from his second cousin by marriage was enough, Beatriz was installed. Doña Elvira, as always, made a sour comment, 'One will soon not be able to distinguish between the ladies' apartments and the nursery!' Beatriz and I were both over thirteen at the time.

Her arrival greatly mitigated my lot; not only was she my constant companion, Don Andreas began to pay her a great deal of attention—fatherly we both thought at first, for he was well into this thirties and his solemn demeanour made him seem even older. He had power, and even when Alfonso's usurpation cast a shadow on me, simply because I was Beatriz's friend I enjoyed privileges which spite would have denied me. Nobody who has not lived at Court, out of favour and yet bound to remain there, can imagine how things like the allotment of accommodation, of servants, even of food can be affected. I should have fared badly in those days but for the fact that Don Andreas always saw to it that Beatriz was well looked after. He was not a markedly convivial man and his tastes were simple, almost austere, but like other men of the kind whom I was to know later, he derived a vicarious enjoyment from seeing his guests eat and drink. In his private apartments everywhere, but notably in Segovia where his position of keeper of the castle was distinct from his major domo's office, he gave small but delicious feasts, with music and tumblers and jugglers and dancers. It was after one such that I said to Beatriz, to whom I could say *anything*. 'Do you know, Beatriz, I think Don Andreas is in love with you—something in the way he looks at you.'

She said, composedly, 'I hope so. What more could I ask? A man of unblemished reputation, assured position—and fond of me. My aunt, had I stayed with her, could not have done better for me. And in fact, by getting me to Court, she probably had this in mind.'

'And you are agreeable?'

Perhaps Doña Elvira was right in her denunciation of reading as a thing that might addle the brain. So many of the stories, and quite a few of the Chronicles, were concerned with love. Everybody knew that this had nothing to do with marriage, but I would have wished for Beatriz, as I certainly wished for myself, marriage to a man whom it would be possible to come to love.

'You think him too old? I prefer older men. They are more indulgent. Of course being so old Don Andreas may not wish to wait until I am sixteen. My father said that was the earliest age at which he would allow me to marry.'

She sounded so calm, so cold-blooded about it. Quite rightly, I admitted. And it was. absurd of me, unlikely to have a husband at all—since who would bother to arrange a marriage for me?—to think that I would like a young man, handsome, soldierly, merry, and of course ready to look at me as dotingly as Don Andreas looked at Beatriz. Still, dreams cost nothing, and if uncommunicated do not expose one to ridicule.

In 1466 a husband was found for me!

Not since I became the sister of the usurper—that is two long years—had I set foot in the King's or the Queen's private apartments and when Henry sent for me my first thought was—something has happened to Alfonso! There had been sporadic fighting between Royalists and rebels in many places and although I knew that neither the Archbishop nor Villena would allow Alfonso, so valuable, to take any undue risk, there was always the chance of accident, of treachery, of poison. Not to mention ordinary illnesses such as smallpox.

I ran and arrived breathless, a little distraught.

Henry said, 'You may sit. I sent for you to tell you ... I have this day received a communication which offers a way out of this whole sorry impasse.'

'My brother?'

'No. No. The Marquis of Villena wrote to me. He is ... he is prepared to desert the rebel cause and that would mean its certain collapse. You realise that?'

I thought—Why tell me? I assumed the correct, interested expression.

'He makes one condition. He is willing to come over, to bring his troops and all his influence, if you marry his brother, Don Pedro Giron, Master of Calatrava.'

People often say, recounting a mild surprise, *I was dumbstruck.* The reality happened to me; for what seemed a long time I lost my voice completely. That Henry, my half-brother, with royal blood in his veins should have considered for a moment something so shameful. Marriage to a commoner and what a commoner! Head of one of the great religious-military orders, vowed to celibacy, but one of the most notorious libertines in Castile. Part of me added—and old and fat, with teeth so rotten that they give off the smell of a charnel house!

When I found my voice it was not mine. Boys' voices break, shift through a time when squeaks and growls alternate and then settle down. I had never heard of a girl having a change of voice, but it happened to me. I said,

'I will never marry Don Pedro,' in a voice tones deeper than my own and with a resonance that surprised me as much as it did Henry.

'Isabel, you have no choice. This is what Villena asks as the price of peace.'

'And you listen to that double traitor! You made him. He betrayed you. Now, having deserted a king, and made another—remember the part he played in that obscene masquerade outside Avila—he is so arrogant, so blown up with pride that he thinks to mingle his blood with ours! Through his brother, *vowed to celibacy.*'

Like all men with a weak case, Henry picked on the irrelevant.

'The Pope would absolve him from his vows,' he said, and looked at me hopefully. 'It has been done before.'

'Even so, I should protest. Up to the altar.'

'That also has been done before. Priests can be deaf on occasion. Isabella, think, you have it in your power to bring peace ...'

'You had it; if you had held to the conditions issued from Burgos none of this would have happened. And you could, even now, with one bold stroke bring ... restore ... Villena would not have made such an approach to you unless he and the rest were tired of this nagging war. You and the Duke of Alburquerque have gathered a huge army—and not struck a blow yet. Defeat the rebels *once*, forgive Alfonso and bring him back as your heir, and that would be the end of it.'

'It would be easier this way.' The stubbornness of the weak showed through. 'And if I order you to do it, it will be done. You have no appeal.'

I said, 'Henry, I have been loyal to you. Before you set spies on me I could have gone to the rebels. I stayed with you because you are King. I had respect for your royal blood. Have you none for mine?'

'I have already answered Villena's letter and accepted his terms.'

'Then only God can help me.'

'God also can be very deaf, on occasion,' Henry said.

I went straight to Beatriz. Her very lips went white.

'That infamous rogue! That fat lecher! I'd kill him first.'

She put her frail hand to her pouch and pulled out a toysized dagger. We all wore embroidered or bejewelled pouches at our girdles; they held smelling salts, scent bottles, handkerchiefs, keys. The dagger startled me. 'I know how to use it, too,' she said, with unbelievable ferocity. 'The throat or the eye.'

I took her wrist. 'Come with me to the chapel, Beatriz. We must pray.'

This was no ordinary praying. Intermingled with the formal words were desperate appeals—God help! God save me! God! God! At first with none of the much-praised submission—Thy will be done. I was certain that Henry's plan must be as disgusting to God as it was to me. Certain that the miracle would happen; Villena would change his mind again; the Pope would refuse to release Don Pedro from his vows; Henry would realise the folly of allowing himself to be blackmailed ... The Archbishop would protest against this infamous scheme ...

Nothing of the kind happened. Watched, even at prayer, by hard-eyed guards, Beatriz and I prayed by day and by night-once through a whole day and a night on end. The Pope gave Don Pedro leave to marry; and the man himself began his journey, coming towards Ocana where the Court then was.

Faith wavered; recovered. I must pray differently—God give strength to bear what is Thy will; help me to be strong and resigned...

Once I caught sight of myself in the glass and thought—No ordinary suitor would want me now, haggard, wild-eyed, but a man intent upon marrying into a royal family would take a princess even if she were a leper ... No hope there.

Coming, apparently with the inevitability of death, Don Pedro halted for the night; he said he felt tired and that his throat was slightly sore. Next day he died. Why has always been a mystery to everyone except Beatriz and me. Croup, some said, but that is a childish disease and does not strike in silence; quinsy, some said, but quinsy takes time to breed and seldom kills. God struck him and delivered me, after I had submitted my will to His.

What could I do, in a tangible way, to show my gratitude, my daily, hourly, never-ending gratitude for this deliverance? I had no money; I could not set up a shrine, endow a religious house or feed the poor. It must be a personal thing, and also something that would be a constant reminder.

I was worn down by the anxiety, the long vigils, the missed meals; in fact when the news came I fainted for the first time in my life. Only very briefly. Beatriz, for all her seeming frailty, had borne the long strain better, and presently came, offering wine-sops, the recognised restorative; small pieces of fine white bread soaked in wine. By that time I had begun to think about gratitude—and here was the answer. The small, daily reminder; not a penance ...

'No wine,' I said. 'No wine ever again. Every time I refrain from it, it will be a reminder of what I owe to God.' And such abstention would cause no inconvenience to anyone else, as eschewing meat would have been, for example. Simply between me and God. I should be reminded to whisper in my mind, 'Dear God, I am thankful,' and God Who knew everything would know that the act gave the words meaning; for I had been very fond of wine.

The Marquis of Villena stayed with the rebels. He said his brother had been poisoned, by whom he did not say, for Don Pedro, coming to his wedding, had been accompanied only by his friends, eager to share the glory. Henry saw that a face-to-face confrontation must take place.

The battle was fought at Olmedo in August 1467 and although it seemed indecisive, both sides claiming victory in the actual fighting, it was decisive in its result, mainly because of Henry's own behaviour.

He had in fact run away from the field and thus condemned himself in the eyes of many of those nobles, hitherto faithful. To the Castilian, great or humble, courage was the cardinal virtue; a king who, when the swords flashed and the arrows flew, rode away and took shelter in a nearby monastery, was no king at all. Better Alfonso, who in a suit of armour made to his small measure, had acquitted himself well; better even the power behind Alfonso, the Archbishop of Toledo who in the thick of the fight, his arm slashed and his horse's reins severed, had fought on. Lord after lord went over to the rebel side, and city after city opened its gates. The fighting in and around Olmedo had been brutal and destructive, something no reasonable citizen wished to see on his own doorstep. Even Segovia, always Royalist, Henry's favourite city, threw open its gates to Alfonso.

Henry, going reluctantly to war, had left us there; Queen Juana, the child Joanna with whom I had not been allowed, since that mock crowning of my brother, any contact; also such ladies as had not thought it wise to ask leave to go home.

On a bright autumn morning I went down and stood alone in the great courtyard of the palace to meet and greet my brother whom I had not seen for more than two years.

How would he greet me? He would be justified in thinking that I should have made an effort to join him; if he had ever received my letter, he might resent it; he might even believe that I had been a party to Villena's plot.

I could hear the crowds roaring in the streets and the church bells ringing, as Henry's favourite city welcomed Alfonso and I stood waiting, unsure.

Alfonso made it all so easy. Swinging down from his saddle he embraced and kissed me. 'Isa, no welcome has given me such pleasure.' He had grown, upwards and outwards, lost the spots and the puppy fluff and gave promise of being a handsome man. He had dignity, too; but as I watched him, acting like a king, being treated like a king, I noticed that in repose his face had a weary look, and every now and then he turned his head or his eyes sharply as though suspicious of something going on behind him or alongside.

During the next few days, with many comings and goings at Segovia, he would have kept me beside him, made much of me, but I would not play, in public, the part of King's sister; nor would I address him as King. I explained this inoffensively as I could and he showed no resentment. He laughed and said, 'Your ideas are very old-fashioned, my dear. Are you proposing to be the only person in Castile to refuse to acknowledge me?'

'While Henry lives. I am sorry, Alfonso; it is a matter of principle. Perhaps, in the circumstances it would be better if I retired from Court altogether.'

He gave one of those sharp, wary looks. 'Where would you go?'

'To Arevalo. To Mother.'

'Wait,' he said. 'Just a few days and we'll go together.'

'How very pleasant that would be. But it is unlikely that they would allow ... I mean, those to whom you are King would not wish you to leave just now.'

Something flashed. 'Who is to tell me what I am to do? I was at Olmedo, Isa, I am entitled to leave like any other soldier. Being King is largely a matter of signing papers, which His Grace knows I hate. I can sign papers at Arevalo as well as anywhere else.' He laughed and told me something about signing papers; the Marquis of Villena had coaxed and wheedled and argued himself into a grant of land and when Alfonso had signed the relevant paper, he had written his name so large that it took up half the page. 'Why so large? they asked me, and I had the answer ready. I said, "It is a large grant." And so it was.'

The alacrity with which everybody agreed that it would be very right and proper for His Majesty and Her Royal Highness to make a visit to their mother led me to suspect that the Archbishop of Toledo, the Marquis of Villena and the great nobles—some of whom, like the Mendozas, had deserted Henry for Alfonso after the battle of Olmedo, were beginning to discover that my brother was not quite so malleable as a boy-king should be.

'If I remember rightly,' His Grace said, 'the castle at Arevalo was not over-furnished. We must send wagons ahead to make it habitable.'

'I don't want that,' Alfonso said. 'I want to go back to it as I remember it.' He was equally positive about taking a guard.

'But Your Majesty; it is essential for the safety of your royal person.'

'And who, Your Grace, would wish to kill me in order to restore Henry?'

'There is always the fanatic, Your Majesty.'

'I will not go about as though I were a murderer with a price on his head,' Alfonso said.

I thought it time to intervene. I said, 'Alfonso, I think His Grace is right. Things take time to settle. I for one would feel more comfortable with a few soldiers about.'

'Very well,' my brother said abruptly. 'Not more than twenty. Chosen by me. And they will lodge in the gatehouse. Do you,' he swung round on me, 'wish to take a retinue of women? If so we might as well remain where we are.'

'I should like to take Beatriz, if she wishes to come ...'

It is impossible, try as one may, to call back the past and perhaps it is a mistake to attempt it. Perhaps the very attempt is a confession that something is wrong with the present.

For Mother's state we were prepared; it was true that she did not know us. She was as Beatriz had described her to me in a letter some years ago, placid, inert, the lines smoothed from her face, her eyes beautiful but empty. She was not unlike a pretty plant, well-tended—by Doña Maria who had hardly changed at all, by the Galician servants who, happy in Arevalo, had brought in relatives. Old Jaime had taken a cold which despite all precautions had gone to his chest; but Theresa was still there with her swollen leg and her ability to make an edible dish out of almost nothing. Not that she needed to now. And of course Don Pedro de Bobadilla was still there, faithful to his duty, delighted to see Beatriz, anxious to hear everything about Andreas de Cabrera, more than Beatriz, or Doña Leanore, had told in letters.

In part we did recapture the happy days. Alfonso particularly rejoiced in his freedom. Two secretaries had come with us and if a courier did come with letters, with papers, Alfonso would grudgingly spend an hour in the room which had been fitted out as an office; and every day he spent a little time with the captain of his chosen guard. Any complaints? Anything to report?

These duties done Alfonso was free to ride about the autumn countryside with me—our escort tactfully inconspicuous. We talked more than we had ever done before, the age difference had lessened sharply. I told him about the plan to marry me to Villena's brother and he burst out, 'That is what I mean. They told me nothing of that. If I am King of Castile, I am King of Castile and my consent is needed. That gross old man! When I go back things are going to be very different I can assure you. Never mind, Isa, I have a splendid match for you in mind.'

'Oh.'

'Ferdinand of Aragon. The Archbishop knows him well and is a friend of his father. He's young, handsome, and like me he started soldiering early. Would you like to be Queen of Aragon one day?'

'If it is the will of God.'

'You have become very pious,' he remarked.

'What I have just told you was an experience, Alfonso. Not lightly to be forgotten. God was my friend when I had no other, bar Beatriz, who was as helpless as I was.'

We were both rather like people released from captivity. I especially rejoiced in being able to ride Sasha again. I had had few opportunities of late—only when the Court changed places; but I had visited her in her stable almost every day, so that she should not forget me, and the boy, Inez de Mendoza, had exercised her for me; he having no horse of his own. He had done it well, too, spoiling neither her temper nor her mouth.

Beatriz did not join in our rides; she had begun to embroider her wedding dress. Don Pedro had given his consent, with some reservation: it would be wise, he said, to see how things settled. Don Andreas had always been King Henry's man; if the King abdicated, or went into exile in Portugal both courses were possibilities—what would Don Andreas' future be? Alfonso promised that Don Andreas should retain his offices, and Beatriz said she was certain that when it came to choosing between going with Henry into exile and staying in Castile with her, Andreas would choose the latter. So she started on her dress, peach-coloured satin, and as the embroidery grew I saw that she was copying the pattern from the little Moorish jacket.

Our holiday went on and on. 'They can send for me when they want me,' Alfonso said. 'The day will come when they cannot get on without me—and then I shall return in strength.'

The early part of the year 1468 was a lull, a kind of pause, not only to us in our retreat. Henry neither abdicated nor emigrated. There were still towns, mainly small, unimportant and conservative, where he was acknowledged; he and his faithful few moved from one such place to another. The help which the Queen had expected from her brother of Portugal did not materialise.

Then something totally unexpected happened; Toledo, the Archbishop's own city, declared for Henry. Alfonso was suddenly needed, to ride again in the suit of mail made to his measure, to give the appearance of being in command, young, handsome, appealing. The Archbishop and Villena, with a great retinue, swooped down on Arevalo to fetch Alfonso.

All was haste and confusion, but in the midst of it Alfonso said, 'Come with me, Isa. Never mind the way you address me; call me 'Brother', that is the term kings use towards one another.'

I wanted to go; the last months had greatly strengthened the bond of affection between us; but was there a place for me amongst all these milling men? I could ride as far and as fast as any of them, but wherever they camped, or lodged I should need separate accommodation and might come to be regarded as a nuisance.

'I will come, if you really want me, Alfonso.'

'I do. Somebody to talk to freely ... Besides you *hearten* me, for the strangest reason. You believe in the divine right of kings—that is why you are loyal to Henry, though you hate him. When I am with you, I believe in it too. But I apply it to myself.'

No Mother this time to weep and stand, waving as we left; only Doña Maria saying, 'God keep you both, God keep you both,' and Beatriz, torn by indecision and regretting her poor horsemanship. 'I could never keep up. But I will come, Isabella, as soon as I know. Let me know and I will come.'

Even she could have managed the first stage of the journey; it was already late in the day when we set out, and everybody except Alfonso and I and the twenty men who had been kicking their heels in the guard-room, had already done a full day's journey. So we stopped for the night in Cardenosa and did not push on to Avila where the accommodation would have been better for our company. Not for us; Alfonso and I, the Archbishop, the Marquis were most comfortably housed, and splendidly fed, in the house of the most substantial burgher in the little town. He gave of his best. We ate trout, just taken from the river, mutton, or rather lamb, for this was the time for the culling of the flocks, fresh-baked bread, soft cheese and fruit, peaches and apricots and plums, preserved in such a way that their shapes were retained while their flesh was rendered almost transparent. And all washed down—except by me—with the clear, white, slightly stony-tasting wine of the district which I remembered from the old days, and could taste again, in memory.

Leaning across the table, white-linen-spread, candlelighted, the Archbishop said, 'Pope Paul is entirely to blame for the situation in Toledo. Threatening to excommunicate us all, calling us rebels. A purely political move! He has fallen out with the King of France and needs support. From *us* he could not expect it, we won, without help from him. So he makes this desperate attempt to frighten the ignorant, to restore Henry who will then, presumably, be so *grateful* that when he is asked to move against France he will do so. A great many men,' he said, 'seem to lose proper judgement at the age of fifty, as women do at ...' He realised that there was a woman present at the table. 'Once we are in Toledo,' he said, continuing as though there had been no break, 'and the people see that we do not fear a threat, they will change sides again—probably without a blow being struck.'

In this optimistic mood we parted for the night. I lay awake for a time in my very comfortable bed, thinking about excommunication. The Archbishop might view the prospect lightly but it was a thing to fear, a complete cutting off from the Church: and could Alfonso, still so young, be condemned for filling a role thrust upon him almost three years earlier?

Finally I woke to sunshine lying across my bed and the sound of bustle. We had proposed an early start. I was out of bed, my night shift half on, half off when a white-faced servant flung open my door and said, 'His Majesty ... we cannot wake him.'

'Dead?'

'Not quite.'

I pulled the shift back over my shoulders and ran, barefoot. The Archbishop stood on one side of the bed and Villena on the other. In the big bed Alfonso looked small and very peaceful, as though sleeping. His hand, his cheek was warm; his heart was beating. Not dead, thank God, not dead. I called his name, loudly, more loudly. Boys at that age take a deal of wakening.

'We have tried,' Villena said.

'And sent for the doctor,' said the Archbishop. 'Just across the street. Ah ...'

The doctor bustled in and looked and told us what we knew, 'Deeply unconscious.' He tried to bleed Alfonso from the foot. No blood came. Nor from his thumb. Nor from his ear. 'Alive, but no blood,' the doctor said. 'I have never known ...' And then, as we watched, the fearful change took place. Alfonso's lips turned black and fell apart, his tongue, also black, lolled out and his breathing stopped.

It was my first bereavement. There was the stunned incredulity, the realisation of the terrible truth; Alfonso, last night a healthy boy, rather excited about wearing his armour again, now dead.

Through the sound of my own crying I heard the doctor say that there was some pestilence in Cardenosa, but he had never seen it take this course; nevertheless it would be wise to bury the body as soon as possible.

Alfonso was dead and no examination of how and why could restore him to life. I do not think he died of the pestilence which is always lurking, becoming worse in warm weather; he had suffered no fever, no raging thirst and there was not the mark, the swellings under the arms and in the neck, that distinguishes the plague. The question of poison could not be discounted, but who amongst this company, all rebels, would have wished to do away with the figure-head of their cause?

Unless Villena ... He was a very slippery man. He had joined the rebels in a fit of pique, jealous of Beltran de la Cueva; he had made one attempt to be reconciled to Henry and in fact, in the next year did go back and become Henry's man again. He may have seen for himself a better future, rid of a boy becoming more and more wilful. And I may have been concerned; one of those rumours, so light-heartedly started and so eagerly handed on, accused me of Don

Pedro's death—also sudden, also mysterious and for me very timely. A brother for a brother.

I had my grief and my thoughts and my regret that never once had I given my brother the title which would have meant so much to him, coming from my lips. Looking down on the dead body of one whom one loved but had not always pleased, such thoughts will come. And there was another Alfonso had died within hand's reach of a priest—the Archbishop—but he had died without the final absolution, no holy oil, no ritual.

What with the crying which dulls the head and so many thoughts I failed to see what I should have done—that Alfonso's death had political significance for me. When the Archbishop, the funeral over, a little hasty, but correct in every way, said, 'Will you ride with us to Toledo?' I missed his meaning entirely. I said, 'No, Your Grace. I am going to the nuns in Avila.' He looked surprised, and then nodded approvingly. 'Very wise, Your Royal Highness.'

4
Avila, Ocana, Valladolid, Duenas, Segovia. 1468–74

'On morning of 19th October, 1469, Ferdinand, King of Sicily and heir to the throne of Aragon, and Isabella, the heiress of Castile were married at a private residence in Valladolid.'

Imperial Spain, J. H. Elliott

Seven years had passed since the idea of convent life had seemed distasteful to me; I had spent them in a world where horrible things happened and men were ruthless, ambitious, false. I was glad to be away from it, should have been glad to shut it away for ever, but as soon as my mind regained balance I saw that Alfonso's death had brought me very near to the Crown.

I arrived at the Convent of Santa Ana in a heart-broken state, which the nuns, though sympathetic, did nothing to foster. Undue grief for the dead indicated less than perfect submission to the will of God, and of faith. It was *sad* that a young life should be cut off, but Alfonso had been spared the sorrows and troubles which life inevitably brought, his soul was now safe in God's keeping. One must not brood. And the best cure for brooding was work.

All I know of housewifery I owe to those devoted, industrious women. They believed that for an unsettled mind like mine not only work but variation was desirable, so I passed from one activity to another, learning to spin wool, to prepare simple herbal remedies, bake bread, separate honey from the wax of its comb, dry fruit. To this day the scent of a split apricot can carry me back to those peaceful days.

I was actually helping Sister Agnes with the plums on the morning of one of the most crucial days in my life. I wore a lay-sister's dress of unbleached linen—made for a stouter woman—and an apron to protect it. The plums lay in orderly lines on straw mats, drying in the sun and they were turned every hour. Such work, demanding nothing of the mind, offered ample opportunity for meditation, Sister Agnes explained to me: it served the same purpose as a rosary; she herself said a Hail Mary at the end of every second row she turned.

We heard some clatter, but it was muted by distance. Then somebody came running to tell me that I was called to the parlour. I stood up, not knowing exactly what I was about to face. News of the outer world stopped short of the convent walls and I did not even know whether the rebels-against-rebels movement had been put down in Toledo or not.

Inside the walls rank was made little of and I was slightly startled when Sister Agnes, also rising, said, 'You cannot go in your apron, Your Royal Highness.' She untied it and whisked it away. Hurrying from the sunniest part of the garden into the shade of the house, I snatched off the piece of linen which covered my head, protecting it not only from the sun, but also from wasps. It and Sister Agnes's more orthodox headwear had been freely sprinkled with some pungent lotion, oil of lavender and something else less pleasant which made wasps keep their distance.

There are convent parlours that are furnished luxuriously; that at Avila was not one of them. It had whitewashed walls, ornamented only by a crucifix; the floor was bare and waxed to a surface smooth and dangerous as ice; there was a table and two chairs.

The room, not very large, was full of men, faces known and unknown—the Archbishop of Toledo; the Marquis of Villena; the Count of Orson ... Everything blurred a little and the noise was for a moment not unlike the sound of the wasps over the drying plums. Out of it the voice of the Archbishop came loud and clear—'Your Royal Highness, we, your loyal servants and most devoted subjects, come as representatives of all the nobles of Castile to ask you to accept the Crown.'

It would be dishonest to say that I was unprepared. The logical procedure for all those who had rebelled against Henry and acclaimed Alfonso was to come to me; sooner or later they would come, but not, I had imagined, quite in such full, representative force.

What they stood for, all these hard, grave-faced men, was in essence my country, was Castile. I thought of that for a moment, twisting the head-cloth and staining it with my soiled fingers; then I said what I truly believed,

'My lords, the Crown is not yours to offer. So long as he lives, my father's son, Henry the Fourth, and no other, is King of Castile.'

I had said as much to my dear brother, why not to them?

There was difference, however. Alfonso had not been frightened by my denial of his right to the Crown. Now, with my denial of my own right to it, there was the smell of fear in the close clean room. Brave men, all of them, many renowned for valour, but suddenly aware that without me their cause was lost; they had no alternative to offer to the ordinary people of Castile.

The Archbishop, always impetuous said,

'Is it your wish, then, that La Beltraneja should rule Castile?'

'Far from it. The King himself, when you sent to him from Burgos, admitted her illegitimacy and my brother's right to the succession. That right is now mine. To *succeed*, my lords, not to *usurp*.'

I suppose I looked a ridiculous figure in the sack-like garment, my hair ruffled by the snatching off of the head-scarf, my fingers stained, but I knew what I was saying, and I meant what I said, and they recognised it. Several of them looked at me in a way which, if looks could have killed, would have felled me. There was a muttering, a shifting from foot to foot, an exchange of anxious looks, the twiddling of a button, the tapping of a tooth, all the signs of uncertainty.

I said, 'You must return to your allegiance to the King and bring peace to Castile.'

'He would take it as weakness.'

'He would have our heads.'

'We should lose all that we fought for.'

I looked at them all, and then, my eye lingering on Villena, said, 'So far as. I know, His Majesty has never refused an overture of peace. It is my belief that he would accept almost any conditions. The first, of course, a general amnesty. His Majesty is averse to bloodshed.'

The head of the Mendoza family said, 'That somewhat depends upon whose blood!' This remark was received with more laughter than it merited—another sure sign of nervousness.

'His Majesty is also averse to keeping conditions,' the Archbishop said. 'Your Royal Highness mentioned Burgos. Terms were agreed then. Agreed and disregarded.'

'True,' I said, 'but that was before Olmedo. We must try again.'

So we tried again and once again Henry conceded everything. I was to be acknowledged as his heir and given revenues sufficient to permit me to live in a state suitable to my prospects; Queen Juana and her daughter were to be sent to Portugal. No marriage was to be forced upon me, I could choose my own husband, but Henry must approve him.

Accounts of even family bickering can be tedious and political shifts and bickerings are even more so. That morning in Avila I thought I had acted wisely and done well, but events proved me wrong. There is a saying that in order to sup with the Devil one needs a long spoon; I sometimes think that the Devil, sitting down to sup with my half-brother, would be the one to need the long spoon. Henry was so devious; constant, I will admit, in his dislike of bloodshed; no rebel was punished, there were no recriminations, but all the other conditions he either ignored or evaded. I never received the promised revenues, and when Beatriz married was obliged to borrow from the Archbishop in order to give her a suitable gift—my oldest friend, my lady-in-waiting. Queen Juana, supposed to be divorced and exiled, remained at Court. And then Henry did something which affected me far more nearly than the lack of the promised revenues.

When the Archbishop of Lisbon arrived, in winter, the worst time for travel, two rumours ran about. One said that he had come to conduct Queen Juana to Portugal; the other said he had come to tell Henry not to allow himself to be overridden by his nobles, not to renounce his Queen or the child who was, whatever she was not, niece to Alfonso of Portugal.

Neither rumour touched the truth. The Archbishop of Lisbon had come on his master's behalf, to ask my hand in marriage.

'And this time you cannot say anything about royal blood,' Henry said, lolling back in his chair. No, I could not say that. Alfonso of Portugal was royal enough, was indeed related to me on my mother's side. He was middle-aged, a widower, he had a son; and he was now supporting Henry, and Juana, not with twenty thousand armed, ready men, but in another way.

Shuffle me out of the country that was mine, Castile; make me Queen of Portugal and then ... and then ... There was an age-long rivalry, an enmity between Portugal and Castile, nobody, not even my most ardent adherent would wish to see me, in due time, Queen of Castile, with the King of Portugal as my consort. No, no, they would say, better La Beltraneja!

And in Portugal any child I bore would not be heir.

However, I had learned that direct defiance simply made Henry stubborn, as when he was determined to marry me to Villena's brother. So I said, 'It would be a suitable match—except that it comes within the ban of the Church on grounds of consanguinity.'

It was rather like arguing that Don Pedro had taken vows of celibacy; but here I was on somewhat firmer ground. Vows of celibacy could be cancelled in a sentence; consanguinity was a different matter. Long, long before my time the Church had realised that incestuous, or near-incestuous marriages could be dangerous, likely to produce weaklings, squint-eyed, stammering, liable to fits, so the humblest parish priest in the smallest village kept what was known as a 'kin book' in which the lowest peasant's pedigree was recorded. One of the purposes of the Church festivals, and of the secular fairs, was to bring together marriageable couples not within the fourth degree of kinship. But, of course, exceptions were made; it was easy enough to say to a swineherd—Choose elsewhere, it was less easy with royalty, their choice limited; but the Pope could grant dispensations, and they took time; everything in Rome seemed to move very slowly.

My half-brother said as he had said once before, 'That can be arranged.' The Archbishop of Lisbon nodded and said,

'There will be no question of the dispensation being given. On a former occasion His Holiness was prepared to grant one for a marriage involving a far closer relationship.' Tactfully put! There had been talk of Alfonso of Portugal being betrothed to La Beltraneja, his niece!

From this interview I went to the Archbishop. It was humiliating to be obliged to tell him that the King had broken yet another of his conditions; but His Grace, except in moments of anger, was not the man to say, 'I told you so'; petty-mindedness was not one of his faults. He listened and he understood. I said,

'So long as I am unmarried, this kind of thing will crop up. If I avoid Portugal a proposal will come from England! I have been wondering, Your Grace, about Ferdinand of Aragon.'

He looked a trifle dubious. 'Very suitable, if it could be arranged, Your Royal Highness. But ... Well, we will not mince words. The Prince of Aragon is heir to two kingdoms, Aragon and Sicily. The position of King-consort may not appear as attractive to him as it would to a prince whose own prospects were less.'

'You know him?'

'His father better. But, yes, I know him. I do not think that he is a young man who would be happy in second place.'

'Very proud?'

'Proud enough, and in a man no fault. Your Royal Highness. It is not pride so much as that he holds a high opinion of himself.'

'Is *that* a fault? In a man? In a prince?'

'No. No, of course not. But it means that the negotiations would need to be delicately handled. He would demand concessions.'

'Which I am prepared to make. Complete equality between us. Would that suffice?'

'As broad policy. There may be tiresome details.'

'Those I could bear. The union of Castile and Aragon—a Spain united as once it was—should be worth a detail or two.'

'Then I suggest that we send Don Gutierre de Cardenas to sniff the air, and if it is propitious go ahead. He could be informed as to what Your Royal Highness was prepared to concede, and where the line must be drawn. For example, when I spoke of details, one occurred to me. Would you be willing that on all official documents, in all proclamations, the Prince's name should precede yours? That is the kind of thing that will matter to him.'

'It is not the kind of thing that I should bicker about.' What did it matter? Isabella and Ferdinand, Ferdinand and Isabella. A *young* husband, a prince of whom I had so far heard nothing but good; a likely begetter of healthy children, one of whom, God willing, would rule both Castile and Aragon. My son. The Aragonese did not admit the right of a female to succeed.

One thing troubled me a little. When Henry had promised that I should make my choice of husband, I in turn had promised to ask approval of my choice. Did his breaking of his word justify me in breaking mine?

I sought the opinion of Father Torquemada, and when I put the question to him he was silent for so long that I feared a negative answer, knowing that of two interpretations he would always choose the stricter. Finally he said,

'Have you inquired of your own conscience?'

'Yes, Father. It informs me that two wrongs cannot make a right; but that in dealing with a man who consistently breaks every promise, some self-defence is necessary.'

He then said the only kindly thing I remember from him.

'Then you are answered. Your conscience is tender and well disciplined.' Then he must have felt that he had erred on the side of leniency and read me a long lecture. 'If this marriage comes about—and I pray that it will—you must remember: firstly, that it was a gift from

God; secondly, that marital fondness must never absolve you from responsibility—in your private life you must act as wife and be meek and amenable, where affairs of state are concerned *you* are the person to whom God entrusted the rule of this country; thirdly, if God unites Castile and Aragon, the strength of the two countries, thus made one, must be devoted to His purpose—war with the Infidel.'

For a moment I mistook him. Ever since 453 when the Turks took Constantinople there had been talk of a new Crusade—all Christendom against Islam; Pope Pious the Second had urged it, but Christendom had not responded as in former days. Men remembered the old tales of quarrels and failures in earlier Crusades and it had in fact been left to the Hungarians to repel the Turkish invasion of Europe, just as Charles Martell had halted the Moors ... Moors!

I said, 'You mean ... the Moors in Granada?'

'I mean the Moors in Granada. I would ask you to make a promise—not to me—I may not live to remind you—but to God and your conscience, that you will regard the union of Castile and Aragon as a weapon forged and placed in your hand for one purpose only—the re-conquest of Granada, Allah's last stronghold in the western world.'

Something seemed to explode in my head; that sense of purpose, of high destiny to which the young are prone. Don Gutierre, with a long list of proposals and concessions, was waiting to leave for Aragon the moment my confessor agreed that a bargain broken on one side was no longer valid. The future glowed with promise.

I said, 'Yes; I promise, Father. If this comes about, Castile and Aragon one, Granada shall be recovered and restored to Christendom.'

Curiously, from that moment all went well. Henry decided to visit Seville and did not wish me to accompany him. That was punishment for my lack of enthusiasm for the Portuguese match. I could go, he said, to Ocana and stay there.

Gutierre de Cardenas went to Aragon and returned with the glad news that Ferdinand wished to marry me and now regarded himself as betrothed to me. He had, as the Archbishop had foreseen, haggled a little, but the final terms were fair enough. He could not come immediately, his father was old, growing blind and engaged with war against the French, but he would come as soon as he could. He sent me a betrothal gift; a necklace of rubies, said to have belonged to Solomon the Great. That was quite possible: the Romans had sacked Jerusalem in the Year of Our Lord 70 and many veteran Roman soldiers had been given grants of land in Spain—Hispania as they called it. Since then there had been the Crusades, from which few returned empty-handed. From the chain of rubies hung one of exceptional size. Years later an English ambassador was to describe it as being 'as big as a tennis ball'. He exaggerated slightly, but it was a wonderful stone, and I was touched when Don Faderique Enriquez, Admiral of Castile and Ferdinand's grandfather said that in order to send me the necklace Ferdinand must have got it out of pawn.

It was the first thing of any great value that I, Princess of Castile, had ever owned. I wore it every day, fingering the ruby and dreaming my dreams. It should not be difficult to love a young, handsome, soldierly man, with a good opinion of himself, and who seemed well-disposed towards me. Beatriz, whose marriage had been every bit as much an arranged thing as mine would be, seemed to be blissfully happy with her Andreas; she was expecting a baby.

Then things went wrong. Inevitably, Henry heard of my plan and threatened to arrest and imprison me. He also threatened to have Ferdinand turned back, ignominiously, if he attempted to cross the border.

Spain is on the whole mountainous country, with few roads, and those mainly what the Romans made. That is one reason why, when the Moors were driven south at the reconquest, so many small separate kingdoms were established; Léon, now part of Castile, Catalonia, now part of Aragon. A prince coming from Aragon must take one of the few main roads, easily guarded, or wander and clamber on a sheep track which might or might not bring him into Castile. On either side of the border the tracks were inclined to end where shepherds had found enough pasture for flocks in high summer; there were also places where the Castilian trail and the Aragonese trail met in a little market where a ram might be exchanged for a ewe, salt from the salt-pans near Tarragona for some cloth woven in Ocana, or a knife of Toledan steel. Anyone ignorant of the border could be lost for weeks, or fall prey to bandits. Two reigns of weak kings and then a civil war had resulted in much lawlessness.

My anxiety grew. Henry had despatched troops to arrest me. Maybe they had little heart for the task for they advanced slowly, and the Archbishop and the Admiral had time to muster men to the defence of Ocana. The Admiral said he was inclined to think that Ferdinand must be on his way. 'Had he been further delayed, he would have informed Your Royal Highness. He is meticulous in such matters.'

'He may be turned back,' I said, voicing my greatest fear.

'He is not easily deterred. Nor is he one to take risks and run headlong into trouble.'

Through the next worrying days the Admiral set himself to hearten me. With Henry's men so near I began to feel like a maiden in some old story, locked into a tower, sunk into a tranced slumber, awaiting the coming of the knight-errant who would set her free. To cheer me the Admiral talked much of his grandson, always with praise. One day, drawing himself to his full height—he was very short indeed—he said, 'Your Royal Highness must not judge by me. I am the runt of the family.' The thought had not occurred to me; in his presence one was not much aware of Don Faderique's size. He had a noble, handsome head, and, like his grandson, a good esteem of himself; he had an irascible temper. Indeed, as the waiting time drew itself out all our nerves became raw and it was a relief when the Archbishop suggested a move. 'If the worst comes to the worst, this town is not defensible. Valladolid is, and the city is hot for your cause.'

So with what men we had we galloped off through the August dust; the corn harvest was in, the grapes ripening.

As always, a good gallop raised my spirits and the welcome I received in Valladolid was very heartening. People stood in the streets and cheered, not only for me but for lion Ferdinand as well. The match was now common knowledge, and appeared to be approved.

No move was made to arrest me. I used to lie in the night and wonder whether Henry's threats were as half-hearted as his promises, or whether he shrank from a move which would provoke bloodshed, or, shocking thought, whether some picketing force at the border had already intercepted Ferdinand and turned him back, the whole thing kept secret, so that Henry was now laughing at me, enjoying his private joke. The Admiral said sturdily, 'We should have heard from

Ferdinand,' and the Archbishop said, 'I too have my spies.' But anxiety is very undermining and by the time that Ferdinand did arrive, it was the fifteenth of October, I was in a highly emotional state.

It was late afternoon. Don Gutierre de Cardenas came to tell me breathlessly that His Majesty the King of Sicily had arrived at the Archbishop's house. Part of the delay had been caused by the King of Aragon's wish to have his son arrive in Castile as a monarch, so he had handed over the second title. 'For the rest, His Majesty wishes to tell Your Royal Highness the story himself.'

I chose a dress of cream-coloured satin, the better to show off the necklace. How would he find me, I wondered, peering into the glass with that expression of anxiety that is death to all looks. The compliments paid to princesses cannot be relied upon and I knew that I was not even pretty, leave alone beautiful. Every feature taken separately was pleasing, so was my colouring, the Trastamara eyes with their changeable blue-green-grey and bright copper hair, but the total fell far short of Mother's flower-like prettiness, or of Beatriz's fawnlike loveliness, or even Queen Juana's lush, voluptuous appeal. Something heavy which lightened when I smiled. I smiled at myself in the glass and the effect was bad—rather as though I were saying, Look, I have fine teeth!

When we met I forgot myself entirely. To me at that moment he was the most acceptable sight the world had to offer.

He was rather less than my height—but he was a year younger and would grow; his dark hair was already receding—but he had been fighting the French and helms are hard on the hair; his left eyelid drooped possibly as a result of a gnat bite. Apart from these trivialities which my eye noted and my heart repudiated, he was perfect: straight and sturdy, self-confidence evident even in the way he planted his feet, and with such lively, merry eyes, changeable as my own, light brown, flecked with green. Perhaps ever since my poor brother had first mentioned him I had been half in love with the image of him which my mind reflected; now here he was, my deliverer, my husband, the one I could love.

And if anything were needed to complete and perfect the romance it was the tale he had to tell over the supper table. He showed us his hands, old blisters, shrivelled back into rings of dead, darkened parchment, fresh ones, bulging and pearly white.

'I swear,' he said, 'I was the best muleteer and general servant six itinerant merchants ever had.' The six men—all Grandees of Aragon—who had shared his adventure, murmured and nodded; no professional player, bred to the craft, could have done so well. That was how he had come to me; in disguise, acting as mule driver and servant to the six nobles posing as merchants. They had, after one interception and inspection by Henry's men on a passable road, taken to the sheep tracks, been lost, slept at inns which, at best, were no more than hovels and, with high summer over, had hardly anything to offer. 'Not,' Ferdinand said with a bright glance at me, 'that the quality of the accommodation affected me. Every night I slept with the mules. And all stables are much the same!'

It was all highly romantic, and I was eighteen ...

Our marriage was hasty; as hasty almost as those of peasants who have somewhat anticipated the ceremony and, counting on fingers, reckon that many a child is born at seven months. It was hasty, and it was not grand. It took place in a private residence and the ceremony was performed by the Archbishop of Toledo, but it lacked the lavish show, the open-handed hospitality for all which a royal wedding should bring with it. Ferdinand was King of Sicily, Prince of Aragon, I was heir to Castile, but we were poor in exactly what my mother had once called the worst way. However, the Archbishop and the Admiral rose to the occasion and we managed to feed about two thousand.

Then came the bedding. The consummation of a marriage of such importance must be witnessed; done under watching eyes. A relic of the barbaric past, when a bride, perhaps newly captured and taken as token of a precarious peace treaty, might not be a virgin with a maidenhead to lose, might even be already pregnant.

But for Ferdinand I should have found it all immensely embarrassing. I spared a wild thought for my half-brother Henry, married at the age of fifteen to his first wife, Blanche of Navarre. How far had this making a ceremonial of a deflowering, those watching eyes contributed to his impotency? And why think of that now?

Ferdinand was equal to the occasion. His hard young body pressed against mine under the covers, but it was pretence, like the pretence of being muleteer and servant that had brought him to me. He whispered, 'Pretend! Wait a minute, then cry out.'

I obeyed him; he was in command of the situation; I was completely at a loss. I cried out. The Archbishop, the Admiral and two of Ferdinand's Aragonese nobles, withdrew, satisfied, and the night was ours.

Torquemada had known me better than I knew myself when he warned me not to let marital fondness blind me to my responsibilities. I had thought myself level-headed; prone perhaps to a romantic thought or two, such thoughts having as little relation to reality as the garlands on an ox's horns on a spring day are to its draught power. But I was wrong. If during those first months of our marriage marital fondness had ever come into conflict with public responsibility, I dread to think what might have happened. Both Ferdinand and I were entranced by the discovery that duty could be pleasure.

Once he said, laughing, 'And to think ... I had heard so much about your rectitude and dignity, I had seen myself bedding with a cold, marble girl.'

Happiness made me feel goodwill towards all men. I wrote to Henry to inform him, officially, of my marriage. And he wrote back that I was a rebel and he would deal with me as such. Pope Paul had again threatened to excommunicate all rebels.

With that in mind I one day said to the Archbishop,

'It seems strange to me. If the Pope regards us as rebels, why did he grant the dispensation for our marriage?'

'He did not.'

'But you read it out before you married us.'

'Oh, that,' he said casually. 'That was a dispensation granted by Pious, years ago; when His Majesty of Sicily was very young. A blank dispensation. And quite meaningless, since Pious is dead, and his grants, his dispensations and indulgences dead with him.'

I said, 'Do I understand aright? Is our marriage not legal?'

'Legal. Oh yes, fully legal. It is rather confusing to the lay mind ...' He looked somewhat confused himself. 'There is secular law, and canon law; they do not necessarily coincide at all points. Your marriage is legal; it does not carry the blessing of the Church.'

I felt rather sick, but that was nothing unusual just then, the early days of a first pregnancy.

I said, 'Your Grace, am I to understand that we have been—in the eyes of the Church—living in sin for six months?'

He said, irritably, 'That is an extremist view. You may recall that haste was essential. There was no time to apply for a new dispensation. And in any case the Portuguese emissaries were already in Rome, asking for another to enable you to marry Alfonso of Portugal. Think of that.'

I thought of it. I said, 'Did Fer ... did my husband know that the dispensation was invalid?'

'He brought it with him from Aragon. He can read.' Mine was a small world then, and I felt it rocking about me.

Through the dizziness the worldly, cynical voice went on, 'You would be wise not to make too much of this. Unless you wish His Majesty of Sicily to go galloping back to Aragon.'

'Why should he do that?'

'Because this venture has not turned out as he expected. We have lost ground; Henry has gained it. After Olmedo the whole Mendoza family came over to us, now they have turned coats again. There has been no reconciliation. You, in theory heir-apparent, still have no roof of your own.'

A brutal summing up, but an accurate one.

'Upon closer acquaintance,' the Archbishop went on, 'I have come to the conclusion that His Majesty of Sicily is a thoroughly self-seeking young man. All men are self-seeking, of course, but some manage to be grateful as well.'

I knew that Ferdinand resented being under an obligation to the Archbishop and often went out of his way to behave as though no such obligations existed. The Archbishop interpreted such behaviour as ingratitude. When jarring things were said, both men seemed tacitly to claim my support and I was often in a difficult position; my old friend, my young husband. I was becoming adept at turning a deaf ear, or changing the subject. I did so now.

'I should be grateful,' I said, 'if you would make immediate application for a proper dispensation. The idea of an unsanctified marriage is distressing to me.'

'I will do that, Your Majesty. It will take time.' He must have been feeling very spiteful towards Ferdinand that morning, for the next thing he said was almost unforgivable. 'During that time you must not allow this small matter to affect your marital relationship. To do so would be to drive him back into the arms of his mistress.'

Not *into, back into.*

Two shocks in so short a time; and my old friend's eyes sparkling with malice! I was sickened again, but determined not to show my hurt. I groped for some light, careless words.

'I understand that she is very attractive.'

'Reputedly the most beautiful woman in Aragon. And of high rank. Just before her son was born there was talk of a morganatic marriage, but it came to nothing.'

Retrospective jealousy is an absurd emotion. I told myself angrily that I should have known: Ferdinand's behaviour on our wedding night had shown him not lacking in experience. I told myself sternly that it was nothing to be upset about; over and done with: and how many men go virgin to their brides? The sting really lay in the fact that this unnamed woman was beautiful, and that Ferdinand had wished to marry her. With what reluctance had he set out to marry me, expecting a cold marble girl? Did he think of her with regret? Make comparisons?

Fortunately Ferdinand was on a hunting trip that day and away for the night. By the next day I had recovered somewhat and had decided upon a course of action which was to say nothing, either about his connivance at the use of the invalid dispensation, or about his mistress and his son. In fact, it was five years before any public recognition of this small royal bastard was made; he was then six years old and was made Bishop of Saragossa. By that time, without a word having been spoken, it was understood that I knew of his existence.

I think, I hope, that I acted discreetly. I suppose all honeymoons must end—and one must remember that thousands of people miss entirely the joyous experience that I had certainly had and Ferdinand had appeared to have.

Time crept on and nothing happened to release us all—all of Castile—from the deadlock in which we were gripped. Henry, though he had issued threats to treat us as rebels, made no move at all, and the Pope, who had threatened excommunication, had taken no action. So, growing bulkier and heavier day by day, I was still officially heir-apparent, though without income, or residence or any of the appurtenances of rank. It was a curious situation because my child, if a boy, would be heir to Castile and Aragon; if a girl, heir to Castile until she had a brother. A child of such high destiny, conceived in a borrowed bed at Valladolid, was to be delivered in another borrowed bed in Duenas. We moved about in the regions nominally favourable to our cause and against La Beltraneja, or as Ferdinand once said sourly, 'under Carillo's thumb'. And my delivery must be as well witnessed as the consummation of my marriage had been. Under the eyes of watching men. Again barbaric, but not unreasonable; a live child might so easily be smuggled in, substitute for a dead one, or in countries where girls were not acceptable, a boy for a girl. It was the custom, and I must submit to it.

Pain has no measure. I tried to distract my mind from the wrenched body. Think—a boy will be heir to Aragon and Castile; a girl, if I never again submit to this torture, heir to Castile at least. Ask—was it thus for Our Lady in the straw of that stable in Bethlehem? But the moment comes when the mind will not serve. In the end all I could do was to say, 'Cover my face; a towel ...' so that there was some little modesty about it and my tears, my gnawed lips might be hidden from the eyes of men who, whatever they might suffer, could never suffer this.

The midwife sounded disappointed. 'A girl.' Just for a moment I did not care; a monster, a monkey, the relief of being rid of it was so profound.

Ferdinand took the disappointment—if indeed it was a disappointment—very well and said, 'A boy next time.' And I whimpered, 'Never, never again.' The midwife cackled, 'Your Majesty, every woman the first time says that; but if they held to it where would most of us be?'

Perhaps the birth of Isabel spurred Henry into action—not into war as Ferdinand hoped, but into the staging of a great masquerade. Segovia had always been his favourite city and it had remained loyal to him under the governorship of Andreas de Cabrera, Beatriz's husband. At the high altar of the Cathedral in Segovia, Queen Juana stood up and swore that her daughter, Joanna, was the true offspring of Henry's body. Henry withdrew his recognition of me as his heir. But, typically; he shifted; as his sister he would be pleased to see me, to give me the kiss of peace and to greet Ferdinand.

'What can be his purpose?' Ferdinand asked when the invitation came. 'Frankly, I suspect a trick. He had just repudiated you as his heir. Is this a lure to get you into his hands?'

I tried to think. It was difficult to attribute rational motives to Henry; he was like a water-weed, waving this way and that, and yet rooted in something; he was determined to see La Beltraneja accepted.

'It may be a trick in another way,' I said at last. 'To make it look as though we refused a friendly overture and thus justify further steps against us.'

'Isn't that precisely what we want?'

'I suppose so. I would sooner attain our ends by peaceable means ... But in the end, when Henry dies, I am certain the people will not accept that poor bastard child.'

'It would be over my dead body.'

Ferdinand had behaved as well over my repudiation as he had over getting a daughter instead of a son; he did not seem to be even slightly depressed over this new turn of fortune. I admit that I was—the whole argument had gone on too long; uncertainty and shifting policies were ruining the country, *my* country; perhaps it would be as well to refuse to meet Henry, to cease being passive, force him into a move.

It was while we were still trying to decide that a message was brought me; a peasant woman, with lace to sell, insisted upon seeing me. She had been sent away several times, but kept coming back. Peasants, I well knew from riding around Arevalo with Don Pedro, could be extraordinarily stubborn, but not quite in this way. After all, I might no longer be heir to Castile but I was Queen of Sicily. For a peasant woman to insist ... I said I would see the woman.

I knew her at once, good as her disguise was. I said, 'Beatriz,' and she said, 'Isabella,' and we fell into one another's arms. Then I said,

'What is it? What have you come to tell me?' It must be something of importance; peasant women walked, or rode donkeys and it would take something of importance to make comfort-loving Beatriz travel by such means, in winter weather.

'It is really a message from Andreas,' she said. 'He wanted you to be assured that you would be quite safe in Segovia; that he would make your safety his personal responsibility. He has always been very loyal—a King's man through and through—until this last ... When the Queen stood there and swore by the Living Christ that the King had fathered that child, Andreas had doubts ... In short he wants you to come and be seen by the people in Segovia. Andreas thinks of it as the centre of the world.' She gave a little, tolerant, wifely laugh.

'What I can't understand is why this ...' The homespun skirt, short enough to make walking easy, even through a muddy farmyard, the heavy shoes at the end of such delicate legs, the hood and the cloak, mittens to mid-finger; the overall peasant smell, onions, goat, wood smoke.

'It was necessary. Andreas has enemies, being an upright man. He is loyal—as you were loyal to the King, but he is not prepared to accept La Beltraneja. He is looking to the future. He wishes you to be seen. But if Villena or Albuquerque knew that they would tear him to pieces.'

'I see.'

'I must go,' she said. 'It does not take long to sell a few yards of lace ... Please come to Segovia. It really does matter. Henry may not have long to live.'

'Is he ill?'

'Sickly, and forty-nine years old ...'

I went hot-foot to Ferdinand and he nodded, gnawed a nail and said that there might be something in it, but that he didn't trust Henry; he would come only as far as Turegana and wait there with three hundred men in case of trickery. One word, carried by Inez de Mendoza, absolutely to be trusted, and on Sasha, swift as the wind, and Ferdinand would come to my rescue. Once I was inside Segovia I learned that Henry had taken similar precautions—Albuquerque and Villena, that slippery man, once a rebel, now again a King's man, had both posted themselves outside Segovia and with bigger forces; with an equal eagerness to pounce should the slightest thing go wrong.

The whole thing was so fantastic, so absurd, that written in a book it would be scorned. It was a masquerade. One evening, unbelievable as it sounds, I went round Segovia, part of a torchlight parade, riding an ambling grey palfrey, with Henry, King of Castile, walking, holding the bridle. There were banquets, with Henry saying, 'I will sing for you,' and then demanding that I should dance for him. Purposeless; except that after a few days of it Ferdinand thought it safe to come in, and Henry welcomed him as though he had been his brother, long-lost.

They now call that great hall in the Palace of Segovia the Hall of the Pineapples; but it is a misnomer. The pineapple was not known in Europe then; pine cones were, and in that great hall there were four hundred of them, all gold, hanging from the ceiling like stalactites.

But it was Don Andreas's banquet, in a humbler hall, that proved to be more memorable. I looked around; I saw the Archbishop of Toledo, my friend, chatting amiably with the Bishop of Sigenza, a member of the Mendoza family, now on Henry's side, and I had a fleeting thought about the sadness of a world where sides must be taken and people, most of whom wished only to be happy and comfortable, must fight one another for *causes*. At one place at the table sat my goddaughter, my rival, La Beltraneja, grown into a pretty girl with a rather wistful look. I remembered Don Philipino's prophecies and breathed a hasty prayer that they might all be disproved. But he had said one cogent thing, he had advised Henry to separate the child's fate from his own. Had he done so, sent her and her mother back to Portugal, the girl would have had some chance of leading a normal, possibly happy life. On one side at least her blood was royal, any minor prince would have found her an acceptable bride. As it was she had been betrothed several times, none of the betrothals lasting; and sometimes she was Henry's daughter, Princess Joanna, heir, sometimes she was La Beltraneja, a bastard. Small wonder that she wore a wistful look.

Further along the table sat Beatriz de Cabrera, very fine in rose-coloured silk and the string of pearls which Andreas had given her to celebrate the birth of her son, Ferdinand. She smiled when she caught my eye, but I thought that on the whole her expression was watchful—the wife of the host, alert to see that all was well.

Then Henry screamed like a scalded cat and clapped his hand to his side. He bent forward so that his heavy head touched the table. 'Pain,' he moaned and screamed again. 'Such pain ... Like a sword.'

They carried him to a little ante-room and laid him on a couch. The banquet was abandoned and we all stood about while the doctors came and professed themselves puzzled. Ferdinand kept his head; standing by me, grim-faced, he said, 'I have sent for my fellows. I suspected something all along.' Beatriz seemed calm too. 'Did I not say he was sickly? The festivities have proved too much for his digestion.'

Slightly but not much soothed by some drops the doctors administered, Henry still moaned. 'I am dying, I know it ... Fetch Villena, Albuquerque ... Last wishes ...'

Somebody said, 'A priest, my lord?'

'No. No. After.'

He did not call for the Queen, or for the child he had so lately acknowledged as his daughter, or for me, earlier in the evening his 'dear sister', or for Ferdinand, his fellow-monarch. It was to his favourites that he wished to confide his last wishes. They were sent for and arrived, pushing their way arrogantly through the hall. The door of the ante-room was slammed shut. Half an hour later it opened again and Villena came out, jumped on to a bench and shouted,

'Poison! His Majesty has been poisoned. By Don Ferdinand and Doña Isabella and Don Andreas. I call for their arrest.'

A ludicrous situation. As Governor of Segovia Don Andreas was responsible for all law and order—was he supposed to arrest himself? There were men-at-arms all about, but they were *his* men.

Then a booming voice said, 'Nonsense,' and there was the Bishop of Sigüenza, heaving himself up by the aid of nearby shoulders on to the table itself still littered with half-eaten food, half-emptied wine cups. Like all the Mendoza family he was a big man, with an air of authority. 'Nonsense,' he said again. 'How would it profit their Majesties of Sicily to have His Majesty of Castile die in the middle of these most delicate negotiations? And why should Don Andreas—the most loyal of the loyal—act against the master he has served so many years? What of the food-tasters?' he demanded. 'Has one of them suffered?' None had.

Poisoning was never so common in Castile as it was in Italy, but precautions were taken. Every cook was supposed to sample each dish as he completed it—that is the reason why so many cooks are fat while declaring that they eat nothing: then, lest a dish should be tampered with between kitchen and table, it was unobtrusively tasted again before being offered to those important enough to be target for plots.

The Bishop's words carried weight, especially coming from one whose own loyalty was unquestioned; and there was another element too. In the mysterious way that such things have, news of what was going on had reached the people of Segovia and there came a steady roar of voices crying my name and Ferdinand's. Perhaps Don Andreas's plan that we should show ourselves had borne fruit; or perhaps, like him, they were not prepared to stomach La Beltraneja. Crowds are well known to be fickle, but they cannot be ignored. These cries in the night convinced the favourites that Segovia was no longer a place to be trusted and in the morning they insisted upon the removal of the King and the Court. Henry was no longer in pain but he looked ill, unfit to travel. Actually he lived for almost a year more, prolonging the twilight time, the wasted time, during which the question as to who should succeed him dwindled down to a matter of small personal enmities or family feuds, and excuse for rioting at fairs, for raids on sheep folds.

Most of this time I spent in Segovia, happy enough with Beatriz, my child and hers and with Don Andreas, Henry's man so long as Henry lived. I was reasonably sure that there were thousands like him—unwilling to be called rebels, equally unwilling to accept La Beltraneja when the time came.

People have sometimes expressed surprise, and even admiration at the speed and certainty of the way in which—when the time came—I put certain plans and reforms into effect. I had had plenty of time to plan and I saw the necessity; for as time dragged on it became painfully plain that what I should inherit would be a country on the verge of ruin.

5
Madrid, Segovia, Colmen Viejo. 1474–5

'... despue los grandes del reyno juraron alos Catholicos principes, nascio entre ellos una difficil y gran contienda sobre quien de reyno ...'

'... after the grandees of the kingdom had sworn allegiance to the Catholic Prince and Princess, there arose the great and difficult probem as to who should rule ...'

Lucio Marineo

When the time came Ferdinand was in Aragon. He had grown more and more restive as young men do with nothing much in the way of occupation and little to spend. Sicily, our Kingdom, was a poor island and any revenue that could be wrenched from it passed through many hands, all with sticky palms; Aragon, still engaged in the seemingly endless war with France over the two disputed provinces, Rousillon and Cerdagne, could not afford to allow an income to its Prince, heir to the Crown, who had made what had seemed to be a good match—the heir to Castile—and now seemed to have got himself a bad, or at least a tardy bargain.

So, on a hot June day in 1474 Ferdinand said, 'Have I your permission to go to Aragon?'

'My permission?'

'Have you forgotten? Part of our marriage treaty. I must not go to Aragon without your permission.' He smiled, not quite with the old merry look which had made his smile so attractive; just slightly sour, like cream on the turn.

'I have forgotten, or perhaps I did not notice. I was so anxious to have the whole thing settled. But certainly,' I said, in that married way, where two words can sound jocular, 'you have a blank dispensation to go to Aragon whenever you wish, sorely as I shall miss you.' We could joke about the blank dispensation now, since in 1472 the new Pope—not Paul whose reign had been very short, but his successor, Sixtus IV had sent a genuine one. Hedging, he had sent the document that made Ferdinand and me married in the eyes of the Church, and by the same bearer the scarlet, tasselled hat which made Pedro Gonzalez Mendoza, Henry's man, a Cardinal. A sop to both sides in this indeterminate struggle.

So Ferdinand went off to Aragon with a thousand men, all Castilians, men of noble birth and no property; all hopeful of grants of land, carved from the disputed provinces. I said, 'I shall miss you my dearest ...' He was still that to me, and I saw him off with a good supply of shirts and woollen hose so that in the north, in an autumn campaign, he should not sit in damp clothes.

I saw him off with tears in my eyes. It is considered unlucky to watch anyone departing, yet it is a natural impulse. At the last he turned in the saddle and raised his arm in a salute. I waved the scarf I held in my hand.

In that dismal October Henry's first favourite, Villena, died, and like our father who had not long survived the death of his favourite, Henry began to give way to the sickness, long suffered but ignored. Henry died hard; with his insides rotting, and the pain only dulled by opium, he insisted upon hunting up to the date of his death, and he died in his boots which is a simple way of saying without the rites with which Christian souls are sped. As in Segovia when he believed himself to be dying of poison, he refused to have a priest near him; and when those at the deathbed asked him to declare whom he wished to succeed him, me or his 'dubious daughter', he refused to answer. Devious and obscure to the end.

He died in Madrid which is forty-five miles from Segovia, and not easy riding; but the messenger reached me by nightfall. I said, 'God rest his soul!' And Don Andreas said, 'God rest him. A kind master but a bad king.' There was truth in it. My father who was also Henry's father had by all accounts died declaring that he wished he had been born the son of some artificer, trained to the lute; Henry, in a humbler sphere than that to which God had called him, might have been happier: he would certainly have had less scope for his vices and fewer decisions to make and unmake.

I was fortunate in two things: the Archbishop of Toledo was in Segovia at the time, and so was the great Crown of Castile, with Beatriz's husband as its custodian. The Archbishop came to me through the snow of the December night and urged immediate action. 'Villena's son and Albuquerque will proclaim La Beltraneja as soon as the King is buried, if not before. You must be proclaimed tomorrow. Leave all to me, Your Majesty. I can reach enough people to put on a good show.'

I said, 'I think that perhaps before anything else a mass should be said for the King's soul.'

'Yes, yes. I will see to that, too.' He hurried away to despatch messengers. Beatriz and I gave our attention to clothes and Don Andreas unlocked the castle strong-room.

Only of late has black became the colour of mourning; it used to be white, unrelieved by any colour or ornamentation. A plain white dress had a place in every woman's wardrobe. Beatriz had a cloak of winter ermine, another present from her husband, who was as anxious to shield her from the cold as her father had been. The Solomon necklace was in pawn again, the money being needed to outfit Ferdinand for his campaign. 'You must have my pearls,' Beatriz said, 'but they will not make much show against the white.' However, when Don Andreas opened the treasure chest, it was discovered that what remained of the Queen's jewels were there. Some time in the past Henry had been angered because Juana had taken another lover, not one of his favourites. He had taken the jewels, locked up her lover, and then released him because she cried so much. Like everything else in Castile the store of jewels had been depleted—or perhaps Juana had coaxed Henry to give her back the best and the newest but enough was left to make a good show. As the Archbishop had said, wisely, 'Ordinary people like display.' There was a collar of gold set with rubies, emeralds and pearls; not beautiful but showy, and a great jewel, a ruby set around with pearls which could be hung on a chain and worn as pendant, or, threaded on a ribbon, as buckle to a belt. There was a pretty chain, fluid as water, gold links knobbed with turquoise, jade, topaz, aquamarine. 'Very old,' Beatriz said, 'and of Eastern workmanship.'

I wondered had my mother worn these. Curiously, she had always been very reticent about her days as Queen of Castile, as though she were determined not to hark back. So I should never know. I looked at the things which women before me had worn; and I looked at the crown which lay in a leather-covered box with double locks.

I had spent my life in its shadow, but I had never seen it before; the great crown of Fernando, one of my forefathers who had liberated so much of Castile from the Moors. And by a judicious marriage united Castile to Léon.

Always with me, the practical will intrude. I gazed upon this crown; nine great diamonds, seven rubies, seventy-four pearls, all set in thick gold, and I felt awe and reverence; at the same time I thought that Fernando must have been an exceptionally strong man, that Henry, with his long weak neck, had been wise never to wear so heavy a thing, and that I must. Tomorrow. Nevertheless I was awed, looking upon it, for the first head to have worn it was also the head which had produced the code of laws, an emulsification of the old Roman and the Visigothic. I was aware of time, of privilege and duty handed down.

Beatriz said, 'Isabella, you can never wear it. No woman, few men, could.'

I said, 'I shall wear it; just so long as it takes to be acclaimed.'

The snow was all down in the morning, a white world, all in mourning for the dead King who, though we did not yet know it, lay in Madrid, deserted by all but one faithful official, his body left to hirelings.

In a plain white gown, a white fleecy shawl to guard me against the cold, I went to mass in the cathedral; and there the solidarity of Christendom, of the one Holy Catholic Church, was momentarily made manifest. Even the Archbishop, for ten years a rebel against Henry in the flesh, said mass for his soul as though for a brother.

Later the sun came out and the whole world glittered. So did I. It would perhaps be wrong to say that those who crowded into Segovia to acclaim me were truly representative of the country as a whole; but I had, six years earlier, been recognised as Henry's heir and his subsequent shufflings had apparently affected other people as little as they had me.

Throw off the shawl, don the borrowed ermine and every available gem; sit in a chair saddle—that last resort of the infirm or the inexpert who still must ride. Proceed slowly, with the great sword of justice, carried by Don Gutierre de Cardenas, handle uppermost, like a cross, going ahead, and with the Archbishop and an astonishing array of clerics, all in their finest robes, following behind. Now that the moment had come it seemed utterly unreal; such stately processions are necessary but not to my taste. Overdecorated, silent, immobile, I felt like one of those images of Our Lady, or of a saint, brought from its rightful niche to parade the streets. Was that a blasphemous thought?

In the main square I mounted a platform, spread with rugs and tapestries and set with a canopied, throne-like chair; bugles shrilled through the sparkling air; the Archbishop of Toledo proclaimed me, using my title for the first time, and every noble who chanced to be in Segovia, or within reach of the city by night riding, knelt, kissed my hand and took the oath of allegiance. Worthy emotions and noble thoughts should have occupied my heart and my mind, as I lifted the crown from the cushion on which it was proffered and set it on my head, but it was not until by my order—the first of my reign—the procession was re-formed and we were again in the cathedral that I was capable of coherent thought. There on my knees, I thanked God for entrusting me with the Crown of Castile, and prayed that my reign might be peaceful and prosperous, bringing nothing but good to my people, that in all decisions I might have God's guidance and in all actions His blessing and support.

I knew in the first moment that something was wrong. Ferdinand's embrace was perfunctory and flaccid, his kiss of greeting given to the air, not to my lips, mine evaded and taken on the cheek. I thought—A reverse in the campaign that by report had been going well? Annoyance at having to leave a campaign that was going well? Not that he had been recalled; all I had done was to write him a joyful, loving letter, informing him that he was now King of Castile. He had hurried back but of his own accord.

He was off-hand with everybody—not only those of Henry's adherents who had in the last month come hurrying in to offer me their allegiance; to the Archbishop of Toledo he was positively offensive. 'Perhaps *now*,' he said, 'Her Majesty and I can hope to pay what we owe Your Grace.' A rational statement enough, but made in an unfriendly way. I tried to cover it: 'Two accountants working day and night for a week could hardly reckon the total, in money. The less tangible favours we owe His Grace can never be repaid.'

'A seat on the Council should go some way towards it,' Ferdinand said, unpleasantly.

I thought—Cross because I have appointed a Council without consulting him? But nobody can reign, even for a month, without some structure of government. I had chosen my Council carefully, I thought tactfully; it included Cardinal Mendoza, not because he had defended us from the accusation of poison but because he was an able man and his loyalty to Henry had gone beyond death; almost alone he had stayed in Madrid and organised a decent, dignified funeral.

This homecoming, which should have been so joyous, was marred. For the first time in our married life Ferdinand. and I were to occupy apartments, sleep in a bed, indisputably our own. Yet the first thing he said when we were alone together was, 'I should have thought you could have waited until I was here.'

I thought I saw it all; he was peevish as a child who has missed some festivity.

'I only wish I could have done. But, darling, I dared not. La Beltraneja's friends would have had her acclaimed. It was necessary to forestall them.'

'Necessary to have the Sword of State carried in front of you—a woman!'

'It was part of the ceremony.'

'It was a usurpation of my rights.' I looked at him amazed. '*I* am King of Castile.'

'Nobody denies it. In fact your name was ...'

'I mean by right; not by favour. My great-grandfather was King of Castile.'

'I know. But your grandfather was his second son. The Aragonese chose him for their ...'

'I know that. Your descent may be more direct, but mine is more valid. I am the male heir. Simply because Castile has this ridiculous law ... Not that they'll notice; they've had two old women, in breeches! Now they have a young one, in skirts!'

I said, 'Ferdinand, are you seriously disputing ... ? What did you *imagine* would happen when Henry died?'

'That you would have sense enough, taste enough to yield ... Or at least to share ... Am I disputing? Yes! Do you think I've been kicking my heels here for six years in order to get a title—King in Petticoats? That is what they call me. And you saddled me with it; acting so hastily and allowing the Sword of State ...'

I began to cry and that was a mistake. I had not inherited Mother's ability to cry beautifully. Ferdinand was far from mollified. He stamped up and down and said he would not be content until the whole thing was looked into, his rights investigated and justice done. I kept saying yes, and yes; everything should be looked into; he could choose his investigator and I would choose mine.

But inside me something happened. I sat there, a woman weeping because Ferdinand was angry with me in the very moment of reunion after long absence, because just when things had seemed to go right they had gone wrong again; I even spared a tear or two because he had been wounded by a malicious phrase; but inside me there was a hardening. Ferdinand spoke of kicking his heels for six years; *I* had waited for thirteen, sure of my right, such a stickler for all royal rights that I would not even please poor little Alfonso by using a title to whom another had better claim, such a believer in royal rights that I had refused the Crown while Henry was alive to wear it. Now this; another claimant, my own husband!

Now Torquemada's warning had a deeper and darker meaning. Marital fondness must not blind me to my responsibilities.

I tried to be just. When, with the utmost discretion—since any hint of discord between us would so vastly encourage the opposition—we arranged what was called the Concordia to examine our respective rights and Ferdinand named Cardinal Mendoza as his arbiter, I said, 'Would you not prefer a cleric from Aragon?'

'No. I trust the Cardinal, with good reason. My father used his influence, and I used mine, to get him that coveted hat.'

I named the Archbishop of Toledo as my arbiter. And then they both chose to play Devil's Advocate, that age-old office in which a man who believes something is required to argue against it; the Cardinal must espouse my cause, the Archbishop, Ferdinand's. To their credit they produced without much delay a settlement which, reached by such means, must be conclusive. Since Castile admitted the rule of a woman, I was indisputably Queen of Castile, just as Ferdinand by the terms of the marriage settlement, much raked over, was King. There were sops to his vanity; on all documents and proclamations his name was to precede mine; if we were together we were to administer justice as one person, if we were apart each alone was vested with equal authority. There were other details, trivial, but all calculated to deny that hateful epithet—a King in Petticoats.

From the time of his return until the production of this *Concordia*, we had each slept alone. When the Archbishop and the Cardinal offered us their conclusions, I said to Ferdinand, 'My lord, if you are content, I am. Henceforth we shall be two bodies and one will.' That night he came to my bed with a joking twist of the words—two wills, one body. For a little time—for as long as it takes.

Afterwards, instead of the remembered glow of happiness, I had some thoughts, a flash of insight: I knew why so many countries repudiate a woman's rule. In bed the man, the giver, is master, and it is very difficult to assume equality when morning comes and the curtains are drawn back.

There was scant time for such abstract thoughts, none at all in which to carry out the plans and reforms which Ferdinand and I had talked over so seriously—and so amicably—during that long waiting time. By the end of January two rumours were spreading. One was that Henry had, after all, made a will, naming La Beltraneja as his heir, and that Ferdinand and I had bribed somebody to do away with it. The other was that Alfonso of Portugal now recognised his niece's claim and was prepared to fight for her. We threw ourselves into preparations for war.

War demands money.

Under the feudal system the King can call upon his nobles to follow him to war, and they in turn can call upon their retainers, but there are limitations to the length of time for which such an army can be kept in the field; a lord's humbler followers, mainly bowmen, cannot be spared too long from the plough and flail. A force mustered in this fashion cannot be regarded as a standing army, and even while it is in being only the very rich Grandees can afford to support their men without aid from the King. The other source of supply of men, the companies of mercenaries, sell their military skill and their lives just as any merchant vends his goods, for prompt payment. My experience has proved that mercenaries are as devoted and loyal as any other soldiers—so long as they are paid, well fed and left in the charge of their own captains. Any breach in these conditions quickly leads to disaffection. The best, in my day, were the Swiss pikemen who, though on foot, could withstand a cavalry charge. At a given word they form a tight circle, their long pikes forming the 'hedgehog'. They rated themselves highly, were well disciplined among themselves, inclined to resent orders from outside.

Just at this moment a hitherto unfailing source of money dried up as suddenly and completely as a river in hot summer. 'I greatly regret, Your Majesty,' the Archbishop said, looking not at me but at Ferdinand, 'I can contribute no more. I have already strained my resources to the utmost.'

It may, temporarily, have been true; he had been extremely generous over the years; but there was more to it. Ever since Ferdinand's return from Aragon in that black mood, he and the Archbishop had been at odds. Ferdinand would say to me, 'If that arrogant old man thinks he can rule me as he has ruled you, he is mistaken.' And the Archbishop would say, 'Your Majesty, the King dislikes advice—from *me*. The very thing I have suggested and he rejected, he will accept from Cardinal Mendoza.'

These things were said in private, but in public, at meetings of the Council, Ferdinand's preference for the Cardinal was open and tactless. I do not think that the Archbishop resented the Cardinal's retention of the Chancellorship—in fact he had himself advised it, saying that such things were better left in experienced hands and to a man who liked bookwork and routine. Nor do I think that the Archbishop was jealous—as has been said—of that Cardinal's hat; to be a Cardinal implied, to a lesser or greater degree, being a Pope's man, and that Alfonso Carillo never was. So far as he had ever been anybody's man, he had been mine; but Ferdinand had always chafed a little at being under an obligation to so rich and powerful a subject, and more lately had held against the Archbishop the hasty ceremony that had made me Queen, and the result of the Concordia which had confirmed my position. So, in a moment of danger and need, the Archbishop withdrew both financial support and his very influential presence.

Perhaps my fault.

More firmness then, a more positive support from me in Council, and to Ferdinand in private a tactful warning about an ageing man's vanity. But I was then a novice in the handling of men and affairs; I could not forget that Ferdinand had threatened to go back to Aragon if his pride were ever affronted again. Also, I was pregnant once more, and however determined a woman may be to ignore such a condition, the effects of it make themselves felt, an euphoria of mind, a bodily inertia. I have seen a nesting hen sitting close and apparently undisturbed in a farmyard invaded by a hundred hungry men.

However, when, with the Portuguese on our very border, the Archbishop withdrew, not taking leave of me, and went to Alcalá de Henares, where he had a palace, the smallest and least comfortable of his many, I cast off euphoria and inertia.

I said, 'Ferdinand, this breach must be healed. His withdrawal just now is a blow ... a loss we can ill afford. He still wields enormous influence ... I will go to him myself, apologise for any offence I have given,' that surely was tactful, 'and try to persuade ...'

'And what can you offer?'

'Offer? What could I offer that would be of value to him?'

'Sometimes,' Ferdinand said, 'your innocence astounds me—as much as at other times, your shrewdness. See him as he is. A man of infinite ambition, supporting, shaping the Queen of Castile whom he one day hoped to rule—as Alvaro de Luna ruled your father, as Villena and Albuquerque ruled your half-brother. I warn you, Isabella, if you go crawling to him now, you will give him what he wants—the power exercised in England by an Earl of Warwick who makes and unmakes kings according to his whim. Or, even worse, you may humiliate yourself to no purpose.'

'He has been such a faithful friend, for so many years. I cannot let him go now without some effort of reconciliation.'

'Very well. I dissociate myself. He did not make me, and he failed to unmake me, hard as he tried.'

I chose three men, all known hard riders, to go with me; the Duke of Alba, the Count of Faro, the Marquis of Santillana; and as always, good swift riding raised my spirits. My state was not yet apparent and I was not yet heavy and clumsy. As the miles sped away, hope and confidence grew. I thought—There are three reasons why a man will not look into one's face and announce his intention; a physical repulsion, a consciousness of treachery being planned, fear that his heart may soften; in this case the first could be discounted, the Archbishop had looked on me kindly for some fourteen years; the second was unthinkable; treachery to me must imply adherence to La Beltraneja whose legitimacy he denied on clerical grounds, holding that even had Henry fathered her, she was still illegitimate since her conception would annul Henry's divorce from his first wife on grounds of impotency: so that left the third possibility—that in those last Council meetings he had not looked at me, and had gone away without taking leave, because he feared the strength of his own resolve. Face to face he would weaken ...

In the afternoon of the second day, when we were only five miles from Alcalá de Henares, a thought struck me. The Archbishop was proud—or vain—and he was renowned for his hospitality; he might not be pleased to be taken unawares, offended already, he might regard this informal descent upon him as lacking in courtesy; so at a wayside hostelry I halted and sent the Count of Haro on ahead to warn the Archbishop that I was near by and should have great pleasure in taking supper with him. The rest of us turned into the inn, drank water or wine, washed our hands and faces, beat the worst of the dust from our clothes and waited. The air chilled with the going down of the sun in a sky of clear apple green and the woman of the house, hovering respectfully, asked should we be wanting supper. The Duke said, 'I hope not.' The Marquis hazarded a guess at the reason for the long delay. 'His horse has foundered. I never favoured the Andalucian, all show and no stamina! Madam, shall I ride on?' Then we heard the sound of hooves and went out. The Count's horse was in good fettle, but he looked as though a sudden fever had smitten him, he was so pallid and shaken.

'Madam,' he said, and then flinging away all pretence at anonymity which had so far guarded this errand, 'Your Majesty, I cannot find words ... At first he refused to see me, but I insisted. Then he kept me waiting and then he said ... he said he could not prevent your coming but as you entered by one gate he would leave by another.'

It was as Ferdinand had said, humiliation to no purpose. Not merely a rebuff but a rebuff couched in insolent terms. A smack in the face. I could have wept from chagrin, I could very easily have given way to the wave of nausea that rose; but I thought—I have lost one man, there are here three, my subjects, my adherents who must not see me weaken. I managed to laugh. I turned to Alba and said, 'My lord, I think you were a little premature in refusing the good woman's offer of supper.' I gave Santillana a warning look and told Haro that he and his horse had done well. I said they both needed refreshment.

Never show the wound.

My errand had failed, absolutely; but that evening taught me a lesson which was to be useful to me all my life; a way of dealing with men, unless they are fanatics. The truth is that men like to be happy and comfortable. The Duke of Alba, a serious man, sat down to his supper, fretting about the implications of that insolent message. Obviously the Archbishop had turned traitor and if the threatened Portuguese invasion came ... I said, 'My lord, all very true. A problem to be dealt with. Like this fowl which I suspect came out of the Ark with Noah.'

The woman who kept the inn, informed of our change of mind, had quickly killed and cooked an ancient rooster, which should have been stewed, not spitted. It was impossible to praise this tough dish, but it was served with a mess of boiled peas and herbs which was flavourful, so I praised that; the men then said that for so small a place the wine was good and presently we all agreed that the goat cheese was excellent. Despite the abortive errand and the discomfort to which it had subjected us, we had a merry meal and I could see that they were thankful to me for taking the rebuff and the humble fare with good grace.

While we were eating men began to come in from the fields and the folds and gave proof of the mysterious way in which news can spread in an underground way and travel almost as quickly by word of mouth as by courier. In this remote place, so far from the Portuguese border, these peasants knew that Alfonso had massed his men on the frontier and was ready to strike at Zamora.

It was in such fashion that I learned that my inheritance must be fought for after all.

6

Toro, Tordesillas, Cebreros, Zamora, Segovia. 1475–7

'Era muy inclinada a facer justicia.'
'She was much inclined to do justice.'

Pulgar

The Portuguese took Zamora, followed the river Douro as far as Toro and were there besieged by Ferdinand and our hastily assembled army. Ordinarily it is the besieged who suffer shortage of food while the besiegers can call upon the open countryside; but in this case the positions were reversed. Before being shut up in Toro the Portuguese had stripped the farms of everything that could be carried or driven away. I busied myself at our headquarters, Tordesillas, with organising supplies, not only for the army but for the poor, homeless peasants who flocked into the town bringing nothing but hungry mouths and a touching faith that if only they could reach me I should provide. It was soon clear to me that if the war lasted any length of time I must cast my net wider and go literally begging for supplies, for money and for recruits.

Alfonso of Portugal had had La Beltraneja proclaimed as Queen of Castile, but there had been no great flocking to her standard; nor, by the ordinary people, to ours. It was, in fact the wrong time of year—the harvest almost ready to gather; with people remote from the fighting line, food comes first, and below this sensible attitude lurks the feeling that wars can be left to kings, their retainers and those allowed tax concessions in return for military service.

The fact that we had been invaded lent edge to my appeal. The fact that as yet we had had no time to erect a workable structure of government made the making of the appeal difficult. Who, in effect was the head of any given district? Often enough a noble-man—already encamped outside Toro: in the free towns a mayor, or a sheriff, sometimes the two offices combined and sometimes in hot competition with one another; in really remote places the man, or the woman, who owned most land or the largest flock. Although during a short space of time I rode many miles and stayed in no single place very long, I gained an enormous insight into the state of my country; and every evening Pulgar, my secretary—another servant I had inherited from Henry wrote copious notes, often about things highly irrelevant at the time, but one day to be useful.

My companions on this long ride were very mixed, though care-fully chosen. I did not wish to clatter into a market-place or a vil-lage square, asking for men to fight the Portuguese accompanied by young; able-bodied men who might—and to simple minds, should—have been outside Toro, so I could not take my faithful Inez de Mendoza, or Gutierre de Cardenas or the hard-riding Count of Haro. I took, for dignity, the Marquis of Ferallo; a greybeard but tireless, for dramatic appeal a young, extremely handsome young man Don Carlos Montara, the first man to be wounded in this war; an arrow, almost spent when it hit him, had pierced his cheek, inflicting a wound of the kind likely to arouse pity and patriotic feeling but not dismay—not that he would have been a dismal figure had he lost a limb. There was Pulgar, very obviously a penman and two frisky boys of about fifteen, not quite peasants, though their voices were rustic, not quite of noble birth, though they had a patron, quite possibly their father, who had seen to it that they could ride, and had good horses to ride. Frankly they were bait. Join the army and you, too, may have such a horse to ride!

They always went ahead, preparing the way for me. Then there was my reception, a speech, as rousing as I could make it, from the hastily erected platform, from a balcony, from an ox-cart. Over and over again I thanked God for the gift of a voice that could make itself heard, even as sometimes happened, above the bleating of a flock of sheep or the professional loud voice of a town crier, roaring out that I was coming when I was already there.

And so, in July, on a day of sweltering heat, I came to a place of no particular importance. Cebreros. My bulk a little more oppressive now at the end of a tiring but very successful day; promises that cartloads of wheat and barley—all to be paid for, of course—should be diverted from their usual markets and sent to Tordesillas, promises of loans—'Were I alone, Your Majesty, it would be a gift, but I have two grandchildren to consider ...', 'Your Majesty, it is very little, but if it helps to drive out the Portuguese, I and my family will eat bread and onions for a year and be happy.' Every gift, every promise was carefully noted and I tried to give cheer as well as thanks, saying of any contribution, 'This will go far to help in the buying of a Lombard ...' or something of that kind. And of course, I was constantly under observation, being viewed by many of my subjects who had never seen me before. It did not surprise me that I should feel tired and glad to retire early to a bed more comfortable than some I had lately occupied.

I woke in the darkness to pain. Indigestion? Cramp? I had thought myself well on the safe side, heading back now to Tordesillas, and once there no more riding for three months. Now, trapped! Shouting as soon as I knew what ailed me; being most carefully attended, and until the end cherishing a faint hope; many seven-month babies lived, might not this, scant of seven, but with healthy parents, by God's grace survive? Oh God! Merciful father of all the living; Christ the Saviour of the World; Mary, Mother of God ...

'Still-born,' the midwife said. 'It was a boy.'

One must not of God ask *Why*? One must *not* think if ... if only, or reckon the loss not only to Castile but to Aragon; one must not think—Had I sat down, folded my hands in my lap and waited, left Ferdinand to starve outside Toro and the country, un-aroused, to go about its business ... No, no, that way madness lies! Remember your mother. Remember Christ in the Garden of Gethsemane—*Thy will be done*. To that I must cling.

Curiously, a miscarriage can be more debilitating than a live birth. I was obliged to linger in Cebreros for four immeasurable days because as soon as I stood up the floor rocked and the walls spun. To humour me the Marquis and Don Carlos attempted to carry on my work, riding out into nearby villages each day. They met with remarkably little success, 'Though we used your very words, Madam. And your arguments,' the Marquis said dolefully.

By mid-day of the fourth day the world steadied, I rose, dressed myself and went alone to a nearby church and there knelt, bending my will and thanking God that I was restored to health, young enough still to hope to bear a living child—a son, should it please God to so bless me. When I returned to the house in which I was lodged, six men were waiting, asking audience of me.

Two, though advanced in years were still upright and spry, four were young. They all had the true Castilian dignity, and a manner almost courtly, despite their homespun clothes. They all smelt strongly of sheep and had come, I hoped, to offer me a beast or two, to be delivered later on when the flocks were culled.

One of the seniors turned to the other and said, 'You are the elder. Speak for us.'

'We have been away, Majesty, driving the sheep to the high pastures. We have only just heard of the danger. These,' he indicated the four young men, 'can be spared. My son, one of four. My sister's son, she has three.' As he pointed the young men bowed again and I smiled at them, with a little ache in my heart; seven boys in one family.

'My third and fourth,' the other elder said. 'I have six, and the young ones are now capable of sheep tending.' Evidently members of a patriarchal society, where the heads of families made the decisions and young men accepted them.

'They can all walk twenty miles a day, with ease.'

'They are not raw recruits. They are trained in the use of weapons.'

'They can also ride.'

This time I addressed the four silent young men. 'And where did you do your soldiering?'

They left it to the elder elder to answer, which he did, with a rather grim little smile.

'Majesty, in our youth my friend here and I were members of the Sancta Hermandad. It is nothing now, but our young have been reared according to its rules.'

'Oh,' I said. 'I understand.'

I knew from my reading that once upon a time the Sancta Hermandad or Holy Brotherhood had been an institution devoted to the preservation of law and order. It was voluntary and democratic and in many ways not unlike the great military-religious orders, except that it was secular and not celibate. It had declined, its power and its prestige often deliberately whittled away, because nobles disliked an organisation which put justice before prestige; and weak or unpopular kings, like my father and my half-brother, looked askance at a body which could on occasion act as mouthpiece for critical opinion. The Hermandad had dwindled from being an unpaid police force, capable of pursuing and arresting law-breakers, to a kind of secret society, meeting to eat ritual suppers and take now-meaningless vows. In many places it had vanished altogether. But here it was still capable of producing at a moment's notice six strong, disciplined young men at least partially trained. Not only that, but had the Hermandad still been as active as it had been in ancient times—and indeed up to my grandfather's day—a campaign such as this upon which I was now engaged would have been infinitely more easy to plan and conduct.

I said, 'Pulgar, will you write *Hermandad* on your miscellaneous page? And underline it? It carries a thought that I shall return to presently, when things ease.'

He, the Marquis and Don Carlos had had an entirely unrewarding day. The district they had scoured was apparently ruled by a bandit chief who had first call upon every product.

'I have never, Your Majesty, seen people so poor and so terrified. They were being watched—and so were we. My hand never left my hilt,' Ferallo said.

Don Carlos fingered his wound which had now reached the healthy, itching stage and said, 'One old woman was bold enough to cry out, "And what have we to fear from the Portuguese? They could not use us worse." She was soon silenced.'

'How?'

'A goat butted her from behind.'

Whose goat, and by whose hand propelled?

I withheld the information that I had in the meantime gained four good recruits, now on their way to Tordesillas, striding out their twenty miles a day.

Ferdinand must be told—it was his child. So on the fifth day I rode towards Tordesillas, thankful for Sasha's smooth pace, even at speed.

I had left Tordesillas in good hands and, though overcrowded by the latest refugees and the newest recruits it was orderly. The Count of Escalona had kept things moving; the mills ground night and day, bakers and butchers worked in relays; the best of what was available was being sent to the army, the offal, not only livers and kidneys, always acceptable, indeed sometimes regarded as delicacies, but lungs and well-scraped paunches, thoroughly stewed and mingled with beans, at the moment plentiful, made a thick nourishing soup for the refugees.

'Nobody,' Escalona said, reporting to me, 'has hungered, so far. But the news, Your Majesty ... the news from Toro is not good. There has been a falling out, a difference of opinion ... Or so it seems. The lords are tired of inaction. They wish to carry the war into Portugal—raids on the border. His Majesty does not agree. There are difficulties, too, with the Swiss. Three companies, all with notable captains have left—gone in search of a more profitable war ...' And all the time, as he spoke, his eyes, hooded like an eagle's, surveyed me—a receptacle filled and emptied to no purpose, small waisted again but not because a cradle had been filled ... Nothing to be ashamed of, I told myself, and yet there was a sense of failure.

I spent what remained of that day—it was almost evening when I arrived—visiting the wounded and the sick and the places where the refugees were sheltered. There were not many wounded but there was sickness both in the makeshift hospital and the refugees' encampment, the kind of fever, one experienced old nun told me, that often accompanies famine. One starving family, latecomers, had brought it with them and it had spread like fire through straw, not only in these relatively crowded places but in the town itself. 'It is very contagious,' she said, 'and Your Majesty should not take risks. We are all hardened and if it pleases God to call a nun to Himself there is always another to fill her place. Whereas you ...' I noted idly the ambivalence of these remarks; death came when God called, yet risk of death should be avoided. It is an attitude possible only to the truly devout.

In the morning I set out for Toro, taking with me the Marquis of Ferallo and Don Carlos, but leaving Pulgar behind because some of the produce and some of the men I had been promised were beginning to arrive and he had the lists.

In the last few weeks the twenty-five miles of road between Tordesillas and Toro had been well travelled and were thick with dust; in places, where two supply wagons had met, one going out loaded, one returning empty save for a wounded man or two, the fields had been encroached upon. I framed in my mind a rule that in such cases the empty wagon must give place to the loaded one, so that less damage was done.

Presently we met one of the returning wagons—a light vehicle, drawn by two mules. I could see that it was occupied; three men, sick or wounded. I signalled to the driver to halt and reined Sasha in. I had worked quite far into the night, making arrangements to keep wounded and sick apart. I intended to give the driver directions and to speak the necessary, cheerful word to the men. I put on what I call my public manner: it is not a question of insincerity; one cannot always be cheerful, but one must seem to be so; one must also give the impression that one's whole interest is focused on the person one addresses, no matter what more urgent things weigh on one's mind. And a touch of something, not levity exactly—other people's woes must not be taken lightly—a kind of humour, laced with goodwill, does help. 'Dear me, you do seem to have been in the war,' had never so far failed to elicit a grin. It failed now. The three men in the wagon looked at me, dull-eyed. They were wounded, not sick, and so far I had found wounded men more cheerful, more inclined to talk about getting back into the fight and taking revenge, than the ones merely ailing.

I tried again. I said, 'Take heart. The nuns will soon have you back on your feet.' Without speaking one of the men twitched away an empty flour sack. No amount of tender nursing would put him back on his feet. On one, if he lived and were lucky.

'*We* have no guns,' he said.

Actually, in four words he summed up the root cause of our failure in that first campaign against the Portuguese. I was not unaware of our need, I had voiced it, taking a small loan and saying it would help towards buying a Lombard; I was not then referring to a mercenary from Lombardy but to a gun, the weapon which within my lifetime, changed war completely and in the end seemed to give victory not to the righteous, or the brave, but to those equipped with the heavier armaments. That time had not yet fully come, and far be it from me to say that a righteous cause and valour should ever be discounted; but a relatively new weapon must always have a demoralising effect.

I said, 'We shall have guns soon.' That would be small comfort to the man whose foot had been shattered, but the other two were not seriously wounded. 'God restore you all,' I said, and rode on. Sasha's hooves seemed to beat out the rhythm—*We* have no guns.

The next thing we saw on the road was stationary; one of those low, shallow ox-carts, specially designed for the transport of wine casks. The Count of Escalonia had mentioned to me, casually, that the Viscountess of Ebol had sent four casks of wine for Ferdinand and that he had seen it on its way the previous afternoon. The cart was headed towards Toro but there was no sign of the ox or of the driver. And one cask of the wine was missing. Noting these things and wondering what had happened I became aware of the scent of meat roasting and the sound of men's voices. Both came from the side of the road not bordering on a flat field but edged by a steep bank. I set Sasha to it. She was light and nimble and I, after much riding, stamped meals and a miscarriage, weighed less than at any time in my adult life. We were over the bank and into a little vineyard while my escorts, on their heavier mounts, were still struggling on the far side.

There were perhaps fifteen men, all drunk, gathered about a trench full of fire over which hung the carcase of the ox, suspended from two ribs of the slatted cart. They were not—as they might so easily have been—a band of robbers; they were soldiers; weapons, iron hats and leather jerkins lay about. Deserters!

'You rogues!' I shouted. They stared at me, surprised and stupefied. Then one said, 'Stand up. It's the Queen.' One was too drunk to stand and two, having staggered to their feet, fell over again. The one who had recognised me said,

'Your Majesty, not rogues; true men.' The statement was marred by a loud hiccup.

'Then what are you doing here?'

'The war's over. We've been disbanded.'

'Liar!'

In a chorus they told me that it was true. The King had dismissed all the masterless men and told them to make their own way home. 'The lords'll look after their own, likewise the hired captains. Such as us must look out for ourselves.'

I was still disbelieving when Ferallo and Don Carlos came slithering down the bank. They both looked stricken and the healing scar stood out darkly from Don Carlos's bleached face.

'Madam, from the top of the bank ... The road ahead ... Full of men,' Ferallo gasped. Don Carlos, with his younger eyes was able to say, 'Alba's livery. And Santillana's ...'

So it was true.

I thought—No battle or there would have been more than three wounded men in a cart. Perhaps a sudden truce, pending peace moves. And, as so often happens with me, when my mind has more to think of than it can manage easily, it will fix on one small thing.

I said to the least drunken of the men,

'I apologise for doubting your word. Make the most of your meat!' For if there is one thing more rapacious than an army in camp, it is an army disbanded. I rode on to meet it, and to hear what terms had been negotiated.

There were no terms.

'It was completely hopeless,' Ferdinand said bitterly. 'The Portuguese would not come out and fight. Your Castilian nobles would not take orders from me. The mercenaries think only of pay—and loot. And we had no guns. What we did have was the bowel flux—the Portuguese looked down from the walls and jeered, called us Bare-arses, breeches went down so often ...'

'And what now?'

'We must get ourselves organised. We must get some guns. You must tell your nobles that an army can have only one commander.'

He was, after all, an experienced soldier, he should know. It was just possible that those of *my* Castilian nobles who had suggested raids across the Portuguese border could have been right; with their own territory threatened, however sporadically, the Portuguese might have been tempted out of their stronghold. Not for me to say. What I must feel was some gratitude that Ferdinand took our personal loss lightly and did not say, as many a man might—Had you not gone galloping about ... He was pre-eminently a sensible man and saw that my galloping about had been essential if our heir was to have anything to inherit.

We called the Cortes to meet at Medina del Campo and in solemn session they agreed that the Portuguese must be ousted, and that money was needed. But the grant they were able to make was pitiably small compared with what was required. In the end it was Cardinal Mendoza who suggested a solution to the problem.

'There remains in Castile, Madam, one repository of Wealth. The Church. I do not mean individual clerics like His Grace of Toledo. The Church as a whole. Many churches, monasteries and nunneries have a store of treasures, locked away; never seen except perhaps at Easter. Loaned to you for the definite purpose of maintaining your right over the bastard, and for a certain limited time, say three years, such resources might tip the scale. You could buy artillery. Personally,' he said, 'I have no faith in it. To my mind fighting should be done hand to hand, man to man. These things are hit and miss and they as often blow up their handlers as their target, but they are *new*, they make an impression. Those who possess them grow in confidence, those who do not, feel that the odds are unequal. War is a state of mind as well as of body, Your Majesty.'

So, with the blessing of this Prince of the Church, we borrowed Church treasures and bought guns and hired men to use them and to teach others to use them. There was a saying –'A cannoneer must always love and serve God, for every time he fires a gun he may be killed.'

The best guns were made in Germany. A monk of Friedburg was credited with the invention of using that mixture of saltpetre, charcoal and sulphur, now known as gun-powder, for military purposes. The people of Lombardy in northern Italy, threatened by the French on one hand, Austria on the other, had taken to the device and perfected the Lombard, which, when it worked could discharge, at high speed, a ball as large as a full-grown melon, iron, stone, marble or even, when all else failed, a pig's bladder filled with nails and pebbles and sharp little chippings from masons' yards or splinters of wood or old arrow heads. Such a makeshift device—a bag of miscellaneous small articles forcibly expelled by the hot, explosive force behind it—was capable of making its own, minor explosion when it met the cool, outer air.

All the while, in that autumn of 1475 and the first weeks of the new year, I gave the most part of my attention to the resuscitation of the Hermandad, not only because, properly restored, it might bring back the rule of order and law which Castile so desperately needed, but because it offered a uniform framework of government which had been lacking.

I went back to that very ancient unit, the Hundred. Every hundred households were to be responsible for providing and maintaining an able-bodied, armed and mounted man, who in turn was responsible for seeing that the law was kept, and justice done. He was to have, as the mayors and sheriffs had not, the right to pursue a wrongdoer outside a given area, and he had the power to choose his own associates and assistants.

Lawlessness did not, of course, end overnight, but ordinary people saw that something was being done to end the robbery and the terrorisation which they had suffered so long without any hope of redress. And they knew that the Hermandad had my full support, and Ferdinand's. As soon as the Portuguese were driven out, we intended—and allowed it to be known that we intended—to set out on law-administrative circuits in which any person, however humble, could come into our presence and plead his cause.

By February of the next year, 1476, we were ready to attack again, and Ferdinand showed his skill in tactics. He would not go straight for Toro, where, despite the winter weather, the Portuguese might be expecting an attack; he would strike first at Zamora. He was successful there, which meant that the Portuguese supply line was cut. Prince John of Portugal then crossed the border and besieged Ferdinand in Zamora, but he fought his way out; the Portuguese attempted to fall back on Toro. The Portuguese in that city then ventured out and on the first day of March there was a battle of the old-fashioned kind, hand to hand and man to man as Cardinal Mendoza had said.

He was there. He had said to me, 'Madam, you can better do without a Chancellor than without Castile,' and I had given him leave to go. My former friend, the Archbishop of Toledo was there too, fighting for the Portuguese and La Beltraneja, in the murk and drizzle of that fateful afternoon when Castile, led by Aragon, gained a resounding victory.

All this time I was in Tordesillas, again my headquarters, organising and providing. When the news came I walked barefoot to the church of San Pablo to give thanks. The murk and drizzle had turned to snow overnight and it lay thick on the ground, but I did not feel it, I was so elated. Men say that in the heat of a battle they do not feel a wound. I thought of that as I walked, and hoped it might be true—and of horses also ...

The long-drawn-out peace negotiations began. Alfonso and his nephew were in no position to dictate terms, but if a lasting peace were to be ensured we, the victors, must give a little. One suggestion was that Prince John's son, another Alfonso, should be betrothed to our daughter Isabel, now six years old.

Curiously this suggestion cast a bright, harsh light upon a matter which in the hurly-burly of war and contrivance had perhaps not been given its due importance. We had no son; the little girl, happily and safely tucked away with Beatriz in the castle of Segovia might inherit Castile; if she married the young heir of Portugal he might occupy the same position as Ferdinand now did, but the union would be far less equal. Portugal, though smaller, was far richer. It faced the Atlantic and did much trade with England and the Netherlands, it had tapped a source of gold on the west coast of Africa.

One day when we were speaking about the treaty I said,

'It *might* result in Castile becoming a mere appendage of Portugal.'

Ferdinand gave me a peculiar look.

'Have you any reason for taking such a gloomy view? Is anything wrong? Did that mishap ...?' I shook my head. 'Well then, we're both in our prime. All the same, I would no more wish to see Castile and Portugal made one, with Aragon out in the cold ...' His drooping eyelid became more pronounced. 'We'll fob them off with a half-promise. Play for time. We might go so far as, to agree that Isabel should go to Portugal to learn the language and the customs. But presently ... After all, we have not been together much lately. We shall do better now.'

Our marriage was seven years old, and still good. The first wild ecstasy had worn off as it inevitably does; but if we were no longer young lovers we were husband and wife, bound by innumerable common interests and the memory of difficulties and dangers survived. I heard occasionally an echo of resentment in the way he spoke of *my* nobles, who were not always as subservient to him as he thought they should be. I never retaliated by remarks about *his* Aragonese who were, I know, beginning to think that I had failed in a wife's chief duty the provision of an heir. They never said so, of course, but occasionally an Aragonese lady would drag in some story about the effectiveness of a certain shrine or some such thing, the point of which was not lost on me. The result of bedroom talk concerning the future of Aragon should the Queen not ...

Still, at twenty-five I could not look upon myself as a failure in that respect: it was borne in upon me very sharply, however, that I was in danger of being a failure as mother to the one child I had. On my first visit to Segovia after the battle of Toro, Isabel seemed not to know me—a year is a long time in a total of six. She clung to Beatriz and her manner to me was very stiff and formal; yet Beatriz said that she was not shy as a rule. I found Beatriz's son, Ferdinand, much more responsive. Beatriz, as always, was comforting: 'It will wear off when she sees you more often. I may have erred, I wished you to think her well-mannered. I may have overdone "the Queen, your mother". Rather like Doña Maria! I was trying to fit her for life at Court.' I knew Beatriz well enough to hear, in that simple statement, the question. When?

'I wish it could be immediately; but things are far from settled yet. A few places are still holding out for La Beltraneja, and for the Portuguese. Ferdinand and I have decided that the best thing to do is to divide the country between us and either threaten or cajole the recalcitrant places. He will go north and I south. There is this ridiculous, long-standing feud between the Duke of Medina Sidonia and the Marquis of Cadiz.'

'Oh yes. I have heard Andreas speak of them. Two tigers, he calls them. In the old days—when the Court chanced to be in Seville—they could not be admitted on the same occasion; they would quarrel even in the presence of the King. But they will both eat out of your hand, I have no doubt.'

Ferdinand had expressed it rather differently when we were dividing our labours; he said that if he went the likelihood was that the fifty-year-old quarrel would end in a combination against him; northern Castilians he found difficult enough. Southerners were worse, more arrogant than kings. And of course circumstances had encouraged petty kings just as they had encouraged bandits ...

Thinking of my journey, I looked at the daughter who was a stranger to me and meditated the wisdom of taking her with me. Foolish! There would be long rides, irregular meals, haphazard accommodation and perhaps even some physical danger. So I said, 'Beatriz, I must leave her here with you for a while. I trust soon to have a settled establishment.'

'Of which I hope to be part.'

I assured her that as soon as I had a proper Court she should be chief of my ladies-in-waiting.

Before Ferdinand and I parted to pursue our journeys of pacification and unification we received the submission of the last of the rebels. Amongst these was the Archbishop of Toledo, so vastly altered that it was pitiable. He had fought, I had heard, with all his old ferocity at Toro, his red cloak with its white Cross conspicuous even through the murk. I had not heard that he was wounded, or sick, and since he had not appeared before us earlier Ferdinand and I had rather suspected that he had gone to one of the stubbornly recalcitrant towns. Now, looking old and broken, his skin sagging loose on his bones, he knelt with tears in his eyes, begged forgiveness for his treachery and asked leave to renew his oath of allegiance.

Life was hardening me in its relentless way but I was not yet hard enough not to be touched by such a sight. I said, 'Rise, Your Grace. All is forgotten except the long years during which you did us such good service.'

'There was no need to be so gracious to that old traitor,' Ferdinand said afterwards.

'He looked so broken. And he was our friend. In fact we still owe him money.'

'Which I for one do not intend to pay. And I shall be displeased if you do.'

'There will be no question of that.'

'You didn't,' Ferdinand said, looking at me aghast, 'promise him back his place on our Council?'

'No. Even I ... What I did do was to ask him where he had been since Toro. I felt I had a right to ask that. And if he had been, for instance, at Trujillo which still holds out, he could have given me some useful information.'

'True. Where *has* he been?'

'In a monastery. Near Olmedo. Making, he said, his peace with God. He intends to retire and end his days there.'

Ferdinand gave a great roar of laughter. 'Didn't I always say he was the most ambitious man alive? He tried to rule you; I prevented that. He looked to rule La Beltraneja and failed there, too. So now he takes God for his patron! He'll pray harder and fast longer in the hope of being the power behind the throne in Heaven, having missed it on earth.'

The words grated a little, for to tell the truth I had been impressed by Carillo's sincerity—just as I had always been impressed by his kindness and generosity and even the flamboyancy that had made him return me that insolent message. And in me something had stirred; I had thought—After all the trouble and the fret of the world, and the mistakes, the sins, to leave it all and make ready for the Day of Judgement. I thought of the calm of Avila.

But I was not prepared, at this moment, to argue with Ferdinand; we were about to be parted; and Carillo, making his peace with God, needed no support from me. So I managed a conniving smile and said that I hoped His Grace would not suffer yet another disappointment. That was the side of me that Ferdinand liked best, an agreeable flippancy. A kind of light-mindedness and an acceptance of a certain coarseness, so that Ferdinand could say, rolling over to his side of the bed, 'And if when we meet next, you are not big with a boy, I am not to blame. God bless the seed.'

In the morning we took a rather more formal leave of one another; he to go into the hilly country near Salamanca to take possession of, or destroy all the castles, built without licence and still harbouring rebels or bandits. I to go south, take Trujillo, if it would not submit peacefully, and then go on to Seville.

In order to impress the arrogant who act like petty kings some grandeur is necessary, so I was taking a considerable retinue; three ladies, Gutierre de Cardenas, Inez de Mendoza—now my Master of Horse—Pulgar and two other secretaries, and the Master of Calatrava with three thousand horsemen. My preparations were almost complete when my Council requested me not to go; they were concerned for my safety; there might be fighting at Trujillo, and Andalucia was still far from settled, witness the war being waged between Medina Sidonia and Cadiz.

Since the whole thing had been planned in Council and no demur made, I was surprised. Then I saw the truth. They had waited until Ferdinand was out of the way, believing that alone I should be more amenable.

I said, 'My lords, would you have offered this advice to His Majesty?'

There was some humming and haa-ing, and then Cardinal Mendoza said, 'Well, no, Madam. He is a man and a soldier. There is some difference.'

'Not where such things are concerned. I am Queen, and no monarch who wishes to govern can avoid a little risk from time to time. I thank you for your care for me, my lords but I cannot allow your anxiety to affect my intention. Argument would be a waste of time and I have none to spare.'

I returned to my apartments for the last fitting of a gown of cloth of silver. A roll of this beautiful stuff had been amongst the loot from Toro; for me singularly fortunate, for the great Crown of Castile was still in pawn and would stay there until some Portuguese ransoms were paid or some other windfall came our way. But I had a second crown, light-weight and wearable, made of silver, wrought and pierced.

The dressmaker and her assistant went through all the usual, totally unnecessary fussing and my ladies made the usual exclamations of admiration. Doña Mercia lifted the little crown from the box and holding it reverently in both hands, brought it towards me.

'Madam, please put it on so that we may see the effect.'

The effect was very pleasing. It maybe did not justify the fulsome praise, but there was no doubt about it, maturity had improved my looks. Not pretty, not beautiful, but in harmony now, as though Time, like a sculptor, or a dressmaker, had made the tiny, almost imperceptible adjustments. I thought as I stood there of Isabel who was, Beatriz said, exactly as I had been at that age. It was said with love, but it was no compliment. I stood there, hoping that the years would be as kind to my daughter as, in this respect, they had been to me. And then there was a commotion.

'Your Majesty, a courier from Segovia. Most urgent.'

'Bring him in,' I said; and to Doña Mercia, 'Here take this.' I handed her the little crown. Segovia! Isabel? Ill? Or Beatriz?

The man was mud-bespattered and still breathless from hard riding.

'A riot,' he said. 'Mobbing the castle ... Don Andreas ... I just got away ...'

It was almost inconceivable that Segovia, the city that had seen my crowning, should have reverted to La Beltraneja's cause; yet it was possible, because in this uncertain world anything is possible.

'The Princess?' I asked.

'Safe at the moment. It is my master ... Don Andreas ... they want to *hang* him.'

'Why?'

'They say he is too strict.'

'How safe are they?' My only child; my best friend; Don Andreas who had in effect given me the Crown—for on that December day two years ago he could have made difficulties, said that the crown, the sceptre, the sword of justice had been removed....

'The gates closed behind me,' the courier said, mastering his breath, 'but fire ... He fears fire ...'

So did I. For a mob is mindless. A political move in Segovia would have taken account of Isabel's worth, as pawn, as hostage, something to bargain with. As it was, if they took to fire …

I issued orders as a fountain spouts water. 'Get me out of this, give me my riding clothes.' 'Run, find Don Inez. Tell him to have my horse saddled—and his … The Master of Calatrava and the household troops. Quick … quick.'

Inez and I got away first, yelling to the others to follow at top speed. I was mad that night; thinking only that if I could get there before the fire that Don Andreas feared had taken hold of the wooden gates, or a well-directed, tow-headed arrow, all aflame had made an entry—'Smoke them out' was a common phrase …

Forty-five miles between Madrid, which had become almost our capital, being so central, and Segovia, that safe, loyal place. Or so I had thought it, leaving Isabel and Beatriz there.

And Sasha was now seventeen years old—she had been three when Beatriz's father gave her to me. Plough horses, few in number since oxen are cheaper, were still active, if rather sluggish, at twenty; pack ponies, more hurried, dead at twelve, a battle-charger, even if unin-jured, was old at ten. But Sasha I chose to think—I *must* think—was as good as ever; never overridden, always well cared for.

In any case she was my only hope. There had been no time to send on ahead, to order another horse to be ready after twelve or fifteen miles … I sat low, I spoke to her. I said, 'Dearest, you can do it. Do it for me. Try, Sasha, try.' It is not an easy road from Madrid to Segovia, but a man had done it to bring me news of Henry's death. He may have changed horses, I never thought to ask, and he rode in daylight. Sasha and I were travelling through the dark. And through the rain; heavy going, bad going for the Arab breed, bred and reared to tread dust or sand. But at the top of each rise I halted her for a moment, and said, 'Good girl! Get your breath.' And for five, six, perhaps seven times as we halted Inez de Mendoza made up the distance between us on his heavier, harder-breathing horse. And finally even he, my most faithful servant from the moment when he had promised to put me, should Don Philipino cast a spell and make me a frog, into a comfortable pool, with water-lilies, said, 'Your Majesty, wait I beg you. You are outriding me. And the force is far behind. What use will it do, even if it were possible, to ride into Segovia alone?'

I said, 'There is no answer to that. All I know is that I must get there.'

'But I cannot be with you. I beg you wait. Do not go alone.'

I thought, but did not say—I have always been alone. No time to think of that now. Sasha had recovered her breath, Don Inez's mount was still puffing. I said, 'If the others overtake you, Inez, and I should be there to direct them, tell them—and this is an order from me—half into the space before the castle, half to the side, the Street of the Angels.'

I spoke to Sasha and she raced on. Then I asked myself the question that Inez had asked me—What use will it do? The mob would either have worked their will or dispersed at nightfall. I should find the open space deserted ... Or I should find the castle door rammed or burned; Don Andreas dangling from a gallows. Did it matter if I reached the place an hour earlier? An hour later? I only knew that get there I must. Rain began to fall again, a thin drizzle at first, then heavy. Nothing disperses a mob like rain. Rain will quench fire, but the damage will be done by now. Sasha my dearest, my best, keep going, keep going; get me there and I will never ask anything of you again. My hooded cloak was soaked and weighed heavy, I loosened the buckle and flung the garment from me; the silk net that confined my hair went with it and my hair flew wild and wet.

Afterwards everybody said that no horse, no rider could have covered the distance in the time, in the dark and in such weather, without pause. I only know that we did it.

And, I thought, seeing a faint, rosy glow in the sky, all to no avail, for that was the glow of a big building, slowly burning. The mob had fired the castle. Mad, like me, not asking—What use will it do—just set on the doing. And mobs will do things which no single person, a component part of the mob, would ever dream of, but each is individually responsible none the less. I thought—I may even have said it aloud—I swear to God, I will hang them all! If I spoke aloud only Sasha heard. She was faltering now.

The rain had stopped, a mile, two, six. The moon, cleared of cloud, rode high as we stumbled into the city, into the street that led to the castle, black and solid and seemingly intact between the reddish light striking upwards and the white moonlight beaming down.

Torches, little bonfires all crying—Here we are, and here we stay! Just at that moment I was too bothered and exhausted to benefit from the message; in fact it took me twelve years to remember and profit by the lesson the Segovians proffered that night, with the torches and the little fires over which women were cooking in a primitive way.

I did not ride straight into the square. Before I could announce myself and be recognised some rioter might thrust a torch under Sasha's sensitive nose, or under her belly. I knew Segovia well. Before the castle the open space, beside it the Street of Angels, since renamed, and joining them, running alongside, one of those dirty little lanes where ownerless dogs fight over scraps and pigs root in the middens. I guided Sasha into this unsavoury place, dismounted, walked around the sharp corner and mounted the steps. Those within the castle were watchful and wary; with commendable promptitude somebody somewhere loosed an arrow which hung, quivering in the upper part of my arm and then fell. I roared, 'Hold your shafts. I am your Queen!' That alerted the crowd, settled down for an all-night-long siege, and all faces turned towards me, moon-paled, fire-flushed.

Nobody ever made a less queenly appearance; drenched and bedraggled and wounded. I had clapped my left hand over the wound spouting blood from my upper arm, but the blood ran between my fingers; though I felt no pain. One can only feel so much—I felt relief that the castle seemed to be intact, and sheer blind red fury that it should ever have been threatened, that this mob ... Yes, admit it, making an outing of it ... make the little fire and show that you can cook a pancake on it, using a shovel instead of a pan; light and hold a torch ... Let Don Andreas *see*. The King marching off to the north, the Queen about to ride south and we will teach him ... For a moment I hated them all, even the man whose voice spoke the first words of recognition. 'Yes, that is the Queen.' There was a murmur, over which I shouted,

'Who is the leader here?' The murmur grew louder and there was some shuffling and people attempted to push this man and that out into the open space immediately before the castle steps, left clear for fear of the arrows. The men thus pushed, pushed back.

'Who speaks for you, then? Come forward.'

That did elicit some response. Three, five, six advanced, removing their headwear. Then my strength failed. I could not even question or scold them. The blood was dripping on the steps. I must sit down, or fall down, my wound must have attention. I made one last effort.

'I will talk with you tomorrow. Now see that everybody goes home. At once.'

Then the door behind me opened and I fell into the Castle hall. Don Andreas and two or three other men, all armed; behind them Beatriz, with Isabel clinging to her skirts. I just managed to say, 'Sasha ... In the lane,' and then I fainted.

In the morning I was quite restored though rather pallid. I said to Beatriz, 'I shall need no blood-letting for at least a year.'

She, even more whey-faced said, 'How can you joke about it? You might have been killed. Andreas has ordered that archer a flogging.'

'I countermand that order. How could the man know?' Six inches higher, though, and the arrow would have dealt me one of those unstaunchable wounds in the neck and Castile would have had a child for Queen. Amongst all the other thronging thoughts of that morning was the one that I must make a will, strongly advocating that in the event of anything happening to me, and my heir less than eighteen years old, Ferdinand should be Regent.

I had a long talk with Don Andreas who explained that the whole trouble arose from the excellent way in which the Hermandad had been working. More criminals had been arrested in the last six months than in the previous six years—amongst them a group of men who had been working a 'Protection' scheme by which householders and shopkeepers paid regular sums of money in order not to be molested.

'I do not *judge*, Your Majesty. But as Governor it is my duty to see that sentences are carried out. I have done so thoroughly, and that is why I am hated. Individual sums involved may be small, but they mount up, and some wrongdoers offer tempting bribes. And some men—in responsible positions—have lost their integrity. May I give an instance?'

'Do.'

'It concerned a cheesemonger. Bandits, in their hand-to-mouth way of life, value cheese highly; it is easily transported and it keeps well. The cheesemonger with his three donkeys and his son were set upon, a few miles outside Segovia, defended themselves with spirit, using cudgels, broke one robber's leg, but lost their cheese and their donkeys, trudged into Segovia and laid a charge. In former days,' Don Andreas said, 'nothing would have come of it. But the Hermandad went out, made an arrest and brought in three thieves, one the man with the broken leg. The magistrate was in their pay. Do you know what he said, Madam? He said to the cheesemonger, 'You accuse this man of attacking you. How could he, his leg is broken.' The cheesemonger said, 'I know. I broke it with my stick.' 'Oh,' said the magistrate, 'you confess to inflicting grievous bodily harm? I must fine you.' That, to my mind, is a travesty of justice. The cheesemonger came to me and complained and I looked into the matter and uncovered a most unsavoury scandal. I dealt with it. And with others. For that I am hated.'

The six men pushed forward as spokesmen to whom I had said I would talk in the morning, had come to the castle early, accompanied by four others, citizens of the more responsible kind. I deliberately kept them waiting and when, at mid-day, I faced them, I was still angry. I had a number of grudges against them. The fright, the anxiety, the desperate ride, even the wound in my arm—now painful—I could at a pinch have forgiven. But the effect upon Isabel was something I should never forget and found difficult to forgive. After a day of terror, lasting well into the night, that poor child had peeped from behind Beatriz and seen in me, her mother, not merely something to be shy of, in awe of, but something horrifying, a nightmare figure, dripping water and blood. Her horrified screams had gone down with me into the spinning darkness of the swoon. In the morning she could not look at me, tidied and bandaged as I was. I understood because once, long ago, in Arevalo, one of our temporary servants, a young man whom I much admired because he could imitate bird calls and whistle merry tunes, had misdirected the little axe with which he had been chopping kindling wood, and severed the top of the first finger of his left hand. The wound healed, and until he left in one of those general exoduses, he still whistled and made bird calls, but I had never felt at ease with him again. I did not know it then, but the dislike of blood which had activated so much of poor Henry's policy had been part of me then. I had been forced to overcome it; Isabel might, unless God were very kind to her, be forced to overcome it; but the first time makes a mark and there remains an association of disgust, repulsion, completely unjustifiable, but natural.

I had this to hold against the Segovians. And also Sasha's death. She was dead in that filthy lane when somebody went out to bring her in. And she had died alone.

I know that the Church holds that animals have no souls, that God created them, things for man's use. St Francis thought otherwise; it is recorded that he preached to birds and called his humble mount, 'Brother Donkey'. The whole thing is debatable, but nobody who has loved, or been loved by an animal can entirely evade the thoughts that *perhaps* those who live close to us, give us their affection and their trust might be something more than senseless tools.

Isabel, more than ever, and more understandably alienated, Sasha, her valiant effort made and now dead, went with me, in addition to my throbbing arm to confer with the citizens of Segovia at mid-day. I listened to their grievances. First and foremost on Andreas was too strict. By prosecuting the big extortioner of protection money, he opened the way for a dozen others whom the powerful man had kept in check. He had applied too harshly the rules about keeping streets clean. 'Your Majesty, it is surely unjust. I have a bakehouse, as clean without as within, but if a dog dies outside my door; or a donkey, half-eaten with maggots and stinking, falls outside my gateway, am I to be held responsible, subject to a fine if I do not clear it away?'

'And if,' another man said, 'my lamp fails ... Nobody could contend that streets should not be lighted; but if an apprentice, hurrying to his supper, fails to see that the lamp has sufficient oil to last out the stipulated hours, should I be fined, and shamed? I can beat the apprentice, but my good name is lost. Don Andreas is not open to reason, Your Majesty.'

Rancour boiled in me. So far as I could see Don Andreas had never exceeded, or failed in, his duty, and he was hated and had been besieged and threatened simply because he had been applying the law as it stood. It was true, carcases must be removed, but by whom? Who owned a dead dog, a foundered donkey? As for the lighting of lamps and lanterns, a little supervision beforehand was worth any amount of beating afterwards. The more I listened the more I realised that Don Andreas was a man after my own heart; I wished I had a thousand of him. And I was still angry.

Also, by this mid-day, I was in a position to enforce my will. Inez de Mendoza had arrived, and hard after him three hundred mounted, armed men.

Unworthy to think—Had they only been on my heels last night ... No, better this way. No dead, no wounds, except mine. But I must not forget, I must never forget, that last night if wishes could have killed, I would have killed them all. This morning I said, at the end of it,

'So it is your wish that Don Andreas be removed?'

'Yes, yes. He was too strict, too harsh.'

'Then I will remove him. The Marquis of Moya shall henceforth be Governor of Segovia. You accept him? Swear to obey him?'

Oh yes, indeed they would. But from the men who had not taken part in the riot, who had not been there in the square last night there was a little protest—'Don Andreas was strict, but just.' I thought so too, and it gave me a sour kind of pleasure to present to them their new Governor, Andreas de Cabrera, Marquis of Moya, subject to the consent of the Cortes.

Most of them managed to smile; a few laughed outright. But I had not done with them yet. I said to Don Andreas over dinner, 'I shall stay here for two days, administering justice myself. *I will show them what strictness means!* And I wish you, as Governor, to make and enforce a new rule—nobody for any purpose whatsoever is to bring a torch or make a fire within sight of this castle and until I lift the ban any gathering of more than twelve persons, except in church, is to be forcibly dispersed. I will leave you fifty men to strengthen your arm.'

I had trusted Segovia, my own city, and the Segovians had given me the worst fright of my life and indirectly my first physical wound. It healed well: Beatriz had applied salve, almost magical—in fact the 'oil and wine' of the Good Samaritan in the Scriptures, bound together by firm, three-year-old honey—and I was left with only a small, pale scar, invisible when I was dressed and not obtrusive at other times. The mental wound was deeper and longer-lasting.

Certain people could be trusted, or mistrusted; mobs of people could be trusted to some extent, but always with reserve. It was, after all, much the same crowd who on palm Sunday spread leaves under the feet of the donkey Our Lord rode, and on Good Friday howled, 'Crucify him!' and 'Give us Barabbas!'

It was in this mood that I set off for the south—missing Sasha all the way.

7
Trujillo, Seville.
June–December 1477

'Her humanity was shown in her attempts to mitigate the ferocious character of those national sports, the bull-fights, the popularity of which throughout the country, as she intimates in one of her letters, did not admit of her abolishing them altogether.'

W. H. Prescott

I had never been further south than Toledo and I was amazed to find Andalucia so lush under an even hotter sun. In central Castile, once the spring blossoms are dead there are few flowers, except lavender and gorse and such drought-resistant things. In this June Andalucia blazed with wild peonies and asters and roses and oleanders. The Great River, the Guadalquivir, the largest Castilian river to empty its mouth from between Castilian banks, watered this area; and Andalucia was the last province to be taken from the Moors, who were specialists in irrigation. Also Andalucia had the benefit of sudden, brief summer showers, blowing in on a south-westerly wind. It was a different country.

Behind me lay dark Trujillo, which had held out fanatically in La Beltraneja's lost cause, but had surrendered to a slight show of force. Ahead of me lay Seville. Travelling in state, I had sent outriders ahead of me; I had ordered that the Duke of Medina Sidonia and the Marquis of Cadiz should retire to their estates and wait there until I invited them to come to Seville and present themselves at my Court.

A few miles outside Seville a deputation met us; a medley of young nobles, beautifully dressed and wonderfully mounted, and some citizens, more soberly clad. Would I not take to the barge, waiting for me? To enter Seville, Castile's biggest port, by river would give more of my loyal subjects a chance to see me.

'Whose barge?' I asked.

It was the Duke's barge, but he had lent it to the city of Seville for the occasion; would I not please accept this small gesture of loyalty and affection? The combination of youth, all beauty and ardour, and grave civic dignity was irresistible. I agreed to enter Seville by barge and I was no sooner aboard than I realised that a very subtle and knowledgeable mind had been at work. It was a floating bed of roses, crimson, scarlet, pink, golden and white, all sweet scented. And there was a little canopied apartment containing everything which a woman could wish for the repair of her toilet. Somebody had used imagination. Somebody had also been most disobedient, for when the barge drew in to the landing steps, who was there to meet me, with a grave, reverent look and an outheld hand but the Duke of Medina Sidonia himself!

I was sharp with him. I said, 'My lord, you have disregarded my order.'

'Yes, Your Majesty. Of necessity. Had I obeyed and withdrawn, Rodrigo of Cadiz would have been here to meet you and there would have been dead men in the streets and in the river. I beg your forgiveness. I thought only of your comfort—and happiness.'

Happiness as a positive, a *planned* thing had so far played only a small part in my life. Fleeting moments, memories of childhood, yes, happy because they were not unhappy; I had never known the pursuit of happiness as an end in itself, as these southerners knew it. But that knowledge came later. I said, 'My lord, I ordered you to retire to your estate and await my call.'

He said, 'I know. I apologise. I am yours to command; but I cannot hand over Seville to the Marquis of Cadiz.'

'Seville is not yours to hand to anyone.'

'Legally—no. It is Your Majesty's. I have been holding it for you. I beg, do not deprive me of the pleasure of rendering it to you, and of welcoming you to the most beautiful city of your realm.'

He spoke cajolingly and smiled. He was a handsome man in a grave, dignified way, and he might well have been a monarch, welcoming another. I thought—If I show my displeasure and hold to my point, dismiss him summarily, I may alienate him; better perhaps to be gracious, though anger stirred again when with a great flourish he handed me the keys of the castle of Seville.

'Do I need these? Is my own castle locked against me?'

'Madam, of course not. It is a token gesture, designed to impress the populace.'

Later I saw what had been meant by making the entry by barge; the streets of Seville are narrow; in many places with two riders abreast there was no room for sightseers on the ground; but every balcony and every window was crowded and the streets were hung with silk flags and arched with flowers. Where space permitted young girls in white dresses stood, ready to throw more flowers in front of our horses. I was, of course, the centre of attention, but I noticed that amongst the cries for me the words 'Medina Sidonia' and 'Our Duke' could occasionally be heard; and some of the thrown flowers were for him, too.

I said, 'You seem to have endeared yourself to the people.'

'I have protected them, Madam.'

'From my lord of Cadiz?'

'Occasionally from the Moors also.' He looked thoughtful for a second and then added, 'Barbary pirates have also been known to venture this far upriver. On such occasions the Marquis and I joined forces.' He made it sound like an alliance of kings.

He did not, I was thankful to find, make even a token gesture of handing over the palace of Seville to me. He simply said that he hoped I should find everything to my satisfaction. He said that banquets and entertainments and receptions had been prepared but he had supposed that after a day of travel I should prefer to sup quietly and in private. Just a hint of a question there. I gave the desired answer, saying that it would give me pleasure if he would eat with me.

It sounds absurd; I had been born in a palace, I had been Queen of Castile for two and a half years but I had never known such luxury or such delicious food. In central Castile one is too far from any coast to have fresh sea-fish, and with pasture so sparse and short-lived, cows are few, so cream is a rare luxury; the fruit season is short, and the most usual vegetable is the bean. I had never eaten lobster, a sea-fish, cooked in cream, or a vegetable shaped like a thistle head, but four or five inches across, from which one plucked scale from scale and nibbled at the thick base; or another green thing, not unlike a thick wheat ear, of which one ate only the head. I had never seen a white mulberry.

In ordinary circumstances I should have said, 'This is delicious,' and asked its name; but the Duke of Medina Sidonia and I were measuring one another up and I would not give him the advantage of informing me. My ladies would ask and tell me later.

But there were other delicate and pleasing touches. At intervals, through every meal, it is necessary to wash one's fingers in the proffered bowl. Here the water in the bowls was scented, and rose petals floated. The music was different, too. As indeed was the setting; not in an enclosed room but in an arcade of arches, open to the evening air. The musicians were out of sight and I could not see where the difference lay. About this I felt I could ask.

'It is the guitar, Madam. Outmoded now, but here in the south we tend to cling to the old ways.'

I ate two white mulberries, dipped my fingers, wiped them and said, 'Tell me ... Is this feud between you and Cadiz a clinging to the old ways?'

'It could be called so. It is an inherited feud; his grandfather and mine fell out. The cause is forgotten—a field perhaps, a fortress, a ford—some disputed thing; it may even have been a bride. Our grandfathers fought, and our fathers, and so we fight—except, as I told you, Madam, when we make common cause.'

'Is there enmity between you—apart from this inherited feud?'

'No,' he said with the utmost seriousness. 'There are times when I love him as a brother. He is the best ... one of the best fighters who ever drew sword.'

'And who is the best?'

'Madam, I have held Seville and its environs against him for more than six years.'

It was a kind of game to them. Life a perpetual joust; boyish— though that was one of the last terms to be applied to this solemn and completely humourless man: even when he said there were times when he looked on his enemy as a brother he had not seen the ridiculous side to it.

I said, 'My lord, this quarrel is something I deplore. When the King and I were fighting for our lives—the Portuguese on Castilian soil—neither you nor the Marquis came to our aid, or sent aid. Too busy with your family feud!'

'Madam, the Portuguese did not, as strategy might have dictated, mount an attack in the south.' He looked to see if I had understood the significance behind this obvious statement. '*They* fear us, too. And a running feud has certain advantages. We are always ready.'

I told him that once the Treaty was made there would be nothing to fear from Portugal; I remarked how wasteful this private war was, and how displeasing to me and the King; I said, 'I intend, before I leave Seville, to see you at peace with one another. The fact that there seems to be no personal enmity between you, encourages me.'

'The House of Ponce de Léon at peace with Guzman? Your Majesty, I should fear to meet my grandfather in Heaven! He would disown me in the presence of God!' He made this extraordinary statement in all solemnity.

'And yet you do not know how this quarrel began. My lord, you astound me.'

'Three generations is a long time,' he said. 'Nobody asked why, or cared. It will end with us, of course. He has no son. Poor man. Twice married, too. Only three daughters—all illegitimate!' This was not said gloatingly, but with a kind of pity and regret, as a knight might say after a tourney that his opponent's horse had failed him.

I sat there and thought—Is it just this man? Or is this insouciance a characteristic of the south? If so I must learn to understand it, for these, too, are my people.

Presently another thing puzzled me.

I was keeping my promise to administer justice, to be accessible to the humblest of my subjects, and although I had taken the whole thing seriously enough to assemble local men to advise me—since custom often affects law, and customs vary from place to place—most of the cases brought to me were so trivial that I began to think the complaints were merely an excuse to come and gape at me. Day after day, a disputed boundary, a debt not paid, or that perennial grievance, an unfair division of a dead man's property.

I had nothing to complain of; I held my court of justice in another long arcade, with a pool in its centre, a cooling fountain scattering its spray; attentive servants brought me drinks and sweetmeats at intervals. The drinks, like much else, were new to me; one was fruit flavoured, effervescent and sweet; the other was a brown and bitter brew called kaffa. Both, I learned, were of Moorish origin; strict Moslems eschewed kaffa, classing it with wine, an intoxicant, and so forbidden by their Prophet. But even the strictest, the Duke of Medina Sidonia told me, allowed their women to drink it, because women, in the Moslem world, were, like animals, soul-less. I tried it, hated it and then saw its value; it did not, like wine, soothe! it sharpened; it enabled me to give to the twelfth or twentieth case of droning litigation the same attention as I had given to the first.

But something was wrong and I presently spoke about it to the Duke. I said, 'Tell me, does nobody in or around Seville commit any more reprehensible crime than trying to cheat his brother out of an old donkey?'

He then said a thing which cancelled out all the courtesy and the consideration.

'Naturally, Your Majesty, here as elsewhere, there are crimes against the person. Few, because when necessary I have used a hard and heavy hand. Such offences have not been brought to your notice because I should not wish anyone to say, in the presence of my Queen, anything I should not wish my wife to hear.'

I thought—Thank God for Ferdinand who had never shown such squeamish discrimination; who had agreed from the first, from the time when we had no justice to administer, that justice between us should be fair and equal. The one thing Ferdinand had never done, and I was grateful for it, was to try to *shelter* me; the opposite was true; our only real falling out had occurred not because he looked upon me as a pet, but as a rival.

I said, 'My lord, I appreciate your chivalry, but it must not come between me and my duty. I cannot afford to be squeamish, nor must you be squeamish on my behalf. I know the meaning of rape and incest; and I have heard sick men rave.'

The Duke flinched a little. A few days later he had an opportunity to retaliate.

Amongst the entertainments he had arranged a bull-fight and I was obliged to tell him that I did not wish to attend. His first reaction was amazement. 'But Madam, it is in your honour. Three of the famous black bulls, especially bred for spirit and strength, are to be dedicated to you; and fought by three of my best knights—one a near kinsman, renowned for his skill.'

I have lived to see things change, but in 1477 knights met bulls in the bull ring as they met other knights on the tourney ground. The custom of hiring professionals had not yet been thought of; indeed it arose from the fact that I disapproved of the sport and that no young man ever found favour with me because he had killed his bull—rather the contrary. My objection to the whole thing was perhaps unreasonably eclectic. The young man who had fought the bull would be called upon to show courage and endurance in some other activity; the bull had been bred for a specific purpose and in any case was destined to be butchered, soon or late. It was the horses; I could not bear to see horses gored and disembowelled. Once had been enough.

The Duke said, 'It would be an unequalled opportunity, Madam, for the people to see you.' And that fired me. I thought—I am tired of this schoolmaster's attitude underlying the assumption of near-equality; I should have opposed him more from the start, refused to step into his barge, sent him straight back to his estate in accordance with my order. I said, 'I do not wish to attend the bull-fight.'

Then he said, 'If Your Majesty is squeamish ...' and I knew he was remembering the rape and the incest and the things men said when they raved. But I did not retort. At least, I did not argue. I looked straight at him and said, 'My lord, you know my wish,' and left it there.

So, soon after five o'clock on that hot afternoon, I found myself completely alone for a little while. Not really alone, of course; in a palace servants, guards, ladies are always within call, but the court with the fountain was temporarily deserted—even justice must halt for the bull-fight. I sat reading and brooding over the somewhat sketchy records of the work of the Hermandad in Seville and its environs. It had not worked as intended; the effects of the Duke's hand which could be hard and heavy were all too evident; democratic institutions do not flourish under petty kings, however benevolent.

Light began to fade and suddenly I was aware of not being alone. I looked up and saw under the archway a young man, not a clerk, not a servant.

I seldom thought about it but it is true that a monarch, however widely accepted, however popular, does run the risk of assassination. There are one's known enemies and there are maniacs who think they have rights to the throne.

I said, 'Who are you? Show yourself!' For he stood in the shadow.

'Rodrigo Ponce de Léon, Your Majesty,' he said coming forward and dropping to his knee, bowing his head.

I had sent for him to come to Seville as soon as I had been manoeuvred into accepting the presence of the Duke in that city, and that was ten days earlier. I wished to be fair. But he had not come in and I was beginning to wonder if he would, or whether I must send a more demanding message. In the meantime the Duke, who sometimes loved him like a brother, had rather more often dropped a subtle hint. The Marquis might not have received my message because he might be in the city of Granada, he was understood to have a Moorish mistress there. Conversely, his wife might have been restraining him; we must not forget that she was the sister of the Marquis of Villena, who although he had been reconciled after Toro, had not been restored to the high office he thought his by right. 'Despite her childlessness and his infidelities,' the Duke said, 'she has great influence upon him. And is devoted to her brother.' I was not naïve enough to miss the point of such remarks, and I knew that I must not be prejudiced: at the same time, a summons to Court was a summons to Court and the delay must not go unremarked.

'You have been tardy, my lord of Cadiz,' I said. 'But you are welcome.' I held out my hand and he kissed it. A tingling sensation ran up my arm. I thought—It is the beard! Though many men wore beards.

'I wished to come into your presence alive,' he said simply. While I was pondering the significance of that remark and wondering how to reply, he said, 'And I am glad to have done so.'

Saying that he looked at me.

There is no word for that instant recognition.

I had been prepared to fall in love with Ferdinand; almost determined to do so and thankful that it was possible. This was so completely different that to use the same expression for it seemed wrong—part of the general wrongness. I knew, even as the colour ran up scaldingly from the edge of my bodice to my hair and then died down again, that this was more akin to the moment when the gunner puts the flame to the gunpowder, and potentially as dangerous.

I looked away; at the papers where the words, 'The Duke intervened' and 'Referred to the Duke', occurred too often in the Hermandad reports. Then I looked up and asked brusquely,

'And how do you come now, my lord? Unannounced and unattended?'

He said, 'Over the wall, Madam. Even here, in the heart of my enemy's territory, I have a spy or two. I was informed that you did not wish to see the bull-fight. I was even told where I might find you, though I did not count upon the fortunate circumstance of finding you alone. I could have come otherwise, of course. In mail and with my men behind me—and then there would have been fighting, and dead men in the streets of Seville. Would that have pleased you?

'You know it would not.'

'Then what could I do? Come unarmed and be dead? Come armed and offend you? Or like this? For once,' he said, 'Medina Sidonia outwitted me. You gave the order; both of us to withdraw. I obeyed it. I went to my castle of Arcos. He stayed here, offering keys and banquets, and flowers and blocking every approach. Yes, I must say he is cunning. There are times when I love him like a brother, sly dog as he is.'

I said, 'I have heard so much lately about brotherly love. Of the kind Cain showed Abel!'

He laughed and I laughed with him. Close to, one saw that his look of youth was deceptive; his face was lined, lines of harshness and of merriment, very different from his rival's impassive look of dignity and pride. Not that he lacked either, it was just that he carried them more lightly.

'With so much love about,' I said, 'one of the tasks I must perform in Seville is made easy. To make peace between you.'

'Your Majesty. I came this afternoon to offer you all that I have! Myself; my castles of Jerez and Alcalá; others which I inherited, or won, or built. I beg you, ask no more. For having seen you, I wish to please ... Do not ask the impossible.'

'You also fear that in Heaven your grandfather would disown you in the very presence of God?' I spoke with irony.

'*He* said that? Madam, I might have said the same, but for the fact that I am so great a sinner that by the time I struggle out of Purgatory Ponce de Léon and de Guzman will be one with Atlantis.'

That statement showed the little extra vision that makes the poet.

I hardened myself; I thought——He has a cozener's tongue; glib, flattering; he is a master of the dramatic gesture, coming secretly in, climbing a wall, when he well knows that if blocked, as he said he had been, one of his spies had only to say the word and I could have sent the Master of Calatrava to protect him. Or gone myself! I thought—a womaniser; twice married, a taker of mistresses—one Moorish; a begetter of bastards. But no amount of thought could undo what thought had done ...

Now, forget the Duke of Medina Sidonia and the Marquis of Cadiz sitting down and drinking wine together, reconciled, not under the pressure of war as in their former frail truces—unless, as God forbid, they regarded me as their common enemy. Here I was in the presence of God and must speak, through my confessor.

'Father, forgive me for I have sinned. I have sinned grievously in that I ...'

Torquemada would ruthlessly have demanded something more explicit; Talavera would have sensed my distress. I have had many confessors, these two stand out in my memory, both good men, great men in their different ways. Neither was with me now; one belonged to the past, the other to the future; and my confessor, that evening in Seville was Alfonso of Burgos, a good priest but not unduly curious. When, hesitant, stumbling, I confessed to sin in the mind he did not ask in what way. Possibly he thought it was pride in my achievement, and it *was* an achievement bringing these two hereditary enemies together. In different circumstances I might have been proud; but I knew, and could not bring myself to say it that I had been guilty of a sin which only Our Lord, in His infinite understanding, both human and divine, had ever recognised and condemned. And even He did it indirectly.

It is in the Gospel as written by St Matthew, attached to the Sermon on the Mount; it reads thus—

You have heard it said by those of old time, Thou shalt not commit adultery. But I say unto you—That whosoever looketh on a woman to lust after her hath committed adultery with her already, in her heart.

It is a *hard* saying; those who cannot read are happily unaware of it; those who never probe below the surface of what the Church teaches, can happily ignore it. But I knew, and God knew, how, speaking words that anyone could have overheard, Rodrigo of Cadiz and I had looked upon one another that afternoon. I sinned then, and now again, not making a full confession, unable to find the words, taking some trivial penance. Not even told in the routine phrase to 'avoid the occasion of sin'. That rule, however, I laid upon myself and held to. Never, never to be alone with him again; never again to share that moment of laughter, more intimate than any physical contact, or to think, as I had done when he made mention of lost Atlantis—Here is a man after my own heart.

Dear God, on the great Day of judgement, count this, in Thy infinite mercy, to my credit. I did try ...

Ferdinand—the north subdued—came south in August and I was able to offer him Andalucia at peace. I was pleased to see him, he seemed pleased to see me, and we spent some time in merrymaking, travelling about the beautiful countryside and being royally entertained everywhere. The Duke and the Marquis, no longer rivals in arms, competed in other ways. In Rodrigo's castle of Arcos we ate from solid gold plates: at the Duke's castle the wine, and my fruit juice, were served in beautiful, stemmed glasses from Venice. Better than cups of gold or silver, as he himself remarked, holding his glass between him and the candles, because served thus it could please the eye as well as the palate.

Ferdinand managed to offend both men almost immediately by requesting them to swear that they would live at peace. Their replies, made at different times, and places far apart, were identical, 'Your Majesty, have I not given my word?' All Castilian nobles, Ferdinand said, were intolerably arrogant, but these were the worst of all, and of the two the Marquis was the worse. Possibly some slight jealousy may have prompted this speech; Rodrigo's Marchioness had an almost unearthly beauty, inherited from her father who, as a young man, had stolen poor Henry's heart, but in her etherialised. I never saw such truly golden hair, such truly whiterose-petal skin: it was always with astonishment that I saw her sit down and consume ordinary food. And of course, she was young. This was the time when Ferdinand was beginning to develop a wandering eye and in every case of it about which I knew, first-hand or hearsay, it rested on someone very young and very fair.

Desire which cannot have its way takes some curious forms. It is quite possible that my son was conceived at Arcos, of a father and a mother who both wished to be in another bed, with another partner ...

God forgive me that thought!

8

Seville, Toledo, Medina del Campo. 1477–81

'Enel ano del nascimiento de nuestro senor Jesu Christe de mill quatrocientos y ochenta; mucho sacerdotes y othros varones Zelosos y amigos dela religion Christiana y fe Catholica, ausaron alos principes Catholicos como auia por todo SPA A muchos hombres de los Judios que se auian tornado Christianos ... se boluian a su ley antigua y cerimonias Judaicas.'

'In A.D. 1480 many priests and other zealous, respectable men, friends of the Christian religion and Catholic faith, advised their Catholic Highnesses that all over Spain many Jews who had become Christians had reverted to their old law and Jewish ceremonies.'

Lucio Marineo

The remainder of that year, 1477, and the first months of the next were very busy, mainly concerned with undramatic things such as the reform of the currency. We reduced the number of mints from 150 to five and ordered a uniform coinage so that the same money was acceptable, and had the same value from end to end of the country. This greatly encouraged and briskened all trading processes. So did a uniform scale of weights and measures.

We set up, not only a Court, but a proper home life.

Isabel's future was now under consideration and when she was nine she was to go to Portugal, not to be married but to learn; so I had only a year in which to enjoy her company and, if possible, gain her affection. I never did so though I think that I was more indulgent to her than to any other of my children. Between her and me there stood always the memory of the lost years when I had been too busy to give her much attention, and the horror of that moment at Segovia on the night of the riot. Even the fact that I loved reading and she did not, seemed to alienate her. I wanted her to be well-educated. The fact that I had not learned Latin, the universal language of scholarship and diplomacy, when I was young, had been a handicap to me, lessons are not so easily absorbed when one is mature. Isabel regarded her tutors, her books as something imposed upon her by 'the Queen, your mother' and therefore something to be resented.

'Doña Beatriz knows no Latin. I don't see why I need to.'

'Doña Beatriz is not going to be Queen of Portugal.' I put a stealthy hand on my waist as I thought of the possibility of this pretty, surly little girl being Queen of Castile, too. Please God, a boy. Let it be Thy will that Castile and Aragon remain united.

Later in the day I said to Beatriz, 'My dear, would it be asking too much to ask you to take a few Latin lessons?' She looked surprised but gave the answer I expected, 'If that is what you want me to do.' I explained why. Then I carried the thought further. Why should not every lady-in-waiting study something, even if it were only a standard form of their own language? They came from various parts of the country, pronunciation, even grammar varied. And there was a man, Antonio de Nebrija who had come home from Italy some time before and brought the German art of printing with him. He was said to be planning a Castilian book of grammar. That would take years to complete, but he could print a few simple excerpts. They could be studied; so could French, music, embroidery as an art, rather than as the whiling away of an idle moment. Something *real* to do would act as an antidote to the gossip and the card-playing.

Years later somebody whom I was prepared to love told me saucily that my Court was more like a schoolroom than a Court. I took it, not as an insult, but as a compliment. I had quite obviously succeeded in making my Court as different as possible from my half-brother's which had so shocked my young eyes and ears. I had even considered such trifles as the length of pages' hair. The pretty-boy look had gone; every page in our Court had his hair cut once a week, level with the lobe of his ear.

Alongside all this somewhat pedestrian activity ran two more important things, and with both Father Torquemada, my confessor again, was concerned.

Once in the shock of self-revelation, down in the south, languorous and sensual, I had momentarily wished for his flinty judgement.

Yet, back within his astringent ambience I did not confess to sin in the mind and invite his probing question, his harsh penances. Because, for one thing, it was over, this fleeting lust of the eye, of the flesh. A gravid woman is not troubled by lascivious thoughts. Nor is a celibate man, set on his course, likely to think—This woman is pregnant and should be spared.

On the first momentous occasion, confession over and penance decreed, Torquemada eyed me sternly and said, 'You wish for a son?'

'Of course. Only a prince could hold Castile and Aragon together.'

'That is a worldly opinion. Christ said that His Kingdom was not of this world.'

'I know, Father but ... But worldly responsibilities are given us by God. Castile is my responsibility; its permanent union with Aragon is a matter of great importance to me.'

'Rightly so. Yet there is a disunion within Castile itself. One of which you seem to be unaware. I am speaking now of heresy, Madam. I think that this moment, when you are asking and hoping for a supreme favour of God, would be an apt time to show that you deserve it. By restoring and greatly enforcing the power of the Holy Office.'

I lived to see it known as the Spanish Inquisition, and to have it closely associated with my name, blessed or cursed ... But in 1478 it was still known as the Holy Office and had almost three hundred years of existence behind it. Its function had always been to inquire into, and if necessary root out, heresies; it operated in every Christian country. In the thirteenth and fourteenth centuries it had been the instrument for hunting out the Albigensian heresy that had flourished in southern France. It had taken action against the Knights Templar. It had been active in Germany and Italy; less so in England because it was a Papal organisation and, as such, unpopular there. In Castile it had fallen into desuetude, largely because my ancestor, Alfonso the Wise, had disapproved of it.

I now said to Torquemada, 'That needs thought, Father.'

'Why? To a good Catholic I should have thought the eradication of abominable heresy was a duty that should come before all others.'

That could not be denied; but I hesitated. I disliked the idea of persecution for itself; and I had read enough to know that the persecution of the Albigensians had ruined the thriving province of Provence. I also disliked the idea of letting into Spain an absolutely unbridled power, appointed by the Pope and responsible to him alone. It was improbable, but not impossible, that the Holy Office, once established, could accuse even me of unorthodoxy and haul me away in the night. The officers of the Inquisition rode high above all secular law; they could arrest without making a charge; everyone arrested was held to be guilty until proved innocent—a direct reversal of common law; trials were held in secret; the chief Inquisitor was both accuser and judge, and all the ordinary laws of evidence were flaunted. People not usually accepted as witnesses—women, children, slaves—were allowed to testify against, but not for the accused; and there was never a plain clear verdict of 'not guilty'. The taint of suspicion clung for the rest of his life to anyone arrested, even if the evidence against him were so weak as to warrant no penalty.

To gain a moment I asked was heresy indeed so rife.

'The whole country is riddled with it. Three-quarters of the so-called Conversos are Jews-under-cover, and practise their rites in secret. It is against them that Holy Church must be active, and *armed*.'

I knew about the Conversos, too.

When the Moors held Spain, they and the Jews had lived peacefully alongside one another—their faiths were in fact not so very disparate. When our forefathers reconquered the country, piece by piece, the Moors had somewhere to run to—Granada, Africa; the Jews had nowhere. So they stayed and were offered magnanimous terms; they could be baptised, become Christians and enjoy every citizen's right; or they could hold to their own religion and suffer some restrictions. The unconverted Jew must live, with his fellows, in certain areas of towns and cities; he was not allowed to own land outside such areas; he must wear his own distinctive dress; must not give his children Christian names. Against these mild disabilities must be set the fact that while the Christian religion forbade usury, the Jewish religion allowed it; so specialising in money-lending and in pawn-broking, and kindred pursuits—until the currency reforms in money-changing—many open Jews became very rich.

The Conversos had become integrated with Christians and were now almost indistinguishable; but they too had prospered in other ways. Dependent upon their wits for survival, they had used them well, and become doctors, lawyers, teachers, secular scribes. My chief secretary, Ferdinand Pulgar, and two others, Fernando Alvarez and Alonso de Avila were all from Converso and good Christian families.

'I am concerned,' Torquemada said, 'with the souls of those who for motives of sordid gain, *pretend*; who kneel at the altar, take the Body of Our Lord into their mouths, unbelieving, and then go home, to observe, in secrecy, the rites of a religion that denies His divinity. I fear for them. God's infinite mercy may extend to the heathen; perhaps even to the Infidel, to the genuine Jew, reared and confirmed in error. But for those who keep the Sabbath and go to church on Sunday, who regard the Passover as a festival, and yet observe Easter, there can be no mercy; unless some effort is made to save them.'

'And you think that the institution of the Holy Inquisition, and some persecution would do that?'

'Most assuredly. Brought face to face with the penalty of wrong-thinking *on this earth* a man must think of the hereafter. The Holy Office, properly organised, could bring many souls to God.'

I took, rather shamefully, refuge behind Ferdinand. I said, 'In this, as in all matters, the King must be consulted.'

Ferdinand said, 'Times have changed, you know. Burning heretics has ceased to be a popular pastime. A stiff fine. In really stubborn cases a confiscation of all property. It could do no harm. The genuine old Jew with his kaftan and sidecurls would go on his way, untouched. So would the genuine Converso. Only the frauds, the ones who wish to have it both ways, would be affected. Oh, and the exchequer, of course.'

Disloyal to think—Always most reasonable and always with a mind to the money-bags.

'And,' he said, 'it would please the Pope.'

With Sixtus IV we were not in high favour because I had been fighting for the ancient right of a monarch to make clerical appointments. Cardinals, yes—they were his concern, but on a lower level

I had always thought and said that the monarch on the spot knew better what man was suitable for high office in the Church than the Pope who knew nothing of the man, or the country, and who might, badly advised, or overpersuaded, appoint a man, already with a full burden of offices, to, say, a bishopric, which the appointee had never seen, and never would, since he intended to sit in Rome, hands cupped for the next benefice. There had been altogether too many of these chance appointments.

In my—I will not say fight with Sixtus, debate is the better word—I had always been handicapped by the knowledge that it was he who had given the full dispensation for the marriage between Ferdinand and me.

'It is always good diplomacy,' Ferdinand said, 'to give way on minor points.'

'You think the restitution of the Holy Office a minor point?'

'On the whole, yes. It can only affect a very small minority. The *relapsed* Conversos.'

'Of them Torquemada said three-quarters of all ...'

'He exaggerated. All Dominicans do. But even at that estimate, very few.'

Even so I hesitated. I talked to Cardinal Mendoza who, like Ferdinand, was of the opinion that it might be wise to show earnestness concerning heresy as a means to gaining the right of appointment; but, he did not press. In the end I thought of the fundamental differences between the Order of St Dominic and that of St Francis. There had even been a time, long ago, when the Dominicans had regarded the Franciscans as heretics.

I chose as my adviser Father Talavera, a man whose gentle, modest manner concealed a first-class mind, a strong streak of something which in a more worldly character would have been called shrewdness. He did not contradict Torquemada's statement that heresy was existent and that heretics' souls were in peril, but he said,

'Could not persuasion be tried first, Your Majesty? Some Conversos—especially the young—are open to confusion. The Jews have very strong family feelings. An Orthodox Jew may *regret* that his son accepts Christianity, even while understanding the social reason for the act. Only in rare instances is the family tie completely severed. Children are born and presently see their parents practising Christianity, other grandparents practising Hebraism; they may even see their parents, for the sake of peace or out of civility, joining the Hebrew rites when in the grandparents' home. What are such children to think? To believe? Since you seem to wish for advice on this matter,' he said diffidently, and waited, 'then I will give it. A determined campaign of persuasion, combined with some education in the Christian doctrine, aimed particularly at the young.'

This was welcome advice. 'Would you undertake the organising of this campaign?'

'Most willingly. It is particularly suited to my Order, and to Franciscans who are accustomed to preaching in the open.'

But when I told Torquenaada of this plan he scoffed.

'Madam, how many Jews did Our Blessed Lord Himself persuade? *Twelve*; of whom one betrayed, and another denied Him.'

I said, 'Oh, Father! The man who climbed into the sycamore tree; Joseph of Arimathea; the young man who went away and sold all he had.'

'Exceptional cases; recorded because they were so exceptional. The Jews are an obdurate people. The story of Masada may not be known to Your Majesty, not being in Holy Writ ...' That was a sly dig at me for having made reference to the Gospel stories. Tactfully I remained silent and allowed him to tell me the story I already knew. Some years after Our Lord's death and resurrection, the Romans had decided that the time had come to conquer the Jews completely. Masada had held out not to the last man, but to the last but one, who killed the wounded, the women and children and then himself, so that when at last the Romans entered the place it was a necropolis.

When Torquemada had finished I ventured to say, 'There is a slight difference. The Romans were not attempting to convert the Jews, but to enslave them.'

'A splitting of hairs, Madam. The strength of the resistance is the point. We have, here in Castile, another Masada—that of the heretical spirit—which it is our duty, as Christians, to subdue. And it will not be done by gentle persuasion.'

In the end I compromised. The pope was approached for a Bull authorising the setting up of the Holy Office, and in every church, in every market square, the campaign of gentle persuasion and enlightenment began. I could only hope that the latter would be so effective that the former would not be needed.

When summer began to scorch the hot dusty central plateau, we all went to Seville again, and in that beautiful place, in that beautiful palace, on the last day of June 1478, my son was born.

Second births are popularly supposed to be easier than first ones; for the sake of women everywhere I hope that this is so. For me it was not. In some ancient play a woman is made to say that she would rather stand three times in the front line of battle than bear one baby. I cannot know whether she spoke from experience of battles, and I myself have never been allowed to stand in the front line, but I agree in principle. All through a hot long summer day, under those watching eyes ...

But worth it! The midwife said, 'A boy! Thanks be to God. A prince.' Ferdinand, not given to the easy expression of emotion, broke down and wept tears of joy.

In a ceremony of the utmost magnificence, he was given the name Juan. He seemed healthy, and once the red, crumpled look had worn off became very pretty with silvergilt hair, truly blue—not Trastamara—eyes, and an appleblossom skin. From the first he had his own household. My experience with Isabel had taught me a lesson; a mother, however busy, must see her child at least once a day, but since so many ailments are handed about like gifts, Juan was with the Court but not part of it, and his household were subject to strict rules; nobody, for instance with a cough or snuffle, a rash or a headache was allowed to go near him. The rules were strictly enforced by the governess of his retinue, a remarkable woman, Doña Joanna de Torres, who combined the gentleness of a dove with the courage of a lion. Juan had his own doctor, Nicolas de Soto, a man of high reputation, who, for the first six months, enjoyed a sinecure.

Trouble began when he was weaned. 'It is nothing,' everybody, even Beatriz, said. All babies at this time suffered digestive disturbances, lost weight, cried. But Isabel had been with me when she passed through this phase and she had not been affected. 'Oh yes,'

Beatriz said, 'girls are easier to rear. I had anxious times with my Ferdinand.'

Anxious times! This was a life inestimably precious, not only as most children are to their parents, but to Spain; and it was housed, say what they liked, in a body growing increasingly frail. Despite all precautions, Juan caught colds, not simply snuffles and sneezes, but always developing into a low fever. 'A common accompaniment to the cutting of teeth, Your Majesty,' Dr de Soto said. A little bleeding, a little purging, some soothing pain-killing drops ... But even when the teeth were, with the utmost difficulty, cut, it was a very fragile, pallid little boy who could now call me 'Mother' and his governess 'Ama'.

One day Beatriz said to me, 'I have no wish to decry Dr de Soto, but I think a Moorish physician might do better. Hear me out, Isabella ... It is not only that so many drugs came with them from the East. They have a different attitude towards the study of anatomy, the framework of the human body. They are allowed to make studies, forbidden by our Church.'

I said, 'But there is nothing wrong with Juan's body. If he could eat more, and digest more of what he does eat ... Very well, find me a Moor.'

'I have him, waiting. Otherwise I should not have spoken.'

His name was El Said; a grave, taciturn man with dark, sad eyes. He stared at my child and finally approached him and said, 'Would you please bite my finger?' Juan, with a child's dislike of strangers, bit him with right good will. Dr El Said examined his finger with care and then said, 'As I thought. A slight malformation of the jaw. It will worsen with age. His teeth do not meet. Chewing is difficult. That is why ordinary food is indigestible to him. It accounts, also, for the difficulty in the cutting of the teeth. Ordinarily one gum, working against the other, helps. But that is bygone and we look to the future ... Food put through a sieve, or chopped very finely. And always bland because this little prince cannot chew, which is the first process of digestion. Properly nourished he will grow stronger, and if the slight deformity mars his appearance a beard will conceal it.'

Juan's health markedly improved.

Then one morning when I made my first visit, I found him playing with a string of cheap-looking blue beads to which was attached a flimsy silver pendant of curious design.

He was, of course, the recipient of numerous presents, but they came through recognised channels; nobody was allowed to give him things directly, and this particular thing I disliked the look of. If the string broke he could swallow a bead, and the pendant had what might have been spines.

'Who gave him that?' I demanded of his governess.

'That,' she said, 'is a mystery. It appeared in one of his shoes and nobody admits to putting it there.'.

'It looks dangerous to me. It should be removed.'

'I thought so, too. But he has taken an unaccountable fancy to it. Madam, he will scream.'

'Better he should scream than choke,' I said. 'Darling, let Mother look.'

'No.' He gripped the thing defensively. I spent a moment coaxing and trying to persuade, then loosened his fingers. He screamed with rage, pulled at the beads and broke the string. I held him, struggling and yelling while Doña Joanna swiftly gathered the scattered beads. Through the din I asked whom had she questioned about the necklace and she replied, 'Everybody.' Coming from her it meant *everybody*, from the highest officer in the household to the kitchen scullions.

I was left holding the little pendant, the design of which puzzled me; it could have been a fowl's wishbone, crossed with other bones. Its very aimlessness said 'Moor' to me, for strict Moslems, like the Jews, were forbidden to make the representations of anything, they must confine themselves to patterns; even so this seemed to be a singularly unfinished pattern.

I showed it to Beatriz, telling her where I had found it, and how much the little mystery of its appearance worried me, since if one thing could be brought in secretly, so could others.

'Whoever did it meant well,' she said. 'It is an emblem of good fortune.' She fished into the neckline of her bodice and hauled up a gold chain from which hung a cross and the emblem, identical with the one I held except that it was more substantial and made of gold.

'My grandmother gave me this, just before she died.'

'Your Moorish grandmother?'

'Yes. But she was a Christian. She had been baptised. She said it would bring me good luck, good health and good teeth. And it has.'

I said, 'Beatriz, you surprise me. So superstitious!'

'But, dear Isabella, it *has*. Look how fortunate I have been! I have had your friendship, my son, a kind husband and never a toothache.' The order of her catalogue of blessing, though flattering to me, had its own significance.

'Beatriz. Did you put it there? Do not be afraid to tell me.'

'Afraid? Isabella, I have always admired and respected you, and served you when I could. I have never feared you.'

'Of course not. That was a stupid thing to say ... It has upset me a little to learn that someone has had access to Juan's apartments, and placed a heathen symbol—however well meant.'

'I don't think it is a heathen symbol. My grandmother died when I was very young, but I assure you, she was a Christian.'

I could see, in the eye of the mind, the old Moorish woman, about to die, wishing to pass on something of the belief in which she had been reared, to the little granddaughter who had inherited her dark, straight hair, her black, lustrous eyes.

'Ah,' Father Talavera said, looking at the little trinket with something like awe. 'The Fish Symbol of Our Lord. I have heard about it, but never seen it before.'

He then told me a most romantic story. When, in the years immediately after Our Lord's death, the Christians in order to survive were forced into secrecy, they needed some simple symbol, intelligible even to the illiterate as most of them were. The cross was too obvious. So a certain affinity between two Greek words had been usefully exploited, and the fish symbol came about. What had looked to me like a fowl's wishbone, held sideways, was the outline of a fish; the crisscross lines might, to the uninitiated, represent either its skeleton, or some meaningless scribble, but the cross was there, twice, three times, cunningly concealed.

'To a persecuted minority it was a symbol of hope and unity, Your Majesty, in those troubled times. It could be drawn very quickly and amongst the wall-scribblings, escape notice, but it spoke to the believer. It said—A Christian lives in this house; or, more vaguely—A Christian has passed this way and left a sign for all to see. And it should not be forgotten that without such devices, the roots underground, the Church could never have been founded. I mean,' he said, working his hands together in the way he had when troubled in his mind, 'it was well said that the blood of martyrs was the seed of the Church; but if every Christian had gone into the arena, or been used by Nero as a living torch in what ground could the seed have rooted? I think of this often ... The survivors, in their inglorious role, going secretly about, scribbling this on walls and doors and wine casks, or even in the dust, were also serving God's purpose. This may even be heresy—of a sort. The fact remains, if St Peter, in that courtyard by the fire, had not denied Our Lord, he would hardly have lived to become the rock upon which the Church was founded.'

I said, 'But the decision was not his, Father. Earlier that evening Christ had told him—before cockcrow Peter would deny him three times.'

'True. True. The same thing could be said of the betrayal ... Of all Holy Writ, I find hardest the statement that evil must be done, but woe will come to him who does it.'

On the verge of a dizzying and dismaying thought, I shied away and took refuge in practicalities, but, as with a very different man, in very different circumstances, I had again that feeling—Here is a man after my own heart. I decided that I would like Father Talavera for my confessor.

Life went on; work went on. Isabel left for Portugal where I knew she would be well looked after by my mother's sister Beatrix. She went happily and the thought occurred to me that since, with girls, parting was almost bound to come, perhaps it was as well that there should be no close ties to be ripped apart, giving pain on both sides. Isabel had her future, the almost certain prospect of being Queen of Portugal—something that appealed to her pride; I had Juan. I also had, in a fashion, the six little nobly born boys installed as part of his household, as playmates, presently to share his lessons. And I was pregnant again. This time without overmuch concern as to the sex of the child. Either would be welcome. A second son could take title of King of Sicily and be given a Duchy in Castile or Aragon; a second daughter would for some years at least be a child to cherish and enjoy, but not to clutch at too closely.

What came was a changeling child.

It was November 1479 and we were in Toledo, where in the New Year the biggest and most representative Cortes of our reign was to meet as soon as the roads were passable.

Toledo is known as The City of Steel; the river there has some quality that hardens steel. And it is a beautiful city, largely because it has not been destroyed, as so many were, in the Reconquest. But in November, in the time of the winter rains, it can be chilly and bleak, though on that particular afternoon in the little room I called my 'cabinet' a good fire burned and there were many candles.

Pulgar shuffled papers. Some of them concerned the setting up of the Holy Office in Castile. As my one-time friend, the Archbishop of this City of Steel had said, things in Rome moved slowly, but approving letters, the promise of a Bull from the Pope, had that day arrived. The thought that the idea of resolute persecution had yielded something more tangible than the campaign of gentle persuasion, did something to depress me and when Pulgar, all his papers in order and himself ready to withdraw, hesitated and said, 'Your Majesty, would it offend you if I were impertinent?' I said, lightly,

'My dear Pulgar, I doubt if you could be. But the sight of you trying to be impertinent would be a diverting spectacle on such a dull day.'

He had, from his Converso-Jew ancestry, those dark eyes which to those of us of lighter colouring always look sad. In addition, years of faithful work, to my half-brother and then to me, had given him a melancholy hound's look. But he had a sense of humour and could laugh; when he did it was as sudden and gratifying as the sun sending a beam from behind a sullen cloud. Today he did not laugh or even smile. He put his hand on one group of the carefully assorted papers and said,

'Your Majesty; it will not end here. The Holy Office, once established, will not be content with false Conversos. Any official, of any grade, must justify his own position, his existence. May I give a humble example? A copying clerk, his real work done, will busy himself, ostentatiously sharpening quills, rearranging papers already in good order. The Holy Office, once established, having dealt with a few relapsed Conversos cannot be expected to say—*This is a job well done,* and then disband, putting every member out of employment, out of position. Out of power. They are only men, Madam.'

Low down discomfort struck; I thought—I have sat long enough in this hard chair, heavy as I am. I eased myself a little, putting the weight on my elbows, on the chair arms, and shifted.

I said, 'I know. But I am prepared. I decided, when the question of heresy and the Holy Office first arose, that I would rule—every heretic must be defended by a qualified lawyer. That must be written in, Pulgar.' Then his face changed, not a smile, not a laugh, the grimace of one tasting vinegar when he had expected wine.

'And where will they be found, Madam? These qualified lawyers? Most of the able are themselves Conversos. Once this thing is under way,' he tapped the papers, 'few will dare. And they will be so overworked that any suspect, guilty or not, will spend months in gaol; and *gaols being what they are*, dead before he faced the tribunal of the Holy Office.'

The condition of gaols was something I had never considered seriously and now was not an apt time. Pain lanced me. Slightly early, I had thought perhaps on All Souls Day ...

Hurried into the world with the minimum of ceremony, born perfect, no crumpled baby look, my daughter Juana. She was born with a cap of soft dark hair, which pleased Ferdinand. 'She has my colouring,' he said, with naive pride. So far as hair was concerned this was true, but when her eyes lost the slaty-blue of the new-born they turned as green as emeralds. Ferdinand petted her from the first and was full of plans for her future. 'You shall be Empress, my pretty one, if I can manage it.' It was true that the Archduke Maximilian of Austria, who would almost certainly become Emperor when his father died, had a son, Philip, just that right amount older. It was true that Ferdinand was becoming adept at diplomacy so far as it consisted of playing off one power against the other. He was not too scrupulous about the means he used to gain an end, and when an ambassador one day said bluntly, 'Your Majesty, my master complains that you have twice lied to him,' Ferdinand laughed and said, '*He* lies! I have lied to him three times!' I do not doubt that he confessed his lies, just as he confessed his breaking of the marriage vows, for he was pious in his way, but his successive confessors were indulgent and never imposed upon him, so far as I knew, any penance that really hurt. One who did so would not have lasted long.

I was up and in perfect health again by the time the Cortes met, to approve amongst others two measures designed to reduce the pride of the nobility and increase the power of the Crown. One forbade the use, in any form, of any of the emblems of royalty. Over the years by marrying younger princesses or princes half the great families in Castile and Aragon had become related to the ruling houses and thus claimed—wrongly—the right to quarter the royal arms with their own. For months after the ban was announced, painters and embroideresses would be busy, correcting such anomalies. The other step towards placing more power in our hands was the rule that as each Master of the great Orders died his title reverted to the King. There would, in time, be no more Grand Masters with practically limitless power, based partly on the strength of the military forces they commanded, and partly on the huge estates held by the orders producing huge rentals. Ferdinand would eventually hold all the resounding titles, and choose his own deputies.

In fact, by the end of the year 1481, Spain was united, slowly growing in prosperity; the Holy Office, not yet too rigorous, was dealing with heretics; the Hermandad was imposing the rule of law.

And in this palace and that, as the Court moved, the heir to it all was growing. Not a very clever little boy, but extremely conscientious. Only perhaps to me, his mother, did his health give reason for concern. Now and again I noticed that whereas a romp made his little companions flushed and hilarious, Juan would turn pale and quiet. 'An hour in bed,' Doña Joanna would say, 'and he will be restored. He always tries too hard. He wishes to excel.'

Juana, a year younger, but in all but age far older, also wished to excel, but she did it effortlessly. I think there can never have been a child so precocious. At ten months old she had a vocabulary, not of a baby talk but of ordinary words; at a year she walked, and well;

none of tentative, stumbling steps, the holding of a supporting hand, the grasping at anything that offered support. It really seemed to me—who saw her twice every day at least—that one day she was not walking at all and the next strong and sure on her feet. One day, shortly after she became thus fully mobile she walked to a lute left lying on a bench. She could not, of course, lift it. Nor did she try. She plucked a string and seemed to listen, her small pretty face attentive, but half-smiling. It was almost as though somebody invisible were instructing her ... Silly to think that any other child, made free of a lute, would have made a jangling discord. Silly to think that after that one tentative note what followed was unnatural. 'Juana is just very *clever*,' Beatriz said. 'She has watched and listened. All children are imitative as monkeys.'

She meant well but the word *monkey* is to me uncomfortable. Monkeys are not native to Spain, but with Africa so near they have been imported, as personal pets, as a spectacle for the populace. And in neither capacity did I like them; they always looked to me to know more than they should and to be burdened down with what they knew and could not communicate. All other animals have innocent eyes ...

However, very soon I had more to worry about than Beatriz's injudicious choice of a word. I had the Moors to deal with.

9
Wherever the war was. 1481–5

'Correctly it may be said that, from 1483 onward, Isabella became the soul of the entire enterprise ... proved herself to be one of the ablest quartermaster-generals in history.'

Decisive Battles of the Western World, J.C.C. Fuller

The Christian reconquest of Spain had halted on the borders of Granada and that region had remained an independent Moorish kingdom, but a tributary kingdom. In 1476, when Ferdinand and I were fighting the Portuguese, the King of Granada, Muley ben Hacen, had withheld his annual tribute and sent instead an insolent message—'The mints of Granada no longer coin gold but steel.' The message was clear and we were in no position to do anything but accept it.

It may even be that in persuading the Duke of Medina Sidonia and the Marquis of Cadiz to cease their running feud I had undone some of that instant readiness for combat which the Duke said was a deterrent to all enemies. In December of 1481 Muley ben Hacen crossed the border and attacked a town called Zahara. All the men in the town were slaughtered, the women and children carried off into slavery. There was always a demand for fair-skinned young females in the harems of well-to-do Moslems; Muley ben Hacen's younger and favourite wife was a Christian girl, taken in some earlier raid and given a Moorish name, Zoraya.

The news reached Ferdinand and me in the bitter winter at Medina del Campo where we had gone to keep Christmas and we hurriedly took stock of our resources and began to formulate a policy.

I did not go lightheartly into this war; the Civil War of the Succession and the Portuguese War had taught me how horrible warfare can be; however righteous the cause it does not protect men against wounds and death and sickness, fields from ruin, the economy from disruption. Yet this war was inevitable. 'Death to the Infidel' had been a battle-cry in the old days and I had more than once given my word that as soon as Spain was united and the power to do so was placed in my hands the Moors should be driven out. There were other pressures than those that were national and personal. The invasion of the Turks—blood-brothers to the Moors—had not ceased with the fall of Constantinople. All around the Mediterranean, and deep into eastern Europe, the Crescent was threatening the Cross; it was every Christian's duty to engage in the so-called Holy War, whenever, wherever he could.

In all the Councils and in all the private conversations I held at this time there was only one dissident voice and that not very aggressive. It was an echo from the past. Once, in an unguarded moment, I had said to Ferdinand that Aragon's war with France was not Castile's war. Now, in private, he told me that the war with Granada was not Aragon's war, and in public gave evidence of his lack of real enthusiasm by emphasising the difficulties of the campaign; the cost. He would sometimes sit in silence when a 'fighting' speech had been made; and then, as though after long deep thought, say, 'We must not underestimate ...'

I did not underestimate the difficulties—one of which lay in the fact that in the south there was no road suitable for the passage of an ordinary cannon, leave alone a Lombard; and I knew from my visits to Andalucia—the latest recovered province—how strongly the Moors fortified their towns and how many small, rock–like fortresses there were in the border country. It would take artillery to subdue them. The roads—or rather the lack of them—would also affect supplies. Fertile and lush as the valley of the Guadalquivir was it could not support an army for long without help from the corn-growing north.

I did not underestimate.

I was heartened, however, by the assurance of all churchmen, Cardinal Mendoza, level-headed and concerned with costs, Father Torquemada, the Infidel must be subdued, Father Talavera, the Infidel must be conquered and converted, and dozens of others, that this was a Crusade, something that God and the Pope would bless, something that Christian history would remember.

I was heartened, too, by a message, brought hot-foot from the south—'Your Majesty, Zahara is avenged.' The Marquis of Cadiz, with a friend, the Count of Miranda, had taken the Moorish town of Alhama, a small town, well within the borders of Granada, and very rich for a place of its size since it made textiles, everything from cobweb gauze veiling to carpets. And it had been taken without any modern weapon at all. A few intrepid Spaniards had scaled its walls, opened its gates.

So perhaps, not so difficult after all! And very rewarding. The Moors—or so it began to be said—were effete and decadent; too much lolling about in warm baths, too much energy expended in the women's quarters. One brisk, determined campaign ... And what one victory of Cross over Crescent would do for the whole of Christendom!

Thus began the war which was to drag on for ten years.

In the first year of it I bore another child.

We all look forward with blind eyes, backward with sharp hindsight. To this pregnancy I had been able to give hardly any attention; there was no time. I do remember thinking when Ferdinand and I had taken up our headquarters in Cordoba that I should have preferred not to be seen by Rodrigo of Cadiz in this state, bulky, heavy-footed. But there was no help for it.

My third daughter was born with comparative ease; but the birth did not bring the usual relief or the reduction in bulk. After some miserable hours Doctor Ribas Altas came and asked leave to examine me. He said, 'There is another child, but it is dead; it can make no effort. I will prepare a draught which I hope will be effective.'

It came, bitter as gall. Beatriz said, 'I only wish I could drink it for you.'

I said, 'I only wish you could,' and gulped down the brew. Thirty-five hours later—in pain one counts hours—I was delivered of the dead baby—a boy.

The little girl was named Maria, and slipped almost unnoticed into the family; a healthy baby, an amiable, rather stupid child, always in danger of being overlooked. Ferdinand did not lean over her cradle and predict a great future—in fact for a Princess of Castile her future was curiously unplanned, though it turned out to be, thank God, a happy one. I loved her, but in her early days my limited time in the nursery seemed to be consumed by Juana, charming, wayward, much spoiled not only by Ferdinand but by everyone who came into contact with her. In fact, of my three girls, not one had been the daughter I had sometimes dreamed of, as perhaps every mother does: Isabel was haughty and hostile, Juana clever, beautiful and changeable as the wind, Maria slowwitted and shy.

I was thirty-one when Maria was born and the end of my child-bearing days was in sight if it had not actually arrived.

It was soon after Maria's birth, while I was still in Cordoba and Ferdinand had gone to join the Duke of Medina Sidonia, the Marquis of Cadiz and several other notable captains at the seat of war, that I was invited to an *Auto da Fé*. This ceremony which means, literally, an *Act of Faith* was the culmination of a trial before the Inquisitors. The *Auto da Fé* is now as common as a bull-fight, but it was a novelty then and to attend was regarded as a religious exercise.

My secretary Pulgar, who can be pig-headed at times, has often said to me, 'Your Majesty, you and I must be the only able-bodied people in Spain who have never watched an *Auto da Fé*.' I know what he means by that, but in fact, on that hot sunny morning in July 1482, he sat so near me, on a lower level, that I had only to lean forward and downward in order to tap his shoulder.

This Act of Faith was performed in a pleasant little market town between Cordoba and Seville. I was there on my usual errand—raising supplies.

The church bells began to ring at six o'clock in the morning, and rang steadily for four hours in order to summon the crowd and give people time to assemble. The open square in the town's centre might have been decked for a saint's feast day, or for the celebration of a victory. For me, my attendants, and some local notables there was a raised platform, tiered, so that I sat alone, and with an awning as protection from the sun. Every window and balcony was decorated with flowers and banners and much of the square was thickly carpeted with the leaves of sage, believed to be a guard against the summer plague, and therefore, by association, in the minds of the ignorant, against all evil.

Supervising my dressing that morning Beatriz had said, 'Will you wear the little crown?' and I had replied that I would dress as for church, so I wore on my head the stiffened cone that upheld the veil of lace. As she placed it in position she said, 'Are you all right? You look very pale!' I retorted, 'So do you.' She said, 'It is the bells. They make me feel dizzy.' I said I did not mind the bells; it was the thought of men burning ...

I had managed to extract, by positive *demand*, a kind of half-record of the events that had led up to this day, but even I, Queen of Castile, could not be supplied beforehand with the Inquisition's findings. Six men and one woman, all of the same family, had been arrested. The woman, rightly, had been dismissed; she was able to prove that she had never been baptised. She was therefore an 'Open Jew' and as the law stood then, not a heretic. The six men, all Conversos, had been accused, and tried; the results of the trial could not be divulged, even to me. But some must have been condemned, otherwise there would have been no *Auto da Fé*.

Beatriz said, 'I have prayed and prayed, Isabella, that those condemned may at the last moment repent. They can ... Priests plead with them, up to the very stake.'

That was true; to the very end the priests did plead; all good earnest men, to whom a convert, a penitent, meant more than a dead man, punished, and an erring soul hustled into eternity untimely. But on that summer morning I sensed what I had feared—the brutality of a crowd. They had not left their beds early and trudged miles and stood for hours in order to hear some heretics recant.

Once, in the early days of my reign, I had said to Cardinal Mendoza that I would like to ban bull-fighting, and he said, in his sensible way, that to do so would be to deprive ordinary people of the excitement which all men crave and which ordinary labouring lives do not provide. So I had passed that over, merely making a law, often evaded, that the bull's horns should be covered with a blunt casing.

Now I smelt the distinctive smell of the bull-ring, of a crowd out for excitement at whatever cost.

But the creatures which this crowd had come to see sacrificed were not soul-less animals, I must remind myself. They were men, with free will, who had chosen the wrong belief and were therefore heretics. As a good Christian, I should try to share the feeling of this crowd ...

The procession began. The bells stopped, giving way to a silence more deafening momentarily than the din, and from one of the side streets leading into the square came the censer bearers, some monks chanting the Miserere, the green banner of the Holy Office borne ahead of a file of clerics, all in their finest robes, and finally the six accused. One old, rather shuffling man, two in their middle years, three young. They were curiously clad in one-piece garments, a pointed hood attached to a loose, all-enveloping cloak. Three of the garments were black, decorated with applied tongues of flame, or imps of Hell, in scarlet; the other three were yellow marked with crosses. All the men wore ropes around their necks. The black-clad ones were accompanied by a bevy of priests, holding up crosses and ceaselessly exhorting; the yellow-clad ones walked between armed guards.

The procession came to a halt before a platform, lower than the one on which I sat. There, immobile and stern, sat the officers of the Inquisition.

Beatriz, her head level with my knee, turned and said, 'There is still time.' I am sure that she was praying, as I was—God, of Thy mercy, make them recant.

Mass was said. Then a man with a most resonant voice read out the names of the accused and their offences. In such a solemn moment, with the scent of incense and of trampled sage and of blood-lust filling the square, each single offence sounded trivial; eating meat on Christian fast-days; eating only meat of birds or animals which had been slaughtered by the cutting of the throat; observing the Jewish Sabbath—our Saturday—by purification rites performed on Friday evening; preparing a dead body for burial in the Jewish manner. Yet since these acts had been performed by people who had been baptised and publicly professed the Christian faith they were proofs of apostasy.

The bull-voiced man had a sense of timing; after each charge he paused so that the crowd could groan, or hiss, or spit—or in a few cases cross themselves.

Three had confessed, repented, regretting their abominable sins; they were to suffer a public whipping, pay some heavy fines and wear their yellow penitents' robes for six months. Three had remained obdurate and were to burn.

I tried to divert my mind by wondering who the witnesses against them had been—at least one must have had most intimate knowledge of the family. I also made a mental note that the man with the splendid voice should be made Town Crier—unless he already occupied that office. But these thoughts were also trivialities; there stood the three men who were to burn; the blood would boil in their veins, their flesh would sizzle; and all for what? A mistaken adherence to a faith which was outmoded, its purpose served, as soon as Christ our Lord was born in the Bethlehem stable.

The three penitents were marched away in the direction from which they had come. The whippings, the fines, the wearing of humiliating dress would not expiate their fault; they would always be under suspicion, and the yellow robes would hang on the walls of the local church, a reminder for ever.

The three unrepentant ones were taken in another direction along a side street which led to the edge of the town where the stakes, the faggots and the fire waited. I had no need to mingle with the rabble, now all agog. A respectable citizen had put his house at my disposal; I had only to leave my platform, cross the square, enter his house and there from an upper window, see all.

I could perhaps have managed it, but for the fact that as the three condemned moved to their doom, they began to chant, one voice answering the other antiphonally, and Cardinal Mendoza, offering his hand to help me to a lower level, proffered the information that this was the Jewish rendering of a Psalm. The twenty-third to be exact—'The Lord is my shepherd ...'

I then had a thought so shattering that it almost paralysed me.

Suppose the inconceivable happened, and all the Moslems, the Turks, the Berbers rushed to the aid of the Moors and we lost this war and I were given the choice—Renounce your faith or burn. Should I be brave enough, resolute enough to go singing to my fate?

For I think the only time in my life I took refuge in female disability. Only a bare month out of childbed. I said I did not feel well enough ...

'In truth,' Beatriz said, 'it is not a *painful* death.' Distressed herself, she was anxious to comfort me.

'How can one know? No burned man, really burned, ever rose

from the dead to tell us that.'

'The smoke kills. At least it was so with Andreas's aunt. She was bedridden. A log rolled from the hearth and set fire to a chair. It was quickly extinguished; the fire did not touch her, but she was dead.'

I could not bring myself to denigrate the comfort of this story by voicing the thought that for a bedridden woman the shock could have been enough; so I said, 'I hope it is so with them.' And then I wondered whether that could be a wrong thought: perhaps even for heretics suffering on this earth might mitigate those in the hereafter.

I never again attended an *Auto da Fé*, and since Pulgar, like myself, shirked the final scenes of this one, he holds that we have never been present at one.

That year's campaign against the Moors went badly; the Moors proved to be tougher adversaries than they were reputed to be and they had a style of warfare new to us. They never engaged in a set battle and they used mounted archers. While we were besieging a town a group of cavalry, mounted on very swift light horses would emerge from nowhere, do what damage they could with their slashing, curved swords and then gallop away, turning in their saddles as they went so that they faced their horses' tails and let fly a shower of arrows. All too often poisoned arrows. By the end of summer, though we had held on to Alhama, we had failed to take Loja, after a long siege. In October Ferdinand and I were back in Madrid, rising money, recruiting men, organising a Pioneer Corps to work on the roads. The Duke of Medina Sidonia, Rodrigo of Cadiz and Gonsalvo of Cordova—another brilliant soldier—could be trusted to keep the frontier. We were preparing for what we now knew might be a long war.

The Pope sent us his blessing and a great silver cross to carry into battle; he also sent letters approving of the work of the Holy Office. This was now so busy that in Seville alone 298 people burned, and four times as many recanted, which was very good for the revenue. Ferdinand was strict but just over the confiscation of property and on several occasions when children were to be left without any means of support, ordered part of the fines to be remitted. He also offered me, without realising it, a splendid opportunity of disassociating myself from the whole business. He suggested putting Torquemada in charge of the Holy Office in Aragon as well as Castile. I welcomed the idea. Torquemada's energy and fury were beginning to disturb me, the more diffused they could be the better, I thought. So I said, 'Could we at the same time set up a separate secretariat to deal with the whole business? It is becoming burdensome.' Ferdinand agreed and that meant that I need not even read about it, need not learn how many towns and cities now had a permanent place for the burnings—sometimes permanent stakes, stone figures of the Apostles.

Pilate washed his hands, too!

Isabella Trastaniara, you *must* not think this way! You *must* not think that to the Roman and to the Jews, Christ was the heretic of heretics ... Busy yourself; for thoughts melancholic or eccentric work is the best cure.

So I busied myself with things as diverse as riding down to a place called Cambril where the Pioneer Corps, aided by a great force of locally recruited labour, were literally moving a mountain, to seeing that Ferdinand's fancy for the youngest, prettiest and silliest of my ladies-in-waiting came to nothing. That I did by writing a very tactful letter to her mother, saying that Doña Lucia was too eager, undertook more than she could accomplish, and should; I thought, return home for at least a year, at the end of which time, unless other arrangements had been made, she would be welcome back. I wished not to hurt the girl's most estimable parents, nor the girl, guilty of nothing more than silliness ... That was the exercise of tact which life had forced upon me. I much more enjoyed my visit to Cambril where a good part of the force of six thousand then at work on the roads were labouring, men hacking away at the red sandstone, women and children carrying the hacked stuff away and throwing it into the valley on either side to level up the declivities. Old men, past hard physical work led laden donkeys away, old women cooked over camp fires; simple, rough food which I shared. Nobody, not even the Romans, those great roadmakers, had ever undertaken such a task in Spain. And in Toledo, in Huesca, cannon and Lombards were being made by Spaniards, one day to travel this new road, the cannon on wheeled vehicles, drawn by picked mules, the Lombards on sledges pulled by oxen; no wheeled vehicle could support a Lombard's weight, and oxen, though slow-footed, pull low.

One day, next year, or perhaps the year after next ... One day ...

The war, left simmering in the south, being prepared for in the north, erupted here and there; in principle even far to the north, in Navarre where it was suggested that the King of Navarre should marry La Beltraneja—now twenty years old and a professed nun. We knew what that meant: the King of France, Ferdinand's born enemy, was prepared to back this impossible marriage and the poor girl's claim to the throne of Castile. It ended in nothing because Phoebus, King of Navarre, died, but it did show that far from all Christendom rushing to the aid of, or at least, encouraging, a Christian country at war with the Infidel, they were all willing to take a sly bite from behind. Cynicism is an ugly thing and unbecoming to a Christian, but it sometimes seems to me that it is forced upon all but the very simple by the process of experience, just as the years bring the wrinkles and infirmities of old age.

Certain events stand out. In March 1483 there was not a battle but a massacre. Rodrigo of Cadiz and the Master of Santiago with a large army, were ambushed in a narrow valley at a point where men were marching almost in single file. There was a terrible slaughter and Rodrigo lost two nephews and had barely escaped with his own life. Ferdinand was disgusted. 'I thought he was supposed to know the Moors so well! He should know the terrain, he is a rash, impetuous fool and when I return to the war he will have no place at my Council.'

In the next month the Count of Cabra and Rodrigo retrieved the situation. The Moors were so encouraged by what 550 guerrillas had done to an army of Spaniards that they ventured out and attacked them near Lucena, where they were soundly defeated. One of their most famous leaders, Ali Atar, was killed and the young King of Granada, Abdallah, was captured. (His father, Muley ben Hacen had not died, he had been deposed and it was his mother's intrigues and insistence that had made Abdallah king.)

Rodrigo sent a long despatch and some advice. He was holding Abdallah until he knew our wishes, but he strongly counselled letting him go. Zoraya had offered a king's ransom but this was not the main consideration. Back in Granada the young man would do harm to the Moorish cause, his kingship being a matter of dissension already. As a soldier he was useless, harem-bred and spoiled by his mother; as a focus of intrigue between his supporters and those who felt that his father had been unjustly treated, he might be invaluable.

'I must admit,' Ferdinand said, laying down the despatch, 'that for a soldier, Cadiz writes well.' Ferdinand had his own conception of the soldierly handling of a pen, terse, very slightly inarticulate. 'What do you feel about this?'

Say that I thought Cadiz's opinion should be seriously regarded and I should rouse opposition. Faced with opposition I was prepared to argue, but if argument could be avoided I was willing to hedge a little.

'It needs thinking over,' I said, my mind already set. 'What do *you* think?'

When we were alone Ferdinand often thought aloud, putting one side of a case, then the other, logical, sensible, and completely deceptive in that anyone else, listening to his musings, would have thought him indecisive. He now said, in a breath, 'Naturally he knows more about the Moors than we can ...They ambushed him unawares.' And, 'If we hold Abdallah we lose the ransom money and in addition shall be obliged to keep him in some kind of state. Cadiz may have his own reasons for suggesting this, that Moorish mistress of his may have used influence.' Ferdinand argued with Ferdinand, until, picking up every argument in favour of Rodrigo's proposals, and repeating them, I was able to say, 'You have convinced me that it would be advisable to let him go.' I had decided that upon first reading the despatch, not because it was Rodrigo's opinion but because I hoped that, quarrelling amongst themselves, the Moors would be weakened and the war shortened. It was a dispute about succession, and dispute about my own had shown me how disastrously inward strife can affect a country. Once Ferdinand had reached his decision I was able to make *my* contribution. 'The ransom offered is handsome, but money is not enough. A king should be worth a thousand ordinary prisoners. Let us ask for the release of a thousand Christians.'

'And confer a Dukedom on Cadiz? You would approve of that?'

'Wholeheartedly.'

Then, in September of that same year, Rodrigo, helped by the Count of Puertocarres, captured Lopero and incidentally caused me some heart-searching.

'Cadiz should receive some mark of approval—something that he would use,' Ferdinand said in a burst of generous feeling. 'He does not use his new title; he is wealthier than we are at the moment. We have no such order as the Golden Fleece or the Garter. I think I shall send him my royal robe; with permission to wear it once a year, on the anniversary of Lopero.'

This was quite out of character. For one thing Ferdinand had not debated with himself, either silently, or aloud; for another it was he who was always complaining about the arrogance of *my* Castilian nobles, and who had most fully approved of the law that made any use of royal insignia illegal. Now here he was, suggesting the giving away of his own royal robe.

But—cynical again; several of the families thus obliged to alter their emblematic honours were our relatives, noticeably the Enriques. Could this be the first move in the restoration of such favours, subtly disguised? Make one exception ... The old Admiral of Castile was dead, his son had taken his place, let him win one battle at sea and the precedent set, the painters and embroideresses could get busy again.

I said, 'It would cause jealousy, Ferdinand. And create a precedent.'

'How? I have not so many royal robes to give away. Cadiz has held the fort, carried the war into enemy country. He will be needed in future and should be ... encouraged.' The significance of that remark was only revealed later. At the moment I was more concerned with Ferdinand's suggestion that it would be an agreeable gesture if I sent a royal robe to Rodrigo's wife! The idea of that woman who already had so much, peacocking about ...

I showed, I hope, no sign of the revulsion I felt. I said, I hoped calmly, 'I think that might be rather too much. The Count of Puertocarres was also active at Lopero. I will send my royal robe to his Countess.'

'An excellent idea,' Ferdinand said. 'He must be encouraged too.'

Again I missed the point. It was not until December of that year that I understood.

10

Tarazona, Toledo, Cordoba, Seville. 1484

'.. este noble caballero Duque de Cadiz merecen ser escribas ... era un caballero que la placia mucho la geometria.'

'this noble cavalier the Duke of Cadiz deserves to be written about ... he was a cavalier who found much pleasure in geometry.'

Andres Bernaldez

'No hera a lindado, por que devia ser hijo de alano, o de castra de alano y de lebrel.'

'He was not pretty because he was the son of a mastiff, or of mastiff breeding and of a greyhound.'

Oviedo, writing of Bruto, the Prince's hound

Too greatly astonished to be cautious, I said, 'You cannot do that!'

'And what is to prevent me?' To that there was no answer. That small careful clause about his not going to Aragon without my permission had been waived long ago, even before his father died and he became king, in 1479.

I said, weakly, 'It would be such a shocking thing to do. So false! The church has lent us money; the Pope has granted Indulgences to those who have helped with labour and material, all in order to fight the Moors, not the French!'

'That,' Ferdinand said, 'is the beauty of it. We are ready and they are not. The French believe we have our hands full with the Moors. They will get a surprise and I shall regain the lost provinces.'

'Two wretched little provinces, so fought over as to be worthless!

Full of mongrel people who speak French or Spanish according to which flag flies. Are they worth our good name?'

'Rousillon and Cerdagne belong to Aragon. Don't exaggerate, Isabella; and don't shout! I told you it was a secret. Good name does not enter into the matter. I'm not abandoning your so-called Crusade. One lightning swoop on the French and I shall come south to join you.'

'Join me? You mean that I ...'

'I am not suggesting that you should mount a warhorse and wield a sword. But an army needs a head. I have no doubt that your Castilians will obey you more willingly than they have ever done me. Besides, the Crusade must go on; think of all that Church money and all those Indulgences ...' Voice and glance were sardonic: I had taken the wrong line. I tried again.

'Ferdinand, please. I spoke in haste. Defer this plan for a year. Who knows, by this time next year we may have Granada, with all its wealth and resources; and the surprise will be equally good then.'

'It can never be so good again. A new king, a child on the throne of France. Alliances and policy uncertain. There will never be so good a moment. Believe me I have given long and careful thought to this. Without saying a word to anyone.'

Long and careful, certainly. It was with this defection in mind, I saw suddenly, that Rodrigo had been encouraged by honours, and Gonsalvo of Cordoba, a second son and poor, by more tangible gifts, and the Duke of Medina Sidonia by places and offices about the Court for some of his numerous relatives.

'And I am not thinking solely of two wretched little provinces populated by mongrels,' Ferdinand said. 'I am thinking of the children. A victory over France might help Maximilian to make up his mind about the marriages. We've nothing yet, not even a verbal agreement.' Maximilian had not only a son, Philip, just the right age for Juana, but a daughter, Margaret, just right for Juan; tentative proposals had been made, including the mutual eschewing of dowries for the two girls. But as Ferdinand said, nothing definite had come of them yet. (Sometimes when I thought of it I wondered whether Maximilian could be waiting to see which way the civil war in England went. The Low Countries, part of the ramshackle Empire, and a very rich part, had very strong trade links with England and if once the English could stop cutting one anther's throats there might be rich matrimonial pickings to be had from that quarter.)

I tried to make Ferdinand see that the conquest of Granada would give Spain equal prestige in the eyes of the world, but he would not listen. One will in two bodies, two wills in one body no longer held good. And yet, in the end we were at one, united in the absolute necessity to deceive the world. Any whisper of dissension between us now would greatly encourage the Moors and discourage those in the south who were expecting vast reinforcements as soon as the roads were passable; and of course any hint of the cause of our dissension would alert the French. In secret discussions we divided our forces—all too easily done, for at rock bottom the recovery of Granada was still Castile's aim, the recovery of Rousillon and Cerdagne a thing dear to every Aragonese heart.

In public Ferdinand and I gave no sign that we had ever differed. No two people can ever have been more elaborately civil to one another, and the most astute spy could hardly have read any significance into the fact that I left Tarazona first, in full paraphernalia. I had my children, my ladies, my Court; the Lombards were already on their slow, difficult way, so were the lighter cannon; we should pass them on our way. Feasible enough that Ferdinand should wait a little, ready to follow presently with a few light guns, with foot-soldiers riding pillion to mounted men.

We parted amicably, even affectionately. Only a few Aragonese nobles, who had been taken into our confidence, knew the truth. Only Juana made a fuss. She gave way to one of her hysterical paroxysms—with her everything was extreme—and cried and clung to her father and refused all comfort. I said to Ferdinand, 'God keep you and prosper your cause,' and he said almost the same to me, adding the reminder that in any dispute I was to give most weight to Cardinal Mendoza's opinion. But between us, in private, there had been acrimonious exchanges. My continued disapproval of Ferdinand's plan he had put down to stubborn short-sightedness, and that fired my temper and I had retorted with the word 'dishonourable'.

I approached this, which might be called a new job, with considerable trepidation. That I had been able to persuade and argue the

Duke of Medina Sidonia and the Marquis of Cadiz into ending a feud which they half regarded as a game, and must both have known in their hearts was not benefiting either of them, was no guarantee that I had enough power over men to take command of a dozen such men, all experienced soldiers. Ferdinand's warning about allowing the Cardinal to be arbiter in any dispute had struck a chilling note.

Apart from such thoughts shared only with Beatriz who had a strong romantic streak and who said wouldn't it be wonderful if this campaign, while I was in command, proved to be an outstanding success, the long journey southwards was pleasant, resembling a prolonged holiday outing. Everywhere the good results of careful planning could be seen. The roads had been widened, levelled where possible and in places made completely new. We suffered no lack of provisions or accommodation because halting places had been scheduled and sixty thousand mules had been plying to and fro with stores. They were all good, strong animals, too; obtained, I admit, in a somewhat arbitrary way. It would have been uneconomic to take a mule from the plough, or from a trader's pack train, so I simply passed a law that no woman should ride a mule. This made all the animals upon which burghers' and landowners' womenfolk rode quite useless to their owners and therefore available to me. They were mostly young and all in good condition, and since my feeling for horses extended to mules I took care to keep them so; loads and their rations were measured, the lame and sick not worked.

I had given equally careful thought to the preservation of my reputation in these unusual circumstances. Chaste living is not in itself sufficient guard against scandal and it would be impossible for me to go about surrounded by women—I could not take Beatriz with me into the Councils of War, for example, so I appointed Don Gutierre de Cardenas and Don Inez de Mendoza as special *aides-de-camp*; they were both to accompany me everywhere, or if for any reason prevented, to find a substitute. In addition one of my secretaries, usually Pulgar, was with me. I think that he had shared my fears about dissension and my ability to deal with it, for one day he said, 'It is marvellous to see so many fierce men drawn from all parts of the country, living as one family!'

That was true, as far as it went; they could agree and be mightily civil to one another, *so long as I was there*. It was this knowledge that took me into the actual battle line, and into armour.

I was not the first woman to wear it; the French girl, Joan of Arc had worn it, so had at least one other woman I had heard of, though I did not know her name; she had fought at the Battle of Toro.

The first battle that I ever *watched* was not far from Antequera, and I can no more give an account of it than can anyone else who has been present at a battle; all noise and confusion, with purpose and order behind the apparent muddle. An arrow actually struck me and glanced harmlessly from my steel corselet and I was grateful to Cardinal Mendoza who had insisted that if I went in sight of the enemy I must go mailed because I should be a target, lethally marked.

It was a walled town, with the usual protective gateway above, and the flanking towers overlooking the approach to the gate, made of six-inch-thick timber, protected on the outside with iron plaques and on the inner side by bars of iron. I hesitate even to think this, but I do think that in the taking of that town there was an element—because I was there—of showing off. Despite the deadly arrows from the towers—the archers able to take leisurely aim because those who man or command a battering ram must necessarily move slowly, the battering rams moved in again and again, even when their covers of dried hide had been destroyed.

A battering ram is a heavy tree-trunk mounted on wheels and nosed with a heavy iron cap; it has along its sides handles which those who propel it can grip—often they are no more than long nails driven in with a few inches left projecting, and as a rule those who man it are slightly protected by a kind of canopy of hide, not so heavy as to impede progress, but capable of deflecting an ordinary arrow. A well-directed one with a head of flaming tow can, however, set the canopy or the necessarily light wooden struts that support it, afire. And the men who handle rams cannot wear mail, all their strength must be devoted to the pushing ...

On this occasion the Moors were cunning. About midafternoon they unbarred the gate so that the battering ram then in use, meeting with no opposition and violently propelled, ran into the town, carrying those who manned it with it; and out streamed the white-clad horsemen with their flashing scimitars and, presently their arrows. In a matter of moments they had done great damage and then they vanished. Pursuit was impossible though our cavalry was ready; a horse capable of carrying a man in mail or half mail is of necessity heavier and slower.

We took no prisoners. The procedure agreed upon was that once this town, guardian of an open stretch of country, was taken, we should try to make a way straight southwards to the coast. Not immediately to Malaga, immensely fortified, but to some place where supplies, sent by sea from Seville and Jerez, could meet us. A great saving of time and effort, and a great blow to the Moors, since a Spanish corridor, from Antequera to say, Marbella, would cut the Kingdom of Granada in two.

With such an enterprise in mind prisoners would have been nothing but a nuisance, mouths to be fed. So the women and children, a few old or disabled men would be left to live in the taken town. On what?

I have a thrifty housewife's mind and the wanton destruction appalled me. I had that day watched my first battle, afterwards I saw what a victorious army can do. I knew of course; I knew all the terms, 'ravaged', 'laid waste'. But now I saw it and it was horrible.

And so, that night at the Council table, I fell out with all this happy family, as Pulgar had called it. Congratulations first and then the question: 'My lords, is such destruction necessary?'

The just-budding vines—this was May—were being rooted out, olive and almond trees were ablaze, horses and mules were in the fields and vegetable gardens, trampling what they did not eat.

My lords, with one voice, said, 'Yes.'

It was necessary for as many reasons as could be counted on the fingers of a hand.

It showed the enemy what to expect.

It prevented the enemy closing in behind us, sustained by what the unravaged land might have provided.

It was recognised custom.

It pleased ordinary soldiers; an occasional orgy of destruction raised spirits and helped discipline.

It would help to keep the conquered area subdued, people

engrossed in the hunting of just enough to live on had not spirit enough either to rebel or conspire with rebels.

I said, 'You make a wilderness and call it peace!' Only Cardinal Mendoza looked at me sharply and said softly, but with a warning tone, 'Tacitus said *we*, Your Majesty.' Ignoring both the correction and the warning, I said, 'To me it all seems a very great pity.'

'It is war, Madam. Like the loss of my thumb,' said the Count of Cabra cheerfully, holding up his bandaged hand.

They were all against me; I could see by their faces. I had struck a discordant note. The evening after a battle was a time for jubilation, for making light of wounds, even for forgetting the dead, and not for bemoaning the destruction of enemy property. For the first time I felt—was made to feel—out of place.

Then Rodrigo of Cadiz said, lightly, 'Your Majesty, it *looks* far worse than it actually is. Most of those trees will bear again next year; fields and gardens, quickly replanted will give a harvest this year. When Medina Sidonia and I were at odds we destroyed one another's property with the *utmost* regularity, with no lasting result.'

They all laughed. I knew in my heart that he, without seeming to do so, had offered a crumb of comfort. Something made me reject it. I said,

'Surely, my lord, that is argument against rather than for such policy.'

There was more laughter—they would have laughed at almost anything that evening. But the Duke said, 'Your Majesty, our hope and belief is that when the trees and fields bear again it will be to *our* benefit.'

I could have said, 'It must stop.' And it would have been stopped. I was the Queen. But there would have been a consequent loss of good fellowship, their arguments overridden. So I protested no further. I said, 'God send that you both be right my lords, that the country may recover and that it may be ours.' Goodwill, the pursuit of a common purpose was restored. Later, in private and with a smile, I gave Cardinal Mendoza a very gentle, small knock. He was a most admirable man, a splendid Chancellor; he was Cardinal, and Archbishop of Toledo, Primate of Castile since Carillo died; he was sometimes called the Third King of Spain. He must not, however, grow presumptuous.

To him I said, 'I thank you for correcting my misquotation. I came late to the study of Latin, as Your Grace knows.'

He coloured slightly, but held to his point. 'It was not the Latin, Your Majesty. I thought the separation from your leaders by the use of the word *you* somewhat injudicious.'

'And my argument, too? Is that why you did not lend your voice in my support?'

'I, too, have been a soldier, Madam, I know how men feel. I was greatly relieved that you did not forbid the destruction. Had you done so it would still have occurred, 'by accident'. And an evasion of a rule in one respect can lead to others in other spheres.'

'Half the damage done this afternoon was done by drunken men. I shall issue an order against drunkenness and see what effect that has.'

He looked at me very dubiously indeed. 'It will be a most unpopular measure.'

'We shall see.'

In fact, at that moment, it would have taken a good deal to make me unpopular with the common soldier who looked on me not only as a commander but as a mother; they knew that their welfare was of paramount importance to me; they knew that my army was the only one in the world to have properly equipped hospitals right there on the field. Hitherto badly wounded men had been left to die where they fell, lucky if a priest went out to say the last prayers and administer the last rites: those less severely injured had been lucky if they could hobble or crawl, or be helped by a friend to some place where aid could be found. I had started a service for the wounded, in a modest way, by transport in carts from Toro to Tordesillas; now I took the hospital to the wounded. I provided them out of my own money; six large, rather handsome, tents, equipped with proper beds and other comforts. I had a staff of doctors, and surgeons, well paid and allowed quite high rank in the army hierarchy; I had appealed to religious houses for monks and nuns who had some infirmary experience; lay sisters and brothers were welcome, too, and often some of the camp-followers were willing to help, sluts though they usually were. (It may well be that women like that should not be tolerated and encouraged, but nobody in his right senses could expect an army of fighting men to live like monks.)

The soldiers took my ban on excessive wine-drinking very well; there were many breaches of it of course, but not the wholesale rejection which Cardinal Mendoza had feared; far from it; and since sober men are less destructive than drunken ones, the kind of damage that I so much deplored was lessened by at least half.

That campaign lasted for forty days, and was entirely successful. By the end of the first week in June I was back in Cordoba.

My daughter Isabel was there too, back from Portugal, and in a very bad mood indeed. In October, she would be fourteen and, she herself considered, of full marriageable age. She could not see why she had not been allowed to remain in Portugal, celebrate her birthday and to be married there. She loved Portugal and all things Portuguese; everything there was better than in Castile. Most of all she loved Prince Alfonso, who was to be her husband and that, at least pleased me, little as the rest of it did. She was deaf to all argument and quite obtuse to such concerns as the dowry demanded, the necessity for some ceremony to surround the linking of a Princess of Castile with a future King of Portugal. She was, poor child, unaware of deeper and darker currents, of the fact that six long years must pass before ...

Juana, thwarted in a far less concern, would have flown into a temper, cried, coaxed, cajoled, refused to eat or to wash, laughed and cried again; Isabel reteated into haughty reserve and the making of acid remarks; even Beatriz whom she had once loved, could only reach her indirectly by saying such things as, 'A wedding dress takes time to prepare, Isabel. Shall we attempt the embroidery ourselves, or leave it to hired women?'

Beatriz never failed to oil any wheel that creaked in my life which was a business of wheel within wheel, some of them spinning in opposite directions.

The first Lombards arrived—two of them, outpacing the others, how or why I never understood. All I knew, was that at one moment they had arrived safely, and then at the next moment—or so it seemed, time passing so rapidly in a busy day—Don Inez was saying,

'Your Majesty, the Marquis of Cadiz has seen the Lombards and embraced them as though they were his brothers. But he has thought of an improvement and would like you to be present at an experiment which he is about to make.'

I said, 'Come with me,' and walked out into the blazing sunshine. Stripped to shirt and breeches, sweating and soiled, Rodrigo paused in what he was doing to the great gun, smiled and bowed.

'As soon as I saw it, I knew it had potentialities that have never yet been thought of ... the old trebuchet married to this beautiful thing. I should have asked permission? Forgive me.'

I knew what a trebuchet was, a device for slinging stones, rather more forcibly and farther than a human hand could throw.

Lombards rode on their sledges, were dragged into position and there left, their open mouths ready to propel whatever they had been fed with. At their own level. This one was already tilted, slabs of stone forced under the front of its platform and cocking its mouth into the air ...

'What I must know,' Rodrigo said, 'is how much gun powder is need to force the ball upwards. All things tend to run level or down ...' He stood away and eyed the tilted muzzles. 'Angle of fifty degrees. Ummm. Another handful, I think,' he said to the gunner with the box of gunpowder. The man ladled it out reluctantly, and said,

'May I speak, my lord? If the ball *refuses* to run uphill, the Lombard may explode and then you ...'

'Be quiet, fool!'

I said, 'Are you proposing to fire this Lombard yourself?'

'Who else would? Your Majesty, I have selected a place from which you can see all, in perfect safety.' He pointed to a little tower, part of the city wall, overlooking the open space to which the Lombards had been brought to rest after their long journey.

'Have you ever fired a gun, my lord?'

'No. But this good fellow has explained the principle.'

I said, sounding pompous, 'If anything happened to you, my lord of Cadiz, it would be a great loss to our cause.'

'It is for the cause that I am doing this. Look, Madam ...' He pointed outwards. The open, dusty sunbaked space was bordered by one of the irrigation canals, beyond which there lay, as outside so many city walls, the patchwork of vegetable gardens and the low hovels of those who tended them and brought, every day, fresh products into the market ...'If I am right, the ball projected from this angle should clear those houses, *and* the trees ...Think what that would mean. Instead of battering away at outer defences we could shoot into streets, *over* town walls ...Think of the shock!'

I said, 'It would not compensate us for the best leader of cavalry ...'

'They come a dozen a ducat! Your Majesty, nothing will happen to me. I have no wish to die in my bed, but I doubtless shall, God in His Infinite wisdom having decided long ago that no wish of mine should be granted ... I pray you excuse me, they have the brand ready ...'

Don Inez and I retreated to the tower. The entrance, the stairs, the little watch-place smelt of soldiers—it is as distinct a smell as that of a church, a convent, a blood-lusting crowd. A bleak, masculine smell.

Don Inez said, 'Your Majesty, sometimes mere noise can make stones fall. I think ...' He reached for the wall where some steel hats hung, rubbed the inside of one vigorously with his sleeve and offered it to me. I put it on and turned to the opening in the tower wall. From this height I could see more of the countryside at which Rodrigo was aiming his experimental shot. The houses!

I roared, 'Stop! Hold your hand!' and turning to Don Inez said, 'Run! Tell him those little houses must be cleared of people.' Don Inez ran and Rodrigo, receiving the message, looked towards me and grinned, a flash of white teeth in a dirty face, and waved his arm reassuringly. Don Inez ran back and gasped, 'My lord of Cadiz had thought of it. And promised to pay for any damage done.'

One of the gunners ran up and handed Rodrigo a flaming brand and then scuttled away. Sweat broke out where the leather padding of the steel pressed on my forehead, and on my upper lip; it crawled between my breasts, and along my thighs; not the sweat of a hot day, or of exertion. I dared not look. I must watch. God, be merciful, let nothing happen to him: Santa Barbara, patron saint of gunners, shield him: I leaned against the wall for support. There was a flash, a great boom and a rush of smoke so dense that I could not see what had happened on the ground; but out of the smoke and into the air, the white marble cannon ball soared in a great arc, clearing the canal, the cultivated strip, the little houses and the trees behind them.

'It worked,' Don Inez said in a way that told me that he had been holding his breath. There was the Lombard in the clearing smoke, and there was Rodrigo, jumping and waving his arms. I thanked God and made up my mind to eat no meat for a week; a gesture of gratitude, a penance for the fear that was lack of faith.

I ran down the stairs and into the open, leaving Don Inez to hang the hats back on their pegs. Rodrigo was coming towards me. I held out both hands. I was unable to speak for a moment. He took my hands and kissed them both. My hands were wet and tremulous, his were steady and dry.

'I was so worried,' I said. My voice had a quaver, mid-way between laughing and crying.

'It worked,' he said. 'And I am happy to offer Your Majesty this small device.'

Don Inez joined us, and the gunners and their helpers emerged from shelter. He sent them to find the ball, measure exactly the distance between the gun's mouth and the place where it fell, and to assess any damage it had done.

There could be no assessment to the damage that a few minutes' violent emotion had done to my peace of mind ...

Nowadays among my ladies I had a scholar. Her real name was Moira Beatriz Galinda, but partly in honour of her learning, partly to distinguish from *my* Beatriz, she was always known as La Latina. Her father had been a famous Latinist and had taught her all he knew, and she said, without boasting, and with a certain bitterness that she was now a far better scholar than he had ever been. But Castile, though it would accept a woman's rule, was not yet ready to appoint many women to university posts. I had engaged her, primarily, to teach my children and such of my ladies as chose Latin for their subject of study. But one day she said to me, brusquely as was her way, 'Your own Latin offers room for improvement. You have what I call a working knowledge of the language. The same might be said of the Spanish of a peasant who can communicate with his neighbour. Of the beauty of the language, of its great literature, you know nothing.'

No truer word was even spoken. And it would certainly set a

splendid example if I also became a pupil. So La Latina began to teach me, not with the others, partly because I already had a working knowledge and partly because, having so many other things to see to, I could not keep regular hours. It was thanks to La Latina that I was able to misquote Tacitus.

However, one day I said to her, 'You know I have been thinking—if we ... when we take Granada, just a smattering of Arabic would be of more use to me.'

'Very sensible. I am completely ignorant of it at the moment. I have no doubt I could acquire a working knowledge of it in a month.'

'A month, Doña Latina?'

'Given someone to talk to, and a book or two. The facility for acquiring languages is a gift. Some people can juggle plates, or walk a tight-rope.'

In this brisk, forthright manner she set about the business. She found a family of Christianised Moors with a grandfather who still spoke Arabic. 'A barbarous tongue,' she commented, 'so much tongue clicking! And of course the old man is ignorant in every other way. It is rather like trying to learn Castilian from a mule-driver.'

Still, she had persevered, and coming south with us had been completely delighted to find that Rodrigo of Cadiz and Gonsalvo of Cordova both had far more than a working knowledge of Arabic. She was not young and to put it kindly, plain of face; she despised clothes and all other devices for the enhancement of her appearance, but at any gathering where one or another of these two men were present she would edge her way near, speak a greeting in Arabic and start a halting conversation. Her Castilian and her Latin were so pedantic that her faulty Arabic was regarded by both men as amusing.

By this time at least half of my ladies were more or less in love with Rodrigo—a fact I found secretly shaming since it made it seem as though I had succumbed to something very ordinary. And it may be that the gift of emanating a sexual attraction is on a level with a talent for juggling plates.

One evening after La Latina had held Rodrigo's full attention for an hour, Doña Mercia said sourly, 'perhaps we should all begin to learn Arabic!'

Soon after the episode of the Lombard, I found on my table a small book, bound in white leather, stamped with gold. It was in Arabic, not many words to a page, and each page with a border in patterns of gold, blue and scarlet. None of my secretaries or pages had seen it before or knew how it had arrived on my table amongst the official papers. When I showed it to La Latina she said, 'What a beautiful thing.' Then she opened it, frowned in concentration, tried another page and then looked up. A little triangle of crimson burned under each of her eyes.

'Where did Your Majesty obtain this?' I told her how I had found it.

'One can only hope that someone ignorant of the language thought the cover would please you.'

'Why should we hope that?'

'It is not suitable reading,' she said primly. She closed the book and placed it out of sight under some others.

'Why not?'

'They are love poems. Quite lacking in reticence,' she said even more primly. 'And now to work ...'

I was inattentive that morning; aware all the time of the pretty book hidden by duller ones. I wondered what it was that could have brought a blush to La Latina's withered, spinster cheek. Would she hand me back the book when the lesson ended? Could I ask for it back? Was I right or wrong in suspecting Rodrigo—known to have a Moorish mistress? Would he have dared? The answer to that, at least, I did know. And under it all was a sense of something that had been missing in my life—romance, that heady, frothy brew. Nothing to do with marriage; I knew hardly anyone, except Beatriz, who had been both wooed before marriage and adored afterwards, but almost every woman, not positively ugly, had at one time or another been the object of a hopeless adoration—it had to be hopeless in order to be romantic. It was all as stylised as a dance. Knights carried the lady's favour into a tourney, dedicated a bull to her, hired musicians to play under her window. Ladies lavished languishing glances, dropped flowers. Unmarried ones gleefully counted their conquests, such evidence of popularity enhanced their prospects of making a good marriage. Married ones, provided they kept to the rules, had nothing to fear from a husband's jealousy; men liked to think that they owned something other men coveted. I have heard a husband say, 'Oh yes, my wife is very fond of dogs; she has six puppies on a string at this moment.'

This kind of thing had never happened to me. At Henry's Court I had been out of favour; then I was Queen, happily married, and with no time for dalliance. And what had sprung up between Rodrigo of Cadiz and me seven—incredible thought!—seven years ago in that quiet courtyard on the afternoon of the bull-fight was a different thing altogether, though it contained some of the same elements.

La Latina did not return me the book. And at the first apt moment when Arabic was mentioned, I said casually but clearly, 'I have acquired a vocabulary of a few ordinary words. I can never hope to read it. I am too old.' La Latina was there and she did not say as could have been expected of her that one was never too old to learn; look at her, still learning easily. She said nothing; there were the usual sycophantic murmurs, repudiating my statement that I was old. Queens can no more be old than they can be ugly. Then Rodrigo said, 'I agree with you, Madam. I have just celebrated a birthday, my fortieth or my forty-first—nobody bothered to note the year of my birth—and I find learning comes hard.'

'You learned how to manage a Lombard,' Gonsalvo of Cordola said.

'Ah yes. *Hands* remain teachable ...'

That was the way it was with us. Never a word that meant more than it said to the casual, listening ear, but different to the hungry, wayward heart.

There was also the little business about the dog. There had been a little good-natured banter about Rodrigo's 'mongrels' as the other men called them, neither mastiff nor hound. He said that a cross-breed was not a mongrel; a good cross-breed inherited all the virtues and none of the disadvantages of both breeds; the best of his combined the strength, the loyalty, the guard qualities of a mastiff with the fleetness of foot, the keen sight and the hunting abilities of the hound. There was laughter and argument, talks of tests and bets, and Rodrigo said his very *best* dog was not available at the moment.

Then one day he brought me the puppy and begged me to accept it. 'I chose him most carefully, Your Majesty. So far as I could judge the pick of the litter. But, if you will forgive me for saying so, not a dog to be handed over to kennelmen; these dogs need the personal touch.' Hounds and mastiffs were gifts freely interchanged between nobles, between monarchs: during one of the lulls in the war between Aragon and France, Louis XI had sent Ferdinand a pair of greyhounds with golden collars.

This was by no standards a pretty puppy; it had the loose-limbed, innocent-eyed look shared by all young things, but its head and its paws were too big. However, I accepted it, with appropriate thanks. Rodrigo said, 'Once he realises that he belongs to you, Madam, you will belong to him and he will defend you with his life.' There is more than one way of making even such a simple statement. He gave the puppy a little push towards me. 'His kind give their hearts only once,' Rodrigo said. The puppy moved towards me, sniffed at my skirt, nudged at me and looked up with beautiful amber-coloured eyes. It wore a collar, not of gold but of soft leather, with a plaque of gold, and a buckle. A collar which could be adjusted to the dog's growth. The plaque was beautifully engraved with the arms of Castile and the words, 'I am the servant of Isabella the Queen.' I stroked the silky head.

The dog remained my servant all that day, until at evening I went into Juan's apartments. Boy and dog fell in love with one another at first sight. Juan, not unnaturally, assumed that I had brought the puppy as a gift, and crying, 'Oh, Mother, how beautiful! Thank you! Thank you!' went down on his knees and embraced the animal who did not sniff at him at all; he put out a long pink tongue and licked Juan's face and neck and ears, making little whimpers of delight and wagging his tail so violently that his whole body was in motion.

My son, looking up with shining eyes, said, 'What is his name? Is it on his collar?' I stooped swiftly and released the buckle. 'No, darling. It is for you to name him. This,' I crushed the soft collar and plaque into a handful, 'was only a temporary thing.'

'Then I shall call him Bruto. Oh, the most beautiful present I've had in my whole life.'

There developed between Juan and Bruto much the same relationship as had existed between Sasha and me, but closer in that one cannot share one's bedchamber with a horse. Don Diego de Deza,

Juan's tutor, was at first inclined to disapprove of Bruto's presence during lessons, but later even he admitted that the dog's behaviour was impeccable, he made no disturbance and demanded no attention. All that was necessary was that he should have access to the out-of-doors now and then.

The transfer of ownership suited me very well. It broke what might—if only in my imagination—have been a link; I need not think, as I had on that first morning, that every time I fondled the animal or read the collar's inscription ...

And it was all so reasonable. Even the time fitted in. I could say to Rodrigo, 'My lord, it was not only that the Prince and the dog formed an affinity at first sight, but changes are pending which Bruto may help to bridge. My son has outgrown his little companions. In lessons, in every game or sport, by trying so hard, he has excelled them. And for a Prince, that is not good. I am therefore obliged to bring in some boys a little older and stronger to share his household, and to make this plan work, send the young ones away. With Bruto he will feel less bereft.'

'His Royal Highness is fortunate in having so considerate a mother,' Rodrigo said.

In June, coming hard on the heels of the courier sent to announce his coming, Ferdinand arrived. His mood was gloomy and indeed he had suffered humiliation at the hands of his beloved Aragonese. The Cortes in Aragon had refused to raise funds or even to lend moral support to the war against France. I felt sorry for him and made the very least of *our* successful forty-day campaign and said, 'How fortunate for *us*; we needed you here!' I said, '*Now* we can really move against the Moors.' I said, 'Let Granada once be won, and then we will tackle the French.' The rift between us might never have been. And, momentarily displeased with Aragon, Ferdinand tended to be rather less critical of 'my' Castilians. I handed over the command to him and his wounded spirit was greatly restored by the success of the next onslaught. The Moorish town of Alora was taken after a siege lasting only nine days and the policy of destruction ravaged the countryside almost to the city of Granada itself. But Granada was not to be taken that year.

II

Ronda, Cordoba, Loja, Malaga, Saragossa. 1485–9

'.. 1485 a 11 de Noviembre, commenzo de llover hasta el dia de la Natividad.'

'In 1485 it rained from the a 11th of November until Christmas.'

Bernaldez

'Columbus however ... was a self-taught and extremely persuasive geographical theorist, with some knowledge of hydrography and a grounding in navigation.'

The Age of Reconnaisance, J.H. Parry

It was said that the end of the world was to come in the year 1500. This was not merely astrologers' talk; there were scholars and church-men who believed it; fifteen hundred years was a millennium and a half and this fact was regarded as significant. When, in July of the year 1478 there was an eclipse of the sun many people believed that some slight miscalculation had been made and that the end was at hand.

I was better informed than most. Cardinal Mendoza said, 'There have been eclipses before, Madam, and there will be others.' Yet even I found it eerie. No sunset, no twilight; darkness falling perceptibly on a bright March day, and everything seemed to stop. No bird sang. A chill fell everywhere.

When the world ends, will it be like that? Darkness at noon?

The eclipse passed and all the people who had run to churches and knelt, wishing to be found in the right place and in the right posture, emerged, relieved, slightly shamefaced. But the eclipse, though it did not bring about the end of the world, did bring about the end of ordinary, predictable weather. No story, handed down from father to son for generations, no records, however old, made mention of such weather as we suffered for the next few years. Lack of rain is Spain's curse in summer but all through these stricken years, floods were the danger. Rivers swelled and swept away homesteads and livestock. Even in places secure from flood, great damage was done when the rain fell heavily enough to break down the stone walls that upheld those painfully-made little fields and vineyards on terraces cut out of the hillsides. The result was shortage with a consequent rise in prices of which the Aragonese, who had suffered less, took full advantage.

There were brighter aspects. Before any attack on Granada, the city, could be contemplated, two other places must be taken, Loja and Ronda. Rodrigo suggested a feint attack on Loja to cover a real assault on Ronda, and that was successful. There were other, minor victories, too; enough to keep hope high and the army in good heart.

Also in that year of tempest and flood, 1485, I bore my last child, my fourth daughter, Katharine, the one who was to prove to be my true daughter.

Isabel, as the year 1486 came in, grew more fretful. This year she would have her sixteenth birthday and her future was less clearly charted than she would have liked. I hesitated to tell her that her father was holding his hand in the hope of a French match—a daughter in exchange for Rousillon and Cerdagne—it sounded so mercenary; I tried to soothe her by pointing out that she was not yet sixteen, and that our present situation did not allow for the dowry, the wardrobe, the retinue needed: the war must go on. She said, 'Alfonso would take me in my petticoat!' That was illusion, but to say so would be hurtful. I was therefore compelled to say, 'But that is not how your father and I wish you to go, Isabel.'

Juana, seven in 1486, was still a mixture of extreme precocity and childishness, mingled with something for which there is no exact word. La Latina thought highly of her but admitted that she had difficulty in distinguishing between the trivial and the important: she also seemed me to have difficulty in distinguishing between the real and the imaginary. More than once she would say of a room, or a town, or even of a stretch of road, 'This is a bad place,' and act like a frightened horse. Questions—and we all, Beatriz, La Latina and myself were anxious to *know*—elicited no more satisfactory answer than that she had had a dream about this room, this town, this road. Juana did suffer from bad dreams, bad enough to justify the term nightmare, but they seemed not to end when she woke.

Maria, placid, well-behaved and self-contained, might have seemed to be the ideal child if only there had not lurked behind these admirable qualities a vacuity.

I could not know, I could only hope as I looked at the face of my latest born that she would be as different from her sisters as they were from one another.

Since Ferdinand had resumed command of the army I had stayed in the background, concentrating upon the neverending problem of supplies and how to pay for them. I was thus engaged one afternoon in May 1486, together with Cardinal Mendoza and two of his accountants, when I was told that a man, bearing credentials from the Count of Medina Celi, wished to see me. I looked up from the rows of figures, too many of them on the debit side and said, 'Let him wait.'

I thought I knew his errand—a veiled complaint about the conduct of the war. Ferdinand, his confidence now fully restored, was not always inclined to take advice, and if ignoring advice led to a setback, I was always informed, quite courteously. Medina Celi was with the army and I was prepared to receive one of those communications in which was embedded the phrase, 'It might have been better if ...' Sometimes suggestions were made point-blank, 'Would Your Majesty not agree that it would be wise ...' Such situations called for the utmost tact and evoked in me a good deal of suppressed irritation.

The afternoon wore on. After two hours the Cardinal rose and begged to be excused, he had an appointment. I used one of my evasive devices and asked him, on his way out, to take whatever message Medina Cell had sent, as I was. too busy to receive it myself. Some fifteen minutes elapsed and then the Cardinal returned and said,

'Your Majesty, I think you would enjoy talking to this fellow. He tells a good tale.'

'What about? The war?'

'Oh no. He is an old sailor. He has been telling me about a voyage he made with the Portuguese to the Guinea coast.'

That aroused my interest without causing me any elation. Castile had once owned a footing on that coast, said to contain a gold-mine, but the Portuguese had taken it.

I asked the Cardinal to send the man in.

He did not look like a sea-faring man; nor like anyone connected however loosely with Medina Cell who was famous for the elegance of his retainers. This man wore a doublet, once blue but faded on the shoulders to greyish-white; his breeches were patched, his shoes clumped. In the doorway he looked like a peasant, but as he advanced and made a courtier's bow, I saw that he was not a peasant, and as he straightened and faced me, I found myself looking into the haughtiest face I had ever seen. All but the eyes; steely blue, the eyes of a man of action, but modified by a far-seeing, an almost mystic expression.

I said, 'You have something to tell me?'

'For your ear alone, Your Majesty.'

That old bugbear, the hired assassin.

'I carry no weapon,' the man said, 'except my tongue, and these,' he produced from under his arm, with its frayed sleeve, a roll of paper. 'But I do not propose,' he said, arrogantly, 'to propound my plan within the hearing of clerks who would run away and talk. If you wish—I realise that precautions are necessary, I take my own and am willing to comply to yours, a thousand times more needed ... If it should be your wish, order that fellow ...' he indicated one of the accountant clerks, 'to tie my hands together, behind my back.'

With slightly exaggerated politeness, I asked the two young men to withdraw. 'Leave the papers,' I said, 'I shall not be long.' The man's manner had already antagonised me; I intended to waste no time on him.

The clerk who had been referred to as 'fellow' said, 'We will wait in the ante-room, Your Majesty.' I noticed that he did not quite close the door.

'Now,' I said, 'what is it?'

'I can make you the richest monarch in Christendom.'

An alchemist! That explained the shabby, hungry look. An alchemist without a sponsor must buy his own materials and equipment. It explained, too, that visionary look in the steely blue eyes.

I said, 'If it concerns turning base metal into gold, spare your breath. I have no faith in such things.'

'Nor I. No, what I wish to tell you has nothing to do with magic; it is compounded of seamanship and plain common sense. May I expound my theory?' Without awaiting permission he unrolled his papers and spread them on the table, over the depressing lists, and began to speak, rapidly, spitting a little as he talked. He not only thought, he *knew* that by sailing due west he could reach the East, India, Cathay, the Spice Islands ... The world, he said, was shaped like a pear, not flat as the ignorant thought. I was not so ignorant, but I did not interrupt him to say so, for when he was in full spate one might as soon think to halt a waterfall. One of the papers he spread before me, much worn and scribbled over, was a map of the world as seen by Toscanelli.

'The Portuguese,' he said, pointing with a long, slender finger to a point where the charted coast of Africa ran into 'Terra Incognita', 'believe that they might find a passage somewhere to the south here. They might do it. Every year they creep a little farther, and we are told that God made a division between earth and water. If it is there, the division, they will find it and the wealth of the Indies will be theirs. But I could forestall them! By my reckoning, I could be in India within two months; even if they find a clear passage, it would take them six months.'

He talked and he talked, and finally I said, 'What would you need in order to conduct this experiment?'

Ready with his answer he said, 'Three ships. Three is the minimum. Beyond the Pillars of Hercules the sea can be tumultuous—that accounts for the tales of ships devoured by monsters, or dropping over the edge of the world. The few who ventured were either lost or returned so battered ... Yes, I need three. With good crews, and provisions for two months ... For the return journey we can provision in India. I also need goods for trade.'

His maps, spread out and not weighted down, curled again trying to resume their tubular form, and under them lay the papers with their inescapable message—we were not merely poor, we were on the brink of insolvency. And with such a vast and cunning move against the city of Granada pending ... Every ship bigger than a fishing boat, every man who knew bow from stern, most desperately needed; and what would keep three ships on the ocean for two months ...

I said, 'I am sorry. You have an interesting, possibly workable theory. I cannot afford to sponsor it just now.'

'I offer you the mines of Golconda, the riches of the East and you cannot afford three little ships?'

'That is so.'

'Then I must try elsewhere. I intend to do it. I came to you first because we were born in the same year, under the same star. I thought our fates were linked. Was I wrong?'

'It would seem so. As the maps he had spread contracted themselves, more and more of those desolating figures were exposed. And I thought of our latest plan in the war against Granada, a combined attack, by land and sea, on the great port of Malaga. Granada, the province, had been partly ravaged; Granada, the city, still supplied by Malaga could hold out for years.

'It is so little to ask. Three small ships. A modicum of faith. In your stars—and mine. I know I can do it. Will you not reconsider?'

He had a way of looking not at one, but through one, at something beyond, far away.

'I am sorry,' I said again. 'I cannot spare even one ship, however small.'

'You wish me to carry my idea to Portugal? To England?'

'It is not what I wish. It is a matter of what I can afford. I am committed to this war.'

'And every soldier must eat meat every day! And mules kept fat as butter!' he said savagely. Then, abruptly and disconcertingly, he began to cry, dashing his frayed sleeve across his eyes and talking all the time, jerkily. He said I did not believe him, was simply pretending to. Nobody would ever believe him, until he was dead and in his grave; then somebody would try his way and know that he had been right. Or, worse still, somebody would laugh in his face and then go behind his back, try his way, reach India and get all the credit.

If indeed we shared a birth date, he was thirty-five years old. A man. But he was not unlike Juana when her will was crossed, except that he made considerably more noise. It reached the ante-room; the watchful clerk opened the door a little wider and looked at me questioningly. I nodded and he came forward.

'I do not need to be thrown out,' the man cried. 'I will go. I will go to every Court in Europe. To the Sultan of Turkey if I must. Our Lord walked on water—if only I could I would walk there and prove that I am right.'

There is something contagious about such wholehearted conviction.

I said, 'I can do nothing now. But I will think about your proposition, and if you do not find what you seek, once this war is over ... What is your name?'

'Christopher Columbus.'

I did think about him, on and off, in the months that followed, and I heard about him too—but never what I half-feared to hear. So far as we knew he had found no sponsor either in Portugal or England or anywhere else. His secret project was no longer secret. In my Court he had three staunch supporters, Cardinal Mendoza, Talavera and Don Diego de Deza, Juan's chief tutor. Others, notably Ferdinand, were scornful, more concerned with the man's past than with his future. 'He is a professional liar,' Ferdinand said. 'He cannot tell the truth even about his parentage. One day the son of a weaver, the next the son of a wine-shop keeper, the next of such high birth that he can call the Admiral of France his cousin.' It was true that everything about Columbus smacked of mystery, his birthplace was uncertain, so what about his claim to have been born on my birthday? He was married and had one legitimate son, he also had one illegitimate, yet he frequently appeared, it was said, in the garb of a Franciscan friar.

He dropped to the background of my mind when the siege of Malaga began.

Malaga was Granada's great port, situated on the Mediterranean and doing vast trade with Syria, Egypt and Africa. It was to be besieged by the Castilian navy on the seaward side, by the Spanish army on the landward. Everyone felt moderately certain that once Malaga was taken, Granada itself would capitulate. In this hope, as soon as our forces were deployed, Ferdinand offered the city honourable terms if it surrendered without fighting. They were not accepted; and as the time went on I began to see signs that this Holy War might end as so many former crusades had done. By 1487 the war had been going on for six years and all save born fighters like Rodrigo, Medina Sidonia and a dozen more were tired of it. I could tell by the excuses offered to me as I sat in Cordoba where those wishing to withdraw came to take leave. A wound, not very disabling, some family problem, business on some distant estate which could not be handled by wife or steward. I made a point of talking to, supping with, every lord who wished to withdraw and all too often the talk—and some wine—revealed that behind the ostensible excuse there was a dispute of some kind and that Ferdinand was usually concerned, if only indirectly.

I tried never to show either dismay or displeasure. I said, 'My lord, you will be sorely missed.' Or, 'What cruel irony, to have fought so long and so well and now to be forced to withdraw when victory is so near.' Sometimes such cunning worked and the man went back prepared to fight again. More often it did not. And I was skilled now at reading the significance of the question evaded, the unfin-ished sentence, the averted eye. All was not well at Malaga. In fact, when a man, half-dead from hard riding, brought me a letter from Ferdinand I opened it expecting to read of some shocking disaster. What I did read was a simple, terse request that I should go at once to join the army.

I left immediately, leaving Beatriz, Cardinal Mendoza, Talavera and the rest of my retinue to follow at a more reasonable pace. 'And Isabel, if she cares to,' I said. Isabel hated even talk of the war which she regarded as an obstacle to her marriage.

Greeting me heartily but hastily, Ferdinand said, 'I was obliged to send for you, to kill the rumours.'

'What rumours?'

'Two. The Moors have been encouraging themselves by saying that you were too sick to sit on a horse; indeed some went so far as to say that you were dying. Our own men have been discouraging themselves by saying that you had stayed apart and ordered me to give up the siege.'

'I will show them all,' I said.

I had myself buckled into my mail as a sign that I had come to participate, but for easy recognition, especially from a distance, I rode bare-headed. Don Gutierre de Cardenas carried my standard before me and I made a slow progress through the town of tents which formed our camp. Never, not even on the day of my coronation had I been so heartily acclaimed. 'Castile! Castile for Queen Isabella!' 'Malaga for Queen Isabella.' Some men even wept. 'All will be well now that Your Majesty is with us again.' 'Now we shall take Malaga!' The shouts and the blowing of bugles brought the Malaguenos out to see what was happening; close as beads on a string, heads appeared along the battlements and at arrowslits in the towers. For their benefit I rode on to higher, clearer ground, half-way up a little hill, and turned my horse about, showing my full face, both profiles—anything but my back. The horse I rode was a true battle-charger, trained to rear and strike with his forefeet and though I had never been in combat or used a horse in such a way, I put him through his paces now; an ostentatious gesture, meant to convey the fact that I was not only present but intended to fight.

Afterwards Ferdinand said I had been a bit foolhardy, but he could have said worse things, for the reception given me by our army must have been mortifying to him. I was not flattered by it—I knew it for what it was, part superstition, the men choosing to regard me as a symbol of good fortune, and part the result of a trait in human nature to which, when any situation has become static, any change is welcome. It was not only those who magnified wounds, family problems and other affairs who were tired of the war ...

On paper, on maps, in discussions about a council table, Malaga appeared to be in an untenable position, beset on both sides. But the Moors were desperate now; they knew that the fall of Malaga meant the fall of Granada. And a great port, accustomed to handling vast stores and well warned beforehand that siege is likely, will cram its warehouses and its cellars. Posturing on that hillside, looking across at the city—very beautiful with its rose-red or white buildings and an abundance of trees, I realised that *perhaps* we were the vulnerable ones. We were now deep in hostile territory, behind us that deplorable swathe of ravaged country; a great force to be fed and armed by what the long trains of mules could bring. We were an army lacking in the cohesion that desperation brings; and an army in which the sick men in the hospitals outnumbered the wounded ones. Camp fever had joined us, partly as a result of the unseasonable weather, partly as a result of slackening discipline: the latrine trenches were not used as they should have been, nor as often renewed. My rule about drinking wine only on certain occasions was not observed, and gambling was not only rife but fierce. When two men fought and almost killed one another over a throw of the dice I forbade gambling completely.

Bustling about like a housewife in those first few days I might have lost popularity, but truly God was with me.

One morning, under covering, protective fire from the bastions that ringed the city, a group of Moorish horsemen emerged, shouting, inviting battle. As always, Rodrigo of Cadiz was first in the field, and there was a brisk engagement which I watched. The attack seemed to me to be half-hearted. The clash and thrust of steel lasted only a few minutes, then the Moors withdrew, leaving two dead, and—unusual for them—several prisoners. Foolishly, I ventured to hope that this assault was a gesture raid; *we have done our best and made no impact*. Ferdinand, more experienced, thought otherwise, he said, it was exercise for the horses, cooped up in the city, losing the use of their legs.

By this time Beatriz, Cardinal Mendoza, my daughter Isabel and various officials and secretaries had arrived, and been installed in what I hoped were healthy quarters, above the main camp. Beatriz had insisted upon joining me. 'I have a suggestion to make, when you have time to listen,' she said; and the Cardinal had also come down into the camp where there was some danger of contagion. 'I am seasoned,' he said.

We all dined together. Then Ferdinand went into the sleeping compartment of our royal pavilion to take the little sleep which in the south was usual. It was hot, despite the rain, a heavy, humid afternoon. Beatriz said, 'I will tell you about my idea later. It is something which might evoke mockery.' She too went away and Cardinal Mendoza and I were left to discuss ways and means. Could we ask for *gifts*? Not taxes which, once given, might be repeated. Gifts. The sale of indulgences for those who aided and supported the crusade against the Infidel had reached its limit, but it had revealed the fact that in Castile there was more wealth than was apparent. Many haggard, ragged peasants, many sombre-clad burghers—*I just manage to stay alive and keep my business going*—had responded valiantly and might, just possibly, be persuaded to dig under their hearth-stones or open their strong-boxes once more. 'A Gift to End the War,' the Cardinal said, trying over the phrase. He had a way with words. I said, 'That would sound well in the mouth of a towncrier.'

At that moment Rodrigo of Cadiz came in and I congratulated him on the morning's performance. He laughed and said,

'It was nothing, Your Majesty. A mimic battle. I took six prisoners, all as cover for one who *wished* to be taken without obviously playing the traitor.'

'What does that mean?'

'That the people of Malaga are divided. Many now regret having refused the honourable terms. So they have sent this fellow—he calls himself a soothsayer—to tell you how the city may be entered and taken without further fighting. I have him outside. His name is Ibrahim Algerbi. Have I permission to bring him in?'

On the verge of saying, 'Yes,' I halted. This might be a matter of great importance; and while I could not prevent the army from behaving as though my arrival had saved the day I could, and must, refrain from doing anything that would seem to diminish Ferdinand's authority. So I said,

'Later. His Majesty is asleep now.'

Rodrigo bowed and withdrew.

Almost immediately there was a commotion; men shouting, a woman screaming. With a speed unbelievable for a man of his years, the Cardinal snatched up Ferdinand's sword which lay on a chair, and dashed out of the pavilion. I followed. The Royal Pavilion formed the centre of a group of smaller ones, set as close together as the ropes and stakes that anchored them would permit, and the noise was coming from the nearest. Inside—it was not very spacious—were two men in Rodrigo's blue livery, Rodrigo, the Cardinal, Beatriz, Don Alvaro of Portugal, and on the ground a white-clad Moor transfixed by two swords. There was also a chess table at which Beatriz and Don Alvaro had been playing. Now Don Alvaro lay slumped across it, bleeding profusely from a great gash on his head. There was blood too on Beatriz's stomacher. I pushed my way to her and cried, 'Are you hurt?'

She said, 'No. The stiff embroidery saved me.'

Rodrigo turned and hit both his men and cursed virulently.

By this time there was a small crowd outside the tent and I shouted, 'Run to the hospital and fetch a doctor.' Beatriz and I bent over Don Alvaro, pressing the gaping edges of the wound together and trying to staunch the flow of blood with our sleeves. The Cardinal tugged Ferdinand's sword from the body and wiped it on the Moor's white turban. As he did so he said to Rodrigo, acidly,

'You should strike yourself, my lord of Cadiz! Offering to bring an enemy, an armed enemy, into the Queen's presence.'

'He was not armed. Do you take me for a fool? He was stripped and searched. I saw to that.'

'Then how do you account ...' The dead hand still held a knife. One of the buffeted men, his face already swollen and lopsided, said, 'My lord, he took it from his mouth.' To this extraordinary statement nobody gave due attention at the time; we were too much engaged with the reality of what had happened. What emerged was that Ibrahim Algerbi, soothsayer though he claimed to be, had made a mistake; he had expected to be brought into the presence of the King and Queen of Castile and to strike two swift, fatal blows. He had seen a man and a woman, both finely clad, intent upon a chess game and slipped away from the two men who were to guard him, 'Like an eel,' one of them said, hoping to escape the flogging that Rodrigo, administering those blows to the faces of the men he thought careless, had promised.

Superficially no great harm had been done; plastered and stitched Don Alvaro would mend and would live to boast that he had once been mistaken for the King. Inside that walled city those who sent Ibrahim Algerbi out, to be captured, to act as assassin, would know that he had failed and be discouraged. As for me, I attained that added value of something almost lost. Our Lord, with his divine understanding of man's nature, made reference to this very human attribute when He spoke of the almost lost sheep, more valued than the ninety-nine, and of the Prodigal son, more valued than the one who had always been there at table, at bed time. Because they had so nearly lost me, and Ferdinand—though his danger tended to be overlooked—there was a great upsurge of loyalty and love which exceeded even that of my welcome. I swear that if on that afternoon I had issued an order that every man was to stand on his head for two hours they would all have done their best to obey. The pavilion that served the camp as a chapel was crowded with men, thanking God on their knees for my escape, and the ground in front of the Royal Pavilion was heaped high with small gifts, flowers, fruit, things made by skilled fingers during the idle, waiting hours, treasured mementoes long cherished.

Votive offerings? Perhaps; for behind it all lay the conviction that I had been lucky. And indeed I had been if the primitive, pagan idea of good fortune can be equated with the Grace of God.

Inside the pavilion I was a woman dealing with two very angry men. Cardinal Mendoza thought and said that Rodrigo had been culpably careless, and Ferdinand, waking to the tumult, agreed and said, 'I have a good mind to show my displeasure by not supping with Cadiz this evening.'

All the great lords took turn at entertaining. They were not dependent upon those plodding mule trains carrying grain and meat preserved either by salting or smoking. They could offer delicacies supplied by their estates, or brought in from outside the ravaged area by swift scouting parties.

Had Ferdinand had some reason other than anger for not attending Rodrigo's banquet, I should gladly have acquiesced, I still found the sight of him, the sound of his voice disturbing.

There is a fever which lays its victim low for a day or two and then disappears, leaving him weakened, but sound; then at unpredictable intervals and without warning it will recur. Sometimes the intervals are so long that the sufferer imagines himself to be permanently cured. He never is.

It was the same with me, with my weakness of mind, my wayward heart. I would think to myself—of course it is over, it never was anything real, and given no sustenance it is dead: I am thirty-six years old, with a daughter of marriageable age, three other children growing up; I am happily married; I am too busy to indulge in fancies. Like the fever victim, I enjoyed long spells of immunity, then a glance, a smile, a turn of phrase would strike home and wake the secret, guilty passion. I avoided Rodrigo as far as I could; typically, on this morning I had not gone to him, or sent for him to come to me in order to congratulate him, as I should have done with any other captain.

But now I knew that I must disregard personal feelings. If Ferdinand and I did not take supper in Rodrigo's pavilion everybody would know why, and there would be great rejoicing among those who were jealous of him. That would be a bad thing. It would also be bad if Rodrigo took offence and decided to withdraw. He had sustained a slight wound in that morning's affray, a gash on the cheekbone; he could, as others had done, make the most of it and decide that only at Arcos, in his native air, would that wound heal. I refused to take into consideration how deeply our failure to eat at his table, without some acceptable excuse, nothing to do with that day's doings, would hurt him.

I protested, beginning lightly. 'We should miss a good meal. I have heard talk of venison. A stag brought from Arcos in a cart and being fattened as it rode.'

'Just the kind of thing he would think of! He must always outdo everybody else. Not that a fresh dish would not be welcome.'

Ferdinand's attitude towards food was ambivalent. He could enjoy it, or ignore it as circumstance dictated. Soldierly.

From this small beginning I went on to larger issues, and Ferdinand who, apart from Rousillon and Cerdagne, was eminently sensible, finally agreed that we would go and eat Rodrigo's venison.

My feeling that if we had stayed away Rodrigo would have been almost ostracised was justified by the flurry that ensued. The most-honoured guests enter last and quite a number of the people whom Rodrigo had invited had been waiting to see which way the cat jumped; if we went, they went, and there was a great scramble for the places.

It was a very splendid feast, and, fittingly, the last of its kind. Rodrigo had brought in not only the venison, but his gold plates and candlesticks. There was fish, also, and it was too fresh to have been brought from any part of the coast that was not, in theory at least, in Moorish hands. The Count of Escalona made a seemingly innocent remark about this dish. But it was not innocent, it voiced something underlying, something that Ferdinand's presence and mine, at table, had cloaked, but not quelled ...

'My lord of Cadiz, you appear to have contacts denied to the rest of us.'

Rodrigo said, amiably, 'There are dozens of little places where the people are fishermen first and Moors second. They can no longer supply their main market, Malaga, and are glad to sell what they can, where they can.'

There and then, at his table, full of his food and his wine, those who hated and envied him began to attack Rodrigo, covertly. Knowing the Moors so well, how strange that he should have been deceived by Ibrahim Algerbi. Also, what a coincidence that the would-be assassin had fallen into the hands of one of the two men in our camp capable of understanding his false tale. Oh, but should one not make some allowance for occult powers, how otherwise, if strictly searched, had the fellow managed to conceal a knife? Men, if they give their minds to it, are quite apt with the sly innuendo—supposedly a woman's weapon. Only Cardinal Mendoza made a forthright, challengeable statement. Still angry, he said, 'The truth is the man was *not* searched.' That really was giving Rodrigo the lie and would have called for a duel had it come from any other man at the table: with the possible exception of Ferdinand; protected by his priesthood and his age, the Cardinal was safe. And he said only what others thought.

Rodrigo, who had missed nothing of the sly talk, his face flushed, his eyes glittering, banged the table with his fist, so that all the golden platters jumped.

'He *was* searched. I saw to it myself. Are you ...' his glance swept the table, 'trying to imply that I would take an armed enemy into the Queen's presence?'

'But for the Grace of God that is precisely what you might have done,' the Cardinal said. I thought—This has gone far enough! I learned forward and looked along the table to where Beatriz sat. I gave her a meaningful glance and then said, in my carrying voice,

'My lords, the Countess of Moya has a perfect explanation of the mishap which concerned her so nearly. Beatriz, tell this company what you told me ...'

Beatriz said, 'My lords, when the Queen told me what one of the guards had said—that the man took the knife from his mouth, I remembered seeing a man at a fair. *He swallowed a sword.* I was young and full of wonder and to content me my father approached the man and ordered him to explain. The blade was most cunningly made in segments which collapsed into one another.'

The Count of Escalona said, 'A fair-ground trick. Is it relevant? It was not a collapsible knife that struck poor Arevalo and threatened you.'

I said, 'My lord of Cadiz, is the knife handy?' It was and when it was brought it looked like any other knife, rigid, shining, all in one piece. Rodrigo offered it to me but I said, 'Take it to the Countess of Moya.' Beatriz took it with distaste—it was, after all the weapon that had struck a man down in her presence and deflected, left blood on her stomacher. But in Beatriz resolution never failed. She said, 'A Damascus blade,' and gave her attention to the handle which was short in proportion to the blade. Then she said, 'I was right!' and plunged the knife at the table. The segmented blade collapsed into the handle and it was plain to us all that what remained could have been easily concealed in the mouth of a determined man.

They passed it about—a new toy. Cardinal Mendoza, as forthright with apology as with accusation, said, 'I withdraw my accusation of carelessness, my lord of Cadiz. Even I ...' Wiping the handle on his napkin, collapsing the blade in the way that Beatriz had demonstrated he placed the whole thing in his mouth, withdrew it, gave the handle a twist and stabbed a melon. The supper party which had begun badly and grown worse, ended hilariously.

'Thanks to you, Beatriz,' I said.
As always, back to those early days in Arevalo, she was herself, cool and self-contained. She had screamed when the assassin attacked, but afterwards had not become tremulous, or tearful from shock; nor had she talked about the event, as most women would have done. She now said, calmly,

'I am glad that a childhood memory served. It encourages me to mention something you may think nonsense. I think it would be worth while to try bells against the Moors.'

'Bells?'

'You know how I dislike them. That is my Moorish blood.

Counteracted, of course by my Christian faith and upbringing. Bells do not actually frighten me, they just make my head ache and give me a feeling of uneasiness. They might cause panic in full-blooded Moors. I admit,' she said, forestalling ridicule, 'that is a fanciful thought.'

'Well worth trying,' I said.

I set about collecting bells and mustered forty-eight. They were a strange assortment: the chapel-tent provided two, both of silver; the makeshift convent in which the nursing nuns lived, lent one, also of silver; several lords owned bells for the summoning of servants, again silver, sometimes silver gilt; but many mules had bells attached to their collars. I commandeered them all and handed them to the boys of my choir and some other non-combatants, explaining that the object was not to make a tunable noise but the loudest, most jangling din.

We tried the experiment just before the next major assault. The noise was astonishing, and so was the result. On that first morning the Moors who manned the guns and the arrow slits simply fled. Unimpeded, our Lombards lobbed balls over the walls and Gonsalvo of Cordoba was able to undermine one of the forward-standing towers, place gunpowder in the cavity and explode it, demolishing the whole tower. Several men, including Gonsalvo himself, were injured by lumps of flying masonry, but not seriously; there was not a gun fired or an arrow loosed from the city. It seemed incredible that forty-eight bells should have paralysed the defenders, but it seemed to be the moment for a determined attack. The scaling ladders and the battering rams were brought out. However, by that time the Moors had recovered and were retaliating fiercely. Some scaling ladders were unhooked and the men on them sent crashing to the ground; in other places boiling water and boiling oil, blazing brands and another fiery thing, called Greek fire, of which the Moors had the secret and we had not, met the would-be invaders. Our losses were heavy that day, and there would be more, for it is a fact that whereas an ordinary wound, quickly and properly dealt with, will often heal, and even an amputation may be survived, men suffering extensive burns almost always die.

Next time we tried the bells the Moors tried to hearten themselves by jeering. 'Where are the cows?' they shouted, and made lowing sounds. But though they were prepared to defy their fear, it existed; I knew by the horses. When a group of cavalry did venture out the rider's fear was communicated and the horse was restive, no longer controllable by voice, or pressure of knee so that hands were free for fighting.

The siege went on. The unseasonable weather continued and as the days shortened we began to give serious thought to our plans for the winter. Abandon the campaign and go north, taking the army to the food as in former years or stay here, bringing food to the army? Even Malaga's stores must be running low, and I had received a completely unexpected windfall. On the morning after that almost-disastrous supper party in Rodrigo's pavilion, he had sent me all his gold and platters and dishes and candlesticks. With a letter—'Your Majesty, until last evening I should have said that my devotion and allegiance were absolute. By proving me not a liar, however, you so much more greatly endeared yourself to me that I beg you to accept this gift—a small token of immeasurable gratitude.' A letter which anyone might read. I handed it to Ferdinand, saying that if he approved I would send the gift, packed as it was, to the mint in Seville.

'Except for the candlesticks,' Ferdinand said. 'Somebody told me that they were part of the furnishings of Solomon's great Temple. Three of the ten he is said to have made. To any pious Jew, a pious Jew pawnbroker, they would have value, more than their weight in gold.'

So the seven-branched candlesticks went to the pawnbroker, the tableware to the mint and the siege continued. The walls of Malaga were damaged, but never breached, partly because the Moors were so adept at making repairs in the night. Once they made a dawn attack and Ferdinand rushed out without armour and would have been killed but for Rodrigo's prompt action, and once, in another assault, one of the arrows, dipped in wolfsbane or some other poison, brought Rodrigo's horse down. The horse in its death agony rolled and Rodrigo had a broken collar-bone and two broken ribs. He refused to stay in bed. I went myself to urge him but he would not listen, repeating what he had said, trying the high-throwing Lombard, that he wished above all things not to die in bed, and therefore, because his wishes were never granted would probably do so. 'But not yet,' he said.

Then there came a time when no horsemen, under cover of heavy fire and showers of poisoned arrows emerged and Ferdinand said, 'They are eating their horses.'

Dogs, too?

To Arabs dogs are not faithful friends, they are scavengers. But, outcast as they are, they are still responsive to the moon and to the attraction, mysteriously conveyed, over great distance, to a bitch on heat. Now, from inside Malaga, no dog bayed the great white August moon; and the cats of the city, nightly visitors to our camp, ceased to come. Yet the Moors held out until on a late August morning, a dull enough day to have been November, the small section of the gateway intended for the ingress and egress of foot passengers, opened and four men, carrying the white flags of truce emerged, accompanied by a venerable man. We immediately hoisted similar flags and Ferdinand sent men running to call Rodrigo and Gonsalvo who understood Arabic. Their tongues were not needed; the emissary spoke good Spanish.

A crowd had gathered, but Ferdinand dismissed them curtly. 'To your posts. This may be another trick.'

The old man was not humble. He bowed perfunctorily to Ferdinand, me, Rodrigo and Gonsalvo and said,

'Our leader, El Zegri, realises that we can hold out no longer. We are eating palm leaves. We are therefore forced to accept the terms offered.' He managed to say that as though he were conferring a favour on us.

'The terms I offered in April!' Ferdinand exclaimed. 'Acceptable now! Not to *me*! Nor to those with me. Honourable terms, rejected with scorn. My terms now are those of unconditional surrender, and that means the enslavement of every man, woman and child in Malaga and the confiscation of all property.'

'So,' the old man said. 'El Zegri foresaw such a contingency, and told me to say that if his acceptance of the honourable terms once proposed, should be rejected, every Christian prisoner within the city will be hanged, and the city set on fire.'

'Tell him,' Ferdinand said, 'that if one hair on one Christian prisoner's head is touched, every man, woman and child in Malaga will be put to the knife. That I swear.'

'I will convey the messages. Those who carry ill news,' he said with something near a smile, 'cannot count upon tomorrow. But the day will dawn and at about this time tomorrow an answer will be delivered.'

All that day a strange silence hung over the camp. All day I—and how many others?—could not draw a full breath. I felt as though I were wearing a breastplate too small for me. Our thoughts centred upon the Christian prisoners who had so nearly reached the end of their ordeal and might even now be being hanged. Hanging is a quiet form of execution, so the lack of screams could not be taken as evidence. The fact that the city had not been fired was proof that one part of El Zegri's threat had not been put into execution.

We remained on the alert all day for fear that the people of Malaga might prefer to die in a last, fated attack, rather than immolate themselves in the flames, or live on in slavery; but nothing happened.

I spent some time trying to persuade, to coax Ferdinand into adopting a less severe line, but he was adamant. The harsh fate he planned for Malaga would shorten the war; when he called on Granada to surrender, offering honourable terms, they would accept at once, wishing to escape a similar fate.

The whole problem of slavery troubled me. Our Lord never spoke of it, yet fifteen centuries of His influence, through the Church, had eliminated it in Christian countries in the west. Serfdom still lingered, but a serf was tied to the land and had certain rights within the law. Serfs were not liable to be torn from their families and put up for auction like cattle.

I could only hope through that endless, quiet day, that when he was confronted by the people who had held out so staunchly that they were reduced to eating palm leaves, Ferdinand's kindly streak would come uppermost and that he would relent, as he had relented over the pauper heretic children. We had come a long way from the one will in two bodies; and my arguments gained no support from anybody. Cardinal Mendoza, like the rest of our Council, agreed with Ferdinand that the fate of Malaga would end all resistance; even my gentle confessor said that slavery *might* be a means of hastening conversion and the consequent saving of souls. This was an argument that I was to hear again in a very different context.

When the venerable man arrived punctually next day to say that the city accepted unconditional surrender, Ferdinand did make one concession—the product of a subtle mind rather than of a tender heart. One venerable man and forty families of his choosing would be free to leave, after our entry into the city, and they could go to Granada. 'There,' Ferdinand said to me, 'they will talk of life in a besieged city; they can explain what it means to eat palm leaves. And if Granada is stupid enough, despite all, to resist, forty families will help to consume their supplies.'

We then began to make preparations for the occupation of the city. We tried to ensure that every contingent of the army was represented; and they were given strict orders. No massacre, no looting. They could search for, and confiscate any weapons and separate males from females; they were to make Mooors drink from every fountain and well and pool in the city—a precaution against poison—and then set guards. They were also told to clean up the streets where necessary.

After these chosen soldiers went the clergy, headed by Cardinal Mendoza and preceded by the great silver cross which the Pope had sent. 'Madam,' the Cardinal said, 'with my own hands I shall fix the cross to the highest point of the largest mosque. I shall sanctify the edifice and set up the altar.'

Moorish towns had been taken before, but never so ceremoniously.

I said to Ferdinand. 'What about food?'

'What about food?'

'For the Malaguenos. Days ago they were eating palm leaves.'

'Yes. We don't want them dead of starvation. Will you see to it, bearing in mind they should not be feasted.'

Our resources did not permit of much feasting; and two of our staple foods, smoked ham and pickled pork would not be acceptable to strict Moslems. I did the best I could and the third party to enter Malaga took food, bread already baked by the army bakers, salt beef in casks, hard cheese.

Then, fourth and last, Ferdinand and I rode in at the head of our army.

It was a great, a glorious occasion, but I do not remember it with pleasure, except for the liberation of the Christian slaves who had plainly been the first to suffer from the shortage of food. But the Moors had suffered, too, dark eyes, like Beatriz's, overlarge in starveling faces, those I recall and also the curious way the Arabs have of expressing grief, not a groan, a muted ululation—aaay, aaay. The ordinary people may not have been informed of the terms, or did not understand them, or hoped that they would be mitigated. When, in the great central square Ferdinand made, through an interpreter, an announcement of what was going to happen to them all this infinitely mournful sound broke out. It depressed me, as once in an earlier campaign, the ravaging of the countryside had done. 'It is war, Madam.' True enough! I could only hope as I knelt in the mosque which was henceforth to be the Cathedral of Malaga, that the people of Granada would be affected as Ferdinand supposed and that this might be the beginning of the end.

Ferdinand disposed of the slaves carefully. One-third of the Malaguenos were to be exchanged for an equal number of Christians, sold over the years into Africa where many of them had been villainously treated: a hundred able-bodied men—those who had manned the defences to the last—were to be sent as a present to the Pope. 'He has a weakness for exotic things and people.'

And that was true enough. Sixtus IV who had sent us the great silver cross, and his blessing, and who had tried to preach a general campaign, a new Crusade against the Infidel, was dead, and in his place was Innocent VIII who was actually contemplating a treaty with the most vigorous Moslems, the Turks. He might well accept with joy a Moorish guard.

'Pretty girls,' Ferdinand said, 'can be even more easily and usefully disposed of. Fifty to the Queen of Naples, I suggest.'

It may well be that I have a limited mind, set on the unification of Castile and Aragon and, if it could be achieved, the conquest of Granada. I had given little thought to Sicily, that unprofitable island, or to Naples with which it had once been loosely linked. A relative of Ferdinand's had taken the extreme step—much as my half-brother Henry attempted with La Beltraneja—of forcing an illegitimate line to succession. He had had better fortune, but deep within Ferdinand, as I well knew, the recovery of Naples ranked second only to the recovery of Rousillon and Cerdagne. The present Queen of Naples was by all accounts a dominating person and it was just possible that by worldly reckonings the gift of fifty pretty slave-girls might have some effect.

'And thirty to the Queen of Portugal,' Ferdinand said. Well, her goodwill was also to be courted, for after the long and cloudy advances and retreats that might have brought about for Isabel a French marriage instead of the Portuguese one which she dreamed of, Isabel was finally committed to Portugal.

Then all the Grandees who had fought with us were to have the pick of the slaves in order of and in proportion to their rank. This done a system of ransom was inaugurated. A Malagueno fortunate enough to have a relative or friend in Granada or Almeria or some other part of what remained of the Moorish territory, could be ransomed for ready money. There were 450 Jews resident in Malaga and the Chief Rabbi of Castile ransomed them all. Even so a good proportion of the population was left, slaves without a personal owner, to keep the city going and the docks working under the strict eyes of Spanish officials and overseers. Every bit of property was forfeited and Ferdinand and I were able to pay off some of our long-standing debts.

This, the most deliberate and thorough sack of a great city to have taken place since Alaric took Rome, did not have the hoped for effect upon the Moors; in fact it worked in the opposite way; instead of saying—*Look what happened at Malaga, we must give in!* the Moors who were still unconquered said—*Look what happened at Malaga, we must hold out!* We still had a hard and bitter struggle ahead of us. The Turks were pushing westwards, had actually taken Otranto in Italy, and dominated the Mediterranean; what remained of the Moorish kingdom in Spain plainly held on in the hope of support from their fellow-Moslems.

The taking of Malaga and the subsequent arrangements brought us into autumn and we ended that campaign and went north to see to business not concerned with the war. We went to Aragon, taking Juan, now nine years old, to be recognised and acclaimed as heir-apparent by the Cortes there. There had been a time when the Aragonese had been as grudging of real allegiance to me as my Castilians were to Ferdinand, but all was changed now. I was the mother of their future King and anyone with half an eye could see that I had given them a good one. Juan was handsome and like my brother Alfonso, tall for his age. That slight malformation of the jaw did not detract from his appearance, it lent his face a look of determination; he was well educated, and perhaps more important, profoundly sensible. Even his slight disability about chewing he concealed, chopping his meat small while apparently giving no attention to it, listening and looking about the table. I was truly proud of him. Of them all if the truth is told. Isabel could throw off her sulkiness on occasion and be charming in a dignified way; to look on Juana was to love her, in what I can only call an etherialised way; anxious to please, she was as near an angel as this poor world could produce; in a bad mood she could be frightening; and there was Maria, sturdy and placid, Katharine healthy and happy. Yes, I was proud of my family; and proud, in a way, even of Ferdinand's illegitimate son, now eighteen years old, very dignified and quite unspoiled by the two conflicting influences of his life; the privilege that had made him Archbishop of Saragossa at the age of six, and the taint which gave anybody born in wedlock an advantage, the right to look upon him as a bastard. He also, like Juan, had inherited his father's sound good sense.

They were happy days. The Cortes of Aragon who had refused to support the war against France, made a grant for the war against Granada. And our ambassador to Flanders, Juan de Fonesca, came back with a firm marriage offer. Juana was to marry Philip—already known as The Handsome.

Ferdinand's overtures to England had also been well received. There the civil war had ended with the triumph of Henry Tudor, the Lancastrian claimant to the thone; he had married the nearest Yorkist claimant, and she had borne a boy, Arthur, to whom Katharine was now betrothed. The year difference in their ages was on the wrong side, but could be overlooked; I was a year older than Ferdinand and it had never seemed to matter.

So, apart from the war, nagging on in the south, all seemed to be well as the year 1488 slipped into the year 1489.

Baza, Almeria, Seville, Santa Fé, Granada. 1489–92

'... con mucha profia dandosa priessa de dia y de noche dentro pocos dias la edificaron con sus muros y torres a cavas, y baluartes y puertas y otras cosas necessarias.'

'... with much tenacity, working speedily day and night, they built it in a short time with its walls, towers, ditches, bulwarks, and other necessary things.'

'... embiaron a don Goncalo Fernandez de Cordoua que era mu conoscido entre les Moros y entendia su lengua.'

'They sent Don Fernandez de Cordoba who was well known amongst the Moors and who understood their language.'

Lucio Marineo

Time, outwardly so precisely measured, seven days to a week, twelve months to a year, is not constant when reckoned by other means, against the yardstick of memory for example. Stretches of time in which nothing very memorable happens, seem to slip away.

The war went on; in 1489 we took Baza and Almeria, on terms far less stringent than those imposed at Malaga. After that we waited for offers of submission from Granada, but none came.

1490 was the year in which Granada must surely fall. It was also the year when it was plain that Isabel's marriage could be no longer deferred; the proxy ceremony was arranged to take place in Seville in April.

We wished to make the occasion as splendid as possible, so Ferdinand and I 'borrowed' back some of the pawned jewels. We were still short of money, partly because of the weather which had continued to be so bad that we were forced to buy grain from abroad, even from as far away as England, a very expensive operation. Most of our Grandees outshone us, and for once I was glad and tried resolutely not to think of the value of jewelled hat ornaments, and buttons and belts, necklaces and stomachers, in terms of wheat and barley and mules. The people of Seville also threw themselves wholeheartedly into making this a splendid occasion; spring there is a flowery time and every balcony, window and doorway was decorated; narrow streets were spanned by floral archways; the fountains spouted wine and there were free feasts for all. The weather was kindly, too.

The custom of marriage by proxy probably dates back to times of such unrest that the bridegroom could not afford to be absent from his country, and the bride might well reach her destination to find that her betrothed was dead, taken prisoner, or compelled by circumstance to wed elsewhere. It was a ceremony of mime, but as legally binding as a real wedding. Alfonso's chosen proxy stood by Isabel in the Cathedral of Seville and spoke, and acted, exactly as Alfonso himself would have done. There followed the token consummation. Isabel lay, fully dressed on the bed, the proxy lay beside her. Custom demands a token intimacy; usually the proxy bridegroom unbuckles his knee-band. The whole thing is watched by representatives of both countries and as many other people as can crowd into the room. On this occasion the proxy bridegroom, flurried perhaps, perhaps a little flown with wine, unbuttoned his breeches, and not at the knee. For a moment my heart bled for Isabel, always so prim and dignified and easily offended; but she showed an admirable spirit; she laughed and jumped from the bed, saying in Portuguese for the benefit of some of the onlookers—'Now I am Crown Princess of Portugal indeed.' It was exactly the right touch. Every Portuguese in the assembly pushed forward, knelt, kissed her hand, assured her that she was their Princess indeed and well-beloved. It was her great moment, the one for which she had been waiting so long. It would be superseded only by her actual wedding night. I prayed in my heart that she might be happy, might find Alfonso the husband fully as agreeable as she had found Alfonso the playmate, years ago.

Another thing I remember about Isabel's wedding, was that

Christopher Columbus was there, in the company of the Duke of Medina Celini. He was wearing Franciscan garb, as I had heard, and he still looked hungry. He also looked haughty—and scornful. I could well imagine that he was thinking that a king and queen who could afford to give a daughter such a wedding could well have afforded the three ships and the stores he needed for the pursuit of his dream. If indeed he did think so he little knew to what shifts we had gone in order to send a Princess of Spain to her adopted country in seemly fashion. I remember thinking—Next year, if all goes well. If Granada surrenders, as God grant it will ...

And so, back to the war.

If a city can be said to be impregnable the word should be used of Granada. It is not merely walled, it is doubly, in places trebly, walled with walls of such thickness that every entrance is deep and dark as a tunnel. It is built into the mountainside, and slightly above it is the fortress-palace of the Alhambra, very strongly fortified and difficult to attack, even by the high-throwing Lombards which must stand on level ground. Dragged up and placed on a slope the balls they fired were just as likely to make, not the soaring parabola, but an up and down flight, more injurious to those who fired than to those aimed at.

Rodrigo of Cadiz, ever ingenious and a student of geometry, did his best and once, with infinite pains, hauled a high-firing Lombard to the top of a siege tower; but a siege tower is meant to bear men and small guns. Under the weight of the Lombard and the explosion and the recoil the siege tower collapsed. Rodrigo, faithful to his belief that no commander should ask a hireling to do a job he was not prepared to do himself, was dragged out of the wreckage with a broken leg, a smashed wrist. When I visited him in the hospital tent, he said, 'I think I have now broken every bone in my body. But they mend. And even a broken heart beats on. I shall live to see you ride into Granada.'

Shortly after that there came a moment when it seemed very unlikely that I should ride in Granada or anywhere else.

Ferdinand and I, by mutual consent, no longer shared a bed. We had reached that stage in life where we no longer delighted, but disturbed one another. I suppose it comes to us all and I am truly sorry for all those couples forced by circumstance to occupy one room, one bed for the whole of their lives—unless there is some link between them, other than that of the flesh. I slept, I admit, badly. Insomnia is popularly supposed to be the mark of a bad conscience, but so far as I knew, so far as I could, I had always obeyed the dictates of my conscience; and when I woke, with a jerk, in the darkness, it was certainly not to a consciousness of sin. It was to an awareness of everything going on outside this quiet place where I lay wakeful. I saw, in my mind, the most crazily assorted things: all earth as I knew it, under a star-flecked sky, thousands of soldiers in the camp around me, thousands of people locked in Granada, awaiting the inevitable end; I saw the tumbling uncharted sea and shared Columbus's dream; I saw all that had been done, all that remained to do. I would try to lie still, try to sleep again, but sleep would not be recaptured; the impulse to turn from side to side would become irresistible and sooner or later I would move. However cautiously I did so, and however soundly asleep Ferdinand seemed to be, he would wake with a soldier's inbred alertness. 'What is it?' 'Nothing.' 'What woke you, then?' 'Nothing.' 'Then go to sleep.' I would try, and the impulse to move, resisted, would set my limbs twitching with movements that I could not control. I longed to leave the bed, make a light, walk about, read.

One day Ferdinand said to me, 'Tell me truthfully. Do I snore?' He did. He could be snoring, could wake when I stirred, and, assured that all was well, sleep and snore again.

'It may be that my snoring wakes you,' he said. 'Then you fidget and wake me. Shall we try sleeping apart?'

I said, 'We could try ...' Ridiculously, it seemed to be the end of something. I knew very well that he had been unfaithful to me many times; there were two little girls in a convent at Madrigal, and one, a sweet child, known as Joan of Aragon, at Court, by my wish, company for Katharine; but ... But despite it all, his wandering eye, and my wayward heart which had at least made me understanding and tolerant, he had always come back to my bed and though in these later days, passion had been stilled, he would often, before he fell asleep, throw a heavy arm over me; or I would hold his hand.

An end to all that ...

However, we tried sleeping apart and Ferdinand said he slept better, while my wakeful hours were less trying. When I woke and saw everything, and everybody in a crazy whirl, I could make a light, move about and read or even write. So we held to the arrangement and I was alone when I woke with something more than the usual jerk, to find myself in a blazing inferno.

How the fire started we never knew. I had wakened and read a little that night, but I had blown out the candle before I returned to sleep again. It is *just* possible that somebody, extraordinarily skilful, had shot in the night from the wall of Granada, a flaming arrow with tow head, or some of that Greek fire. If that were so and the aim was to kill Ferdinand and me, it was almost successful. Ferdinand and I escaped in our night-clothes and stood, shivering in the cool night air, watching the great pavilion which had served us as reception chamber, dining hall and sleeping apartments, blaze and shrivel into blackened ruin. The children's quarters and the ladies' were untouched. Ferdinand and I had escaped with our lives and nothing more and even our night-clothes were singed and blackened because, in that moment of panic, we had both run inwards, towards each other, he shouting 'Isabella,' I screaming, 'Ferdinand,' instead of making for the nearest available exit.

That may be what true marriage means.

Ferdinand was more easily refurbished with clothing than I was. All the lords came forward proffering breeches, tunics, shirts and they all seemed to fit him more or less. For me it was not so easy, I had always been somewhat taller than average and since Katharine's birth I had had no waist. I was not fat, I simply had no waist and I lacked the resolution necessary for enduring the tight strapping into an iron-nenforced corset which, persistently worn, might have restored the contours of youth. 'Bad enough,' I said to Beatriz, 'to squeeze myself into my armour.' So now there was nothing to fit me until Gonsalvo of Cordoba came along and offered me some of his wife's clothes. And they fitted better than any others, not because she was ill-proportioned and lacked a waist, but because she was a large, a magnificent woman. And all her clothes—those she could spare even—were magnificent, too. The day-shifts and night-shifts were of a fabric so fine that each garment could have been pulled through the circle made by one's thumb and first finger; the petticoats were so much laced and embroidered that they could have stood alone, and all the skirts and bodices were of satin, smooth and close-grained as fur. I said, 'Don Gonsalvo, will you thank your wife for me and tell her that these are far better than those I lost in the fire—better than any I have ever owned.'

And it was in borrowed clothes that I stood, later that day, and looked down upon the blackened remains of what had been the royal pavilion.

A perfect cross, outlined in black on the red earth. The long, all-purpose space, the transverse to left and right, my sleeping chamber, and Ferdinand's, and behind the transverse, exactly in line with the main pavilion, the cooking annexe. A perfect cross. Inside my head, as I looked a thought sparked, like gunpowder in a pan when the brand touches it off.

And so Santa Fé was born. And so it stands, the town of Holy Faith, to this day; added to and extended, but a cross for all who have eyes to see.

Building a town in the shape of the cross had a religious motive, but building a town there, fronting Granada had practical good sense behind it, too. We intended to maintain the siege even if it lasted through winter, and life under canvas, even in the southern winter was neither pleasant nor healthy. Immediately behind Granada rose the mountains, snow-capped for much of the year: they provided the cooling airs which so pleasantly mitigated the heat of late spring and early summer, but in winter they emitted icy blasts. I visualised snug stone barracks that could be heated without risk, a proper hospital, a proper church instead of makeshift tents. I thought of paved roads instead of paths between tents where one waded through mud—and, when the latrine trenches flooded, sometimes worse than mud.

Nobody opposed my suggestion much. Cardinal Mendoza whose post as Chancellor made him very much aware of money did say that it would be costly, and Ferdinand asked where I thought the money would come from. I was obliged to think very hard about that. Labour posed no problem—the workers who could shift a mountain to level a road, could erect buildings. Rodrigo of Cadiz who had made a study of geometry offered to plan the new town. Money. Money.

The scheme that the Cardinal and I had been thinking over, 'A Gift to end the War', had brought a moderate response, but that was four years ago, and could hardly be repeated. The gifts had *not* ended the war, and it is only simple human nature to desire to see something for one's money. As usual I thought—God help me; and as usual I added to my ritual prayers, the kind of appeal which a child might make to a parent, an appeal to be answered, or ignored as the parent sees fit. I never directed a thought, or a prayer to God without adding—If it be Thy will.

The answer to this prayer came, as such answers often do, in an unexpected, indirect way. I woke in the night, with that jerk, that instant precipitation into wakefulness and the whirling view of all that was going on in the world. And—as though an actual voice had spoken into my ear, the words came. Civic pride!

Civic pride and the spirit of competition. The gifts to end the war had gone into the common fund and how much Toledo gave, how much Madrid were merely figures in an account book. Now, visited by inspiration, I saw every city and town in Spain being not merely willing, but anxious to give, because their gifts would have a lasting memorial; the Seville Hospital; the Carmona barracks ... down, down, even to the paving of the streets. The humblest village would wish to contribute a paving stone, so long as the gift had visible shape and was recorded. I could hardly wait for morning when I could present this—I thought, God-given—idea to men who thought twice about everything, and slept well at night.

They all approved. 'But,' Cardinal Mendoza said, 'Your Majesty must remember that it will take time. To send out the appeal, and for thick-headed burghers to understand and respond and for the money to be collected.'

I was so sure that for once I abandoned caution; I said, 'We will build first and collect afterwards. I have trust in God ...'

A trust fully justified. The labouring men agreed to work for three months, drawing army rations for themselves and their families, their wages to be paid at the end of the stipulated time. The cities of Andalucia, the first to be approached, Seville, Cordoba, Jaen, Zahara, responded to the challenge in a way that set the pace for all the rest. There were quarries in the nearby hills, and not too far away an ancient, long-deserted city, once occupied by the Romans built largely of marble and hitherto looked upon only as source of cannon-balls, spheres meticulously cut and chipped into roundness by those skilled in the art. Now, with Santa Fé a-building it yielded other things, pillars and paving slabs, even fountain heads.

But Santa Fé served another and quite unexpected purpose. More than the massed might of the Spanish army, more than the bells, more than the daily exchange of artillery fire, it dismayed the Moors. We were here to stay; that was the message that the new town conveyed. From the ramparts of Granada, from the towers of the Alhambra, higher on the hillside, any Moor could look out and see that this winter we did not intend to withdraw and recuperate. Any Moor with long sight could see something else. What Rodrigo had told me—about the rapid recovery of a ravaged countryside in these parts, was true. There would be a harvest this year, and we should reap it.

But October came and so far there had been no sign of weakening in the beleaguered city. One afternoon I set out to inspect the new barracks, already occupied soldiers first; and the hospital, almost ready for occupation. A battle of a kind was in progress, our Lombards, in Rodrigo's charge, throwing missiles that could at best only reach the suburbs of Granada, and the Moors firing back, inflicting with their rather lighter guns and their arrows enough casualties to keep my gatherers-up-of-the-wounded busy and the hospital tents full. Ferdinand was receiving a delegation from Aragon where the Holy Inquisition had been very ill-received; in fact there had been riots, in one of which an officer of the Inquisition had been killed.

The new barracks were stark; quickly built, hastily whitewashed with a limestone preparation popularly supposed to deter lice, but compared with tents and blankets on the ground it offered luxury in so far as every man had a bed; every twenty men had access to clean water and to a 'necessary house', a vast improvement on the latrine trenches. Soldiers vary, like other people; there were crucifixes and crudely painted pictures of Mary and the Christ Child hung on the freshly whitewashed walls. There were also rude, almost obscene signs and words scribbled here and there, and half-obliterated by hasty scrubbing. With another woman, even dear Beatriz, with me, I should have been embarrassed; but I never took women with me on such errands. On this afternoon I had Inez de Mendoza, and Gonsalvo of Cordoba and two of his young officers.

Towards the end of one of those passages with the clean whitewash and men-without-women-smell, Gonsalvo halted and threw open a door. 'This, Your Majesty, is *my* room.' It was small, bare as a monk's cell; the hard, regulation bed, a stand for his armour, the chest which served the double purpose of clothes-container and table; a crucifix on the wall. All to be taken in with a glance. But he held the door, seeming to invite me. I said, 'Somewhat bleak, my lord, but a cover on the bed, a rug on the floor ...'

He said, almost in a whisper, 'Madam, please enter. I need, most urgently, a private word with you.'

I looked at him and thought—And am I supposed to stand while you speak your word; or to sit on your bed? The truth was, of course, that I had been among men so long, on such a down-to-earth footing that though they never failed in real respect there were times when they regarded me as one of themselves and brushed aside the finer points of propriety. I never did; and even now, forty years old and lacking in waist I was as prudishly careful as I had ever been. I cannot remember any occasion on which I have ever been alone in a room, with the door closed, with any man except Ferdinand. The result of such caution is that even my enemies, though they have said unkind things, have never said a scandalous word.

I said, 'Don Gonsalvo, if you can spare the time, walk with me to the hospital. I am anxious to see how the work goes.'

A better place for a very private conversation would have been hard to find. In the middle of what was to be a big ward I sat on a block of untrimmed stone and in the midst of the noise of carpenters, masons, plasterers at work, listened to a plan almost as fantastic, and to me just then, of far greater importance than that of Columbus. Don Gonsalvo asked my permission to go into Granada in Arab guise and conduct negotiations for peace with the Moorish King, Abdallah. I said,

'How do you know that he would be willing to meet you?'

'My lord of Cadiz has certain contacts.'

'How maintained nowadays?'

'By arrow, Madam. At certain times, from a certain tower an

arrow, bearing a message is shot. There is great dissension in the city. Abdallah wishes to capitulate; a man called Musa is determined to hold out. And so is Abdallah's mother. That is why he must move so secretly.'

'Why you, Don Gonsalvo? If my lord of Cadiz has such friends there, would it not be safer for him?'

'It breaks his heart that his eyes are the wrong colour. His beard he could dye—or indeed leave as it is; their Prophet used henna on his beard, and some of them still do. But a blue-eyed Arab ...'

I looked at his, dark, and glowing with enthusiasm. 'But how will you enter?'

'By a secret tunnel, under the walls.'

'And then? I mean how will those within be alert to your arrival?'

'Cadiz will see to it.'

'How? Does he also send arrows bearing messages?'

'Madam, sometimes tricks learned in time of peace, for personal reasons, can be turned to good purpose for war. This I tell you in confidence ... Many, many years ago Cadiz had a Moorish woman as mistress. She was a woman of rank, strictly guarded, as they all are and she, and he, devised a language of signs—whether it was safe for him to make a visit, or when it would be. They were young and ardent,' Gonsalvo said, almost apologetically, 'and anxious to exchange ... other messages. It still works; he can stand in the open and communicate with her.'

'Then why the arrows?'

'The tower has but a narrow opening; the gestures the lady might make would not be visible, Madam.'

I tried to think coolly; closing my mind to the romantic element of the story, refusing to think how skilled Rodrigo was in the hidden approach, the message concealed. I thought—What a *peculiar* way to conduct a peace negotiation! I looked for trickery.

Finally I said, 'Do you think it a safe venture? My lord of Cadiz must be to the Moors a marked man. And love has been known to turn to hatred. Or again, suppose this woman is motivated by the simple wish to see him again, and instead you appear. Might that not mean danger for you?'

'I understand that she is now old—women of that race age quickly—and mainly concerned for the well-being of her children.'

'His?'

Gonsalvo gave me a sharp look.

'Quite impossible! Consider the risk of a blue-eyed baby being born in a Moorish harem! No, Cadiz believes, and so do I that all but the extremists in Granada realise that there is no hope for them. And they wish to avoid the fate of Malaga. I need your permission to go, and some idea of what terms you would offer.'

He spoke as if he expected me to tell him there and then. 'About that,' I said, 'His Majesty must be consulted. And our Council.'

He looked displeased.

'There is some risk that this might misfire. It is more or less a harem intrigue, at the moment; notoriously unpredictable. If the whole Council considers it and I fail, my lord of Cadiz and I are going to be laughing-stocks.'

'If on the other hand you succeed I shall be faced with the difficulty of explaining why I connived in a harem intrigue without consulting the King.'

'I see. Would it be possible to tell His Majesty and nobody else until I have made my first visit and tested the ground?' I agreed to that.

Ferdinand was willing to do anything which would end the war, and the reports he had received that afternoon of affairs in Aragon had disturbed him. He was always ready to call 'my' Castilians arrogant, but it was now his ordinary people who were getting out of hand; defying him, the Pope, the Holy Inquisition.

'The truth is, I have been away too long. This sounds a crackbrained scheme, but it might be worth trying.' He fingered his beard and his left eyelid drooped. 'The Moors are perverse enough to handle an affair of such magnitude through a harem intrigue: that I grant. It costs nothing. It commits us to nothing. Yes, we'll let them try. As I look at it we have no need to state our terms, yet. They have made the first approach. Gonsalvo need only say that we are willing to talk, and find out, as far as he can, upon what terms they are willing to surrender. Then the next move is ours.'

Ferdinand was, without doubt, a most skilled diplomatist. When that left eyelid of his lowered, almost obscuring physical sight, it looked inward and saw far. Once I said to him, idly, that I wondered why he did not play chess—a game at which I was a numbskull—and he said, without any pride, that it was because he had never found anybody worth playing with.

One thing concerning terms of surrender we could at least offer, even in this early stage. Some time earlier emissaries from the Sultan of Turkey, who called himself the Grand Turk, had come to us with a dire threat. Unless we ceased to make war on the Moors, part of Islam, he would order the massacre of every Christian within his wide domains and desecrate all the holy places in Jersusalem.

I admit that I was frightened; Ferdinand was not. He said, 'This is an empty threat. The Grand Turk knows very well that if he put it into effect, it would start the Crusade which has been half-heartedly preached throughout Christendom. This is a gesture, calculated to ensure rather better terms for the Moors when we win. We'll send a soft answer. Some concession that will cost little.'

Our soft answer was carried by a man called Peter Martyr, another of the remarkable men whom our Court seemed to attract; he had originally come to help with the education of Juan and his young companions, but he was a linguist, a man of imposing presence, known to wield a golden tongue and a ready pen. We sent him to Egypt, where the Grand Turk then was, with the offer of a bargain, purely religious. If the Grand Turk spared the Christians and the Holy Places, we—though bound to proceed with the war—would guarantee religious freedom to any Moors who, in future, fell into our hands. That seemed to suffice.

So now, in good faith we could arm Don Gonsalvo with the assurance that the Moslems of Granada would be allowed to practise their own religious rites.

Abdallah asked more; much more. He wanted the whole province of Granada restored to its former status, a subsidiary, but independent kingdom as it had been before his father, Muley ben Hacen, had refused to pay his tribute and attacked Zamara.

'Then what, in the name of all the saints, have we been fighting for these ten years?' Ferdinand demanded. 'And what would he take as bait? The title of King of Alpujarras?'

When Ferdinand said that it sounded like a joke—faintly sour. The Alpujarras was a rugged mountainous region, lying far south of Granada, bordering on an inhospitable, rocky coast with not a single port. To be King of Alpujarras was to be exiled amongst primitive people, leading most primitive lives with a few sheep and goats, and, if Rodrigo was to be believed, practising a religion far older than even Christianity or Islam. They worshipped trees and streams, indulged in witchcraft and human sacrifice...

I said to, Rodrigo, 'But how can you know all this?'

'Because the south-facing slopes of those mountains grow the best mulberry trees, and therefore produce the best silk. Once a year the people of the Alpujarras would come down to trade ... Islam, as Your Majesty knows, is not a proselytising faith; the Moors never interfered with the people who sold silk in cocoons, or little girls ... Lucky enough, we can only think, to be pretty enough to be marketable ...'

I thought—Was *she* one of them? That woman, old at forty, now sitting there, somewhere in the beleaguered city, spinning a web of intrigue.

Astonishingly enough, Abdallah accepted this mock title. Probably he had no notion of what the Alpujarras was, for his next concern was how much money, how large a retinue he would be allowed to take with him. Ferdinand was disposed to be generous about money since Abdallah also mentioned that he would be prepared to hand over the city in six weeks—the end of a costly war: as for retinue, he could take anyone who wished to go with him. At this Rodrigo protested, half-jestingly.

'Perhaps it would have been wise to have kept hands on Abdallah's mother. She is a fire-brand. Quite capable of organising a flock of sheep into rebellion.'

She must have been a woman of character; she had made her son king, she was so entirely against the idea of capitulation that the negotiations had to be kept a secret from her until the last minute; and yet she was one of the few who chose to accompany him to uncomfortable exile.

January 2nd, 1492, was a bright, brittle day, sunny but so cold that the sun seemed to give out chill rather than heat. Ferdinand and I, in our finest clothes, headed the procession drawn up outside the gate of the Alhambra through which Abdallah and his retinue were to emerge. In the crystal clear light the palace fortress and the city it guarded glittered like mother-of-pearl.

Behind us was the great host of the Spanish army; and our family, Juan, now thirteen and a half years old, Juana twelve, both old enough to be properly mounted; Maria and Katharine—young to be present for this was a great occasion, something they might remember all their lives—in a muleborne litter with Doña Ines, their governess-duenna. And away, and behind all the nobles of Castile and Aragon, plumes and banners tossing.

Abdallah rode out with his mother and perhaps fifty followers. Certainly no more; the pitiable number who preferred exile with their King to life under our rule, even with religious freedom guaranteed. I looked with especial interest at the woman of whom I had heard so much, who had attained such power, such authority. And there was nothing much to see. Just a little huddle of filmy veiling and furs in a chair saddle perched on a bony horse.

Abdallah halted his horse beside Ferdinand and said, 'Here are the keys, Sire. Go, possess your Alhambra and your city.' It was as symbolic a gesture as Medina Sidonia's handing me the keys of Seville, all those years ago, but with a difference. As he spoke Abdallah broke into tears, and from within the bundle of gauze and fur which might well have been a load of merchant's stuff, a voice spoke, clear and chill as the sunshine, saying the bitterest words I ever thought to hear from any human tongue.

'Weep son. Weep like a woman for what you would not defend like a man,' said Abdallah's mother.

With those few words she had, somehow, marred my glorious day. I could have borne his tears—who would not weep, handing over the most beautiful city in the world, having brought a long war to inevitable defeat and made the best bargain possible? But there was something so *cruel* about those incisive words, spoken at such a time … The memory stayed with me, pushed aside as one pushes a busy fly, but, like a fly, returning.

Outwardly the fall of Granada marked the end of the Holy War, a triumph for Christendom and something to be celebrated from

Rome to London. It was something more than the mere halting of the Islamic invasion; it was an advance of Christendom's frontiers. Admittedly, in order to prevent the slaughter of Christians, the desecration of the Holy places in Jersusalem, we had promised the Moslems freedom to worship as they wished; but I had made Talavera Bishop of Granada on the very day that we took possession of the city.

By the terms of the treaty, freedom of religion was to be allowed, but in Castile Talavera's campaign of gentle persuasion had not been entirely unsuccessful, though, to judge by the mounting activities of the Inquisition, less successful than we had hoped. It might even be true to say that the Inquisition had outpaced the campaign of gentle persuasion. Here in the south, Talavera might do better and he could certainly be relied upon to be gentle.

It was a time of change. The end of the war. Cardinal Mendoza, who in 1487 had scrambled about amongst the towering roofs of Malaga and fixed the great silver cross with his own hands, had sorrowfully admitted that he was no longer capable of such exertion, and it was Gutierre de Cardenas who had placed the cross on the highest tower of the Alhambra. 'But, no longer able to climb,' the Cardinal said, 'I can, thank God, still see and hear, write and reckon. I hope to die in your service.' Such a hope, expressed by a man of sixty-three, might well be fulfilled and did not imply undue morbidness of thought; but it was saddening.

Also sad was what had happened to my daughter Isabel. After little more than a year of blissfully happy married life, she was back with us, a widow. Alfonso had had a fall from his horse and died. She was truly heart-broken; life for her, she said, was over, she would never wear anything but mourning clothes again. She isolated herself from the life at Court and from the family life which was its centre. She spoke of entering a convent. The failure of our relationship was exposed by the fact that she turned from me, not to me. 'Nobody who has not been widowed can possibly understand.' Even Beatriz who had once been like a mother to her was no longer acceptable company—not being a widow. Isabel surrounded herself with women who were able to declare that their hearts were buried in their husbands' graves. Ferdinand said, sensibly, if heartlessly, 'What she needs is another husband. We must look around.' To that I replied, 'Not yet. We must give her time.' I did not oppose Isabel's idea of becoming a nun, for to have done so might have precipitated her decision: I simply accepted, within the Court, the existence of her conventual way of life.

With the fall of Granada our financial difficulties ended, if only for a time. Ferdinand and I felt rich enough to give each other presents; his to me was a bracelet made of small golden arrows set slantwise on a band of rubies, emeralds and diamonds: I gave him a golden chain, almost a collar, a wide mesh of interlinking rings, resembling chain mail. Both ornaments were intended to be mementoes of the struggle in which we had been engaged for ten years.

The time had now come for expansion; for the implementation of all those plans, promises, half-promises that were preceded by the words, spoken aloud or said inside the head—When this war is over ... But even so I did not seek out Christopher Columbus, he came to me; this time amongst the myrtles and the early roses of that fairy-tale palace, the Alhambra, and this time with Ferdinand by my side.

The years had changed Columbus little except that his sand-coloured hair had whitened. His eyes still looked through and beyond the one he spoke to—on this occasion me, virtually ignoring Ferdinand. Inwardly he had altered.

I opened by saying, 'And you have not yet found a sponsor?'

'Dozens, but none suitable. Noblemen, merchants. They cannot give me what I need.'

Not unwilling to show my good memory, I said,

'Three ships, capable of braving the Atlantic; stores for two months and some goods for trade with the Indians.'

'I know better now. Ask little and you get nothing. That is the lesson I have learned. I asked so little and promised so much, everybody suspected the value of what I offered. Part of God's great design, of course. I realise that now. He intends you to be Queen of India as well as of Granada.'

Ferdinand said, 'And what do you ask now?'

'A royal commission. Plainly God did not intend me to go on this great venture as a simple sailor. I must go as Admiral, as Viceroy.'

'You ask the impossible,' Ferdinand said. The word *Admiral* stung him. It was a title, a rank, reserved exclusively for his relatives, the Enriques family.

'Impossible because, on one side, I am not of noble birth? Was Our Lord? Was Mary, Queen of Heaven?'

'That verges on blasphemy,' Ferdinand said.

I interposed. 'Titles such as you request are not ours to give. The Cortes would have to be consulted.'

'And by the time they had done their mumbling another year would be lost. Unless I sail in August at the very latest ...' I feared that he was, once again, about to break into tears and that would have added contempt to the distrust and distaste with which Ferdinand already regarded him. Only once had Ferdinand ever had tears in his eyes, so far as I knew, and that was at the moment of Juan's birth; even then he had not allowed them to fall. But this time Columbus did not weep. He said, looking beyond me, 'August. No later. We know God orders the winds, but why should He perform miracles because we were hesitant?'

I said, 'Or over-demanding?'

He looked straight at, and through me. 'Or fools. I was a fool to offer you the gold of Golconda, the riches of the East. I offer you now what I should have done then, the salvation of human souls without number.' He began to speak quickly; the people in India, in the Spice Islands, in Cathay were far deeper sunk in error than the Moslems; they worshipped idols, they worshipped their ancestors; they worshipped cows. They must be taught, converted, baptised.

'And how can I undertake so great a task, unless I go armed with some authority?' He waited. 'Which you are not prepared to grant.'

'Only the Cortes,' Ferdinand said again.

'Then will Your Majesties give me leave to withdraw?'

'The man is mad,' Ferdinand said. 'Admiral! Viceroy! Insolent, too. Asking such honours in advance. If he'd taken what we were prepared to lend, and come back with something to show for it ...'

I said, 'I asked Talavera, and Reza and the Cardinal to give a little thought to his plan, when he first proposed it to me. They all think it feasible, and Talavera did speak of the need to convert the heathen.'

'That argument touched you,' Ferdinand said, almost teasingly. 'Time for that when he gets there—if he ever does.' For him, plainly, the thing was over. I had, a little late, but not, perhaps, too late, a thought, which I tried to put tactfully.

'You were right,' I said, 'completely right about the Cortes. Would it be possible to call him back and say that we would ask their approval? Before they could give or withhold it, he could be on his way.'

'That would serve for *Admiral*. What about Viceroy?'

'Could that not be left until whether we knew what was there to be a Viceroy *of*?'

'Shrewd,' Ferdinand said. 'Shall we call him back? He can't have gone far. He rode a very sorry mule.'

Fetched back, Columbus accepted the compromise, his scornful look revealing that he knew it for what it was.

'Then I must ask for letters of commission,' he said. 'I must have authority.'

I have felt many things in my time, but I have never felt so *silly* as I did when writing letters into the unknown. In what language? Spanish? Latin? Arabic?

'Greek might serve,' Columbus said. 'Alexander the Great reached the Ganges and left troops behind when he withdrew. That part of India reached from the east is, we know, Moslem, Arabic. The landfall I hope to make, from the west, might contain some people who know Greek. Not that I do. But letters, sealed and signed, in whatever language will give me authority.'

All the scribes scribbled. 'To the King of —' and a blank, to be filled in when Columbus knew the monarch upon whose coast he had landed. And to give the man the authority he needed I forestalled the Cortes; I used the phrase, 'our Admiral, Christopher Columbus'. He, so sure, so embittered by failure, went off jubilant. He had already selected his point of departure, a small place called Palos. He would, he said, clutching the letters to his breast, be ready to sail on the first day of August.

God go with him. Ferdinand and I must turn back to the dull routine of administration, and to something that was not routine; something that seemed then far more urgent than a crazy sailor's dream, or the letters addressed to the King of the Cow-worshippers.

Something real and close to home and to me controversial. The problem of the Orthodox Jews.

13
Granada, Barcelona, Toledo. 1492–5

'.. y no hallaban quien se las comprase, e daban una casa por un asna, y una vina por un poco pano o lienzo, porque no podian sacar oro ni plata ...'

'And they found no one who would buy, and they gave a house for a donkey and one vineyard for a little cloth or linen because they could not take gold or silver out of the country.'

Bernaldez

Later, looking back, I am inclined to think that Pulgar knew how things would go before even I was certain of my own mind. He was no longer a young man, but he was not as old as the Cardinal who had expressed a wish to die in my service, and so far as I knew he enjoyed good health. But one morning, capping his ink-pot, wiping his quill at the end of a long session, he said,

'Your Majesty, it grieves me to say it, but I feel that I have come to the end of my usefulness. My memory is failing; I should like to retire before some forgetfulness on my part causes trouble.'

I was so used to him; he had come straight to me after my half-brother Henry's death, and he was so much more than the word 'secretary' implies; reliable source of information, giver of advice, expert at protocol; so I tried flattery—what should I do without him? cajolery—I would lighten his load; appeal—so much business is pending. Nothing worked. He had set his mind on retirement and retire he would. In the end I gave in and said, 'You have been a most faithful servant, Pulgar. I will give you an estate. Six hundred acres. Wherever in Castile you choose.'

He thanked me and said he would like to spend his remaining years in Granada. And that surprised me; most men given a pension or promised a grant of land make straight for their native place.

'Why Granada?'

'The climate suits me, Your Majesty.'

What he meant, I see now, was the climate of thought, not of weather. He was a Jew by blood; a Converso and a good Christian, but he wished to live in Granada where there were few Jews and those there were hardly distinguishable from the Moors with whom Talavera was dealing, as I had known he would, very gently. And Pulgar did not wish to have any part—even to the reading and writing of letters—in what was about to happen. He was the one who had warned me about the activities of the Holy Office not stopping short with lapsed Conversos.

He had been right.

As soon as the Infidel had been defeated in Granada, there began an agitation—What about the equally Infidel people in our very midst? What about the Orthodox Jews, by the rules not subject to the Holy Office, but who, by simply being there caused so many Conversos to lapse; were a constant source of infection? God, Torquemada wrote, had given me victory over the Moors in order that Spain should be cleansed. And Spain would not be cleansed until these alien people, this alien religion, was expunged.

I was bombarded with accounts of appalling incidents, all vouched for by people who sounded reliable; I could not, personally, hunt down a group of Jews said to have stolen a Christian child in order to sacrifice it. I did not believe that ...At least, I did not fully believe ... my scant knowledge of the Hebrew religion inclined me to think that Jehovah did not accept human sacrifices. But between what I believed and what the ordinary people believed there was considerable disparity. And there was no doubt about it, the Orthodox Jews were everywhere hated—perhaps because they were rich, despite all the hampering rules that controlled where they should live, what they should wear, what trades they might pursue.

Jew. Jew. Jew. I came to hate the word, spoken, or leaping out at me from a page. Now, when I woke in the night, I saw that grave, dignified Chief Rabbi with his orthodox robe and his side-curls, coming to the aid of the Jews of Malaga; I saw in glittering heaps the money which Ferdinand and I had received from the Jews over the years, either as direct loans, or as a result of pawning things.

Yet I could not ignore the mounting evidence of the theory that the Orthodox Jews were, wittingly or unwittingly, responsible for the lapsing of Conversos; nor could I turn a deaf ear to Torquemada's argument that the Inquisition, in punishing obvious heretics was merely lopping branches; 'We must eradicate the root!' he exclaimed. The campaign of persuasion and education had not been successful because everywhere the unbaptised Jew could be seen going about his business and prospering.

Nobody advocated an alteration in the rules governing the Inquisition and proceeding against all Jews as heretics; it would take too long, the lowest reckoning of Orthodox Jews in Spain was 160,000, the highest, 800,000; what was demanded, and demanded with increasing pressure, was the expulsion of every Jew who refused, within a period of four months, to be baptised.

When I considered this demand I could not fail to remember Pulgar's warning about people keeping themselves in employment. Forced baptism would lead to an increased number of Conversos, some of whom would inevitably lapse and keep the fires of the Inquisition burning. Even Talavera, much troubled in his mind, said 'No' to that. Every Jew capable of being converted had been, as a result of the preaching campaign.

While I worried about the rights and wrongs of such decisive action, Ferdinand concerned himself with the economics. The wealth of the Jews was difficult to reckon; the sumptuary laws forbade any display upon the person; the residential restrictions compelled them to live in cramped quarters. Few Christian observers had ever been inside a Jew's house in a ghetto, but there were rumours of hoards of gold and silver as well as of carpets and tapestries and such things, all of great worth. Such things must not be allowed to leave the country, because it would thus be impoverished.

'Then the exiles will starve,' I said.

'Of course not. They can take with them bills of exchange.'

Bills of exchange were actually notes of credit and worked on a system that made it unnecessary for merchants to carry large sums of money on their persons. In a way they were currency, but only in places where the system operated, settled, civilised communities where trade was brisk. How many Jews would reach a place where a bill of exchange was as good as money in the hand? And, another question, was I right in worrying so much over what happened to people who had rejected, and continued to reject Our Lord, Holy Church and all that Christianity stood for?

Beatriz said, 'Isabella, I have never said this to you—and hoped never to be obliged to say it. But when you give way to melancholy, you should remember your mother.'

Stung, I said, 'I see no likeness, Beatriz. My mother's melancholy was the result of hope, long deferred and finally quenched. This is not the case with me. My hopes have been realised—to the full. And I am not *melancholy*. I am indecisive, pulled this way and that; for me the worst state. If I can see what is to be done I manage somehow ...A decision, once made, I can act upon. It is this uncertainty in my own mind. I listen, I take advice, I go to bed persuaded, or almost persuaded, and then I wake and contrary thoughts *will* intrude ...' Reduced by sleepless nights and bothersome days, I spoke irritably. 'This, which should have been such a happy time, the war over, has been spoiled for me by this bickering about Jews.'

'A thought about the Moors might tip the balance.'

'The Moors! What have they to do with it?'

'They have been offered precisely the same terms as our ancestors offered the Jews. Be baptised or accept certain restrictions.'

'That was the policy that Talavera proposed. And I endorsed.'

'I know. But is it workable? My dear, that is the question that should be asked, every day, every night. Is this—or that—workable? Stubborn Moslems can look out and see stubborn Jews flourishing. Exempt even from the attention of the Holy Office. It does not encourage *them* to be baptised, does it?'

Added to everything else this argument seemed to make the expulsion *just* justifiable. We gave the necessary order: any Jew who had not been baptised before the end of July must go into exile. The Church immediately started a passionately vigorous campaign of conversion, but what Talavera had said was proved true. Those who had not abandoned their own religion were not prepared to do it now, even under such dire threat. They began to prepare for their exodus.

Paradoxically, the flood of wealth thus released, profited singularly few people; the whole system of bills of exchange collapsed under the demand; the market for such things as the Jews had to sell became glutted and everything lost value. Barter revived. I heard of Jews giving a house in return for a donkey. As usual those who were better off fared best, even in such a chaotic time; the rich pawnbroker had contacts in Venice, in Naples; the poor shoemaker had probably never been outside the ghetto in which he was born. And, as always with Jews, the family, even the tribal bonds held firm; the fortunate ones who had obtained bills of exchange, and had some known destination, took others under their wing. In many far places, in Italy, Africa, Turkey and Syria, Jews prepared to accept one refugee family would find themselves asked to accommodate six.

The Jews began to disperse on the 30th of July, 1492, and three days later Columbus set sail from Palos. He had his three ships, the *Nina*, the *Pinta* and the *Santa Maria*, the last-named his flagship. I was told that his standard was of silk, blue, Mary's own colour, and that it bore a beautiful painted picture of the Virgin. The messenger by whom I had sent my last wishes for a safe and successful voyage came back and described everything to me. Those who sailed with the Admiral were, the messenger said, very mixed. He had managed to persuade a few hard-headed businessmen, a few well-born youths, hungry for adventure to accompany him, but there had been a shortage of experienced sailors anxious to face an uncharted ocean; some of the crew was made up of men who would otherwise have been in gaol.

Through that August, when I woke and saw all that was going on, I now had two extra visions. The Jews dispersing—and it was impossible not to think of Our Lady, a Jew, going into exile in Egypt, riding a donkey, with the Holy Child in her arms. I also saw the three little ships, mere specks on a tumbling waste of waters, with the blue flag leading.

Then, in late August something happened which diverted my mind entirely. Rodrigo of Cadiz died in Seville. He was, at most, forty-seven years old, and except for the days after that disastrous defeat, had always seemed so young, so exuberant, so almost boyish in his enthusiasms. Now he was dead. They said of a slight fever which he was unable to withstand because of the exertions and privations he had endured in the war. Had I been blind? When he took leave of me, after the victory celebrations he had looked to me exactly as he had done when he first stepped into my life.

My grief was all the worse because I must conceal it. I must behave as I would have done had any other Grandee died; order the Court into mourning, attend the Requiem Mass, say how much he would be missed ...The common people to whom he had greatly endeared himself by his kindliness, his love of justice and his daring, could weep in the streets. Ladies of the Court could shed a few gentle tears, even soldiers could say, 'We shan't look on his like again.' I, to whom he meant so much more, more even than I had admitted to myself, could only grieve inwardly and think thoughts which contradicted one another. I would think about the occasions, numerous they now seemed, when I had avoided the loving look, spoken more sharply or more coldly than had been strictly necessary. At the same time I must think that to have acted differently would have been sinful, and be glad that I had behaved as I did.

I could, of course, pray for his soul; and I did. I could so order things that although he had no heir, the son of his eldest illegitimate daughter, his grandson, another Rodrigo, should succeed to a modified title—Duke of Arcos—and much of the estate.

I do not believe in ghosts, but on one occasion I had a curious experience. I went out—a sentimental errand, but one which called for no explanation—to look at the Lombards which Rodrigo so much loved that he had given them all personal names. And the dog Bruto was with me because Juan was riding in a mock tourney, a pastime which Bruto could not share because he would not stand by and watch; he would participate, quite uncontrollable if he saw Juan threatened in any way. And I was the only other person with whom Bruto would even take a walk.

The great guns stood where they had done when Granada capitulated. Other hands had touched them since of course, but Rodrigo was certainly the last person to have caressed them, calling them by name, saying, 'Good girl! You have worked well today.' So I put my hand out and touched the cold metal, and as I did so Bruto crouched, and bristled and whined. Then he turned and ran. And I also, was conscious of something; not frightening, in fact infinitely reassuring, as though that beautiful voice said, 'All is well.'

All in all I was glad when Ferdinand said we ought to winter in Aragon. Travelling is in itself a distraction; the quartermaster and his assistants going ahead to commandeer in places where there is no royal residence, no bishop's palace, some suitable accommodation; beds of varying comfort, meals of varying kinds; and everywhere my family admired and made much of.

We made our headquarters in Barcelona. And there something else happened which served to jerk my mind from fancy to reality.

This was Ferdinand's country and I stood back a little, busying myself with family and social affairs, and leaving such things as the administration of justice to him.

One morning while he was thus engaged, we were watching water-jousting, a sport new to us and one in which I could watch Juan take part without the anxiety I always felt when he was engaged in the ordinary kind where there was always a risk of a fall on to hard ground. The worst that could happen here was a drenching. With Juan there was always another risk, too; he was inclined to exhaust himself, he did so wish to excel and although one could not call him delicate he tired easily. We were all laughing because he had just managed to overset his opponent when there was a stir in the crowd and Don Inez pushed his way to me. He was very white-faced. 'His Majesty has had an accident,' he said. I picked up my skirts and ran, talking as I ran.

'A fall?' I knew that Ferdinand had intended to go riding as soon as the morning's business was concluded.

'He was stabbed, Madam. They say a lunatic ...'

'Badly?'

'I fear so.'

Wounds are nothing new to me, but this was a ghastly one; just between the shoulders, four inches deep and six long. I could hardly bear to look as the doctors set about plugging it. Ferdinand was conscious, groaning with pain, but he managed to say, 'The chain saved me ...' It was true that had the blow struck his neck he would have been a dead man.

He had sat in court all morning and was coming down the stairs at the foot of which his Master of the Spurs waited, spurs in hand. The assassin came out of an alcove and struck his blow. Even as he fell, the blood spouting, Ferdinand retained his sound good sense. He called to the Master of Spurs, 'Don't kill him. Hold him. There may be others.' Afterwards he told me that he did not realise then the extent of his injury—I have heard the same from other men. He merely knew that he had been attacked and that the man who struck him might be part of a conspiracy, and if held might reveal details.

For two days the wound, savage as it was—one of the doctors said that but for that heavy chain, almost a collar, Ferdinand would have been beheaded—seemed to do well. Then it inflamed. Ferdinand became fevered and tossed and raved. All Barcelona, and as the news spread, all Spain, believed that he was dying. There was much superstitious talk of a bell; a church bell which rang of its own accord and could not be stopped when a member of the royal family of Aragon was about to die. Many people claimed to have heard it on that Friday morning. Small comfort to me, watching by his bedside, listening to the rambling, incoherent talk, sleeping, when weariness was too great to be borne, on a makeshift bed in an adjoining room. I prayed most desperately. We had had our differences; had grown out of love as some people fall into it, or grow into it; his eye had wandered; my heart had known wayward moments, but none of that seemed to matter now. He was my husband, the father of my children, my comrade in arms. God, please let him not die now, in the year that has seen peace restored. God spare him ...

One morning, examining the unhealed and suppurating wound Doctor de Soto saw what he thought was a piece of bone protruding. He was not a surgeon, but he did not hesitate; he called for a pair of tweezers and removed the splinter, and then, probing, found another. After that the gash began to heal and the fever died down and soon Ferdinand was able to think about the political implications of this savage attack on his life. By this time, under stringent questionings and some mild torture, the would-be assassin had revealed his name, and his grievance, and nothing more. His name was Juan de Canamas and he believed that he had a better right to the throne then Ferdinand had. He was not concerned with any conspiracy; he was in fact a lunatic, a man of good family but with no relationship to royalty at all. He was, except for his madness, like the two impostors who lately had been troubling Henry Tudor in England.

When Ferdinand had sufficiently recovered to be able to discuss the matter, I asked, 'Why did you instantly suspect a conspiracy? The Aragonese gave you a most loyal welcome. And what would anybody stand to gain?'

'There are always malcontents,' he said. 'People who think that I should not have wasted time and resources on fighting the Moors instead of the French. Who would gain? Ambitious men who think a boy-king easily manipulated. Like your brother Alfonso.'

I said, 'Had he lived, they would have been surprised. Alfonso had a will of his own; and Juan is very like him, not only in looks.'

We then went on to talk about what should happen to Juan de Canamas. As so often happens the most injured person was the least vindictive. Ferdinand said, 'A fellow should not suffer a traitor's death simply because his wits have gone astray. Henry Tudor set one of his impostors to work in the kitchen.' The irony of that act made him grin.

'You can hardly do that with a lunatic. He'd be dangerous anywhere.'

'He could be locked up.'

But public opinion was against such mild measures. All the people who had agonised while Ferdinand lay between life and death, wished to be avenged. The best I could do was to see that the man was confessed, and then cleverly strangled *before* all the slow horrors of death for traitors were inflicted upon him.

As soon as Ferdinand was fit for travel we moved here and there, everywhere acclaimed. We were back in Barcelona in April 1493 when a courier brought news that Admiral Columbus had returned; that he had reached India and was on his way to present himself, and the proofs of his achievement. Stirring news indeed. We prepared to give him the reception—all the Court, all the family—which the occasion warranted.

Was I too proud of my family?

Isabel, after two years of seclusion willing to emerge occasionally, very dignified, a trifle withdrawn, but still pretty and capable of charm when she chose. Juan, every inch the young prince of the fairy tales, tall, handsome and convivial; he really loved people, any people, in a way that neither his father nor I did. Ferdinand and I were alike in that we valued personal relationships and regarded public ones more of a necessity than a pleasure. I had achieved a certain rough-and-ready comradeship with soldiers, in camp, in hospital, but my son had more than that, a general, all-embracing goodwill, difficult to define, but potent.

Then there was Juana, so beautiful with her heart-shaped face, her cloud of dark hair and green eyes and unpredictable moods; but charming, too. And Maria, very amenable, quite unremarkable, though she had some talent for playing the harp. And Katharine who grew day by day more like me—or so I chose to think; the daughter of my heart.

Yes, I was proud of them. With so many dangers lurking for the young it was no small achievement to have reared all the five born alive. In my children I had been singularly blessed. They stood ranged about us as we sat, in chairs of state to receive Columbus.

The double doors were thrown open. The man who had followed a dream and attained it, walked in, followed by six young Indians—or so we assumed. Quite different from the dark men of Africa. These were the colour of cinnamon, had noses as beaky as Columbus's own, and dead black hair. Columbus led them towards us, with a gesture indicated that they should kneel, and then knelt himself.

A harsh, authoritative voice rang through the hall.

'Hail Mary, full of grace. Hail Mary, full of grace,' it said.

In that emotional moment we all responded; 'Blessed art thou amongst women and blessed is the fruit of thy womb, Jesus.'

Columbus said, rising, 'A talking bird, Your Majesties.' And that was exactly, and absurdly, what it was, a brightly feathered, hook-nosed bird, perched on the wrist of one of the Indians.

'Hail Mary, full of grace. Hail Mary, full of grace,' it said, and would have gone on had not Columbus made a gesture and the Indian who held the bird silenced it.

One by one the speeches of welcome and congratulation were made; one by one the gifts from the distant land presented: a bowl containing grains of gold; some curiously fashioned ornaments, also of gold, cloaks made of feathers.

Juana said, 'I want that bird.'

A distinct breach of etiquette; when it came to the apportioning of gifts, or of precedence, she was fifth in line. As a matter of fact the gaudy bird was presented to Juan, but within an hour Juana had coaxed it from him. 'You have Bruto,' she said. 'You can't have another pet. Bruto would die of jealousy.'

The reception over, Ferdinand and I and the Cardinal retired to a quiet place to hear Columbus's account of his voyage. He told it with gusto: how he had somewhat underestimated the length of the journey and how the crews grew frightened, almost mutinous, though he had falsified the distances and kept two log books, one for himself, one for others to see. 'And then, when hope was almost dead, we saw birds again and knew that land could not be far away. Birds and floating branches.' He had not, he admitted frankly, reached India, only some off-shore islands, of which he had taken possession in our name. The natives, he said, were friendly but utterly idle because the climate was so good and the land so fertile that no work was needed. He had brought specimens of some of the fruits that grew in the islands, but they had all rotted on the return voyage.

He had lost his flagship which on an island called Haiti had run aground on a sandbank and could not be refloated.

'But nothing was wasted. We made a fort of her timbers, and forty men are there now. Your Majesties' first colony. The seeds of a great Empire.' His eyes wore that far-seeing look, and then sharpened. 'But it must be guarded. Now that my discovery is known, the Portuguese will cease to look for a passage around Africa and turn to the West.'

'We could hardly forbid them to do so,' Ferdinand said.

'The Pope could; and should do so at once,' the arrogant man said. He then went on to speak feelingly about the people of the islands, indolent, but amenable, and, so far as he could observe, without any organised religion of their own.

'No cow-worshippers, Don Christopher?' asked Ferdinand.

'There are no cows in the islands; no goats, sheep, pigs or horses. And the vegetation is, to be honest, not what I expected.' He frowned in a puzzled way. 'I looked for the things that we associate with the East; cloves, nutmegs, cinnamon. They were not there. Nor do the people and their way of life accord with any of the travellers' tales. I am inclined to think now that the world is larger than we thought and these off-shore islands may be farther from the mainland than I supposed. On my next voyage I propose to go farther. India is *there*, I'll stake my life upon it. And the gold is there—as you have seen from what I brought back. The reason it was not more is that the people value it only as decoration and are too idle to dig. They must learn to labour.'

'But not by forcible means,' I said. Now in bright daylight I had that feeling of looking down on the earth and I saw the islands, the people in them, the trees dropping gifts into idle hands. The Garden of Eden before the Serpent entered and Adam was condemned to live by the sweat of his brow and Eve to bear children in pain?

This was a fanciful thought, but I held to it, and when the Admiral sailed again—this time with thirty-five ships—he, as our Viceroy, had strict orders; the Indians wherever found, in the islands or on the mainland, were to be treated kindly, not enslaved. They were to be converted, gently. The Indians whom Columbus had brought back with him, now knew a little Spanish, and had been baptised; they would serve as interpreters and missionaries; and twelve ardent priests sailed on that voyage, too. I also sent seeds, or small plants of everything that Spain had and these Islands of Paradise had not; wheat, barley, melons, beans, oranges and lemons. I sent animals too, cows, bulls, goats, pigs and hens...

Dear God, knowing the secrets of the heart, You know I meant well and not ill to those islands and to the mainland, should Columbus ever reach it. I did my best and I could not know then that only the swine would thrive.

All seemed well. Pope Alexander VI, in the Vatican, reached for a map and drew a line, a hundred leagues west of the Azores. Then he issued a Bull; west of that line all rights of exploration, colonisation, annexation of land belonged to Spain; east of it to Portugal.

When the Bull arrived and the scribes were making copies, one for Portugal, I said to Ferdinand, 'It is only one line. If we move to the west and Portugal to the east, we shall meet, one day. And what will then happen?'

He laughed. 'Time enough to worry about that when it happens. I'm no mariner but I think it would be in the middle of some ocean or desert, where they might be glad enough to meet and exchange a cup of water for a slice of bread.'

He had never seen, in his mind, what Columbus saw so vividly, but now that the voyage had been made, and successfully, his imagination was stirred.

A few days later, while Columbus was still being fêted, I came across the first real evidence of what was going to be a great worry to me in days to come—Juana's lack of genuine religious feeling. She was walking up and down a long gallery, playing cup-and-ball. She had the bright parrot on her shoulder; she was counting her successful catches. 'Nine, ten, eleven ...' The bird said, 'Hail Mary, full of grace ...' With the ball in the cup, poised for the next throw, Juana paused and said, 'Go on, you know the rest.' The bird said, with less assurance, 'Hail Mary, full of grace, blessed art thou ...' Juana tossed the ball and caught it and said, 'Twelve.'

I said, 'What do you think you are doing?'

'My penance. Father Andreas set me twenty Hail Marys for missing Mass.'

'And do you usually do your penance and play cup-and-ball at the same time?'

She looked at me with no sign of guilt or shame.

'Not until I had Haiti; he is saying them for me.'

'Put the toy down, Juana. Put the bird down. Come and sit by me.' I sat down on a bench. Juana reluctantly placed the bird on the back of a chair, the cup-and-ball on the seat. The parrot moved restlessly, shifting from one scaly foot to another.

'Be good, now,' Juana admonished. Eyeing her with a bright, disconcertingly knowing eye, the bird said, 'Blessed art thou amongst women and blessed is the fruit ...'

'He is learning,' Juana said, and came and sat by me.

I tried to explain, though well aware that she *knew*, reared as she had been, the meaning of confession and of penance; I told her that what she had been doing was an insult to Our Lord and to His Mother.

'But the Hail Marys were being *said*.'

'By a *bird*, with no feeling, no understanding.'

'Is that so different from clicking the beads of a rosary? I think nobody can say more than one Hail Mary with feeling and understanding.'

'Child, if you cannot see the difference, I fear for you. Surely you understand that when such a penance is set, you are supposed with each repetition, to repent your fault and resolve to do better in future. You say you missed Mass. Why?'

'I didn't feel like it.'

'Apart from that being a dreadful thing to say, Juana, it is high time that you realised that we all have to do things we do not feel like doing. I do it every day.'

'Do you? What things?'

'Many things. But we are not talking about me. We are talking about you. You are going to occupy a very high position and the first thing a person of high position must learn is to subjugate personal feelings to the common good.'

'Then what is the use ...? I have made up my mind that once I am married, I shall do exactly what I like.'

Up to that moment she had looked at me, innocently, limpidly with her beautiful eyes, but as she said that something moved in their clear depths. It was as though another person—or at least another entity—looked out at me. It was to it that I spoke, sharply.

'In that case, Juana, you will not be married. I do not propose to have Spain shamed, as we should be if you went to Philip, to Flanders, to Burgundy, to Austria, wilful and selfish, and impious.'

Whatever it was that looked at me, glared, and retreated. Juana said,

'I am sorry, Mother. Had I known I was doing wrong I should not have done it in your presence.'

I said, 'My darling, you cannot always be in my presence. But you are, always, in the presence of God.'

'I will try not to offend again. Mother, I am very sorry.'

'Of your sorrow you will give proof by returning that bird to Juan.'

'Oh no! Haiti is mine. Haiti belongs to me.'

I made a mistake then; I thought—The penances Father Andreas set mean nothing to her; she is fourteen this year, she must learn.

I said, 'You will give the bird back to Juan.'

'But Juan has Bruto. The only birds he cares for are falcons ... Mother, do you mean it?'

'I usually mean what I say.'

She went to the chair, the parrot with a joyful squawk jumped upon the slender hand she extended, and clawed half up her arm. She stroked its head, bent her own and nuzzled the bright feathers; and I thought of what Sasha had meant to me, of what Bruto meant to Juan. I thought—Two days, long enough to let the lesson sink in, then she shall have him back.

But even as I thought it, she moved her right hand and with a swift, almost expert action, broke the bird's neck. Across the limp bundle of feathers the *thing* in her eyes looked at me with hatred before tears quenched it. Her sobbing fits had always been violent, and almost reasonless; this one was extreme, and appalled as I was by so violent and ruthless a gesture of possessiveness, I was moved by pity, by dismay. I tried to take her into my arms, but she resisted, pushing me away, crying over the dead thing. 'Haiti, you were mine. I loved you. Oh Haiti, Haiti ...'

I made another mistake. This display of hysteria must stop. The general belief was that a smart slap across the face was a cure; but I could not bring myself to apply it. So I did worse.

I said, 'Juana, unless you show some self-control I shall order you not to make any public appearance for a week.'

It was the worst threat I could think of; she loved the admiration and adulation that any public appearance inevitably brought her.

She said brokenly, 'I don't want to. If I hadn't welcomed Columbus I should never have seen Haiti.'

To discuss Juana with Ferdinand was useless; he could see no wrong in her; La Latina, herself a model of self-control, was prepared to allow much latitude to one who learned so quickly and so well; and

Beatriz said that the child was at the difficult age; before she was married she would have settled down. Even Father Andreas, while admitting that he wished the Princess would take her religious duties more seriously, said that she had an admirable character, was tender-hearted, charitable, honest.

Her behaviour, however continued to be extravagant. When Philip of Austria sent her his portrait, set in diamonds, she went into ecstasies over it, kissing it repeatedly, pressing it to her heart. 'Oh, you can see why he is called the Handsome. Isn't he handsome? Am I not fortunate?' In all royal portraits one must allow for the artist's wish to flatter, but even so something emerged in the portrait, a dull, heavy look; a handsome, rather stupid young man, I thought. Not that it mattered perhaps, Juana was clever enough for three, and there is a kind of solidity that goes with stupidity. Would he be kind? Patient?

Juana began to wear the portrait on a chain around her neck; showing it to everybody. 'Am I not fortunate? If I were free to take my choice of all the men in the world, having seen this, I should have chosen him!' After a few days I became exasperated. I said, 'Really, Juana, this is not modest behaviour. And the portrait is far too large to be worn like that.' It was about five inches long and four wide.

'You are right, Mother. As usual. And it is in the wrong place.'

Next time she appeared she wore a green sash, slantwise across her breast with the portrait pinned to it. 'Over my heart,' she explained to everybody.

It is strange but with the arrival of the portrait and Juana's unashamed adoration of it, Ferdinand changed.

'You make yourself a spectacle,' he said, eyeing the sash and its ornament with disfavour. '*And* you're laying up trouble for yourself. He's only a man, after all.'

'I wouldn't want to marry anything else, would I?'

That was the kind of pert retort which usually provoked her father to laughter; but not on this occasion.

'You're making yourself a laughing-stock,' he said. 'People are asking, if you behave like this over a portrait, how will you act when you meet the man? Go take that thing off and let's hear a little less about Philip the Handsome.'

Whatever it was stirred in her eyes, but she obeyed.

I said, 'I am glad you spoke. She has always taken more notice of you.'

'Thanks be to God, she has beauty. Even so, you or somebody should tell her. Men like to hunt a bit, even with their wives. And fawning bitches get kicked ...'

Fawning, jealous, possessive, hysterical, and due to leave us before she was seventeen.

'We know so little about him. His character. Ambassadors so seldom tell one the things one longs to know.'

'He's bound to be spoilt,' Ferdinand said, uncomfortingly. 'His mother died when he was four, and left him Burgundy. He's had no education worth speaking of. But he's young and healthy and handsome. They should get along—if she can be persuaded to show a little restraint. She'll be Empress one day, and it's time she cultivated a little dignity.'

From a hitherto doting father, these were harsh words. I think that Ferdinand resented being ousted from first place in his favourite daughter's affections. But that was all to the good. His open partisanship had helped to make her what she was.

The year 1495 began sadly for us with the death of Cardinal Mendoza. He was only sixty-six. I say *only* because as one's own age advances one's standards of what constitutes old age change. Once I should have thought anybody aged sixty-six ripe for death. He *had* ailed a little in that a weakness of the bladder had made long sessions and long ceremonies no longer possible for him; but his final illness seemed sudden and brief.

On his death-bed he asked me to consider as his successor, a man who was already my confessor, Jimenez de Cisneros, an office to which the Cardinal warmly recommended him, and which he only accepted on condition that he should not live at Court, but in the nearest monastery; his ascetism was more severe even than that of Torquemada.

I might have suspected the Cardinal's interest in Cisneros as being paternal, but for their ages. The Cardinal, in the fashion of his time, had had several mistresses, who had borne him a number of children, all well provided for. He had, like so many others, managed to reconcile vows of celibacy with an evasion of them and the one order of mine which he had not wholeheartedly supported was that which insisted upon such vows being kept. He had said, 'Madam, it will cut deep, and lead to trouble.' And it was true that over four hundred clerics, faced with a choice of giving up their concubines or leaving their various Orders, had gone to Africa and turned Moslem. I thought them no great loss and said so, but Cardinal Mendoza said, with a man-of-the-world, tolerant smile, 'Your Majesty, had such a law been enforced when I was young and foolish, you might have missed a useful Chancellor.'

Now, clever, tactful, brave and tolerant, he went to his grave, and Cisneros, quite the least tolerant of men, took his place.

Cardinal Mendoza had appointed me as executor, and his will provided for a foundling hospital, much needed. Long ago, in that cave-like room, Don Philipino had said that a baby could be picked up from any midden; I had never forgotten that; but I had tried to remedy the sorry situation, too many children and girls unwanted, by working through the established convents, most of which now had some accommodation for such unfortunates.

Cisneros, accepting with reluctance the posts of Chancellor and Archbishop of Toledo, gave immediate proof of his austerity by dismissing servants, selling silver and tapestry and horses. Mendoza had kept great state; Cisneros lived like a monk. The Pope rebuked him for causing unemployment and penury. Mendoza had been known as the Third King of Spain; Cisneros became known as the Iron Chancellor. As Primate he could issue orders to any cleric and he soon forced Talavera to stricter measures against the Moors in Granada, and he also ordered a great burning of Arabic books; only those dealing with medicine survived. His views were much in accord with those of Torquemada; heresy must be exposed and rooted out. So the Inquisition, which I had been told would fall into inactivity if every Jew were expelled, instead flourished and expanded and became infamous.

That Cisneros was a sincere man nobody could deny; he was a good Chancellor, too; but he was a man who inspired respect rather than affection and I never ceased to miss Mendoza.

14

Laredo, Burgos, Saragossa, Seville, Granada. 1496–1500

'The physicians recommended a temporary separation of Prince Juan from his young bride, a remedy, however, which the Queen opposed.'

Zurita

In 1496 Juana set sail for Flanders to marry Philip of Austria. She went as well prepared in every way as was possible. I had talked to her, very frankly. There were things I said with difficulty, even distaste; it is not easy to tell an ardent sixteen year-old bride-to-be that the time may come when her husband may be unfaithful, and that acceptance and dignity are a woman's only resource.

I chose those who were to go with her with the utmost care; her chief lady-in-waiting was Beatriz's niece. I saw her off from Laredo with a mixture of hope and doubt and trust in God. She had of late been more amenable, had settled down as Beatriz had foretold.

The Spanish fleet that carried her to Flanders was as splendid as any that ever sailed. It was to serve several purposes—to deliver a Princess of Spain; to impress upon all who saw it that Spain, so lately racked and impoverished by war, was now great; and to bring back Marguerite of Austria to marry Juan, heir to united Spain.

Ferdinand did not come to Laredo. He was already deep in the complicated moves against France which were to obsess him more and more as time went on, with Italy, especially Naples, the proving ground.

The autumn gales broke early that year; Juana left in August, but it was not until October that she was safe in Flanders, safely married. I could imagine her impatience. And it was while I was waiting news of her arrival that I heard of my mother's death. To grieve would have been hypocritical; it was the end of thirty-four years of vegetable existence and by the grace of God, the beginning of a new life, in Heaven. I had visited her from time to time, but she never knew me; all I could do was to see that she was well-tended, kindly treated—which all mindless people were not, though, here again, trying to work, as with the abandoned children, through institutions already established, I had done what I could to mitigate their lot.

Our fleet was obliged to overwinter in Flanders, and setting out in March 1497 was almost wrecked in the Bay of Biscay, but it survived and put in at Santander. Ferdinand and Juan rode post-haste and met Marguerite and I waited at Burgos.

This girl, presently to take my place as Queen of Spain, was pretty—not beautiful as Juana was, but prettier than any other daughter of mine; fair, colouring much like Juan's, plump but shapely, a very compact little figure. And she had a lively wit, backed by the most astounding self-confidence. On that first night in Burgos, when I had welcomed her—yes, perhaps a little solemnly, for she had almost been drowned, she said, over the supper table,

'I was anxious not to be washed up, dead, anonymous, the body of a well-dressed woman, so I wrote my own epitaph and pinned it to my sleeve. It would sound nothing in Spanish.'

She could speak our tongue; she said she had learned a lot from Juana, but she spoke it with a lisp, very attractive, like a child. Juan, in love at first sight, said, 'Tell us.'

'In French? I wrote—

> *'Ci-gît Margot, la gentil damoiselle,*
> *Qu'eut deux maris, et si, mourut pucelle.'*

We all knew enough French to get the meaning of that; A lady of birth, twice betrothed but dying a virgin. She had been formerly betrothed, a French marriage planned and then rejected because Anne of Brittany had Brittany as her dower.

A girl who in imminent danger of death could describe herself thus; no *real* identity, no mention of her being Archduchess of Austria, Maximilian's daughter, was something to be reckoned with.

I recognised this and set out to woo her. Because of the mutual moratorium over dowries—and because Maximilian had no money—Marguerite had come to Spain ill-provided; so I showered her with gifts. I gave her the ruby necklace supposed once to have been Solomon's. I said to Ferdinand, 'You do not object, do you? It is, after all, only a matter of time. When I die ... And I do so wish to content her.'

I hope that none of my daughters behaved in their new homes as Marguerite of Austria behaved in Spain. Nothing contented her and she made no attempt to hide her feelings. She had come from a gay, glittering, profligate Court and found ours dull, stiff, boring. Her malicious remarks were often sparked with wit but that did not make them less hurtful. When some jibe elicited laughter only from Juan, who was completely infatuated with her, she congratulated him on being the only member of the family with a sense of humour. She poked fun at our fashions and introduced some of her own, more French than Flemish, and almost indecent. She said bold things, with an innocent look. 'I understand, Madam, that you like your ladies to attend classes. May I enrol with Peter Martyr's?' Peter Martyr was at that time conducting a school for young men of noble birth.

We gave her the most splendid wedding imaginable and she remarked upon the absence of carriages—the only conveyance fit for ladies. In the whole of Spain there was no carriage, but Juan promised her one as soon as it could be built. It was a lumbering contraption, a roofed four-wheeled wagon, in fact, which required six horses to draw it, and even then could only be used on flat ground.

She was a disappointment to me, and to Katharine, now twelve years old, and greatly missing Juana to whom she had been devoted. I was compelled to mask my disappointment, for Juan's sake, but Katharine discovered within herself an unexpected talent for making tart retorts.

With the ordinary people, Marguerite was immediately popular. She was pretty, a princess from far away who had come to marry their beloved Prince; she was gay, and on public occasions very charming. And there was a fairy-tale quality about these two young people, so young, so fair, so obviously in love, and allowing the fact to be seen.

I told myself that she was young, would settle down; and that in any case there was no need for her to be earnest, hardworking, serious-minded as I had been compelled to be. She was Queen by marriage not by inheritance, and once Juan could give his mind to something other than his delight in his bride, he could undertake all the duties for which he had been trained, almost from birth. Still, it was on the whole with relief that I saw them off on a long honeymoon tour which was to include all the towns and cities which we had given Juan as a wedding present; Salamanca, Zamora, Toro, Arevalo, and in the south, Jaen and Ronda.

Ferdinand and I were free to turn our attention to a marriage of a very different kind.

When King John of Portugal died, leaving no issue, and his elder nephew Alfonso being dead, he was succeeded by Alfonso's younger brother, Manuel. Almost as soon as Manuel was crowned he sent a message that he would like to marry Isabel, his brother's widow. Isabel was still in her mood of having done with the world, and Ferdinand and I were obliged to reply that the Princess did not wish to remarry and that we had no intention of forcing her to do so. But Manuel, in a way flattering to Isabel, did not choose a bride elsewhere, and early in 1497 renewed his offer. Isabel, after much thought, said she might consider it, on condition. 'What condition?' I asked, and she replied solemnly, 'That Manuel expels all the Jews from Portugal.'

I should not have thought that she was sufficiently interested in outside affairs; and the request put me into a curious position. I could not very well decry the suggestion that Manuel should do precisely what we had done; on the other hand five years had proved to me that Spain had suffered from the expulsion, and gained nothing. The fires of the Inquisition still burned and the Jews had left behind a gap difficult to fill, both in business and in the lower ranks of officialdom; they had been particularly efficient as tax collectors.

I tried to explain all this, but Isabel simply said,

'You did it yourself. And if, as you now say, expelling the Jews brought disadvantages, if Manuel is still prepared to do it, it will be proof of his devotion.'

'Has he not already given that? Renewed proposals in the face of rebuffs?'

'Manuel was always jealous of Alfonso. He now has the Crown

which would have been Alfonso's had he lived. He wants me as well. And for the same reason.'

'Are you setting a hard condition because you do not wish to marry Manuel?'

'Mother, I have said that I am willing to marry him; if he accepts my condition.'

Manuel accepted. The Pope granted a dispensation necessary in the case of a man marrying his brother's widow. Then Isabel gave further proof of her lack of enthusiasm by saying that this time she wanted no show at all for her wedding. She did not even need a new wardrobe; she had so many clothes so little worn. I remembered, with a pang, her first wedding-dress, so lovingly and hopefully embroidered.

I said, 'Darling, you can hardly wear the same wedding dress.'

'No. I suppose not.'

All in all I had an idea that Manuel was to have a cold bedmate.

Despite Isabel's request for no show, Ferdinand tried to insist that Marguerite should come from Salamanca and be present at the proxy wedding to take place at Alcantara.

'And not Juan?' I asked, puzzled.

'If he came it would mean another household.'

'That could be supported. It would be better than parting them, just now.'

With his left eyelid almost closed—to me a sure sign—Ferdinand said, 'For a reason which I do not wish to discuss with you, my dear, I think that a short parting would be a good thing.'

I said, 'Ferdinand, what reason? What are you concealing? They have not ... quarrelled.'

'Far from it! Very well, if you must know ... Doctor de Soto told me, privately, that Juan was overdoing it. You know what he is, he must always do more and better. And the girl is insatiable. He needs a little rest; time to get his breath back.'

I suppose we are all rather like horses in blinkers, seeing only so much, the limited view of our own experience. I, too, in my time, in borrowed beds had been insatiable, but always compliant to Ferdinand's will; if a bed meant more than a sleeping place, the man decided. Surely.

Yes, I was blind. I actually said, 'Those whom God hath joined, let no man put asunder.'

Ferdinand said, 'Isabel, in some ways you are singularly innocent. Doctor de Soto said that in his opinion the marriage should not have been consummated for at least a year.'

'Within a year I hope there may be a child.'

'I hope so too,' he said. And we left it there. In September we took Isabel to the border again, with no show, and after the quiet proxy wedding, that made her Queen of Portugal after all, I was quite inexplicably forced to take to my bed. Inexplicably because I felt tired in a way that the leisurely journey, the simple ceremony could not warrant. I was bone weary. I remembered an old soldiers' motto—*You can go a long way when you're tired*. I had very often gone a long way when I was tired, but this was different. Now my bones seemed to melt under their burden, and when, clutching a bed-post or a friendly hand I tried to force them to it, as callous drivers force failing mules, I was back in that rocking, spinning world I had known after the miscarriage at Cebreros—with this difference: there was now no urgent demand for action. I could lie in bed, weak and yielding for two days, three, a week if necessary.

I slept a good deal, or lay in a half-doze, troubled by none of the thoughts or scenes in the head which I associated with being in bed and wakeful. I seemed to lose count of time. Beatriz was with me; other people came and went. Once I heard a voice say, 'She has come to an age ...' I thought, yes, forty-six, the watershed of a woman's life; but I will not be ruled by it. I had always defied the lunar calendar, made little of pregnancies and their aftermath of weakness. I could defy this, given a little resting time.

It seemed a trifle odd that Ferdinand had not looked in upon me. I knew he hated anything to do with illness, but I was not ill. Once I said to Beatriz, 'Where is Ferdinand?'

Settling my pillows she said, 'He has gone to Salamanca.'

'Why?'

'Is this not the time of the great Autumn Fair there?'

I thought—Of course, the wedding so cheerless, and me taking to my bed, he needed some gaiety. And naturally he would be anxious to see Juan. Beatriz answered my unspoken question.

'He would have said goodbye, but you were sleeping ...'

She stood there, pressing her linked hands to her waist, as though in pain. 'Isabella, I have never lied to you and I cannot now. They said not to worry you, but the truth is, Juan is ill. Very ill, fevered and coughing blood.' Tears filled her eyes and brimmed over. She had her three sons and loved them, but my children had always been, in a way, like her own.

God. God. Always there; always listening.

'Beatriz, help me. Pray with me.'

She got me to the *prie-dieu* and knelt with me.

No orderly prayers now, just the simple petition. God, spare him. Mary, Mother of God who stood by the Cross, pray for my son. Intercede for him. Christ lay Thy healing hand ... I had prayed with passion to be delivered from Don Pedro de Giron—and that prayer had been answered. I had prayed with passion that Ferdinand should recover from the assassin's blow—that prayer had been answered. This, a prayer, urgent and passionate beyond comparison surely could not be disregarded. I prayed until I was unconscious and as soon as I recovered and found myself in bed, crawled weakly out to pray again.

Useless. Even as I prayed my son died; in his father's arms.

When God is lost all is lost, faith, compassion, tears. Ferdinand, aged by ten years, said brokenly, 'If only you had listened to me.'

I said, 'Remember, he was my son, too.' I repudiated all proffered comfort. I was sunk in that despair, the dark night of the soul which is the ultimate sin.

It sounds absurd, near blasphemy to say that the only creature who shared my dumb misery was the dog, Bruto. But it was so. Juan was to be buried in Avila. On its slow way to its resting place the coffin halted in various churches and was surrounded by mourners, surrounded by candles. Always the dog was there, crouched by its foot. He never fouled a church, he would rise and go out when necessary which was not often, since he ate nothing and drank little. When the last rites were over I put my hand on his neck and said, 'Come with me; Bruto,' and he understood. From that moment he never left me. We were together, we were alike, dumb, stricken animals.

Even Marguerite's announcement that she was pregnant did

nothing to console me; I thought—another child to be cherished and taught and snatched away! I acted, yes, I did act as the situation demanded. I said the right things—that the child would comfort her; that she must take care. Meaningless words because I was sunk in a morass of meaninglessness. And had I been otherwise, hopeful and forward-looking, praying for a boy, heir to united Spain, I should only have invited another blow. For with all the care—and I admit that Marguerite was very careful—she miscarried, producing something so shapeless ...

Peter Martyr expressed it exactly in one of his busy little letters. 'A formless mass of meat.'

The darkness which I had believed to be absolute, deepened. There were things to be done, I did them; papers to be signed, and I signed them. I moved about, busy with this and that, mother still to Maria and to Katharine, to Isabel in Portugal, to Juana in Flanders; and I never once in this dismal time missed a Mass or broke a fast day. I even prayed, aimless repetition, like that poor parrot.

My Court, lacking perhaps in frivolity, had always been happy; now my gloom pervaded it, even when the mourning time was done and I could not blame Marguerite for fleeing from it. Other people left, too. I had lost all interest in my appearance but occasionally I caught an accidental glimpse of myself in the glass. *Who is that ferocious-looking old woman?* Myself! My hair was whitening rapidly, loss of flesh had made my face sag into lines less expressive of sorrow than of surliness.

Then one day, in Toledo, Cisneros interrupted the official business which were discussing, dismissed the clerks and turning to me, said, 'Madam, I think the time has come for me to remember my priest's office. You are yielding to despair and that is a sin against God.'

I could only say, 'I know. I have even confessed it as a sin.'

'And been heard with sympathy; given nominal penances?'
I nodded.

'I am now going to say something to you that may well give offence. Hear me out, even if afterwards you dismiss me. Ask yourself whether, at the back of your sorrow and despair there is not rebellion? Anger with God who did not answer your prayers. The kind of anger you would feel if some official disobeyed your orders.'

'That is a shocking thing to say.'

'The truth often is. Your faith has been tested and it has failed. It is not that God has withdrawn from you, but that you have withdrawn from Him. How can He comfort your sorrow or restore your serenity of mind until you regain your faith?'

'I have never failed in a religious duty.'

'Gestures any well-trained monkey could perform; words any parrot could say. Ask yourself, have you ever, since the Prince's death, said from your heart—Thy will, not mine be done, and been grateful to God for considering you worthy of such a testing experience? No? Then how can you hope to be healed?' Afterwards I thought how suitable that this man of iron should tackle me thus, in the city of steel. 'You have,' he said harshly, 'only suffered a very ordinary human experience—the loss of a beloved son.'

'Juan was much more than that. He was the living symbol of the unity of Castile and Aragon; and he would have been a good king; he was trained from birth ...'

'And you think that God, omniscient, omnipotent, maker of Heaven and earth, is less capable than you of judging what is good for Castile and Aragon? I do not underestimate the difficulty of your position; for many years you have been like the centurion in the Gospel, you have said to a man, go, and he goes; to another come, and he comes. But you cannot command God!'

He went on, brutal, logical; he spoke of Our Lord's prayer in the Garden of Gethsemane—Father, *if it be Thy will*, let this cup pass from me. And of His final cry from the Cross, sure proof that Christ has tasted every human experience, even that of despair—My God, my God, why hast Thou forsaken me? He stripped me to the bone. And finally he said, 'I am not now your confessor, I cannot set you a penance, but I can, and I will, suggest what could be a beneficial exercise. It would be to go to the Leper Hospital, not to think that you founded it, and that, thanks to you, the lepers are well fed and cared for. Look straight at the most afflicted of all, and say to yourself—In the eyes of God this leper and I are one; His will be done on earth as it is in Heaven.'

It was true that I had founded the Leper Hospital; I had felt so sorry for the sufferers of this dread disease, not only maimed, and incurable, but outcast, feared by everybody, even their closest kin. They were driven out, must wear a bell that tolled 'Unclean! Unclean!' and depend for sustenance on gifts laid out in certain places just outside towns. There was hardly a sizeable place that did not have its Leper Stone.

But, though I had tried to gather them together and make provision for them, at a time when I had little money to spare, I tended to avoid the Leper Hospital. Wounded men in army hospitals either mended or died; for lepers there was no hope of mending or of swift death.

When I obeyed Cisneros and went, and looked upon a face eyeless, noseless, and thought, as I had been told to think, that in the eyes of God there was no difference between us, that we were both subject to the divine will, I did experience a feeling almost mystical, an expansion of that 'All is well', that I had known as I stood by the Lombards. Give all over into the hands of God who knew best what was good for Castile and Aragon. Let trust replace worry, faith remove doubt.

Such elevated feelings seldom last with me; but it was a beginning: I began positively to practise resignation. Grief remained, but I managed even to see, dimly, what was perhaps God's plan for Spain.

With Juan's death my heir was Isabel. Ferdinand had none, since Aragon did not recognise a woman's right to succeed. However, learned men hunted through ancient law books and found precedent for a compromise. Isabel could not be Queen of Aragon, but her son, if she had one, could become King. And we had already heard that Isabel was pregnant. This succession, if it came about, would unite the whole peninsula.

In ordinary circumstances I should have advised Isabel not to travel at all, since even a litter is subject to jolting; but my hand was forced, by, of all people, Philip of Austria who from Brussels issued a proclamation in which he claimed to be heir to Spain. This was such a palpable absurdity that it seemed hardly worthy of refusal. Juana was heir to nothing so long as Isabel was alive, and he had no shadow of a claim. Still, the eyes of Europe were on us; invalid claims may sometimes be used as political weapons, and it did not seem sufficient merely to issue a contradictory proclamation. Ferdinand and I wrote to Manuel and Isabel inviting them to come to Castile in order that she could be acknowledged as heir, and we called the Castilian Cortes to meet in Toledo in April in order to acknowledge her. All went well there. The few months of marriage and the expectation of motherhood had vastly sweetened Isabel's disposition, she was gracious and dignified in public and in private far more friendly to me than she had ever been since early childhood. Even when she said, 'All I fear is that twenty -seven is rather old for a first childbirth,' she seemed not to blame me, as once she had done for the delay in her first marriage. In fact she said, 'I should have accepted Manuel when he first offered.'

Since the Aragonese Cortes would not acclaim Isabel, but were willing to acclaim a boy baby the moment he was born and since the birth was due in August, we moved by very gentle stages to Saragossa, just over the border of Aragon and settled there. Apart from performing truly necessary duties I devoted my whole time to Isabel, fussing over her and as the time drew near, encouraging her and like all mothers, making light of the ordeal while quietly making arrangements to mitigate it as far as was humanly possible. In these few months Isabel and I established a proper mother-and-daughter relationship such as I had never hoped to attain with her.

When the time came this child, heir to Castile whatever its sex, to all Spain and Portugal if a boy, must be born in public view and I remembered how much being watched had added to the agony. I had Isabel's bed hung with gauze, the finest that the silk workers of Granada could produce. It is in itself transparent, the view is not occluded by one layer of gauze; two, especially if of differing colours, while still not obstructing the view can give an illusion of privacy.

She said, inside the gauzy tent, 'I am frightened.'

I repeated the comforting lie. 'There is nothing to be frightened of, darling. A sharp wrench or two; soon over. Soon forgotten.'

I remembered, with the utmost clarity, every childbed I had ever lain upon—perhaps because I have a trained memory, supple and quick, compelled by circumstance to be absorbent of facts and fig-ures, of faces and names. It may be true that women not forced to remember anything but household matters, do more easily forget.

Isabel said, 'Don't leave me, Mother.'

'I shall be here all the time. I shall hold your hand. You may wrench mine, squeeze it, bite it if you like.'

It was the easiest possible delivery. Her hand tightened on mine a few times and I said, 'I am here, darling. You are doing well. Soon over now.'

She gave a little moan. The midwife said, 'A fine boy. Thanks be to God.' Isabel's hand went limp in mine. I leaned over her and said, 'Darling, you have a son.' And as I spoke her lifeblood gushed out and she died.

Do not think, do not dare to think that she was given back to me only to be snatched away again. God, God, even to this I will, I must, resign myself.

There was poor Manuel to be comforted; he could hardly bring himself to look at the little boy—'The instrument of her death,' he said harshly. And there were, again absurdly, matters of priority to be considered. A clash between decent mourning for the dead and the proper celebration of the birth, the baptism of a living Prince.

The little boy, heir to Castile, Aragon, Granada and Portugal was the living image of my son. I was happy when Manuel asked whether he could be left with me. 'He has no mother,' he said.

The child had been held aloft and recognised by the Aragonese Cortes in Saragossa; in Ocana back in Castile the Cortes, so recently acclaiming Isabel, had recognised her son; and now, much as I wanted to keep the baby I felt bound to ask, 'Should the Portuguese not see him?'

He said, violently, 'Would my nobles doubt me when I say that I have a son—and no wife?'

'I will tend him well,' I said.

I thought—The south, Seville, Granada. I thought—None of those journeys that perhaps undermined Juan's health in the early days; no lessons until he is at least six years old; and no challenge. Hindsight is very sharp and unkindly; I saw now that in always forcing Juan into competition, demanding that he prove himself, I had made an error of judgement. It had resulted in his needing to prove himself the best lover ...

This little boy never had need to prove himself. From the first he was a pet. He had not only a doting grandmother, a grandfather as doting as a busy man could be, but two aunts, Maria and Katharine, both young enough to be playful, old enough to feel motherly.

As young Miguel learned to crawl, pulled himself to his feet and toddled and stumbled about in the palace at Seville, or under the alabaster arches of the Alhambra, Ferdinand's interests and mine diverged more than ever. Grief for Juan had not brought us together, because Ferdinand, in his heart, blamed me for what had happened, and perhaps he was right. Defeating Philip of Austria's ridiculous ambitions brought us temporarily together again, but once that was done he began to look outwards, while in all but one respect my view narrowed to good government in Castile and domestic affairs.

The exception in my case, was the world to the west.

Admiral Columbus—his title to this rank had been confirmed—had made his second voyage successfully and returned as self-confident as ever; he had succeeded, he said, in reaching the mainland, of which he had taken possession in our name. But he confessed himself to be puzzled, because though he was certain that he had reached India, again neither the fauna, the flora nor the people resembled in any way what he had heard or read about either India or China. With that far-seeing look in his eyes, he repeated his theory that the world was bigger than had hitherto been believed and that this coast of Asia was far from that part of India reported in travellers' and merchants' tales. Both India and China were said to be populous and civilised in a way, whereas the land he had touched upon was uninhabited—swamp and forest. 'But there are great rivers which offer access to the heart of the mainland; and with time, and God's grace, I shall reach it.' Of the gold that he had promised, and which he was sure was there, he still had scanty evidence. When I asked what had happened to the fort and the forty people he had left behind when the *Santa Maria* broke up, he gave me an astonishing answer. 'There was no sign of them. I fear they may have been eaten.'

'Eaten?'

'Some of the islanders practise cannibalism. Indeed their own name for the whole area is *carib* which means *cannibal*.' An incongruous note in the Earthly Paradise which he had described on his first return. But he explained this by saying that there were many tribes, differing vastly, in fact alike only in one thing—their incorrigible idleness.

He set out again, undeterred, having persuaded me to give both his sons some minor office in my Court.

But I was no longer dependent upon him and him alone for reports of how our new colonies were faring; disappointed people were beginning to drift back to Spain and much of their news was disquieting. The good husbandry which I had planned for when I sent seeds and plants and domestic animals, had never even begun. The Spanish settlers had not gone to the islands to farm, they had gone to find gold. The natives were idle, even when amenable, and many were not; even those originally friendly were now hostile. They were also far less easy to convert than had been expected since they had seemed to have no religion of their own. In fact they had, a very old and evil one.

Bribed by gifts, some submitted to baptism, and then continued to practise their own religion in secret: a vast supply of heretics in the making.

Just as disturbing were complaints about Admiral Columbus as an administrator; nobody questioned his ability as a navigator, though there was an increasing tendency to query his findings, but as a Viceroy he was utterly misplaced; he was never there, he thought of nothing but further exploration; he had no ability to get on with people; in any dispute he was always violently prejudiced in favour of one side and would not listen to the other. He was intolerably arrogant—even to the well-born.

And there were the sicknesses; fevers unknown in Europe; one that turned a white man as yellow as the gold he sought; and another which sounded to be a cross between smallpox and leprosy. And if the islands gave white men what was called Yellow Fever and the Great Pox, the white men took to the island such things as measles and the sweating sickness which killed off the natives in hundreds.

It was all very discouraging. I could understand that Admiral Columbus, his gaze fixed on far horizons, took small note of such things, but I must. I cast about in my mind and came to the conclusion that what I needed in the west was an impartial investigator, a sound, down-to-earth man, not interested in gold, or distant places. And I had one to hand. A relative of Beatriz's; Francis Bobadilla. A younger son of a good family, he was a landless man, of the kind referred to as 'a poor squire', and he had for some years held a post at Court, one of those where a corruptible man could enrich himself, since even my close scrutiny could not close every loophole. Don Francis had been content with his comparatively modest salary; he was a devout man and in appearance and manner and everything else he strongly resembled Beatriz's father, that practical man who had done so much to make our exile in Arevalo more comfortable than it would have been without him.

I think that had I sent for any other Court official and asked, 'How would you like to represent me in Hispaniola?' I should have received one of two answers. From ambitious men that glint in the eye belying the modest, Your Majesty does me too much honour; or, shuffling—My health, my age, my family ...

Don Francis said, 'Your Majesty sets me a hard task,' and stood for a moment wearing a far-away look that very closely resembled Columbus's own. Then alert common sense took over.

'Hispaniola is the chief island? The centre of control?'

'So I understand. Part of the island is still known as Haiti, but whoever inspects Hispaniola must inspect and report upon all, the islands now charted and named, and all other lands still to be discovered.'

He thought again and then said, without either pride or modesty, 'I think that, given sufficient authority, I could do it.'

I said, 'Don Francis, you shall have all the authority that I can give.'

'There is Admiral Columbus, Your Majesty's Viceroy, to be considered.'

'He should welcome any arrangement that sets him free to explore. He is not interested in day-by-day administration. That is what I ask of you. Law, order, justice. Your activities should not impinge upon his, but rather supplement them; just as those of the governors of cities supplement mine.'

He said gravely, 'Activities may not conflict; interests might. And if you will forgive me, Madam, if the governor of a city displeased you, you could dismiss him. What would happen if I, as your emissary, displeased the Viceroy, your representative in this New World? I am not trying to be difficult; I will serve you to the best of my ability, but I hesitate to put myself into the hands of an overbearing and unreasonable man. It might limit my usefulness if nothing else.'

In my mind I made a comparison between this sensible, responsible man, and Columbus the dreamer, the arrogant. In a small ship, in an Atlantic gale, I knew which of the two I would choose to take charge, but as an administrator of New Spain ... So I said,

'Don Francis, if you accept this post, I will arm you with a commission, giving you, in such a contingency, overriding powers. I trust you to avoid, as far as possible, any situation which would render the use of them necessary.'

'I will do my best, Your Majesty, in that, and in every other direction.'

I felt no sense of being treacherous towards Columbus of whom it might almost be said that he was self-appointed. He had called himself Admiral and Viceroy before he had made a single discovery. And as an administrator he had, judging by all reports, failed.

I went on to talk about what—after the conversion to Christianity—concerned me most about these new subjects of mine—slavery.

Over and over again, in written reports, and in interviews with men who had come back from the islands, I had come across the distasteful word. Only force would make the natives work, they must be enslaved before they could be made industrious. One gruff old man of business had bluntly told me that the only revenue likely to come out of my new realm would come from the sale of slaves. And even a priest, dying of fever, had in his last lucid moment dictated a letter to me, the gist of it was that until the people were robbed of their liberty they could never be converted.

So now I told Don Francis that I disapproved of slavery and hoped that he would work against it.

'As a general policy, I share Your Majesty's feeling. I must confess to a similar distaste for cannibalism, arson, murder. I think it is possible that we, living in a civilised country may underestimate the difficulties of people trying to make way in places that have never known any law. Here we have ways of dealing with criminals, we have gaols, fines, executioners.'

I thought that over too and conceded that persistent cannibals and criminals might, as an extreme measure, be enslaved. 'But it is not to become a profitable *trade*, Don Francisco. I do not wish human beings to be marketed like cattle.'

Irony again. The native islanders, enslaved for this or that reason, and compelled to work, either on the few farms or in the many mines which were being started at about this time, simply lay down and died. As workpeople they had absolutely no value at all; as slaves, on the pet-dog level, dressed up, pampered and displayed, they fetched high prices, and there was a slave market in Seville.

When I first heard of it I sent a man called Oviedo, another one I trusted completely; he had joined Juan's household as a page and was a man of high intelligence and complete integrity. He now served me, partly taking Pulgar's place, but, being younger and more active, undertaking other duties too. He had orders to investigate, discreetly but strictly, the extent of the slave trade and, where possible, to discover for what crimes the Indians had been condemned to lose their freedom. He reported difficulties with language and in some cases could ascertain no facts at all, but said that the offences were mainly of a trivial nature, and civil rather than criminal.

'Not,' he said shrewdly, 'that too great credence should be placed on this evidence. Nobody with a slave to sell will advertise the fact that he is a cannibal, a murderer or a thief, Your Majesty.'

I was left with the feeling that the rule I had made was being evaded; and in any case, whether the Indians' crimes had been glossed over, or whether they had committed only petty crimes against a system of laws which they probably did not fully understand, I considered a slave market to be a disgrace to a Christian country. I ordered the trade to cease and that all Indians in Spain should be returned to their homes. This was an unpopular measure, since the slaves had cost money and were regarded as property, but I pressed on with it, saying that the forfeiture of a slave's worth could be regarded as an act of personal loyalty to me. A number of slaves expressed a wish not to be repatriated, and their reasons shed an unfavourable light on the conditions in the islands, they had no families to go back to, all were dead, either of sickness, or of the digging.

Now and again I entertained the thought that had I not had little Miguel to rear, and multifarious other duties to perform, since Ferdinand was so preoccupied with diplomatic affairs, and with war, I would have taken ship myself, and visited my distant realms. As it was I must trust in Francis Bobadilla and in God.

15
Granada, Toledo, Madrid, Segovia. 1500–3

'While Ferdinand was thus triumphant in his schemes of foreign policy and conquest, his domestic life was clouded with the deepest anxiety in consequence of the declining health of the Queen and the eccentric conduct of his daughter, the Infanta Juana.'

Prescott

Ferdinand's foreign policy lay like a rock under shifting tides of what appeared to be vacillation, change of direction, change of method. His aims, which never varied, were to get the better of France and to obtain possession of the Kingdom of Naples which had, by way of a bastard, been lost to his branch of the family. He needed allies, Henry of England, Maximilian, the Swiss, the Pope. All in turn made promises, made gestures, made excuses.

Firm believer as I was in legitimate succession, I supported Ferdinand in his wish to regain Naples; and it was indeed one of 'my' Castilians, Consalvo de Cordoba, who was the leader and the hero of the Italian wars and who was, despite Ferdinand's personal dislike to him, appointed Lieutenant-General of Naples and the provinces, when peace eventually came.

One strand what should have been a strong link between Spain, Flanders and England was frayed by Juana's behaviour. The English were bound, as I once said, 'by ropes of wool' to Flanders, English fleeces went to Flanders where they were made into cloth and sent back. Juana, wife of Maximilian's heir, chief lady in Flanders, was also a Princess of Spain, and Henry of England sought her goodwill by writing friendly, flattering letters. Never answered. This hardly surprised me for she never wrote even to us, her parents. Through other channels we had to learn that in 1498 she had borne a daughter,

Elinor, and in 1500 a son, Charles.

Did she not wish to befriend Spain: did she not dare to? That I shall never know. What I do know is that the people who were sent with her to Flanders were villainously treated from the moment that the Spanish fleet brought Marguerite to Spain. Philip dismissed all her ladies, so carefully chosen, all her officials, even Father Andreas, her confessor. By the terms of the marriage treaty, perfectly usual terms, a bride's retinue should be supported by her husband's country; Juana's people were simply dismissed—and stoned in the streets, left to make their way home as best they could. Even those who had resources, independent incomes or pensions due from Spain for past services, were not allowed to use their assets, and incredible as it may sound, many actually starved to death.

And from Juana, so far as I could learn, not a whisper of protest. It seemed as though when she sailed from Laredo she had severed all contact with Spain.

Think tolerantly—She is under Philip's thumb, infatuated; think furiously—Is this my daughter? Think, with mounting worry and fear—What of her marriage? And what of her soul? Disquieting bits of information seeped their slow way in. Juana had ordered a dog of whom Philip had been especially fond to be killed. She had attacked a lady upon whom Philip had cast a favourable eye with a pair a scissors, inflicting enough damage to ensure that no man would ever look upon her with lust again. Of Juana I could believe it all, remembering the parrot.

Once—it must have been early spring, but in the south spring comes early and in the Alhambra the air was already rose-scented, I watched Miguel, twenty months old and now quite strong on his feet, retrieving a soft woollen ball thrown by Maria and Katharine, and I thought—Only this one little life stands between Juana and the Crown, the Throne of Castile! A terrible thought which I put away. The little boy was healthy; he resembled Juan in build and colouring but he had never given the anxiety which Juan had given in *his* early days; thanks, perhaps to the more equable climate, he had never even had a cold. Why worry?

Katharine said firmly, 'That is enough. Into bed with you.' Maria lingered and said, diffidently, 'Mother, amongst your many letters today, does one concern me?'

My correspondence that day had been bothersome and typical of the time, from Henry of England a demand that Katharine, with her dowry, should be sent to England immediately; from our Ambassador in England a shrewd, not over-scrupulous, but intensely loyal Converso Jew, a hint in warning, written in cipher. He suspected, he wrote, that Henry Tudor was secretly negotiating a marriage between his son, Arthur Prince of Wales, and Marguerite of Austria, Juan's widow. Alongside this he wrote that Princess Katharine must learn to drink wine, since English water was undrinkable. And there was also a request, from Elizabeth of York, Henry Tudor's wife, expressing the hope that Katharine was learning French since that was the language in which she and her family conversed most easily.

I had been pondering these contradictory letters as I watched the children play. There were also, awaiting my attention, about twenty other papers, letters and documents, amongst them the regular despatch from Portugal, the inquiry, often at third hand, about Prince Miguel's health and well-being. A mere formality. On this day I had not even broken the seal.

'From Manuel,' Maria said, as I fumbled. 'He wrote to me some time ago that, if I were agreeable, he would approach you and ask your consent to our marriage.'

I was astounded, yet I must conceal my astonishment and ask myself why this move should seem so astounding. She would be eighteen in June, though she looked and seemed younger—younger indeed than Katharine. She was healthy, pretty enough, a Princess of Spain, and free to marry. She had, for no obvious reason, never been caught up in the tangle of marriage negotiations.

I broke the seals of the letter, spread it, read confirmation of what the child had said. She watched me with composure. 'Does he ask for my hand in this letter?'

'He does.' I was still slightly disconcerted and took refuge in a kind of bluff heartiness.

'You appear to have accepted him already, my dear.'

She coloured. 'Oh no, Mother. I only wrote that if you agreed I should be willing to marry him. I hope you have no objection because I am very fond of Manuel, and so sorry for him.'

I said, 'I have no objection; nor, I am sure, will your father. The

Pope may need some persuasion.'

'Manuel thinks otherwise. His Holiness gave permission for Manuel to marry his deceased brother's wife; Manuel thinks that to obtain permission to marry his deceased wife's sister would be a comparatively easy matter. In fact I think he has already applied for the necessary dispensation.'

I was again astounded; this shy, rather backward-minded little girl, conducting what could only be called a clandestine correspondence concerning what could only be called dynastic matters. A mole, working in the dark!

'How long have you and Manuel been writing to one another?'

'A long time, but not often. When he went back to Portugal he wrote and thanked me for my sympathy, when poor Isabel died. He said, Mother, not criticising, please, Mother, you must not think that, but ... well, he said everybody else was more concerned with the baby being acknowledged and all that kind of thing ...'

In a way it was true; I had myself felt the conflict between grief for the dead and plans for the living and possibly the latter consideration, being of a practical nature, had taken first place. 'All that kind of thing,' was outside the scope of Maria's understanding, so her sympathy had been uncomplicated.

'And then,' Maria said, 'he wrote me another letter, nothing much, but saying that he remembered; and the third, the one I mentioned. Asking and explaining,... and saying that he would write to you. So I waited, and now he has ...'

There are lamps, brass or silver, with bodies that hold oil, and wicks, and draught-excluding shades of glass; they stand about, less promising than a branched candlestick, but when they are lighted ... As Maria said, 'And now he has,' she glowed like a lamp, newly lit.

I was so happy for her; a little self-reproachful for not having recognised earlier the character concealed by her meek, undemanding, child-like behaviour: a little sad, because I thought that when she went to marry Manuel she would take Miguel with her. She was his aunt, married she would be his stepmother and I had no doubt that she would be kind and loving; but I should miss him.

Arabic, that alien language, lends itself to aphorisms, succinct and apt. 'Guests, like fish, stink on the third day.' Unkind, but true. 'Danger never shows its face where it will be recognised.' I saw danger's face, thinking I should lose Miguel, but that did not happen. Manuel said he was content to leave my grandson with me, where he was thriving so well: and the daughter whom I had always regarded as stupid, said, 'Mother, I think that Manuel fears being *reminded*. Of Isabel.'

So that expected danger did not show its face. Something, not perhaps a danger exactly, but an affliction and a nuisance, did strike me, just as I was making ready to make my third journey to the border in order to give a daughter to Portugal.

Is there an ailment known to woman more humiliating and disgusting than sores on the legs? And what is the complaint associated with? Elderly peasant women who have borne thirteen or fourteen children, have been kicked by donkeys, mules, angry husbands. At least two-thirds of the old, poor women for whom, in varying ways, I had tried to make provision—even down to the ordering of linen sheets, worn thin, being given for the making of bandages—suffered from what they called 'bad legs'.

A few little open sores that were indicative of nothing serious; they could have been gnat-bites, unthinkingly scratched. A cooling lotion; a purge; a bleeding, a—to me utterly humiliating—test of the urine. Nothing availed, nothing explained. There I was, in my forty-ninth year, saddled with a burden that short of a miracle, I must carry for the rest of my life. And one which I must bear, if it could be so contrived, in secret, Beatriz my conspirator. She never once failed me. The poor women with bad legs were dependent upon bandages, having no stockings. I had dozens of pairs of stockings, linen in summer, fine woollen stuff in winter, and now Beatriz ordered more, so that I could always wear two pairs, the outer ones to go to the washerwomen in the ordinary way; the inner ones she sometimes washed with her hands, sometimes burned. Keeping the secret was less difficult than one might imagine; both Ladies of the Bedchamber and body servants being willing to do as little as possible, accepting my, 'That will do. I wish to talk to the Countess of Moya,' or Beatriz's, 'You may go; I will complete Her Majesty's preparations for bed,' without question.

The condition varied in virulence and handicapped me less at some times than others; it was, I remember, very bad just when I was making ready to ride with Maria to the Portuguese border, as I had twice done with Isabel. The utmost I could manage was to go with her to the edge of Santa Fé, now a fast-growing town. To her it mattered little; she was so entranced at the prospect of marrying Manuel that she would happily have dispensed with any escort at all.

We remained in the south. The improved roads and the courier service which I had organised in the interests of war, served equally well in peace, and made government from Seville or Granada possible. It was not a peaceful summer. The more stringent measures which Cisneros had forced upon Talavera had driven the Moors into sporadic rebellions which gave the Iron Chancellor his opportunity. When Ferdinand, in a few swift actions, had quelled the uprisings, it was: accept baptism or leave Spain. The Moslems proved to be less stubborn than orthodox Jews, and few chose exile, which proved, Cisneros said, with certainty but without complacency, that severe action brought results where mild ones failed.

In June Miguel developed a troublesome little cough, not associated, as coughs usually are, with the rheum of the common cold. I remember the day when it began; I was working in my usual place, by the fountain and pool in one of the courts at the Alhambra, and he and Katharine were playing hide-and-seek amongst the columns of the arcades. A bout of coughing brought on by excitement—Katharine always contrived that he should have no difficulty in finding her, while she found him only after so prolonged a search that sometimes he became impatient. A summer cough, bought on by dust, though these intricacies of marble and alabaster and water were surely the least dusty places in Spain in midsummer. He coughed, he seemed breathless, the pink on his cheeks seemed deeper. I said to Katharine, 'Play some game which means less running.'

Miguel had never had, as Juan had done, his own household, so my doctor was the first to be consulted; then Ferdinand's; then a reputedly clever converted Moor; all had palliatives to suggest, not one could explain why a little boy should cough when he ran—or wake with a cough in the night; should cough whenever he laughed—which he did often, being a merry child, easily amused.

I had him moved into my own bedchamber and kept a candle

burning all through the night so that if he woke, coughing, I could be there in the time of a heart-beat, raising him, giving him a spoonful of the most effective mixtures, holding his small starfish hand until he slept again. Sometimes during the night I thought he felt hot to the touch and suspected some kind of fever, but it was always gone in the morning, and sometimes I suspected myself—of over-anxiety. What puzzled us all was that even after a broken night, he seemed so lively, always ready to play, to laugh, to eat; a sure sign; everybody said, that there was nothing seriously wrong.

But he died in the night. I had waked, as was my habit now, several times, but he had not coughed once that night. I thought—He is better; and gave thanks to God. But when the dawn light dimmed the candle and the moment came when merry and lively, anxious for the day to begin, he should have been climbing on to my bed, sometimes to the detriment of my sore legs, nothing stirred.

Miguel had not coughed because he had died in the night and lay there, still and beautiful as a freshly-plucked flower.

This time I did not turn away from God; possibly that kind of despair can only be suffered once in a lifetime. I tried to turn away from the world, and as a token of withdrawal, I wore always the coarse, rasping habit of a Franciscan nun under my outer clothing. The world, however, held on to me, with hooked claws, with sharp fangs; I was still Queen of Castile and must again do my best for my country.

Juana and Philip were now heirs-apparent; they must come to Spain and be acknowledged by the Cortes; they must stay and become acquainted with the country over which they were one day to rule; they must learn the business of government.

I foresaw no difficulty at all; Philip's father was still alive, he could be spared: and they had both seemed eager enough to assert a premature claim when Juan died. However in return for a formal invitation for them both to visit Spain, and a personal letter, as fond as I could make it, to Juana, we were brought the information that to visit just now was impossible; Philip was far too busy with affairs of state, and Juana was again pregnant.

I seemed to be no longer capable of anger, but Ferdinand was infuriated.

'What affairs of state?' he demanded. 'Running Burgundy! Or hob-nobbing with the French? That is what I suspect. He could have come, had he wanted, and left her behind. *She* could have come; all this to-do about pregnancy. Pregnancy never hindered *you!*' It was, I think the only time that he referred favourably to my fortitude; and it was too late; no compliment, direct or indirect could please me now.

I said, 'We must write again, saying that they will be welcome at any time convenient to them.'

But there came to my ears—the way such things do—that Juana had said that she would as soon go to Hell as to Spain. Such rumours should be treated with caution; one went the rounds about *me* and what I was supposed to have said when Juan died—God gave him and God has taken him away; blessed be His Holy Name. Anything further from the truth would be difficult to imagine; but rumour is inclined to give what people ask of it, what they wish to believe. Juana may not have said those actual words, she may have said that she did not wish to go to Spain just then.

What Ferdinand had said about hob-nobbing, with the French, could not be denied. The next news that we heard from Flanders was that Juana's son, Charles, one year old, had been formally betrothed to Princess Claude of France, still in her cradle.

'Pleasant news indeed,' Ferdinand said. 'With Aragon and Castile—at war with France. I don't know, Isabella. There are times when I think about my one boy ...'

His illegitimate son, now thirty-three years old and himself the father of a son. Natural enough to think of him, to think that bastardy had not precluded the boy from high office in the Church—as by rule it should have done; that vows of celibacy had not prevented the young man from begetting ... Why, with so many rules defied, stop at the idea of putting him on the throne of Aragon? All I could say was that it would provoke civil war, half Aragon in favour of the bastard, half accepting Juana's Charles, as they had accepted Isabel's Miguel. I said, 'Look at Naples and what the crowning of an illegitimate son led to there.'

I was fighting for unity, for peace, while I prepared to face another parting; this time from Katharine, my true daughter. Henry Tudor could be no longer fobbed off. Isabel had left, once happily, once determinedly for Portugal; Juana had left most happily for Flanders, and presently Maria, equally happy, though less excited, or perhaps excited in a more quiet way, had gone to Portugal too. None of these partings had been a wrench. Parting from Katharine would be—and we both knew it.

One evening, alone with her, poor child, I broke the reserve of a lifetime and told her that nothing, nothing in this world was worth aiming at, worth struggling for. I told her that if she wished to renounce the world before she had tasted its Dead Sea-apple fruit, she should have my support. She could go to Avila and be a nun.

It was fifty years speaking with their sad, experienced, disillusioned voice, to fifteen, ardent and hopeful. She answered gently; a nun should have a vocation; she had never felt any desire for a religious life. She was prepared to face the world.

So all that was left for me to do was to arm her as well as I could. I hoped her retinue, her duenna, Doña Elvira, her ladies, her chaplain, the cavaliers of her household would meet with better treatment than Juana's had met with in Flanders. She took with her half of the most munificent dowry that any Princess within recorded time had ever taken to any husband.

She was different from the others; she wrote me long letters; how charming and fond her young husband, Arthur was; what a wonderful wedding she had had, how green England was, even in mid-summer. All the things which a mother wishes to hear. But there again, a little too late for me. The Arabs have another saying, 'The world is a bridge; build no house on it.' In my half-century of life I had built so many houses and seen them topple that now I could not look forward with any certainty of joy. Hope and pray.

The folly of building houses on this bridge of a world was fully exemplified for me by Columbus's third return. Francis Bobadilla, falling back on the commission I had given him, had arrested Columbus and sent him back to Spain *in chains*.

I think perhaps that the climate in the islands is unfavourable to white men; they seem to go mad there. Certainly Columbus was not of sane mind when, landing in Cadiz, he refused to have his fetters removed, and insisted upon coming symbolically chained as he was into my very presence. And was Francis Bobadilla quite in his right mind when, instead of acting cautiously, slowly and with tact, he had taken possession of the Admiral's house, servants, properties and proceeded to denounce him for severity, maladministration, venality?

The charges were possibly true; they were no more than had been made, unofficially, at an earlier date, and which had inspired me to commission an investigation. But what a clumsy way for a seemingly discreet and reasonable man to have gone about the task of restoring law and order!

Rumour again lies when it says that at this meeting Columbus and I both wept. He did, but I had reached the point where if I had been informed that the islands had sunk under the sea I could not have squeezed out a tear.

He wept, and freed of his chains—so loose that they did not even have to be struck off—launched into a glowing account of his latest discovery.

'I know now that I have not found India; but I have found a way to it. The rivers I spoke of, thinking they offered a way into the mainland of Asia, lead into what I can only call another continent. But there is a narrow neck of land through which, given time, I could find a passage into the Indian Ocean. As da Gama found his way around Africa.' He spoke with great bitterness. '*He* was not bound down by sentimental rules and people in power more concerned with a cannibal's so-called freedom than with a discovery that might change the world. I was forced to turn back for supplies and the moment I set foot in the islands I was arrested, and chained. A waste of time—of which we have so little, you and I.'

It is usual for men, accused of any misdemeanour, to round upon their accusers, charging them with even worse things. Columbus scorned such tactics; he did not even say that Bobadilla was untruthful; he used the words 'misinformed', 'misguided', 'inexperienced', and over and over again complained directly or indirectly that Don Francis put the interests of the natives before those of the colonists. In this, of course my emissary was only shaping policy to my wishes, but such was Columbus's personality and persuasive tongue that before this interview was over I was beginning to ask myself had I been right? Had I also been misinformed and misguided? I wondered that particularly when Columbus described the magic-worship in the islands; the horrible rites, the incredible beliefs. He said that he knew for a fact that the natives could *will* themselves to die, and frequently did so, rather than do a day's work; their most skilled practitioners in the magic even claimed to be able to restore life to the dead. 'Against such a religion—if so it can be termed—the Church can make no progress unless allowed to adopt stern measures.'

I heard accounts of the islands from other tongues, of course; and it was noticeable that nobody, of whatever rank or occupation, spoke ill of Bobadilla; no aspersions were cast upon his honesty, his industry, his good intentions. He was simply the wrong man for so difficult a post.

I gave this whole problem much hard thought. Juan's beloved Ama, who had remained at Court and who had always been one of Columbus's staunchest supporters, I think because Juan had derived so much pleasure from his stories, helped me correlate every scrap of information I could gather. Ama sorted it all, labelling some 'known fact', some 'dubious' and some 'unlikely'. One known fact emerged very clearly, there were not enough Spaniards in the islands and many of those there were not of the best kind, too many adventurers, anxious only for gold. So I set myself to another recruiting campaign, men from the class to whom land meant more than money. I managed to persuade 2,500, all of good family, to go with the announced intention of cultivating the soil and establishing estates. One difficulty I had to overcome was the fact that Columbus, though on the whole admired, was not trusted, and that rumours of what was called Bobadilla's weakness had spread and been exaggerated; another was that Columbus, though eager to sail again and seek for this westward passage, much objected to having any dealings with Bobadilla after the way he had been treated. So I appointed a Governor, Nicolo de Ovanda, whose special responsibility would be to see the new settlers established, and the new voyage of exploration provided for. I was not unaware of the possibilities of dissension which this action might provoke, but it was the best thing I could think of. Government is never easy, and government at long range is like gunnery, hit or miss.

Meanwhile Juana had borne her third child, a girl, and had given her my name—surely a good sign. Isabel of Flanders was born in June 1501, and together with congratulatory messages and presents—Ferdinand and I, despite the silences and the rebuffs, always behaved correctly—we sent a renewed invitation, saying that we hoped Juana and her husband would come to Spain as soon as she was well enough to travel. They left Flanders in November and could offer as excuse for passing through France, the difficulty and hardship of a sea voyage in winter.

'I don't like it at all,' Ferdinand said, scowling. 'Suppose Louis of France took it into his head to hold them hostage. Juana in exchange for our gains in Italy. I must confess I should be tempted to do it myself.' Every now and again he would display to me, with a disconcerting flash of honesty, something of what went on in his shrouded mind.

In fact the King of France received Juana and Philip with much honour. An escort of cavalry met them at the border, conducted them to Paris, where people were killed by the crush to see them; and then to Blois, where Louis XII waited. There were jousts and stag-hunts, all the entertainments that one monarch can offer to another. Of what went on behind the scenes, we heard later.

Their journey south was delayed by foul weather and they did not reach Toledo, where Ferdinand and I waited to receive them, until May of the next year, 1502.

How to remember, how to describe this meeting with my daughter, my heir, after six years, or my first meeting with Philip the Handsome?

Juana was, if possible, more beautiful than ever; my mother's eye said—Thin! But the slight paring away of mesh, especially on the face, had merely made clearer the beautiful lines of cheek and chin and brow; and the pallor—she had apparently not adopted the fashion of false colouring—merely emphasised the darkness of her cloud of hair, confined in a golden net, studded with pearls, and the brilliant green of her eyes.

And she wore Spanish dress, the modest-necklined, fullsleeved, tight-waisted fashion which Marguerite had derided.

I had intended to be ceremonious, until I had tested the ground. I had even been slightly cunning, choosing to have on my left hand Ferdinand's bastard daughter, Joanna of Aragon. (This, my dear, is how to deal with a husband's infidelities!) But at the sight of Juana, standing there, so beautiful, wearing Spanish dress, plainly donned to please, I ignored the protocol by which the visiting royalty is supposed to make three formal bows before the one visited can step forward and offer greeting. I went forward at once and embraced her. She did not yield to the embrace and the cheek upon which I implanted a kiss was as cold as stone. And from that moment on, until the end, what looked out at me from the emerald depths of those beautiful eyes was not Juana, it was the other thing; once a vagrant, now in full possession.

When did it dawn upon me that she was deranged? When, less than a week after her arrival in Toledo, in the middle of the festivities we received the news that in England Katharine had been widowed; Arthur, Prince of Wales, had died of a fever.

'How fortunate Katharine is,' Juana said. 'Dead, he can never betray her.'

Was a husband in his grave preferable to one who erred, but always came back—as Ferdinand had done?

And how to judge Philip? This object of adoration. More attractive in person than in portrait; big, handsome, rather bovine, easily pleased, easily amused; a man of shallow nature, rendered slightly uneasy by, and quite incapable of returning, Juana's extravagant devotion. Even Ferdinand, deeply suspicious of him at first, said that politically he was a fool, and that this 'cuddling up to France', as he put it, was the work of his Council. If he could just be kept away from Flanders long enough he would end up as good a Spaniard as anyone not born and bred in our country could be.

The Court had to go into mourning for young Arthur, Prince of Wales, and Philip was plainly restive and resentful of the gloom. Ferdinand did his best for him, taking him away to a hunting lodge where the formalities of grief could be abandoned. Juana, when informed of this pending expedition, behaved atrociously. 'I know what you hunt, and it does not go on four legs! Just because I am pregnant again and useless to you.'

What was so baffling was that although as regards Philip she showed neither sense, discretion nor even ordinary female cunning, in many other ways she was clever. I mentioned, with approval, her Spanish dress—worn on her arrival, then abandoned.

'I wore it to show the French that they do not own us, despite the fact that Philip knelt and swore a vassal's allegiance to Louis. I intended not to kneel to Queen Anne, but they tricked me. As I made the correct curtsey the Duchess of Bourbon put her great beefy hand on my shoulder and forced me to my knees. But I got my own back. We went to church, and at the end of Mass, Anne swept—no, hobbled—out, expecting me to follow, part of her train. I did not follow. I kept her waiting. She stood outside, waiting and waiting until she was half-frozen. And that evening, at a banquet, I wore my Spanish-style dress.'

It was not perhaps the most desirable way of asserting one's dignity and independence; but who was I to judge? I had never been in a foreign Court. And it did at least show that Juana was not Francophile and that she had her wits about her, and that she was not afraid. She was not afraid of anything except losing Philip's affection.

She was shrewd, too. When I told her that I had written to Katharine, expressing my deepest sympathy with her in her sorrow— such a brief, idyllic marriage, little more than a honeymoon—and telling her to come home, to me, her mother, to her father and the comfort of familiar things, Juana said, cynically, 'What a waste of time! Can you seriously think that that old miser would let her go? It would mean returning her dowry. No, my dear mother, the next thing you will hear from England is that a betrothal between Katharine and the new Prince of Wales is proposed.'

I said, 'Oh, that could hardly happen. There is so much difference in their ages. Five, six years. And on the wrong side.'

Juana said, 'Wait and see,' and the hostile thing looked out of the green eyes.

She was right; that is precisely what did happen.

We all know that we are mortal; every morning we should wake with thanks to God that we have lived through the night and have, by His grace, another day ahead of us. But to have one's life-span coolly reckoned and speculated upon does administer a jolt.

Mine came from the Aragonese Cortes. Ferdinand went ahead and convoked it. Juana and Philip followed and were in Saragossa acclaimed, with reservations. I stayed in Madrid, whither we had moved. And there I heard that the Aragonese would accept Juana— or rather her son, Charles, as they had accepted Isabel and Miguel. But ... *But*, if I died and if Ferdinand should marry and on a new wife beget a male child, then that child should inherit.

Putting me into my grave before I was dead!

So far as the Aragonese Cortes could know, I was in good health. I was a year older than Ferdinand, but as a rule women outlive men. Why make a condition about my death?

Easily, but not kindly explained when Ferdinand joined me in Madrid. One of his deep, twisted schemes.

'I needed,' he said, 'an excuse to leave before the Cortes had finished its session. So I said I was concerned for your health and must get back to Madrid with all speed.'

'But why? I am in excellent health.'

'Ah,' he said. 'I wanted to have an excuse for leaving that great silly boy to preside over the Cortes for the remainder of the business. Do you know what that is? Raising funds for the renewal of the war against France! Isn't that a trick to take all? In December he knelt, swearing allegiance to France, and here in less than a year, he is asking the Aragonese Cortes for money to make war.'

He was delighted with himself; he leaned back, the laughed, he slapped his thigh.

It was, in fact the kind of trick constantly indulged in; if it worked it was called high diplomacy, if it did not it was skulduggery. I had never used it; my mind simply did not work that way; but I had, since Miguel's death, come to the sorry conclusion that in this world there was no justice, no certainty of any reward on this earth for honesty, straight dealing, truth or even compassion. Against the rocks of expediency and cunning the frail little waves of would-be virtues made no impact at all. I thought, a trifle sourly, that the worldly-wise, the successful people were those who realised this early in life and never, after youth, suffered disappointment, or disillusion, or even surprise.

Ferdinand had underestimated Philip. Or, it is possible that Juana, very much in some ways Ferdinand's true daughter, had seen through the trick, and though anti-French had not wished to see her beloved fooled. Philip, greatly enraged, galloped back to Madrid, leaving Juana in Saragossa and said he was returning to Flanders at once. Ferdinand and I did our best to soothe him. One would have judged him to be one of those easily swayed, easy-going men, capable of a burst of ill temper but not capable of sustaining it. Another misjudgement. His anger flared hot and then settled down to a cold, impenetrable sulkiness. Argument and persuasion were useless. He had promised his Council that he would be home within a year, and if he left immediately, travelling through France he could just keep his word.

The war with France over those border provinces had been resumed during Philip's stay with us, and when I protested at the idea of making a journey through the actual scene of conflict, Philip retorted, 'Louis would give me safe-conduct. You Spaniards look upon him as a devil, but in fact he is honest and anxious for peace. If you have any terms to put to him, I'll act as your emissary. Think that over.'

Ferdinand sneered. 'Does Louis love you so much that you can persuade him to relinquish all claim to Rousillon and Cerdagne?'

'That is an ultimatum. I was speaking of terms,' Philip said.
Unwarned by his use of *I* and never *we*, I rushed in with what I thought a telling argument.

'Juana is in no condition to travel,' I said. 'You wouldn't like her to be brought to bed in some shepherd's hut, high in the Pyrenees, or in the middle of a battlefield.'

'I am not taking her with me,' he said.

My heart began to flutter. She was still in Saragossa and he spoke of leaving immediately. Who was going to break the news to her?

'Are we expected to tell her this?'

'Of course not. I'll tell her to come to Alcalá de Henares. I'll meet her and tell her there.'

But for the fact that I could no longer ride I should have forestalled him, got there first, supported her under what I knew must be a shattering blow; as it was, I could only write and send the letter by the swiftest courier possible. I urged her to be calm, to maintain control and dignity; I pointed out that she was heir-apparent to Castile and that it would please the people to have one of her children born on Spanish soil. I promised to look after her well.

I was not there when the famous scene took place, but I heard accounts, so exactly tallying, from people of different characters, that I had no reason to doubt the hateful veracity. Juana screamed and shouted, Philip bellowed so that 'the noise of the altercation, even the words, could be heard at a distance of three apartments'.

She screamed that he was abandoning her, just when she was within weeks of bearing his child. She said she had loved and served him all these years and this was how he repaid her. She shouted that she had brought him a kingdom which he hated because he hated her. Philip retorted that he was sick of Spain, sick of her hysterical behaviour and would be glad to get away.

It was not sympathy with Juana that made Ferdinand take his next steps; it was rage and disappointment that the son-in-law whom he had regarded as an amiable stupid boy to be made by careful handling into a good Spaniard, should be deserting Spain, bound on another journey through enemy country, consorting again with the arch-enemy himself.

'He'll need horses at every stage of his journey,' Ferdinand said vindictively. 'I shall order that he is not to be supplied. I shall tell all the towns on the frontier to close their gates to him. He can scramble into France by goat trails.'

How Philip managed we never heard, I have no doubt that he had an uncomfortable journey, but even clambering up goat trails in winter was a pleasant pastime compared with what I was enduring.

I had myself taken—by litter—to Alcalá , there to be confronted by Juana who for most of the time sat sunk into that melancholy which resembled my mother's in its early stages. She emerged from it to weep and wail, to declaim her love for Philip—or her hatred of him, to accuse me of bringing this situation about by insisting that she and Philip should come to Spain. 'You never were human. Nothing ever mattered to you except Castile.' She said the most hurtful things. 'Did I ever ask to own this barbarous country? Did I ask Juan and Isabel and Miguel to die? Give me back my husband and the Devil can have Castile.' Some of these tirades could also be heard at a distance of three apartments, and in addition to being hurt I was shamed. I was so ashamed that even sympathy galled me, smacking as it did of pity.

Cisneros, a stranger, I would have said, to pity, pitied me as he certainly had not when I was grief-stricken. He volunteered to have a talk with Juana, and he had it and was thoroughly routed. 'The Princess,' he said, 'has lived too long in the north where subversive doctrines gain ground every day. The Flemings, the Austrians all have German affinities and the Germans were never civilised by Rome nor fully converted. Some of the things the Princess said to me, Your Majesty, I cannot repeat.'

The only word of comfort and hope came from the doctors. Pregnant women sometimes, often, almost always, suffered some disturbance of mind; once the child was born ...

And what could be expected of a child whose mother often would not eat, slept only intermittently, refused, even ridiculed, all religious consolation? I feared for the child; but when, after the easiest delivery I have ever witnessed, the little boy was born, on March 10th, 1503, he was extraordinarily healthy, a very lusty and compact baby. To Juana he meant nothing, or rather only one thing.

'But for him I should now be in Flanders,' Juana said. 'With Philip.'

But Philip was not in Flanders. For all his haste to leave Spain, for all his promise to his Council, he had not gone to Brussels. He had stayed in France long enough to make a ridiculous pact with Louis, trading on his status as heir-apparent, a pact which Ferdinand instantly and vehemently repudiated. Philip had then moved into Savoy, where his sister Marguerite, Juan's widow, was remarried, Duchess of Savoy. From there he proceeded to Switzerland, and then to Bavaria, 'for the benefit of his health'. He who had, from what I had seen, what I had heard, as perfect health as any man was ever blessed with.

Almost as soon as she was delivered, Juana began to talk of rejoining Philip, wherever he might be, and to be honest, I should have been glad to see her go. The dementia which doctors had attributed to her pregnant state had not been alleviated by a happy, easy delivery. Once, long ago, Ferdinand had spoken of her as a fawning bitch and said that such were liable to be kicked; now she seemed to be a bitch on heat perpetually, and I would have let her go, to make what terms she could with the mate for whom she craved. To such a state of resignation she—and the years—had reduced me.

But Ferdinand said, 'No,' and said it very firmly. Juana was besotted with Philip, Philip was besotted with France. Once let them get together and a peace would be made, a peace that would mean not only the secession of Rousillon and Cerdagne—'for which I have fought since I could first heft a sword, but all that has been gained in Italy. Ask yourself, how would you feel if your hold on Granada depended upon a girl's whim, a girl's eagerness to hop into bed. And a mad girl at that,' Ferdinand said.

That was the first time that the blunt term had been used. *Demented, deranged, distraught, hysterical*, none of them have the finality of *mad*.

'She, not he, is heir,' Ferdinand went on. 'So long as we have her here and under control, Philip can't do us much damage. He lacks the ultimate authority. She must remain here.'

Easily said. Easily said. Busy with other things, busy with his war, he was not called upon to deal with a caged lioness. He was not forced to explain that from Spain, at this moment, there was no exit, either by land or sea; the whole northern frontier a battlefield and every seaworthy ship carrying troops or supplies to Gonsalvo in Italy. That task fell to me.

Sometimes, after a session with her I was so shaken that I could hardly sign my name. My secret affliction restricted mobility and Alcalá de Henares was difficult of access, inconvenient for emissaries and couriers, of whom there were many, not least important those bringing despatches from England where what Juana, now called mad, had foreseen had happened and a very puzzling situation had developed.

Even Doña Elvira, Katharine's duenna and chief Lady-in-Waiting, had managed to confound me. At first, hoping that Katharine might be pregnant, she had written to me that the marriage between Katharine and Arthur had been fully consummated. Then she veered around completely and said she was prepared to swear that Katharine was as virgin as she was born. The second story came after some preliminary negotiations about Katharine being betrothed to the new Prince of Wales: and I rather suspected Doña Elvira of concocting it in order to make easier the obtaining of the necessary dispensation. I was therefore obliged to ask Katharine herself and she wrote to me that she and her boy-husband had lived as brother and sister; that they had agreed to wait a year, because in addition to being a year her junior Arthur was never robust.

Katharine seemed to favour the plan to betroth her to the dead boy's brother and when I wrote that the difference in age worried me a little, replied that she was willing to wait; that Henry Tudor, unlike his brother, was big and strong and seemed much older than his years. She repeated that she was very happy in England, that the King and Queen were very kind to her, she had the company of young Princess Mary, whom she was teaching to play the lute, and that the ordinary people appeared to have taken her to their hearts. She wrote sadly, but not heart-brokenly about Arthur, but in one letter said. a significant thing; Doña Elvira's rules about how a widow should behave were very harsh; she would not even allow her to stand by a window and look out. It sounded to me as though Katharine had retained her lively interest in life.

Then began the tussle about the unpaid half of Katharine's dowry. Henry Tudor had forced extortionate terms on us, partly, I think, as a revenge upon Ferdinand who had once expressed a doubt as to the security of the hold the Tudor had on the English throne. On the other hand the properties with which he had endowed Katharine were vast. It was not a bad bargain—Ferdinand seldom made a bad bargain.

Still, the fact remained that much as Katharine had taken with her when she sailed from Corunna, it was only half the promised amount; and in the intervening time Ferdinand and I had never found ourselves in position to pay the remainder. Nor could we do so now. We seemed to have gone almost straight from the war against Granada to war against France, and having troops active in Italy was extremely costly since it involved the fleet; ships cannot go to sea in other than first-class condition.

Ferdinand had made what economies he could; galleys for instance, were no longer propelled by paid men, they were crewed by criminals who would otherwise have been languishing in gaol, and being an expense to the state. The new system presented great risk of abuse; it was perilously like slavery, since these new oarsmen must be chained to their benches while on the galleys, and kept in confinement when ashore; but they were criminals, expiating their crimes, and they were better fed than they would have been in ordinary gaols.

When our Ambassador in England, Doctor Puebla, first wrote—in the cypher that was so much more legible than his handwriting—that the King of England had raised the matter of the unpaid half of the dowry, Ferdinand was with me in Segovia, back from the battle front in the north and busy, with me, with the question of raising supplies.

'Let them wait,' he said, tossing the letter aside. 'We specified no actual date. Half when Katharine went to be married; half at our convenience. And what more inconvenient moment could the old miser have chosen?'

I said, 'Could we send a little, a token; just to show good faith?' He then said a very illuminating thing.

'For Castile you can answer that question. Aragon cannot spare so small a token as a tinder-box.'

And the same was true of Castile. And something other than the constant drain of war was to blame. Declining trade.

There had been a short, all too short, period of prosperity, between the ending of the Portuguese war and the beginning of the Moorish one when trade had flourished because order had been restored. And that prosperity had not ceased with the war, it had been diverted into other channels; the men who made guns, the men who made roads, the men who supplied the army with its many necessities had all become richer rather than poorer. The penury which had afflicted Ferdinand and me all those years was the result of money spent, and all going into other people's pockets. It was with peace that the decline had set in and the revenue declined, and despite the new war, continued to decline.

Was it the expulsion of the Jews? I had thought so, and I had warned Isabel. Yet Portugal had expelled them, and seemed not to have suffered.

Was it the Inquisition? Did the constant confiscation of property and the imposition of heavy fines tend in the end to upset the balance of things? It was noticeable how many heretics were men who had prospered by their own efforts, a productive section of society, and now either dead or ruined.

Very puzzling, too, was the fact that what those distant islands were now beginning to contribute, seemed to make the money situation worse rather than better. There was little gold as yet, it still had to be found and mined in any quantity, but there was silver. Every nugget and ingot that reached Spain had the strange effect of lessening the value of all the silver coinage minted. On one exploratory voyage Columbus discovered a primitive community where pearls 'were plentiful as pebbles. So plentiful that children played with them.' He sent me some, superb pearls, but of little worth in money, for the simple reason that other men had also sent pearls home and the market was flooded. Only gold seemed to have retained its value and I sometimes asked myself whether, if the colonists ever found gold in any quantity, it would have a similarly deleterious effect on standard values.

So Ferdinand dismissed the request for the remainder of the dowry and began to talk about the progress of the war against the French. He was cautiously hopeful. Gonsalvo de Cordoba was scoring victory upon victory in Italy, and on our border all that was needed was one decisive battle. It was, in fact, to raise funds for this final effort that he had come to Segovia, and I had journeyed from Alcalá de Henares in order to meet him.

The matter of the dowry disposed of—we were to write evasive letters, very courteous, saying in effect, 'presently'—I said,

'I wish I could remain in Segovia; it is so much easier of access; but I feel I must be with Juana and I hesitate to move her.

Ferdinand's attitude towards Juana, and even towards the baby who bore his own name, was one of almost complete detachment. She must be kept in Spain, because elsewhere she would be dangerous; and that was all. For all he felt for her she could have been a parcel of gunpowder which must be kept well away from the fuse that might cause an explosion.

'Why must you be with her? You would be better apart. She worries you; perhaps you worry her.'

'She is so pitiable. And she is a responsibility which I do not feel I should inflict upon anyone else—in her present state.'

'I think, my dear, that you should face the truth. Her present state is her permanent state—until it worsens. I know you do not welcome advice from me, but if she were my daughter ...' He realised the enormity of what he had said, and laughed. 'What a thing to say! My daughter, yes, she is that. I count it amongst my blessings that I never had cause ...'

I thought—Little you know, how often, and how nearly! Put that thought aside; Rodrigo has been mouldering in his tomb these thirteen years: I am an old woman, an old, *tired* woman.

'What would you do?'

'Put her into La Mota.'

La Mota was one of those fortresses, moated and drawbridged, which had once been so numerous that the name of Castile and its royal arms had been derived from them. It stood high just outside the town of Medina del Campo. It could be made comfortable and it had the inestimable advantage, as a place of residence for a woman who suffered hysterical fits during which she did not care what she said or did, of being isolated, with no ignorant, sentimental populace to be appealed to. One of the reasons why I had refrained from moving myself and Juana down to Segovia, Madrid, Toledo was that every now and then, emerging from apathy, from long bouts of crying, she would rush to a window or doorway and shout, 'Help! Help! Good citizens all. Come to my aid. I am being held prisoner.' Such demonstrations, soon over, had not caused much disturbance in a place like Alcalá de Henares; but in a more populous place with more unemployed people, more apprentices, always ready to snatch upon any excuse to make an uproar, such outcries could have resulted, at least, in some broken heads and hacked shins, some people taking one side, some the other.

When Ferdinand said, 'La Mota,' I recognised, almost unwillingly, his good sense.

Carpets for the floors, hangings for the walls, cushions and candlesticks, curtains, musicians. La Mota was transformed from a bleak fortress into a most ... a most comfortable cage. That was what it amounted to; Juana must remain here, until the war was over.

She accepted the move without protest; she was in the middle of one of her withdrawn, apathetic moods; rejected by Philip, not even knowing where he was, what did it matter where she lived? Nobody else meant anything else to her. I handed her whole household into the capable hands of her chaplain, the Bishop of Burgos, a kindly man, and settled myself in Segovia, an excellent place for administration for a woman no longer fully mobile. But I worked, reading, dictating, shuffling the endless papers; helped by Beatriz's unfailing hands to make, when necessary, the correct, impressive appearance. Often the faint noise of the midnight bells, summoning monks and nuns from their sleep, would sound before I retired and sometimes even the next bell, calling the religious to Prime at six o'clock in the morning, would sound before I slept.

'You are killing yourself,' Beatriz said.

'Nonsense. Even my silly little sores are healing.'

Indeed, in that autumn of 1503 everything seemed to be taking a turn for the better. At La Mota Juana was quiet and early in October Ferdinand won the conclusive victory upon which he had counted. The end of the war was in sight; Ferdinand would come home and share the work and the responsibility.

Autumn, like spring, has an effect on one's spirits.

The new Pope, Julius, gave a dispensation for Katharine to marry the young Prince of Wales, *even if*, the document read, she had been Arthur's wife in fact as well as name. In Portugal, Maria, most happily married, became a mother. In Brussels Juana's son, Charles, was nearing his fourth birthday.

And fifty-two was really no age at all. Ten, twelve years, if I could live so long ...

The Bishop of Burgos ordinarily sent me a weekly report from La Mota. Reading these unmomentous accounts I often thought that Ferdinand had been right in saying that I worried Juana as much as she worried me—our separation had certainly calmed her. In fact, week after week there was very little to report, except that Her Royal Highness was in tolerable health, that there had been such and such changes in her household, and such and such expenditure incurred.

But this one, arriving on a cold, slate-grey day in early November, said simply, 'Her Royal Highness is making preparations to leave. What does Your Majesty wish me to do?'

I turned the paper over and wrote, 'Stop her. I will send letter and personal messenger.' I despatched that at once.

I then pushed everything on my table aside and wrote to Juana, a careful letter, for all its haste; I wrote that the war was almost over; soon the frontier would be open, soon a ship would be at her disposal, soon her father would be home. I begged her not to be precipitate or to leave Spain in circumstances which might give the wrong impression to the watching world. Actually, partly by cunning and partly by virtue of great loyalty and discretion on the part of officials and servants, the truth of the situation had been concealed. Even those frenzied calls for help were easily explained. Her Royal Highness was suffering from the after-effects of childbirth; she wanted to be up and about before her doctors thought it advisable.

Only a small number of people knew the truth.

I entrusted my letter to Juana to one of Ama's relatives, Pedro de Torres, as noticeable a fast rider as I, as Don Gutierre, Don Inez, the Count of Henares and others had been in our day; heavier now, slowed by age, all of us. I said to my messenger, 'Ride hard. Deliver this letter to Her Royal Highness, and *say* to the Bishop of Burgos that she must be persuaded against attempting so long a journey in such weather.'

'Your Majesty,' he said, 'is right. I have a countryman's nose. There will be snow in twenty-four hours.'

I said, 'So I thought. Say to the Bishop that she must be persuaded, or, if necessary, prevented, as gently and pleasantly as possible.'

He set off; perhaps an hour behind the rider bearing my first, hasty message to the Bishop. Knowing Don Pedro's horsemanship I thought that he would overtake the first messenger. And always a consideration in bad weather—I now had two missives on their way to La rota; if one for any reason were prevented or delayed, there was hope that the other would arrive.

Fifty miles separate Segovia from La Mota, but by headlong galloping and frequent changes of horses, Don Pedro was back next day with a chilling story.

When he arrived at the castle Juana was in the last stage of preparation, her travelling chests ready to be closed. She had flung my letter away unopened and refused to listen to the Bishop's pleadings.

'His Grace then whispered to me, Your Majesty, to leave the castle and await him on the far side of the drawbridge; which I did. He then made some excuse to leave Her Royal Highness, ordered the gate to be closed as soon as he himself was on the drawbridge, and for the bridge to be drawn up as soon as he had crossed. He had no choice, Madam.' He hesitated in his story and I said,

'He did well.'

'What happened next is not pleasant to tell. Her Royal Highness came down and flung herself at the gate and screamed. She shouted at the Bishop and said she would have him beheaded. She screamed at the soldiers, ordering them to open the gate and lower the bridge. He called orders that things should be left as they were. He was greatly distressed. A crowd began to gather, and Her Royal Highness appealed to them, shouting that she was being held against her will and that she would die at the gate rather than go back into her prison.'

Exactly the kind of demonstration which it had been our object to avoid.

Overnight my sores had worsened, confirming my suspicion that there was some mysterious connection between my physical affliction and my state of mind; I was always worse when worried. I thought—Oh, to be sound and whole, able to ride! But I must go in a jolting litter, at mules' pace. As it was being prepared, something worse than bodily ill swept over me; fear, doubt of myself. I, who in this very city, in the nearby square, had faced a howling mob without a tremor, feared to face, unsupported, my own daughter, flesh of my flesh. If she would not even read my letter, would she listen to my voice? Whom to take with me, to add persuasion, to lend authority?

I chose two men for very different reasons. Cisneros because he was a hard man, unlikely to be distressed by any scene; and the Admiral Faderique Enriques, Ferdinand's cousin, because in the old days Juana had been fond of him and always called him Uncle. She might distrust me, and my Chancellor, but if she retained any sense at all she must know that this fond relative wished her well, and that any argument he put forward would be in her interest.

The journey took two days. The weather was bitterly cold, with a biting wind and flurries of snow. Cisneros and the Admiral had elected to ride—though Cisneros at least was entitled to a litter by reason of his age, which was sixty-eight. Yet they seemed to fare better than Beatriz and I, huddled in the litter under fur rugs.

At mid-day on the second day I asked them to ride on to tell Juana that I would arrive before sunset. The sun dimmed and I asked the muleteers to push the animals a little.

'It will jolt you more,' Beatriz said.

'Jolting is better than anxiety—though I am sorry to subject you to this,' I said.

Cisneros—iron of body as of will—rode back to meet me. The news he brought was bad; Juana, after a day, a night and another day, clinging to the cold iron of the gateway had crawled in a state of collapse into the nearby guard-room. She was there now, refusing to re-enter the castle, refusing to take food, refusing to see the man she had called Uncle. He was part of the plot, she said. Yet something of sense remained; informed that I was on my way to see her she had said that she would sooner see the Devil. She was now in so weak a state that the Bishop thought it safe to lower the drawbridge and open the gate.

And Cisneros, not a man given to pity, thought I should rest, should have a night's sleep to marshal my strength before meeting Her Royal Highness.

I said, 'I must not waste time. Unless something is done she may die.'

'Madam, her life, like all, lies in God's hand. But it might be the best thing that could happen.'

When somebody voices the deepest, darkest thought, the thought one has *feared* to think, one recoils.

All guardhouses smell the same and of all our senses that of smell can most easily evoke the past. Leather and oil, metal, men. By no wish of mine, as I entered the guard-room by the gate of La Mota I was reminded of a hot afternoon, the iron hat heavy on my head and Rodrigo at risk of blowing himself to bits with the high-firing Lombard.

Juana sat huddled, holding her hands to the fire. Her hands were so thin that against the fireglow they were almost transparent. Don Faderique had evidently abandoned his hopeless task and gone to seek shelter and comfort within the castle itself. But Juana was not alone, her Flemish lady-in-waiting, Madame de Halewin was there, looking distraught and tearful.

'I have done my best, Your Majesty,' she said, and indicated by a gesture the rough wooden table against the wall. The candlelight shone on rejected offerings, platters of this and that, drying out and shrunken, bowls of soup scummed over, cups of wine, a dish of the last ripening figs and bunches of grapes of the particular harvest, only just snatched from the first frost. Certainly Madame de Halewin had done her best—and been defeated. (And what a tale she would have to tell, in her lively, spirited way, once she was safely back in Brussels!)

I gave her her due. I said, 'You have done well, Madame de Halewin, and I thank you.' I was stiff from jolting about in the litter, I was sick at heart, but I gathered myself and went forward and put my arm around the huddled figure on the bench and said,

'Juana. I am here. Your Mother.'

'Come to gloat? Don't touch me,' she said in a low, venomous voice. I withdrew my arm and sat down on a bench on the opposite side of the hearth. I decided that after all I wanted no witnesses to this interview, so speaking as calmly as I could I asked Madame de Halewin to take the Archbishop and the Countess of Moya into the castle and see that they were warmed and fed. I then began to talk to Juana, saying only that her behaviour was unreasonable, self-destructive and sure to give rise to scandalous talk.

She gave no sign of hearing me, crouching lower and smaller on her stool and holding her hands to the fire as though communing with it. She looked so frail and so pitiable, her cloud of hair in tangled disarray and her face no longer delicately hollowed, but haggard, mere skin over bone. My heir. I remembered Cisneros's harsh words. I also remembered the lovely, lively little girl who despite all her faults had charmed everybody. I could not renounce her without a struggle.

I had never relinquished anything without a fight. I said,

'Juana, please listen to me.'

She swerved slightly on the stool, withdrew her hands from the fire and wrapped her arms around herself.

'*You* listen to *me*,' she said, and launched into a tirade the details of which I have endeavoured, without much success, to expunge from my mind. There is, I thank God, no record of what she said, except in my troubled memory. More poisoned than those arrows tipped in wolfsbane; and much of it completely untrue. A mad woman's talk. She accused me of caring nothing for my children—I who, having learned my lesson from Isabel, had with endless pains and inconvenience, always made sure that they were with me. She said I knew nothing of love and was jealous of her because she did, and that was why I was keeping her from Philip. She then told me what love meant in words no woman should use; words which the roughest soldier would not in his right senses, and sober, have used in my presence. I was not squeamish, I knew the language of fever, of drunkenness; to hear her, gently nurtured, a Princess of Spain ... Horrible.

'And he wants me,' she said. 'He always did, he always will. No other woman can give him what I can give.' She pulled a letter from the bosom of her gown and kissed it frenziedly, and that gave me a chance to speak.

'Is that a recent letter?'

'He wrote it as soon as he was back in Brussels. And I was making ready to go when that damned Bishop stopped me. By your order ...'

'Juana, I knew nothing of that letter. When I asked you not to leave precipitately I did not even know that he was back in Flanders.'

'Then why did you forbid me to go?'

'I did not forbid you. If only you had read my letter! I merely asked you to wait until the frontier was passable, or a ship free to convey you.'

'I had no wish to read a sermon about my duty to Spain.

You used us all, pawns in the game of power, for Spain. I have been held here, hostage, lest Philip should make an alliance with France. I knew it from the first. And here I shall die. I shall stay here and starve, since life without Philip has no meaning to me.'

I said, 'Juana, you shall go to him as soon as arrangements can be made.'

She gave me a look and turned away to the fire, saying, 'Oh, another trick. This time an underground dungeon.'

'I swear you are free to leave ... Now, in order to be able to travel, you must eat and sleep.'

'What do you swear by?'

'By all I hold holy.'

'My poor woman, you do not even know what that is!'

Juana, my daughter, said that to me. 'The only thing you hold holy is Spain. Swear by Spain and I could believe you.'

'I swear by all I hold holy, and by Spain which I hold dear, you shall leave as soon as possible.'

'I should want that repeated, before witnesses.'

'Come into the castle then, and I will do so.'

'Oh, how clever you are,' she cried, seeming to rear and writhe like a snake. 'No, fetch them here!'

I went to the door to despatch a soldier to fetch the Admiral and Cisneros. The night was blind with snow.

16
Medina del Campo. 1503–4

'.. quando la dicha Princesa mi hija ... no quisiere, o no pudiere
entender en la governacion de ellos ... el Rey mi senor rija,
administre, a govierne los dichos mis Reynos.'

'Should the said Princess my daughter ... not wish to or is unable to
undertake the government. the King, my husband, is to rule,
administer and govern my Kingdom.'

Isabella's Will

It snowed for four days and nights. In separate rooms Juana and I lay,
recovering our health while the blizzard raged. She had been so weak
at the end of it all that she could not walk the short distance between
the guard-room and the castle, but had to be carried by soldiers, and
I was helped along by the Admiral and Cisneros—witnesses to my
swearing. And as though that were not sufficient humiliation for one
evening, half-way across the courtyard I was disgustingly sick.

It was a chill, everybody said; brought on by the two days' ride in
the bitter wind. It could be combated by bricks heated in the oven,
wrapped in flannel and laid on the stomach, at the feet, against the
back; it could be combated by hot drinks, peppered water, sugared
milk and—mulled wine! Beatriz said,

'Unless you take this—as medicine—Isabel, I swear I will leave
you. And then who will look after your stockings?'

I took it, as medicine, wine heated and infused with cloves and
cinnamon and nutmeg—all the things Columbus had thought to
find. It was soothing and made me drowsy, so that I could lie without
going over and over that scene in the guard-room, the scene which
was responsible for my state.

'I shall never forgive Juana,' the Admiral said, admitted by Beatriz
for a five-minute visit on the third day.

'I shall never forgive Her Royal Highness,' said my Chancellor
and the Primate of Spain.

To both I said, 'You must. She was ... hysterical. She had eaten nothing for days. She was light-headed from hunger.'

Then, from one of my wine-induced doses I was roused by the noise of a door closing and there by my bedside was Ferdinand. I did not believe my eyes; I thought I was dreaming. But he looked real; almost completely bald now, and with one front tooth missing.

I closed my eyes, opened them again and he was still there. Brush away this cobwebby curtain behind which you have been skulking! Speak!

I said, 'Ferdinand.'

'My God, Isabel, when you looked at me and seemed not to know me ...'

'I simply could not believe my eyes. Oh, I am so glad to see you! How did you get here? The snow ...'

'Nothing,' he said jauntily, 'to what it was in the north. The great victory at Perpignan cannot be followed up until the thaw comes in spring. So I have time to spare. I went to Segovia and there I heard that you were here—and why. So I came.'

'The first flower of spring was never more welcome. Perhaps you ... Have you seen Juana?'

'No. Waiting for you to waken I have talked with my cousin, with the Archbishop and with Beatriz. They all tell the same dismal tale. We shall be well rid of her.'

'I hoped you would agree,' I said, weakly glad of his approval. 'I was forced to promise. She would have died there by the guardhouse fire.'

He gave a non-committal grunt. Possibly he was echoing Cisneros's thought. Then, in words, he echoed one of mine, 'What did we ever do to deserve *this*? Still, you must not be worried now. You must get better. One thing is certain; she cannot leave yet. The passes are all closed; even the northern ports will be inaccessible for a week or two.'

I almost asked could she not go south and sail from Seville or Cadiz, but I thought—Let Ferdinand handle this; be glad that he is here to do it.

To me that thought was proof that I was suffering from more than a chill on the stomach: it was not my habit to evade my share of responsibility.

I was, in fact, compelled to leave everything concerning Juana to Ferdinand because every contact with her provoked nausea again. I had told those two angry men that they must forgive her, and I endeavoured to do so myself. I did forgive her, I pitied her, I hoped, with all my heart, that she would have a happy reunion with Philip, be healed of her ill, but though I could compel my mind it seemed that where she was concerned, I had no control of my body; the sight of her, the sound of her voice made me sick.

Ferdinand arranged everything correctly; she was heir-apparent of Castile, she was mother of the heir-apparent to Aragon and Castile, she must travel in state. And he was firm with her; when she said she would walk through the snow in her shift to get to Philip, Ferdinand said, 'Any more of such crazy talk, and I'll put you in a safer place than this.' She had sense enough to understand and to regard this threat. And *of course* I welcomed, and was thankful for, any such sign of sanity, but it made some of the things she had said to me less easily dismissed as the ravings of a mad woman.

She left, to sail as before, from Laredo, and there, poor girl, she was delayed by bad weather, so that it was April before she reached Brussels.

By that time I had made what was to be my last journey; thirteen miles to Olmedo and thirteen miles back to Medina del Campo. I went to spend Holy Week of the year 1504 with the Dominican nuns in the Convent of Santa Maria. There I set myself resolutely to put the world away, to share the nuns' religious state of mind as well as their ritual. It worried me that I could not do so more completely; mundane thoughts would intrude.

The misery of that comparatively short journey, the having to be heaved into the litter, and out again, the effect of the jolting, had shown me that my travelling days were done. I was afflicted, but I might live for years, and while I lived I must govern and I could not govern from a convent in Olmedo. With God's help, and with a mighty effort I might get back to Medina del Campo which although not ideally situated, was just feasible. And since stairs now offered an almost insuperable difficulty, I must live and work and sleep on one floor.

What a thought to entertain when one should be contemplating the Agony on the Cross! Had Juana been right in saying that to me only Spain was holy? Dear God, You who know all, know that that is not true.

A set of apartments from which La Mota was not visible; my bedchamber, an office, an audience chamber, various anterooms; to this my physical life had narrowed down and was to become even more circumscribed, until my bedchamber held all; the table which now represented the office, the canopied chair in which I could sit and receive; both within what I called tottering distance. Fortunately the room was large enough to serve the many purposes without becoming muddled and squalid, and when high summer came with its heat and I had some difficulty in breathing, I ordered new windows to be made.

Into this light, airy, busy room, news flowed; good and bad, and mixed. There was the treaty with France—all good; Louis XII's armies, defeated by Ferdinand at Perpignan, and by Gonsalvo at Gaeta in Italy, gave in, and Ferdinand was acknowledged as King of Naples. On the other side of the world Columbus had succeeded in finding, not India, but on the yet—unnamed mainland, the place of gold of which all the legends told. Columbus was preparing to come home and report to me.

From Flanders the news was horrible. Juana had seen one of the ladies of the Court hastily pocketing what she had—rightly—guessed to be a note of assignation; she had demanded to see it and then, satisfied that her guess was correct, had attacked the woman and torn out handfuls of her yellow hair. Philip had rushed in and struck Juana. Scandal enough, and how Europe enjoyed it! And another story, too. In order to show his displeasure, Philip had refused to bed with Juana and had locked his bedroom door. She had assaulted the door, first with a knife, then with a lump of rock, crying, 'Let me in.'

From England the news was not entirely happy either. Henry's Queen, Elizabeth of York, had died, quite young in childbed, bearing a little girl, named for Katharine. And Katharine's letters had hinted at a deteriorating situation. 'I have lost a friend'; 'His Majesty's nature seems to have changed.'

I plodded on, I read all despatches; I dictated and signed letters; now and then, when I felt able, wrote one. Ferdinand never left me;

the two bodies with one will, the running in double harness which had sometimes imposed a strain and a chafing, was ended now. The arrangement, for all its potential dangers, had survived and I was able to say to him one evening, 'Do you remember Pulgar's joke?'

'Did he ever make one? I always thought him a solemn fellow.'

'So he was. But he had humour. He once wrote, sticking to protocol, 'Their Majesties have given birth.' It amused me at the time.'

Something of lightness must be brought in; anything that would make Ferdinand's conscientious visits to me tolerable for us both. I knew I was dying, so did all the doctors, though they could not say why. Dropsy? Certainly that complaint would explain my gross bulk, my insatiable thirst; but the remedy for dropsy was 'tapping' and though I bore the painful punctures with as much courage as I could muster, and hoped for the best, I was not relieved. I was going along the ever-narrowing stony corridor that ends in the grave, and Ferdinand knew it as well as I did. Worse for him ... So I was falsely cheerful and did not let fall a word that might indicate that I was making my will.

To this document I had begun to give serious thought as soon as I realised that my health was unlikely to improve; I started to jot down salient points on the day when I could no longer reach my writing table. I wrote down things as they occurred to me and slipped the papers into a leather wallet kept for the purpose. They could be sorted out in due time.

Most important issue of all was the succession. In the past people had called me tactful, and never had I needed tact more than now. Juana was my heir and I must so name her and that meant leaving my beloved country in the hands of a woman who suffered fits of insanity, and in the hands of her husband, a stupid, selfish man who hated Spain. In what way could the consequent ills be mitigated?

I seized upon a known fact—that Juana and Philip both disliked Spain. Should Juana be unwilling to rule ... Scribble in two significant words, 'or unable', then Ferdinand was to rule as Regent until Charles reached the age of twenty. Surely an acceptable provision. In fact as early as 1502 when I was in good health and Juana and Philip had not been long in the country, the Cortes meeting in

Toledo had respectfully advised me to appoint Ferdinand as Regent; such advice had seemed premature then, but the memory of it was heartening now; I could bequeath, as I had ruled, in accord with the will of the people.

With so little of life left I must still take a long view. After Juana, Charles; if he died without issue, Juana's second son Ferdinand; if the unlikely happened and there was still no male heir, then Elinor, Isabel, and if that branch of the family died out, Maria, her son John; if all else failed, Katharine and her issue.

Katharine!

Reach for another piece of paper and write that the remainder of Katharine's dowry must be paid.

Back to Juana. She had never heeded me much, would a voice from beyond the grave reach her? One never knew. I wrote to express the hope that she and Philip would live in amity, take Ferdinand's advice in all things, observe their religious duties, retain all my well-tried officials.

Officials!

I had a sharp and disquieting vision of a horde of Flemings descending on the country, hungry for posts as they fell vacant. For my next provision I had sound precedent in the marriage agreement between Ferdinand and me, made at a time when the Castilians feared being overrun by Aragonese. I wrote that no foreigner was to hold office in Castile.

I added and altered until, reading through the public part of my will, I was satisfied that so far as was possible I had foreseen every eventuality. So much for the Queen; now for the woman.

Had Katharine been my heir I should have been spared a great deal of writing. A simple request that all my friends and servants and charities should be dealt with justly, as far as possible generously, would have sufficed. As it was I must specify every legacy. It was a long list.

I could make one economy—the last of a lifetime. A vast amount of money is wasted on ostentatious funerals and on great structures of marble and alabaster to stand guard over the unheeding dead. My marriage had been austere, my accession without show; now I ordered myself the plainest possible funeral: only the thirteen candles that stand by any peasant's coffin, and a plain flat slab to mark my grave.

Where?

Here I indulged in sentiment and extravagance. I knew that where the body lies is of no importance; men have been drowned at sea, been torn to shreds by wolves and scavenging dogs. But I had a fancy to lie in Granada, in the chapel of the Franciscan convent that had been grafted on to the Alhambra. I set down this wish adding that I hoped that Ferdinand, in the fullness of time, would be buried beside me; or if for any reason he should be interred elsewhere, that I should be taken to him. For now, coming to the end of it all, I could see that our marriage, governed by such conditions and exposed to such strains as no ordinary union knows, had nevertheless been a good one. From the moment when he returned, victorious, from the north, he had stayed with me, ill and unattractive as I had become. He would have had every justification for going to Italy to be acclaimed and crowned and fêted. But he had stayed with me.

I appointed him my chief executor; the others were all clerics of high-standing, headed by my Chancellor, Cisneros, a hard man, but a just one whose passion for detail would extend to the smallest legacy—and, if I was any judge of men, a signed and dated receipt!

By the 12th of October, with my secret wallet bulging, I sent for Caspar de Crizio, a public notary, to put my covert, night-time scribblings into the language of the law. When that was done I signed it in the presence of seven witnesses; and the seals were attached.

That done I lay back with the feeling of having finished; fifty-three crowded years; not all happy, not all successful, but unremittingly busy; I could only hope that Christ, in His infinite mercy, might say of me, as He did of the woman who anointed His feet with spikenard and dried them with her hair—She has done what she could.

Public life for me was over; retreat now, to Beatriz's tender ministrations, the doctors' hopeless, ritual attentions, the priests' earnest endeavours to make my soul ready to meet God.

There was one echo from the past. As I lingered, wretched now with pain, my Admiral, Christopher Columbus, came home again. This time he did bring samples of the gold that he had promised long ago; but he was too ill to make the journey and come to me himself; he sent his son, Ferdinand. The gold seemed unimportant now but the event did remind me of the Indians and I managed to whisper to Ferdinand, to Cisneros, one final wish—that they should be justly and generously treated. I also wondered whether Columbus, so often called a liar, had been truthful when he said that our fates were linked because we were born under the same star. Were we to go out on the same tide?

An idle fancy, perhaps, and unimportant to me, about to set out on an even more uncharted voyage, but not to an unknown destination. I was going to God, omnipotent, omniscient, who might well judge me, His instrument, faulty in many ways; but Christ would be there, with His knowledge of this world, its difficulties and temptations, and of human nature, so fallible even at its best; and Mary, Mother of God, so gentle and compassionate, would see how tired I was, and say, 'Rest now.'